I0595601

Evert A. Duyckinck, Alonzo Chappel

Lives and Portraits of the Presidents of the United States

from Washington to Arthur

Evert A. Duyckinck, Alonzo Chappel

Lives and Portraits of the Presidents of the United States
from Washington to Arthur

ISBN/EAN: 9783337403898

Printed in Europe, USA, Canada, Australia, Japan

Cover: Foto ©Andreas Hilbeck / pixelio.de

More available books at **www.hansebooks.com**

LIVES AND PORTRAITS

OF THE

PRESIDENTS

OF THE

UNITED STATES,

From Washington to Arthur.

THE BIOGRAPHIES,

BY

EVERT A. DUYCKINCK,

AUTHOR OF THE

"*History of the War for the Union*," "*Cyclopedia of American Literature*," *Etc.*

AND

THE PORTRAITS,

BY

ALONZO CHAPPEL,

From Original Likenesses obtained from the most Authentic Sources.

TO WHICH IS ADDED

THE CONSTITUTION OF THE UNITED STATES; WASHINGTON'S FAREWELL ADDRESS;
FAC-SIMILE OF THE ORIGINAL DOCUMENT OF THE DECLARATION OF
INDEPENDENCE AND NAMES OF THE SIGNERS, ETC., ETC.

NEW YORK:
HENRY J. JOHNSON, PUBLISHER,
27 BEEKMAN STREET.

COPYRIGHT, 1881, BY
HENRY J. JOHNSON.

PREFACE.

THE narratives of the Lives of THE PRESIDENTS OF THE UNITED STATES will ever afford an interesting and profitable subject of study; and this not merely from their elevated position ranking them as rulers with contemporary kings, emperors, and others in chief authority; but, as representatives of a distinct and peculiar social and political organization. The hereditary sovereigns of Europe, succeeding one another by a fixed and absolute decree; educated for their position and following, for the most part, through life a uniform routine of etiquette and State policy, are spoken of in relation to families and dynasties; nor do they always represent the nationality of the countries over which they rule. They may be, as in the case of the Hanover line in England, taken from a foreign country, or as in Greece of the present day, chosen from other countries in obedience to a real or supposed political necessity of European State craft. They may be weak or able, virtuous or vicious, according to their capacity or individual tendencies, without the nation over which they rule being particularly honored in the one case or held responsible in the other. Not so in the United States. Here the CHIEF MAGISTRATE, as it is our glory to call the presiding officer at the head of our system of government, being chosen by the people at short intervals, the nation becomes directly responsible for his intelligence and virtue. The prejudices of party, the accidents of political intrigue, occasional deference to what is termed expediency, may, indeed, direct the election so that the successful candidate may fall short, as a representative man, of the character of the people in its highest and best development. It is by no means to be expected that the best adapted or qualified man will be chosen every four years to the Presidency. In all human affairs it frequently happens that the right man is not in the right place. But generally speaking, making due allowance for inevitable exceptions the country may be rightfully judged by the character of the man deliberately chosen by the people to the post of highest authority. If, for instance, an avowed infidel, or a corrupt man in morals, or one dishonest, wanting integrity in the every-day affairs of life, were to be elected, the nation would be directly humiliated. It would be held up to reproach, and deservedly so, throughout Christendom. If, on the contrary, the list of Presidents shall continue to show men of sound moral character and a high average of intellect, the country will be honored in its representatives.

How much, for instance, at the start was done for us as a people by the choice of WASHINGTON as our great leader, "First in War, First in Peace, and First in the hearts of his countrymen." The nation, after more than half a century since his death, may be said, in a measure, to be living on his virtues. He, more than any other hero, "without fear or reproach," by the purity of his life and the devotion of his whole nature to public affairs, raised the land at once to a "respectable" position, as he was accustomed modestly to say, among the nations of the world. His example has reacted upon the people whom he was called to represent, and doubtless on innumerable occasions has brightened the flame of patriotism and public virtue. Every statesman, and especially every President, must feel himself called upon to follow and privileged in following in his footsteps.

Nor does the example of WASHINGTON stand alone in our review of the Presidents. The ADAMSES occupy a lofty position in our national history, in their private virtues, their devoted patriotism, and independence of character. In JEFFERson the nation had not only a ruler of consummate ability, but a student and philosopher, and a controlling mind among the great men of his century. The great name of MADISON is identified with the foundation of our liberties in the origin and adoption of the Constitution. The strength and manliness of JACKSON, equally illustrated in military and political life, have left their example to invigorate the national policy of our own times. The fame of LINCOLN, consecrated by martyrdom, will be transmitted to posterity with an enduring lesson of public virtues, patriotic devotion, heartfelt love of liberty and magnanimity in the exercise of power. The fate of GARFIELD, cut off by the hand of an assassin at the very opening of his career, will always excite sympathy as wide and deep as when the news of his murder startled the whole world. Others on the brief list have their high and enduring claims to respect.

In the ensuing pages the lives of the twenty-one incumbents who, up to this time, have held the Presidency, are narrated. As a simple record of biography, the story is interesting in its variety of personal details. As an incentive to patriotism in a period more than ever since the days of WASHINGTON requiring the devotion of the citizen, we trust that it is not without its useful lesson.

CONTENTS.

GEORGE WASHINGTON.

WASHINGTON IRVING commences his life of George Washington with a genealogical chapter tracing the antiquity of his family to the eleventh century. Though the transcendent merit of his hero little needs this blazonry, which, as he himself intimated on one occasion, his occupation in active business had given him no time to ferret out, yet it is not to be denied that it is quite in harmony with the character of Washington, that his family should be traced through an ancient and honorable descent. He is placed in history as a connecting link between too great eras of civilization, and it is important to know that the goodly tree of his fair fame has its roots in the one, while it extends its widely spread, still growing branches into the other. He certainly would be less a representative man were his origin unknown, or had he just arrived, a chance comer, to do his work of revolutionizing a nation. On the contrary, he was especially fitted for his great employment by the place of his birth, leaning fondly on the parent country as the Old Dominion, the estates and institutions by which he was surrounded, and the recollections of an elder time which these circumstances implied. In supplying these traditions, Mr. Irving carries us back to the picturesque era of the early days of the Plantagenets, when the De Wessyngtons did manorial service in the battle and the chase, to the military Bishop of Durham. Following these spirited scenes through the fourteenth century to the fifteenth, we have a glimpse of John de Wessyngton, a stout, controversial abbot attached to the cathedral. After him, we are called upon to trace the family in the various parts of England, and particularly in its branch of Washingtons—for so the spelling of the name had now become determined—at Sulgrave, in Northamptonshire. They were loyalists in the Cromwellian era, when Sir Henry gained renown by his defence of Worcester. While this event was quite recent, two brothers of the race, John and Lawrence, emigrated to Virginia in 1657, and established themselves as planters, in Westmoreland county, bordering on the Potomac and Rappahannock, in the midst of a district destined to produce many eminent men for the service of a State then undreamt of. One of these brothers, John, a colonel in the Virginia service, was the grandfather of Augustine, who married Mary Ball, the belle of the county, and became the parent of George Washington. The family home was on Bridges' Creek, near the banks of the Potomac, where, the oldest of six children by this second marriage of his father, the illustrious subject of our sketch was born on the twenty-second of February, 1732.

Augustine Washington was the owner of several estates in this region of the two rivers, to one of which, on the Rappahannock, in Stafford County, he removed shortly after his son's birth, and there the boy received his first impressions. He was not destined to be much indebted to schools or school-masters. His father, indeed, was not insensible to the advantages of education, since, according to the custom of those days with wealthy planters, he had sent Lawrence, his oldest son by his previous marriage, to be educated in England; an opportunity which was not given him in the case of George; for before the boy was of an age to leave home on such a journey, the father was suddenly taken out of the world by an attack of gout. This event happened in April, 1743, when George was left to the guardianship of his mother. The honest merits of Mary, "the mother of Washington," have often been matters of comment. All that is preserved of this lady, who survived her husband forty-six years, and of course lived to witness the matured triumphs of her son—he was seated in the Presidential chair when she died—bears witness to her good sense and simplicity, the plainness and sincerity of her household virtues.

The domestic instruction of Washington was of the best and purest. He had been early indoctrinated in the rudiments of learning, in the "field school," by a village pedagogue, named Hobby, one of his father's tenants, who joined to his afflictive calling the more melancholy profession of sexton—a shabby member of the race of instructors, who in his old age kept up the association by getting patriotically fuddled on his pupils' birth-days. The boy could have learnt little there which was not better taught at home. Indeed we find his mother inculcating the best precepts. In addition to the Scriptures and the lessons of the Church, which always form the most important part of such a child's education, she had a book of excellent wisdom, as the event proved, especially suitable for the guidance of her son's future life, in Sir Matthew Hale's "Contemplations, Moral and Divine"—a book written by one who had attained high public distinction, and who tells the secret of his worth and success. The very volume out of which Washington was thus taught by his mother is preserved at Mount Vernon. He had, however, some limited school instruction with a Mr. Williams, whom he attended from his half brother, Augustine's, home, in Westmoreland, and from whom he learnt a knowledge of accounts, in which he was always skilful. His ciphering book, neatly written out, may be seen among other relics of his early years, in the public archives at Washington. Another juvenile note-book of this time, penned when he was thirteen, contains not only forms of business, as bonds, leases, and the like, but copies of verses and "Rules of Behavior in Company and Conversation," full of homely practical wisdom of the Benjamin Franklin pattern. Some lines on "True Happiness" recite, among other benefits, those of

"A merry night without much drinking,
A happy thought without much thinking;
Each night by quick sleep made short,
A will to be but what thou art."

The "Rules," one hundred and ten in number, are plain, sensible maxims, commonplace enough, some of them, but not the less valuable; minor moralities which add to the comfort as well as the greatness of life, form the gentleman, and assist the Christian. Washington, who was ever sedulously observant of all matters of good conduct and high principle, may well be studied in this elementary exercise of his boyish days. He had early set his mind in these precepts upon kindness, forbearance, self-denial, probity, the love of justice. The youth had also particular instructions from Mr. Williams in geometry, trigonometry, and surveying, in which he became an adept, writing out his examples in the neatest and most careful manner. This was a branch of instruction more important to him than Latin and Greek, of which he was taught nothing, and one that he turned to account through life. All the school instruction which Washington received was thus completed before he was sixteen.

Nor let it be supposed that these sober mathematical calculations constituted all the dreams of the boy. He had other visions of a softer character in the charms of a certain lowland beauty, to whose memory some love-sick rhymes are left in his youthful note-

2

books. It is worth mentioning, this tender susceptibility of one who was all tenderness within, while his grave public duties so long conscientiously required him to present an iron front to the world.

He had, however, to look to some practical work in the scant condition of his fortunes, and we find him early bent upon it. While he was yet at school, a proposition was entertained by himself and a portion of his family, which, if it had been carried out, might have seriously affected the destinies of America. His brother, Lawrence, fourteen years his senior, had served a few years before with the West India fleet of Admiral Vernon, in the land force at the siege of Carthagena, and in honor of his commander, gave the name Mount Vernon to the estate on the Potomac which he inherited from his father. He was now married to the daughter of a neighboring gentleman, William Fairfax, and in the enjoyment of his home had given up military life; but he thought well of the foreign service, and procured a midshipman's warrant for his brother George, who, full of active vigor, with a boyish taste for war, eagerly desired the adventure. Little more is known of the affair, beyond his mother's earnest final interposition—she had given her consent in the first instance—by which his majesty's navy lost an excellent recruit, and his majesty's dominions half a continent, while the world gained a nation.

On leaving school, young Washington appears to have taken up his residence with his brother at Mount

Vernon, where he was introduced to new social influences of a liberal character in the family society of the Fairfaxes. Lawrence, as we have seen, was married to a daughter of William Fairfax, a gentleman of much experience and adventure about the world, who resided at his neighboring seat "Belvoir," on the Potomac, and superintended, as agent, the large landed operations of his cousin, Lord Fairfax. These comprehended a huge territory, embracing the Northern Neck, and stretching over the mountains into what was then something of a frontier region, the valley of the Shenandoah. In this more remote spot resided the owner himself at Greenway Court, keeping up a rude state, and gratifying his love of the chase, for he had brought with him from Old England the tastes of a genuine fox-hunter. Washington, though too young to appreciate the eccentric nobleman's varied experience, was ready to follow him in the hunt, and there was another source of sympathy in the practical management of his vast territory. Surveys were to be made to keep possession of the lands, and bring them into the market; and who so well adapted for this service as the youth who had made the science an object of special study? We consequently find him regularly retained in this service. His journal, at the age of sixteen, remains to tell us of the duties and adventures of the journey, as he traversed the outlying rough ways and passages of the South Branch of the Potomac. It is a short record of camp incidents and the progress of his surveys for a month in

the wilderness, in the spring of 1748; the prelude, in its introduction to Indians and the exposures of camp life to many rougher scenes of military service, stretching westward from the region.

Three years were passed in expeditions of this nature, the young surveyor making his home in his intervals of duty mostly at Mount Vernon. The health of his brother, the owner of this place, to whom he was much attached, was now failing with consumption, and George accompanied him in one of his tours for health in the autumn of 1751 to Barbadoes. As usual, he kept a journal of his observations—he was always diligent and exact in these records from a boy, so that of no one so illustrious in history have we a more perfect picture through life—which tells us of the every-day living and hospitalities of the place, with a shrewd glance at its agricultural resources and the conduct of its governor. A few lines cover nearly a month of the visit; they record an attack of the smallpox, of which his countenance always bore some faint traces. Leaving his brother, partially recruited, to pursue his way to Bermuda, George returned in February to Virginia. The health of Lawrence, however, continued to decline, and in the ensuing summer he died at Mount Vernon. The estate was left to a daughter, who, dying in infancy, the property passed, according to the terms of the will, into the possession of George, who thus became the owner of his memorable home.

Previous to this time, rumors of imminent French and Indian aggressions on the frontier began to engage the attention of the colony, and preparations were making to resist the threatened attack. The province was divided into districts for enlistment and organization of the militia, over one of which Washington was placed, with the rank of major, in 1751, when he was but nineteen—a mark of confidence sustained by his youthful studies and experience, but in which his family influence, doubtless, had its full share. We hear of his attention to military exercises at Mount Vernon, and of some special hints and instructions from one Adjutant Ware, a Virginian, and a Dutchman, Jacob Van Braam, who gave him lessons in fencing. Both of these worthies had been the military companions of Lawrence Washington in the West Indies.

In 1753, the year following his brother's death, the affairs on the frontier becoming pressing, Governor Dinwiddie stood in need of a resolute agent, to bear a message to the French commander on the Ohio, remonstrating against the advancing occupation of the territory. It was a hazardous service crossing a rough, intervening wilderness, occupied by unfriendly Indians, and it was a high compliment to Washington to select him for the duty. Amply provided with instructions, he left Williamsburg on the mission on the last day of October, and, by the middle of November, reached the extreme frontier settlement at Will's Creek. Thence, with his little party of eight, he pursued his way to the fork of the Ohio, where, with a military eye, he noted the advantageous position subsequently selected as the site of Fort Du Quesne, and now the flourishing city of Pittsburg. He then held a council of the Indians at Logstown, and procured guides to the station of the French commandant, a hundred and twenty miles distant, in the vicinity of Lake Erie, which he reached on the 11th of December. An interview having been obtained, the message delivered and an answer received, the most hazardous part of the expedition yet lay before the party in their return home. They were exposed to frozen streams, the winter inclemencies, the perils of the wilderness and Indian hostilities, when Indian hostilities were most cruel. To hasten his homeward journey, Washington separated from the rest, with a single companion. His life was more than once in danger on the way, first from the bullet of an Indian, and during a night of extraordinary severity, in crossing the violent Allegany river on a raft beset with ice. Escaping these disasters, he reached Williamsburg on the 16th January, and gave the interesting journal now included in his writings as the report of his proceedings. It was at once published by the Governor, and was speedily reprinted in London.

The observations of Washington, and the reply which he brought, confirmed the growing impressions of the designs of the French, and military preparations were kept up with spirit. A Virginia regiment of three hundred was raised for frontier service, and Washington was appointed its Lieutenant-Colonel. Advancing with a portion of the force of which he had command, he learnt that the French were in the field, and had commenced hostilities. Watchful of their movements, he fell in with a party under Jumonville, in the neighborhood of the Great Meadows, which he put to flight with the death of their leader. His own superior officer having died on the march, the entire command fell upon Washington, who was also joined by some additional troops from South Carolina and New York. With these he was on his way to attack Fort Du Quesne, when word was brought of a large superior force of French and Indians coming against him. This intelligence led him, in his unprepared state, to retrace his steps to Fort Necessity, at the Great Meadows, where he received the attack. The fort was gallantly defended both within and without, Washington commanding in front, and it was not until serious loss had been inflicted on the assailants that it surrendered to superior numbers. In the capitulation the garrison was allowed to return home with the honors of war. A second time the Legislature of Virginia thanked her returning officer.

The military career of Washington was now for a time interrupted by a question of etiquette. An order was issued in favor of the officers holding the king's commission outranking the provincial appointments. Washington, who knew the worth of his countrymen, and the respect due himself, would not submit to this injustice, and the estate of Mount Vernon now requiring his attention, he withdrew from the army to its rural occupations. He was not, however, suffered to remain there long in inactivity. The arrival of General Braddock, with his forces, in the river, called him into action at the summons of that officer, who was attracted by his experience and accomplishments. Washington, anxious to serve his country, readily accepted an appointment as one of the General's military family, the question of rank being thus dispensed with. He joined the army on its onward march at Winchester, and proceeded with it, though he had been taken ill with a raging fever, to the Great Crossing of the Youghiogany. Here he was compelled to remain with the rear of the army, by the positive injunctions of the General, from whom he exacted his " word of honor " that he " should be brought up before he reached the French fort." This he accomplished, though he was too ill to make the journey on horseback, arriving at the mouth of the Youghiogany, in the immediate vicinity of the fatal battle-field, the evening before the engagement. In the events of that memorable ninth of July, 1755, he was destined to bear a conspicuous part. From the beginning, he had been a prudent counsellor of the General on the march, and it was by his advice that some of its urgent difficulties had been overcome. He advised packhorses instead of baggage-wagons, and a rapid advance with an unencumbered portion of the force before the enemy at Fort Du Quesne could gain strength ; but Braddock, a brave, confident officer of the European school, resolutely addicted to system, was unwilling or unable fully to carry out the suggestions. Had Washington held the command, it is but little to say that he would not have been caught in an ambuscade. It was his last advice, on arriving at the scene on the eve of the battle, that the Virginia Rangers should be employed as a scouting party, rather than the regular troops in the advance. The proposition was rejected. The next day, though still feeble from his illness, Washington mounted his horse and took his station as aid to the General. It was a brilliant display, as the well-appointed army passed under the eye of its martinet commander on its way from the encampment, crossing and recrossing the Monongahela towards Fort Du Quesne—and the soldierly eye of Washington is said to have kindled at the sight. The march had continued from sunrise till about two o'clock in the afternoon, when, as the advanced column was ascending a rising ground covered with trees, a fire was opened upon it from two concealed ravines on either side. Then was felt the want of American experience in fighting with the Indian. Braddock in vain sent forward his men. They would not, or could not, fight against a hidden foe, while they themselves were presented in open view to the marksmen. Washington recommended the Virginia example of seeking protection from the trees, but the General would not even then abandon his European tactics. The regulars stood in squads shooting their own companions before them. The result was an overwhelming defeat, astounding when the relative forces and equipment of the two parties is considered. Braddock, who,

amidst all his faults, did not lack courage, directed his men while five horses were killed under him. Washington was also in the thickest of the danger, losing two horses, while his clothes were pierced by four bullets. Many years afterwards, when he visited the region on a peaceful mission, an old Indian came to see him as a wonder. He had, he said, levelled his rifle so often at him without effect, that he became persuaded he was under the special protection of the Great Spirit, and gave up the attempt. Braddock at length fell in the centre of the field fatally wounded. Nothing now remained but flight. But four officers out of eighty-six were left alive and unwounded. Washington's first care was for the wounded General; his next employment, to ride to the reserve camp of Dunbar, forty miles, for aid and supplies. Returning with the requisite assistance, he met the wounded Braddock on the retreat. Painfully borne along the road, he survived the engagement several days, and reached the Great Meadows to die and be buried there by the broken remnant of his army. Washington read the funeral service, the chaplain being disabled by a wound. Writing to his brother, he attributed his own protection, " beyond all human probability or expectation," to the " all-powerful dispensations of Providence." The natural and pious sentiment was echoed, shortly after, from the pulpit of the excellent Samuel Davies, in Hanover County, Virginia. " I may point," said he, in illustration of his patriotic purpose of encouraging new recruits for the ser vice, in words since that time often pronounced prophetic, "to that heroic youth, Colonel Washington, whom I cannot but hope Providence has hitherto preserved in so signal a manner for some important service to his country."

One lesson of this campaign was deeply impressed upon the mind of Washington, the disobedience, disorder and cowardice of the regular troops compared with the heroic fate of the Virginia companies. He expresses himself in the strongest terms of this " dastardly behavior of the regular troops, *so called*," in his correspondence at the time, and the experience, doubtless, remained with him in after days of doubt and difficulty when the conviction was needed to sustain him against hostile hosts.

The public attention of the province was now turned to Washington, as the best defender of the soil. His voluntary service had expired, but he was still engaged as adjutant, in directing the levies from his residence at Mount Vernon, whence the Legislature soon called him to the chief command of the Virginia forces. He stipulated for thorough activity and discipline in the whole service, and accepted the office. The defence of the country, exposed to the fierce severities of savage warfare, was in his hands. He set the posts in order, organized forces, rallied recruits, and appealed earnestly to the Assembly for vigorous means of relief. It was again a lesson for his after life when a greater foe was to be pressing our more extended frontiers under his care, and the reluctance or weakness of

the Virginia Legislature was to be reproduced, in an exaggerated form, in the imbecility of Congress. We shall thus behold Washington, everywhere the patient child of experience, unweariedly conning his lesson, learning, from actual life, the statesman's knowledge of man and affairs. He was sent into this school of the world early, for he was yet but twenty-three, when this guardianship of the State was placed upon his shoulders.

We find him again jealous of authority in the interests of the service. A certain Captain Dagworthy, in a small command at Fort Cumberland, refused obedience to orders, asserting his privilege as a royal officer of the late campaign, and the question was ultimately referred to General Shirley, the commander-in-chief at Boston. Thither Washington himself carried his appeal, making his journey on horseback in the midst of winter, and had his view of his superior authority confirmed. A bit of romance also has been connected with this tour on public business. At New York he was entertained by a friend in Beverley Robinson, of a Virginia family, who had married one of the heiresses of the wealthy landowner of the Hudson, Adolphus Philipse, the proprietor of the manor of that name. Mrs. Robinson had a sister equally wealthy with herself, young and beautiful, of whom it was said Washington, who was by no means insensible to female charms, and who had also a prudent regard for fortune, became enamored. Indeed, his admiration, says Mr. Irving, is " an historical fact." The story is sometimes added, that he sought her hand and was rejected, but this the excellent authority just cited discredits as improbable. Urgent public affairs called the gallant officer to new struggles in the wilderness, and the lucky prize passed into the arms of a brother officer of Braddock's staff.

Returning immediately to Virginia, Colonel Washington continued his employment in active military duties, struggling not less with the inefficient Assembly at home, whom he tried to arouse, than with the enemy abroad. It was a trying service, in which the commander, spite of every hardship which he freely encountered, was sure to meet the reproach of the suffering public. The disinterested conduct of Washington proved no exception to the rule. He even experienced the ingratitude of harsh newspaper comments, and thought for the moment of resignation; but his friends, the noblest spirits in the colony, reassured him of their confidence, and he steadily went on. The arrival of Lord Loudoun, so unpleasantly satirized by Franklin in his Autobiography, as commander-in-chief of his majesty's forces, seemed to offer some opportunity for more active operations, and Washington drew up a memorial of the affairs he had in charge for his instruction, and met him in conference at Philadelphia. Little, however, resulted from these negotiations for the relief of Virginia, and Washington, exhausted by his labors, was compelled to seek retirement at Mount Vernon, where he lay for some time prostrated by an attack of fever. In the next spring, of 1758, he was

enabled to resume his command. The Virginia troops took the field, joined to the forces of the British general, Forbes, and the year, after various disastrous movements, which might have been better directed had the counsels of Washington prevailed, was signalized by the capture of Fort Du Quesne. Washington, with his Virginians, traversed the ground whitened with the bones of his former comrades in Braddock's expedition, and with his entry of the fort closed the French dominions on the Ohio The war had taken another direction on the Canadian frontier in New York, and Virginia was left in repose.

Shortly after this event, in January, 1759, Washington was married to Mrs. Martha Custis, of the White House, county of New Kent. This lady, born in the same year with himself, and consequently in the full bloom of youthful womanhood, at twenty-seven, was the widow of a wealthy landed proprietor whose death had occurred three years before. Her maiden name was Dandridge, and she was of Welsh descent. The prudence and gravity of her disposition eminently fitted her to be the wife of Washington. She was her husband's sole executrix, and managed the complicated affairs of the estates which he had left, involving the raising of crops and sale of them in Europe, with ability. Her personal charms, too, in these days of her widowhood, are highly spoken of. The well-known portrait by Woolaston, painted at this period, presents a neat, animated figure, with regular features, dark chestnut hair, and hazel eyes, in a dress which, changed often in the interval, the whirligig of fashion has restored to the year in which we write, 1860. The story of the courtship is too character-istic to be omitted. The first sight of the lady, at least in her widowhood, by the gallant Colonel, was on one of his military journeyings during the last campaign, just alluded to, of the old French war. He was speeding to the Council at Williamsburg, on a special message, to stir up aid for the camp, when, crossing the ferry over the Pam-unkey, a branch of York River, he was waylaid by one of the residents of the region, who compelled him, by the inexorable laws of old Virginia hospi-tality, to stop for dinner at his man-sion. The energetic officer, intent on despatch, was reluctant to yield a moment from his affairs of state, but there was no escape of such a guest from such a host. Within, he found Mrs. Custis, whose attractions recon-ciled even Washington to delay. He not only stayed to dine, but he passed the night, a charmed guest, with his friendly entertainer. The lady's resi-dence, fortunately, was in the neighbor-hood of Williamsburg, and a soldier's life requiring a prompt disposition of his opportunities, the Colonel, mindful, perhaps, of the loss of Miss Philipse under similar circumstances, pressed his suit with vigor, and secured the lady at once in the midst of her suit-ors. He corresponded with her con-stantly during the remainder of the campaign, and in the month of Jan-uary, 1759, the wedding took place with great éclat, at the bride's estate at the White House. The honeymoon

was the inauguration of a new and pacific era of Washington's hitherto troubled military life.

Yet even this repose proved the in-troduction to new public duties. With a sense of the obligations befitting a Virginia gentleman, Washington had offered himself to the suffrages of his fellow countrymen at Winchester, and been elected a member of the House of Burgesses. About the time of his marriage, he took his seat, when an incident occurred which has been often narrated. The Speaker, by a vote of the House, having been directed to return thanks to him for his eminent military services, at once performed the duty with warmth and eloquence. Washington rose to express his thanks, but, never voluble before the public became too embarrassed to utter a syl lable. "Sit down, Mr. Washington," was the courteous relief of the gentle-man who had addressed him, "your modesty equals your valor, and that surpasses the power of any language I possess." He continued a member of the House, diligently attending to its business till he was called to the work of the Revolution, in this way adding to his experiences in war, familiarity with the practical duties of a legislator and statesman. He was constantly pre-sent at the debates, it being "a maxim with him through life," as his biogra-pher, Mr. Sparks, observes—and no one has traced his course more minutely, or is better entitled to offer the remark— "to execute punctually and thoroughly every charge which he undertook."

Duties like these from such a man were a graceful addition to the planter's life. After a short sojourn at his wife's estate, he carried her to the house at Mount Vernon, which now became a home. Two children of his wife, by her former marriage, a boy and girl, six and four years old, accompanied her. "I am now, I believe," wrote her husband, to a correspondent in London, "fixed at this seat with an agreeable partner for life, and I hope to find more happiness in retirement than I ever experienced amidst the wide and bustling world."

The occupations and resources of his life at this period have been fondly detailed by his biographers from the numerous memoranda of his diaries, almanacs, and note-books. The humblest proceedings of farm business and the daily management of his affairs are uncovered before our eyes. We may learn the cares and provision of negro labor on the plantation, and the need of watchfulness in the midst of abundance. "Would any one believe," says he in one of these records of 1768, "that with a hundred and one cows actually reported at a late enumeration of the cattle, I should still be obliged to buy butter for my family?" The very items of his housekeeping and personal apparel may be gathered from his orders to his London correspondents, for in the state of dependence in which the mother country then kept her colonies, it was necessary to procure a coat or a pair of shoes from London. Some of our finely dressed aristocratic ancestors must needs have gone in ill fitting garments. Certainly a fashionable tailor of the present day would scarcely be able to supply an order,

3

without great hazard to his reputation, from such a description as Washington sent of himself, as a man "six feet high and proportionably made; if anything rather slender for a person of that height." It was a convenient thing then to have a particular friend with a foot of the same size as your own, as Washington had in Colonel Beiler, when he availed himself in his directions across the water of that gentleman's last, only "a little wider over the instep." We may trace the paraphernalia of the bride in these orders for Mrs. Washington, in the year of their marriage—the "salmon-colored tabby," and the Brussels lace, and the very playthings for little Miss Martha—"a fashionable dressed doll to cost a guinea," and another for rougher, weekday handling, to cost five shillings; and there is the genteel attire for "Master Custis, eight years old," his "silver laced hat," "neat pumps," and "silver shoe and knee buckles"—vanities moderated by the introduction of "a small Bible neatly bound in Turkey, and John Parke Custis wrote in gilt letters on the inside of the cover," with a prayer book to match. Here, too, in the same familiar handwriting of Washington, is an order for several busts for the decoration of the family mansion, now assuming proportions worthy the new alliance which had brought lands and money to its owner's fortunes—"one of Alexander the Great; another of Julius Cæsar; another of Charles XII., of Sweden, and a fourth, of the King of Prussia." A good selection for a soldier who had looked upon the realities of military life. We shall by and by see that same King of Prussia, the great Frederick, sending a portrait of himself with the message, "From the oldest general in Europe to the greatest general in the world."

The daily life of the gentleman planter is all the while going on, the crops of wheat and tobacco getting in, which were to be embarked beneath his eye on the broad bosom of the Potomac on their voyage to England and the West Indies. So well established was his repute as a producer, that a barrel of flour bearing his brand was exempted from inspection in the ports of the latter country. Cordial hospitality was going on within doors, and wholesome country sports without. He had hounds for the fox hunt; there were deer to be killed in his woods, abundant wild fowl on his meadows in the season and fisheries in the river at his feet: and that there might be no falling into rusticity, came the annual state visits, when he was accompanied by Mrs. Washington, to the notable picked society at the capitals, Williamsburg and Annapolis. It was a hearty, generous life, fitted to breed manly thoughts and good resolution against the coming time, when the share shall be again exchanged for the sword, and the humble argument of the vestry at the little church at Pohick, where good, eccentric Parson Weems, inculcated his moralities, for the louder controversy of national debate. In fine, look upon Washington at this or any other period of his life, we ever find him industrious, always useful; his activity and influence radiating from the centre of domestic life, and his private

virtue, to the largest interests of the world.

Fifteen years had been thus passed at Mount Vernon, when the peace of provincial life began to be ruffled by a new agitation. France had formerly furnished the stirring theme of opposition and resistance when America poured out her best blood at the call of British statesmen, and helped to restore the falling greatness of England. That same Parliament which had been so wonderfully revived when America seconded the call of Chatham, was now to inflict an insupportable wound upon her defenders. The seeds of the Revolution must be looked for in the previous war with France. There and then America became acquainted with her own powers, and the strength and weakness of British soldiers and placemen. To no one had the lesson been better taught than to Washington. By no one was it studied with more impartiality. There was no faction in his opposition. The traditions of his family, his friends, the provinces, were all in favor of allegiance to the British government. He had nothing in his composition of the disorganizing mind of a mere political agitator, a breeder of discontent. The interests of his large landed estates, and a revenue dependent upon exports, bound him to the British nation. But there was one principle in his nature stronger in its influence than all these material ties—the love of justice; and when Patrick Henry rose in the House of Burgesses, with his eloquent assertion of the rights of the colony in the matter of taxation, Washington was there in his seat to respond to the sentiment.

To this memorable occasion, on the 29th May, 1765, has been referred the birth of that patriotic fervor in the mind of Washington, welcoming as it was developed a new order of things, which never rested till the liberties of the country were established on the firmest foundations of independence and civil order. "His correspondence," says Irving, writing of this incident, " hitherto had not turned on political or speculative themes; being engrossed by either military or agricultural matters, and evincing little anticipation of the vortex of public duties into which he was about to be drawn. All his previous conduct and writings show a loyal devotion to the crown, with a patriotic attachment to his country. It is probable that, on the present occasion, that latent patriotism received its first electric shock." Be this as it may, he was certainly from the beginning an earnest supporter of the constitutional liberties of his country, and met every fresh aggression of Parliament as it arose, in the most resolute manner. He took part in the local Virginia resolutions, and on the meeting of the first Congress, in Philadelphia, went up to that honored body with Patrick Henry and Edmund Pendleton. He was at this time a firm, unyielding maintainer of the rights in controversy, and fully prepared for any issue which might grow out of them; but he was no revolutionist—for it was not in the nature of his mind to consider a demand for justice a provocative to war. Again, in Virginia, after the adjournment of Congress, in the important Convention at Richmond, he listens to the impetuous eloquence of Patrick Henry. It was this body which set on foot a popular military organization in the colony, and Washington, who had previously given his aid to the independent companies, was a member of the Committee to report the plan. A few days later, he writes to his brother, John Augustine, who was employed in training a company, that he would "very cheerfully accept the honor of commanding it, if occasion require it to be drawn out."

The second Continental Congress, of which Washington was also a member met at Philadelphia in May, 1775, its members gathering to the deliberations with throbbing hearts, the musketry of Lexington ringing in their ears. The overtures of war by the British troops in Massachusetts had gathered a little provincial army about Boston a national organization was a measure no longer of choice, but of necessity. A Commander-in-Chief was to be appointed, and though the selection was not altogether free from local jealousies, the superior merit of Washington was seconded by the superior patriotism of the Congress, and on the fifteenth of June he was unanimously elected by ballot to the high position. His modesty in accepting the office was as noticeable as his fitness for it. He was not the man to flinch from any duty, because it was hazardous; but it is worth knowing, that we may form a due estimate of his character, that he felt to the quick the full force of the sacrifices of ease and happiness that he was making, and the new difficulties he was inevitably to encounter. He was so impressed with the probabilities of failure, and so little disposed to vaunt his own powers, that he begged gentlemen in the House to remember, "lest some unlucky event should happen unfavorable to his reputation," that he thought himself, "with the utmost sincerity, unequal to the command he was honored with." With a manly spirit of patriotic independence, worthy the highest eulogy, he declared his intention to keep an exact account of his public expenses, and accept nothing more for his services—a resolution which was faithfully kept to the letter. With these disinterested preliminaries, he proceeded to Cambridge, and took command of the army on the third of July. Bunker Hill had been fought, establishing the valor of the native militia, and the leaguer of Boston was already formed, though with inadequate forces. There was excellent individual material in the men, but everything was to be done for their organization and equipment. Above all, there was an absolute want of powder. It was impossible to make any serious attempt upon the British in Boston, but the utmost heroism was shown in cutting off their resources and hemming them in. Humble as were these inefficient means in the present, the prospect of the future was darkened by the short enlistments of the army, which were made only for the year, Congress expecting in that time a favorable answer to their second Petition to the King. The new recruits came in slowly, and means were feebly supplied, but Washington, bent on action, determined upon an attack.

For this purpose, he took possession of and fortified Dorchester Heights, and prepared to assail the town. The British were making an attempt to dislodge him, which was deferred by a storm; and General Howe, having already resolved to evacuate the city, a few days after, on the 17th of March, ingloriously sailed away with his troops to Halifax. The next day, Washington entered the town in triumph. Thus ended the first epoch of his Revolutionary campaigns. There had been little opportunity for brilliant action, but great difficulties had been overcome with a more honorable persistence, and a substantial benefit had been gained. The full extent of the services of Washington became known only to his posterity, since it was absolutely necessary at the time to conceal the difficulties under which he labored; but the country saw and felt enough to extol his fame and award him an honest meed of gratitude. A special vote of Congress gave expression to the sentiment, and a gold medal, bearing the head of Washington, and on the reverse the legend *Hostibus primo fugatis*, was ordered by that body to commemorate the event.

We must now follow the commander rapidly to another scene of operations, remembering that any detailed notice, however brief, of Washington's military operations during the war, would expand this biographical sketch into a historical volume. New York was evidently to be the next object of attack, and thither Washington gathered his forces, and made every available means of defence on land. By the beginning of July, when the Declaration of Independence was received in camp, General Howe had made his appearance in the lower bay from Halifax, where he was speedily joined by his brother, Lord Howe, the admiral, who came bearing ineffectual propositions for reconciliation. Having occasion to address the American Commander-in-Chief, he failed to give him his proper title, lest he should recognize his position, but superscribed his letter, "To George Washington, Esq." This was borne by a messenger asking for *Mr.* Washington, who was properly reminded, by the adjutant who met him, that he knew of no such person in the army, and the letter being produced, it was pronounced inadmissible. The messenger accordingly returned, and General Howe, some days after, sent another, who asked for *General* Washington, and being admitted to his presence, addressed him as *Your Excellency*, offering another letter with various etceteras appended to the simple name, urging that they meant "everything." But Washington was not to be caught by a subterfuge. They may, indeed, said he, mean "everything," but they also mean "anything," and he could not receive a letter relating to his public station directed to him as a private person. So the British adjutant was compelled to report the contents of the epistle, which related to the reconciliation; but here again he was checkmated by Washington, who, aware of the nature of Lord Howe's overtures, replied that they were but pardons, and the Americans, who had committed no offence, but

stood only upon their rights, could stand in no need of them. Thus terminated this interview, a most characteristic one, a model for diplomatic action, and even private courtesy, which was highly appreciated by Congress and the country at the time, and which will never be forgotten.

Additional reinforcements to the royal troops on Staten Island now arrived from England; a landing was made by the well-equipped army on Long Island, and a battle was imminent. Washington, who had his headquarters in New York, made vigilant preparations around the city, and at the works on Long Island, which had been planned and fortified by General Greene. This officer unfortunately falling ill, the command fell to General Putnam, who was particularly charged by Washington with instructions for the defence of the passes by which the enemy might approach. These were neglected, an attack was made from opposite sides, and in spite of much valiant fighting on the part of the various defenders, who contended with fearful odds, the day was most disastrous to the Americans. The slaughter was great on this 27th of August, and many prisoners, including General Sullivan and Lord Stirling, were taken. Still the main works at Brooklyn, occupied by the American troops, remained, though, exposed as they were to the enemy's fleet, they were no longer tenable. Washington, whose duties kept him in the city to be ready for its defence, as soon as he heard of the engagement, hastened to the spot, but it was too late to turn the fortunes of the day. He was compelled to witness the disaster, tradition tells us, not without the deepest emotion. An unknown contemporary versifier of the war, in his simple rhymes, has commemorated the scene:

> " Brave Washington did say,
>   Alas! good God,
> Brave men I've lost to-day,
>   They're in their blood.
> His grief he did express
> To see them in distress,
> His tears and hands witness
> He lov'd his men." [1]

But it was the glory of Washington to save the remnant of the army by a retreat more memorable than the victory of General Clinton. The day after the battle, and the next, were passed without any decisive movements on the part of the British, who were about bringing up their ships, and who, doubtless, as they had good reason, considered their prey secure. On the twenty-ninth, Washington took his measures for the retreat, and so perfectly were they arranged, that the whole force of nine thousand, with artillery, horses, and the entire equipage of war, were borne off that night, under cover of the fog, to the opposite shore in triumph. It was a most masterly operation, planned and superintended by Washington from the beginning. He did not sleep or rest after the battle till it was executed, and was among the last to cross.

After this followed in rapid succession, though with no undue haste, the abandonment of New York, the withdrawal of the troops into Westchester, the affair at White Plains, the more serious loss of Fort Washington, and the retreat through the Jerseys. It was the darkest period of the war, the days of which Paine wrote in the memorable expression of the opening number of his " Crisis." " These are the times that try men's souls: the summer soldier and the sunshine patriot will, in this crisis, shrink from the service of his country; but he that stands it now, deserves the love and thanks of man and woman." To inferiority in numbers, with a host at its heels, the American soldiery added the serious disqualifying conditions of lack of discipline and poverty of equipment. Enlisted for short terms, with all the evils of a voluntary militia unused to service, it was, as Hamilton, who shared the great chieftain's solicitudes, expressed it, but " the phantom of a military force." The letters of Washington, at this period, and indeed generally throughout the war, are filled with the anxieties of his position, in which he saw his fame perilled with the welfare of his country. The severest suffering for an ingenuous mind is, perhaps, to bear unworthy reproach, to be misconceived by a public for whom every sacrifice is silently borne and endured. This was Washington's lot, for long, weary years of marching and countermarching between the Hudson and the Chesapeake, husbanding his small, inefficient force, retreating to-day, to-morrow advancing, working the " phantom " with such success in the face of the enemy as to perplex the movements of experienced generals with consider-

---

[1] Ballad Literature of the Revolution. Cyclopædia of American Literature, I. 445.

able forces. Nor was the fault altogether at the door of Congress. That body was, indeed, a popular representation, composed, at the outset, of very able men, and always having such included in its numbers; but it was very loosely tied to its constituency. At present, the delegated power of the representative, where not specially controlled, is absolute; but in the flimsy texture of the unformed body politic of the old confederacy, there was little cohesion of parts or attention to mutual duties. The battles of the Revolution were fought with half-disciplined armies at the will of a half-formed administration. Local State jealousies had to be conciliated, and the people could not appreciate the advantage of an army, firmly handled, as the instrument of its own sovereign authority. The battle had to be fought often and in many parts of the country, according to the immediate necessity and temporary inclination. Much was gained by Washington, but it came slowly and reluctantly, though there were brilliant exceptions in the service. Generally, there was a want of regularity and uniformity. It was somewhat remedied by the extraordinary powers conferred upon Washington at the close of 1776, but the evil was inherent in the necessarily loose political organization.

After the battle of Long Island, there had been little but weariness and disaster, in the movements of Washington, to the end of the year, when, as the forces of Howe were apparently closing in upon him to open the route to Philadelphia, he turned in very despair, and by the brilliant affair at Trenton retarded the motions of the enemy and checked the growing despondency of his countrymen. It was well planned and courageously undertaken. Christmas night, of a most inclement, wintry season, when the river was blocked with ice, was chosen to cross the Delaware, and attack the British and Hessians on the opposite side at Trenton. The expedition was led by Washington in person, who anxiously watched the slow process of the transportation on the river, which lasted from sunset till near the dawn— too long for the contemplated surprise by night. A storm of hail and snow now set in, as the General advanced with his men, reaching the outposts about eight o'clock. A gallant onset was made, in which Lieut. Monroe, afterwards the President, was wounded; Sullivan and the other officers, according to a previously arranged plan, seconded the movement from another part of the town; the Hessians were disconcerted, and their general, Rahl, slain, when a surrender was made, nearly a thousand prisoners laying down their arms. General Howe, astonished at the event, sent out Cornwallis in pursuit, and he had his game seemingly secure, when Washington, in front of him at Trenton, on the same side of the Delaware, made a bold diversion in an attack on the forces left behind at Princeton. It was, like the previous one, conducted by night, and, like the other, was attended with success, though it cost the life of the gallant Mercer. After these brilliant actions the little army took up its quarters at Morristown for the winter.

In the spring, General Howe made some serious attempts at breaking up the line of Washington in New Jersey, but he was foiled, and compelled to seek another method of reaching Philadelphia. The withdrawal of the British troops would thus have left a simple course to be pursued on the Delaware, had not the attention of Washington been called in another direction by the advance of Burgoyne from Canada. It was natural to suppose that Howe would act in concert with that officer on the Hudson, nor was Washington relieved from the dilemma till intelligence reached him that the British general had embarked his forces, and was actually at the Capes of the Delaware. He then took up a position at Germantown for the defence of Philadelphia. Visiting the city for the purpose of conference with Congress, he there found the Marquis de Lafayette, who had just presented himself, as a volunteer in the cause of liberty, to the government. His reception by Congress had halted a little on his first arrival, but his disinterestedness had overcome all obstacles, and Washington, who had schooled himself to look upon realities without prejudice, gave the young foreign officer a cordial welcome. He took him to the camp, and soon gave him an opportunity to bleed in the sacred cause.

Howe, meanwhile, the summer having passed away in these uncertainties, was slowly making his way up the Chesapeake to the Head of Elk, to gain access to Philadelphia from Maryland, and the American army was advanced to meet him. The British troops numbered about eighteen thousand; the American, perhaps two-thirds of that number. A stand was made by the latter at Chad's Ford, on the east side of the Brandywine, to which Knyphausen was opposed on the opposite bank, while Cornwallis, with a large division, took the upper course of the river, and turned the flank of the position. General Sullivan was intrusted with this portion of the defence; but time was lost, in the uncertainty of information, in meeting the movement, and when the parties met, Cornwallis had greatly the advantage. A rout ensued, which was saved from utter defeat by the resistance of General Greene, who was placed at an advantageous point. Lafayette was severely wounded in the leg in the course of the conflict. Washington was not dismayed by the disaster; on the contrary, he kept the field, marshalling and manœuvring through a hostile country, one thousand of his troops, as he informed Congress, actually barefoot. He would have offered battle, but he was without the means to resist effectually the occupation of Philadelphia. A part of the enemy's forces were stationed at Germantown, a few miles from the city. Washington, considering them in an exposed situation, planned a surprise. It was well arranged, and at the outset was successful; but, owing to the confusion in the heavy fog of the October morning, and loss of strength and time in attacking a strongly defended mansion at the entrance of the village, what should have been a brilliant victory was changed into a partial defeat. The action, however, as Mr. Sparks observes, was "not without its good effects. It revived the hopes of the country by proving, that notwithstanding the recent successes of the enemy, neither the spirit, resolution and valor of the troops, nor the energy and confidence of the commander, had suffered any diminution." It was the remark of the French minister, the Count de Vergennes, on hearing of these transactions, "that nothing struck him so much as General Washington's attacking and giving battle to General Howe's army; that to bring an army, raised within a year, to this, promised everything."

Thus closed the campaign of 1777 in Pennsylvania, while Burgoyne was laying down his arms to the northern army at Saratoga. Though it was Washington's lot to endure all the difficulties of the service while Gates was reaping the rewards of victory, the former had his share in the counsels which led to that brilliant event. His letter to Schuyler, of the 22d of July, exhibited a knowledge of the position, and a prescience of the exact result, which show how successfully he would have managed the campaign in person. He notices Burgoyne's first successes, and argues that they "will precipitate his ruin," while he sees his weakness in acting in detachment, exposing his parties to great hazard. "Could we," he writes, "be so happy as to cut one of them off, supposing it should not exceed four, five, or six hundred men, it would inspirit the people, and do away much of their present anxiety."

Had he written after, instead of before the event, he could not better have described the influence of Bennington. To Washington, as the directing head of the national army, belongs his full share of the glories of Saratoga; yet the accidental greatness which fell to the vainglorious Gates was made the occasion of assaults upon the Commander-in-Chief, which would have crept from their mean concealments into open revolt, had not the conspiracy been strangled in its infancy by the incorruptibility of his friends and the virtue of the country.

The encampment at Valley Forge succeeded the scenes we have described. It is a name synonymous with suffering. Half clad, wanting frequently the simplest clothing, without shoes or blankets, the army was hutted in the snows and ice of that inclement winter. Yet they had Washington with them urging every means for their welfare, while his "Lady," as his wife was always called in the army, came from Mount Vernon, as was her custom during these winter encampments, to lighten the prevailing despondency. She lived simply with her husband, sharing the humble provisions of the camp, and occupying herself with her needle in preparing garments for the naked. Washington, meanwhile, was busy with a Committee of Congress in putting the army on a better foundation.

With the return of summer came the evacuation of Philadelphia by the British, who were pursuing their route across New Jersey to embark on the waters of New York. Washington with his forces was watching their movements from above. Shall he attack them on their march? There was a division of opinion among his officers. The equivocal Charles Lee, then unsuspected, was opposed to the step; but Washington, with his best advisers, Greene, Lafayette, and Wayne, was in favor of it. He accordingly sent Lafayette forward, when Lee interposed, and claimed the command of the advance. Washington himself moved on with the reserve towards the enemy's position near Monmouth Court House, to take part in the fortunes of the day, the 28th of June. As he was proceeding, he was met by the intelligence that Lee was in full retreat, without notice or apparent cause, endangering the order of the rear, and threatening the utmost confusion. Presently he came upon Lee himself, and demanded from him with an emphasis roused by the fiercest indignation—and the anger of Washington when excited was terrific —the cause of the disorder. Lee replied angrily, and gave such explanation as he could of a superior force, when Washington, doubtless mindful of his previous conduct, answered him with dissatisfaction, and, it is said, on the authority of Lafayette, ended by calling the retreating general "a damned poltroon."[1] It was a great day for the genius of Washington. He made his arrangements on the spot to retrieve the fortunes of the hour, and so admirable were the dispositions, and so well was he seconded by the bravery of officers and men, even Lee, redeeming his character by his valor, that at

the close of that hot and weary day, the Americans having added greatly to the glory of their arms, remained at least equal masters of the field. The next morning it was found that Sir Henry Clinton had withdrawn towards Sandy Hook. The remainder of the season was passed by Washington on the eastern borders of the Hudson, in readiness to coöperate with the French, who had now arrived under D'Estaing, and in watching the British in New York. In December he took up his winter quarters at Middlebrook, in New Jersey. The event of the next year in the little army of Washington, was Wayne's gallant storming of Stony Point, on the Hudson, one of the defences of the Highlands, which had been recently captured and manned by Sir Henry Clinton. The attack on the night of the 15th July was planned by Washington, and his directions in his instructions to Wayne, models of careful military precision, were faithfully carried out. Henry Lee's spirited attack on Paulus Hook, within sight of New York, followed, to cheer the encampment of Washington, who now busied himself in fortifying West Point. Winter again finds the army in quarters in New Jersey, this time at Morristown, when the hardships and severities of Valley Forge were even exceeded in the distressed condition of the troops in that rigorous season. The main incidents of the war are henceforth at the South.

The most prominent event in the personal career of Washington, of the year 1780, is certainly the defection of Arnold, with its attendant execution of Major André. This unhappy trea-

---

[1] Dawson's "Battles of the United States," I. 408.

son was every way calculated to enlist his feelings, but he suffered neither hate nor sympathy to divert him from the considerate path of duty. We may not pause over the subsequent events of the war, the renewed exertions of Congress, the severe contests in the South, the meditated movement upon New York the following year, but must hasten to the sequel at Yorktown. The movement of the army of Washington to Virginia was determined by the expected arrival of the French fleet in that quarter from the West Indies. Lafayette was already on the spot, where he had been engaged in the defence of the country from the inroads of Arnold and Phillips. Cornwallis had arrived from the South, and unsuspicious of any serious opposition was entrenching himself on York River. It was all that could be desired, and Washington, who had been planning an attack upon New York with Rochambeau, now suddenly and secretly directed his forces by a rapid march southward. Extraordinary exertions were made to expedite the troops. The timely arrival of Colonel John Lawrens, from France, with an instalment of the French loan in specie, came to the aid of the liberal efforts of the financier of the Revolution, Robert Morris. Lafayette, with the Virginians, was hedging in the fated Cornwallis. Washington had just left Philadelphia, when he heard the joyous news of the arrival of De Grasse in the Chesapeake. He hastened on to the scene of action in advance of the troops, with De Rochambeau gaining time to pause at Mount Vernon, which he had not seen since the opening of the war, and enjoy a day's hurried hospitality with his French officers at the welcome mansion. Arrived at Williamsburg, Washington urged on the military movements with the energy of anticipated victory. "Hurry on, then, my dear sir," he wrote to General Lincoln, "with your troops on the wings of speed." To make the last arrangements with the French admiral, he visited him in his ship, at the mouth of James' River. Everything was to be done before succor could arrive from the British fleet and troops at New York. The combined French and American forces closed in upon Yorktown, which was fortified by redoubts and batteries, and on the first of October, the place was completely invested. The first parallel was opened on the sixth. Washington lighted the first gun on the ninth. The storming of two annoying redoubts by French and American parties were set down for the night of the fourteenth. Hamilton, at the head of the latter, gallantly carried one of the works at the point of the bayonet without firing a shot. Washington watched the proceeding at imminent hazard. The redoubts gained were fortified and turned against the town. The second parallel was ready to open its fire. Cornwallis vainly attempted to escape with his forces across the river. He received no relief from Sir Henry Clinton, at New York, and on the 17th he proposed a surrender. On the 19th, the terms having been dictated by Washington, the whole British force laid down their arms. It was the virtual termination of the war, the crowning act of a vast series of military operations planned and perfected by the genius of Washington.

During the remainder of the war, his efforts and vigilance were not relaxed; and he had one opportunity, ever memorable in the annals of political liberty, of showing his superiority to the common ambition of conquerors. In May, 1782, a letter was addressed to him by Col. Nicola, an officer who had the esteem of the army, stating the inefficiency of the existing administration, and suggesting a mixed form of government, with a King at its head, with no indirect appeal to the ambition of the Commander-in-Chief as the proper recipient of the office. To this, Washington replied with the utmost decision, but without the least affectation of doing anything heroic; he simply puts the idea out of the way as something utterly inadmissible, "painful" and "disagreeable" to his mind. He rejects it as a gentleman would an unhandsome suggestion. Much has been said of this matter, and there is reason to believe not unjustifiably, in praise of Washington. "There was unquestionably," says Mr. Sparks, "at this time, and for some time afterwards, a party in the army, neither small in number nor insignificant in character, prepared to second and sustain a measure of this kind, which they conceived necessary to strengthen the civil power, draw out the resources of the country, and establish a durable government." No one felt these evils more keenly than Washington, but he had too much faith in the Republic to despair of a better method of cure.

He knew as well as any that he could not be king if he would; the anecdote is quite sufficient to prove, where proof was not wanting, that he would not if he could.

Another opportunity yet remained to exhibit his control of the temper of the army, and his habitual deference of military to civil government. The occasion arose while he was with the troops at headquarters at Newburg, in the spring of 1783, on the eve of the receipt of the final intelligence of peace. Congress, always dilatory in providing for the army, had shown an unwillingness or incapacity to meet their claims; patient remonstrance had been disregarded; and now a meeting of officers was called, instigated by an appeal of extraordinary vigor, one of the compositions since ascertained to have been written by General John Armstrong, and known as "The Newburg Letters," which threatened serious revolt. It was not the first time that Washington had been called to act in such an emergency. In the withdrawal of the Pennsylvania line from the camp at the beginning of 1781, he had met a similar difficulty, with great prudence and moderation. He now brought these qualities to bear with a quickness and decision proportioned to the crisis. Summoning the officers together, he addressed to them a firm but tender remonstrance, opening his address with a touch of pathos which gained all hearts. Pausing after he had commenced his remarks, to take his spectacles from his pocket, he remarked that he had "grown grey in their service, and now I am growing blind." It was the honest heart of Washington, and the disaffected responded to the wisdom and feeling of his address.

The news of peace arrived within the month, and the army prepared to separate. In memory of their fraternity, the Society of the Cincinnati was founded, consisting of officers of the Revolution and their descendants, with Washington at its head. In the beginning of November, he took leave of the army in an address from headquarters, with his accustomed warmth and emotion, and on the 25th, entered New York at the head of a military and civic procession as the British evacuated the city. On the 4th of December, he was escorted to the harbor on his way to Congress, at Annapolis, to resign his command, after a touching scene of farewell with his officers at Fraunces' Tavern, when the great chieftain did not disdain the sensibility of a tear and the kiss of his friends. Arrived at Annapolis, having on the way delivered to the proper officer at Philadelphia his accounts of his expenses during the war, neatly written out by his own hand, on the twenty-third of the month he restored his commission to Congress, with a few remarks of great felicity, in which he commended "the interests of our dearest country to the protection of Almighty God; and those who have the superintendence of them to his holy keeping."

Mount Vernon again welcomed its restored lord. He reached his home the day before Christmas, and cheerily, doubtless, the smoke on that sacred holiday ascended from the thankful festivities. A few days after, a letter to Governor Clinton, of New York, his old comrade in arms, records the innermost feeling of his heart. "The scene," he writes, "is at last closed. I feel myself eased of a load of public care. I hope to spend the remainder of my days in cultivating the affections of good men and in the practice of the domestic virtues." Did ever conqueror so resign his heart before?

We may not linger, tempting as is the theme, over the simple life on the Potomac, though there is to be studied, no less than in camps and senates, the true nature of the man. Kind, hospitable, sympathetic to every worthy appeal, engaged in the care of his estate, sowing, planting, reaping, the youthfulness of his old family circle renewed in the children of young Custis, who had followed his sister to an early grave, he lived in dignified, cheerful retirement. He even revived his old sports of the chase, though he had no longer the veteran Fairfax to cheer him on with his halloo. The old nobleman had lived to listen to the tidings of Yorktown, when he turned himself to the wall and died.

Here Fame might be content to close the scene in her record of her favorite child. At the treaty of peace he was fifty-one, and had gloriously consummated the duties of two memorable eras in the history of his country, each drawing along its train of ideas—the war with France and the war with Great Britain; a double relief from foreign bondage; the establishment of religious and political independence

His services to either would well supply enough of incident and eulogy for these pages—but two further eras are yet before him. He is to assist, by his all-powerful voice and example, in guiding the nation he, more than any, had formed, through its perilous crisis—the dangerous period when it was first left to itself—to the calm maintenance of civil liberty. It is the youth just freed from the restraint of harsh and iniquitous parentage, putting himself under the yoke of a new and voluntary submission. This second pupilage, to self-government, resulted in the formation of the Constitution. Many ministered to that noble end, far more worthy of admiration even than the previous wars, but who more anxiously, more perseveringly, than Washington? His authority carried the heart and intelligence of the country with it, and most appropriately was he placed at the head of the Convention, in 1787, which gave a government to the scattered States and made America a nation.

Once more he was called to listen to the highest demands of his country in his unanimous election to the Presidency. With what emotions, with what humble resignation to the voice of duty, with how little fluttering of vain glory let the modest entry, in his Diary, of the 16th April, 1789, cited by Washington Irving, tell: "About ten o'clock," he writes, "I bade adieu to Mount Vernon, to private life and to domestic felicity; and with a mind oppressed with more anxious and painful sensations than I have words to express, set out for New York with the best disposition to render, service to my country in obedience to its call, but with less hope of answering its expectations." He must have felt, gravely as he bore his responsibilities, something of exulting emotion as he was borne along to the seat of government at New York by the hearty plaudits of his countrymen. Yet we never hear, in a single instance, then or afterwards, of his exhibiting any feeling, or manifesting any conduct inconsistent with the simplest decorum of a gentleman. He was eminently friendly and social, but calm, dignified, and reserved, superadding doubtless something, as was fitting, to his natural gravity, in thought of the nation which he represented, but far removed from mock greatness.

We have the most authentic means of appreciating Washington at this time, in his private Diary, which has been printed from the first day of October, 1789, to the 10th day of March, 1790. He had been five months seated in the Presidency, his inauguration having taken place on the 30th April. During a portion of this time he had been prostrated by illness, and death seemed at hand. We may pause to note his reply to his physician, Dr. Bard, who could not but express his fears of his recovery: "Whether to-night or twenty years hence makes no difference; I know that I am in the hands of a good Providence;" the very breathing of pious resignation. If aught were needed, news of his mother's death, at Fredericksburg, came to temper the sober joy of his convalescence. The care of setting the machinery of the new government in motion succeeded, when Congress adjourned, and the Diary introduces us to the New England tour, extending into New Hampshire, to which he devoted this interval of leisure. His roadside observations on this journey show his knowledge of agriculture, of which he was always a fond observer, with many simple traits of character by the way, and one famed historic passage in his account of the reception at Boston, where Governor Hancock, slow in appreciating national etiquette, seemed to hesitate whether more was due to himself or to his Presidential guest. We may learn, too, from the Diary, his conscientious scrutiny, in private, of the processes leading to his public acts, and may venture within his sacred hours of retirement and open those doors which were always closed to the world. On Sundays, he attends church in the morning, while at New York, at St. Pauls, and occupies the afternoons with his private correspondence. On Tuesday his house is open to all comers. There are many anecdotes of his residence here and at Philadelphia, of his mode of living during his two terms of the Presidency. He was an early riser, a habit with him through life, and apportioned his day with the strictest accuracy. Economy he always practised on principle, " for the privilege of being independent;" and the story is told of his rebuking his steward for bringing on his table an expensive fish before it was in season. His table, however, was well served, and the affairs of his kitchen, like the rest of his establishment, were conducted with exemplary system. The name of his cook, Hercules, " Uncle Harkless," is commemorated in the " Recollections " of his adopted son, George Washington Parke Custis, who also tells us of the decorum preserved in the stables by the veteran, Bishop, who had been the body servant of General Braddock. The test of his " muslin horses " was, that they should not soil a handkerchief of that fabric. Washington was a true Virginian in his fondness for horses. His cream-colored coach, with six shining bays, was long an object of admiration to the people of Philadelphia. These, and the like anecdotes, are subordinate to the greatness of Washington's public life, but they bring before us the man.[1]

In 1791, Washington made a Presidential tour through the Southern States, similar to his tour to the East, which has also been made public in his printed Diary. He travelled in his carriage along the seaboard through Virginia and the Carolinas to Georgia, when he had the opportunity of traversing many scenes of the war, which he had watched with so much anxiety, and which had been hitherto known to him only by report.

[1] Ample illustrations of this character are before the public in Mr. Custis' Recollections, with Mr. Lossing's notes; the latter's " Mount Vernon and its Associates;" the Northern and Southern Tours of Washington, in his two Diaries, published by Mr. Richardson, at New York, and the late Mr. Richard Rush's review of the Correspondence of Washington with his private secretary, Lear. Irving's Life abounds with fine personal traits of character; Mrs. Kirkland has added much in her excellent " Memoirs " from a careful study of the original MSS. in the Department of State; Paulding's " Life " has something that is not elsewhere, and every student of Washington must acknowledge with pleasure his obligation in little things, as in great, to Mr. Jared Sparks.

Meanwhile, parties were gradually forming in the government—the conservative and the progressive, such as will always arise in human institutions—represented in the administration by the rival statesmen, Hamilton and Jefferson; but Washington honestly recognized no guide but the welfare of his country, and the rising waves of faction beat harmlessly beneath his Presidential chair. One test question, however, rose in those days into gigantic proportions. The example of America was followed by France with enthusiasm in the recovery of her liberties, and the hearts of noble-spirited men throughout the world responded to her efforts for freedom. Washington could not but extend his cordial sympathy, when Lafayette sent to him the thrilling intelligence, and forwarded to his keeping, as a souvenir of rising liberty, the key of the Bastile; yet even then he breathes a prayer for the safety of his friend in "the tremendous tempests" which had "assailed the political ship." In the darker days of the Republic, stained with blood, which succeeded, he watched with trembling the staggering of the ship. It was in Washington's second administration, to which he had been chosen with no dissentient voice, that French affairs really became a home question. The minister Genet then came to America, and prosecuted his insulting attempts to enlist the sympathies of America in the war of his country with England, and violate the professed neutrality of the government. A considerable portion of the people were so forgetful of themselves and their country as to favor his schemes; but no such sophistry or delusion could reach the mind of Washington. He stood firm, and the whole country learnt in time to acquiesce in the wisdom of his decision; but many a pang was inflicted first on the heart of the President, who was keenly sensitive to popular ingratitude. The contest culminated in the struggle over Jay's British Treaty in Congress, and Washington fairly gained a triumph in the vote of approval. There were other public events of importance in his two administrations. The Western Indian War, and the Pennsylvania Whisky Insurrection, both deeply engaged his attention. His emotion on first hearing the news of St. Clair's defeat, exhibited in the presence of his private secretary, Tobias Lear, was one of those bursts of passion, brief and rare, in his life, but fearful in their strength. His instructions to that officer, on parting, had been most careful. He was about to engage in a warfare which Washington had learnt to know so well, in the experiences of his early life, and his injunctions were given with proportionate earnestness. "Beware," said he at parting, "of a surprise;" and St. Clair departed with the startling admonition. When Washington heard of the disaster to his troops, the scene of desolation, with all its consequences, came vividly to his mind with the lurking strength of his own old impressions. "Oh, God! oh, God!" he exclaimed, "he's worse than a murderer! How can he answer it to his country! The blood of the slain is upon him—the curse of widows and orphans—the curse of heaven!" This fervid outbreak was followed, almost instantly, by the rebound, which was truly characteristic of Washington : "I will hear him without prejudice; he shall have justice." Thus, in the very tempest and whirlwind of his rage, in the words of the great dramatist, there was "a temperance to beget a smoothness." Washington was always true to the cardinal principle of justice. In like manner with the Pennsylvania insurgents, he was zealous in the maintenance of authority, but disposed to mercy at the first signs of submission.

As the close of his second administration approached, he turned his thoughts eagerly to Mount Vernon for a few short years of repose; and well had he earned them by his long series of services to his country. He would have been welcomed for a third term, but office had no temptation to divert him from his settled resolution. Yet he parted fondly with the nation, and like a parent, desired to leave some legacy of counsel to his country. Accordingly, he published in September, 1796, in the "Daily Advertiser," in Philadelphia, the paper known as his Farewell Address to the People of the United States. It had long engaged his attention; he had planned it himself, and, careful of what he felt might be a landmark for ages, had consulted Jay, Madison and Hamilton in its composition. The spirit and sentiment, the political wisdom and patriotic fervor were every whit his own. Opening with a few personal remarks in reference to his Presidency, he proceeds enlarging his view to new generations

in the future. His first thought is for the preservation of national unity— that the Union should receive "a cordial, habitual and immovable attachment." The force of language cannot be exceeded with which he urges the importance of this theme by every appeal of sensibility and interest. The Constitution is then commended, as the guardian of the whole, to the national affection and respect, with a warning intimation of the dangers of party-spirit carried to excess. Equally upon governors and governed does he impress his views. At home he calls for the diffusion of knowledge, a respect for public credit, avoiding needless debt; and for our intercourse with other nations, strict impartiality. Let us have, says he, " as little *political* connection with them as possible." This and Union are the main themes of the discourse, which closes with the anticipation of "that retreat in which I promise myself to realize, without alloy, the sweet enjoyment of partaking, in the midst of my fellow-citizens, the benign influence of good laws under a free government, the ever favorite object of my heart, and the happy reward, as I trust, of our mutual cares, labors and dangers."

Thus, once again, Mount Vernon received her son, destined never long to repose unsolicited by his country. France, pursuing her downward course, adopted an aggressive policy towards the nation, which the most conciliating deference could no longer support. A state of quasi war existed, and actual war was imminent. The President looked to Washington to organize the army and take the command, should it be brought into action, and he accordingly busied himself in the necessary preparations. It was best, he thought, to be prepared for the worst while looking for the best. New negotiations were then opened, but he did not live to witness their pacific results. He was at his home at Mount Vernon, intent on public affairs, and making his rounds in his usual farm occupations, with a vigor and hardihood which had abated little for his years, when, on the 12th December, he suffered some considerable exposure from a storm of snow and rain which came on while he was out, and in which he continued his ride. It proved, the next day, that he had taken cold, but he made light of it, and passed his usual evening cheerfully with the family circle. He became worse during the night with inflammation of the throat. He was seriously ill. Having sent for his old army surgeon, Dr. Craik, he was bled by his overseer, and again on the arrival of the physician. All was of no avail, and he calmly prepared to die. "I am not afraid," said he, "to go," while with ever thoughtful courtesy he thanked his friends and attendants for their little attentions. Thus the day wore away, till ten in the night, when his end was fast approaching.

He noticed the failing moments, his last act being to place his hand upon his pulse, and calmly expired. It was the fourteenth of December, 1799. His remains were interred in the grave on the bank at Mount Vernon, in front of his residence, and there, in no long time, according to her prediction at the moment of his death, his wife, Martha, whose miniature he always wore on his breast, was laid beside him. She died within three years of her husband, at Mount Vernon, the 22d of May, 1802.

We need not follow a mourning public in their sorrow and lamentations over the grave of Washington, or trace the growing admiration which attends his name throughout the world wherever it has been heard. His merits and virtues are now proudly spoken of and dearly reverenced in the land of his ancestors, against which he led the armies of his countrymen. Every day it is felt that he belongs more and more to the world. He enjoys that apotheosis of fame awarded to the great spirits of the earth, who have been chosen by Providence to grand national duties; but more than most of them, his memory is the reward of a life of piety and purity, of simple faith and justice, of unrelaxing duty; great in its acts, greater in the heart, inspiring virtues which dictated them.

John Adams

JOHN ADAMS.

The Adams family, with whom private and public worth may be said to be hereditary, may be traced in the earliest annals of the colony of Massachusetts to Henry Adams, who, in 1640, settled at Braintree. His son Joseph adhered to the place through a long life and left a son of the same name who continued on the spot, while his elder brother John, the grandfather of the celebrated Samuel Adams, removed to Boston. This Joseph last mentioned was the grandfather of the second President of the United States.

John Adams, the subject of this paper, was born in the town of Braintree, October 19, 1735. His father was something more than a respectable, he was a useful citizen of the town; he had been educated at Harvard; held the offices of deacon and selectman, honoring the one by his piety and discharging the other with fidelity, and according to a habit not unfrequent with small property-holders in New England, eked out the resources of his farm by shoe-making. Taking care to transmit the benefit which he had received, he provided that his eldest son, John, should have the advantage of a college education. He was prepared for Harvard by the aid both of the Congregational minister and of the Episcopal reader at Braintree, was a good student of his class, which sent many eminent men into the world, and in due time graduated at the age of twenty in 1755. The talent which he displayed in the commencement exercises, attracted the notice of a person present, charged with a commission to supply a Latin master for the Grammar School of Worcester. He applied to Adams, who undertook the task, and shortly after set out on the horse sent for him by the town's people, making the sixty miles' journey in a single day. This transfer from the home sphere was highly favorable to his development: he was thrown upon his own resources among strangers, and doubtless the privations and little vexations of his schoolmaster's life, stimulated his independent nature to further exertions.

The school appears at first to have been very distasteful to his aspiring mind; but he became reconciled to its duties, and doubtless profited by the discipline which he himself administered. "I find," says he, after some months' occupation at this drudgery in shaping the crude material of the Worcester nurseries, "I find by repeated observation and experiment in my school, that human nature is more easily wrought upon and governed by promises and encouragement and praise, than by punishment and threatening and blame"—a sentence which should be grafted in the memory of every schoolmaster in the land.

The pedagogue is not altogether given over to mending pens, the agreeable alternations of birching and feruling or a-b-c-ing the boys, of which he humorously complains, but finds time to store his mind with good reading, makes acquaintance with the writings of such political philosophers as Gordon and Bolingbroke, and is ambitious of the society of the place, always conscious that John Adams should be somebody in the world, and that it is but an act of common justice to himself to take all proper means to secure the position. The house of Colonel James Putnam, an able lawyer of the place, is open to him; thither he frequently resorts, and after awhile, the law securing his attention—he had by this time pretty well argued himself out of the New England orthodoxy, and so given up any thoughts of the pulpit—proposes to study the profession with his friend. Mr. Putnam consents, and Mrs. Putnam makes provision in the house for the student, who is also to continue in charge of the urchins at the school. The legal apprenticeship continues two years, during which it is to be regretted that the Diary is silent, when John Adams takes leave of the population of Worcester, little and great, to seek admission to the Colonial bar. He takes up his residence with his father at Braintree, or Quincy, as it is now called, at the old paternal dwelling, and one day in October, 1758, goes to Boston to be introduced by Attorney-General Gridley, the father of the bar, to the Superior Court, and is admitted Attorney at Law in his Majesty's Courts of the Province.

The attorney relaxes none of his diligence in attention to the old law, in the study of laborious volumes, over which the dust has long gathered in legal libraries. Those were the days before Blackstone, when no republican road had been marked out to the secret places of the profession, when the maxim of Coke, the *viginti annorum lucubrationes*, was still in vogue, when no Lord Brougham or reviser of the statutes had risen to prepare the smooth pathway of legal reform. Reading the entries of these grave old studies, burdened with the traditions of English centuries, from Bracton and Fleta, Coke and Fortescue, we may ask, "Where be his quiddets now, his quillets, his cases, his tenures, and his tricks?" Gone with the old wigs and colonial state, and we need sigh no alas! at the reminiscence.

We see Adams, in these years of opening manhood, lighted along his daily path by the cheerful, pleasant Diary, the man of the world and of society, emerging from the old formalism; the independent thinker, built on the antiquarian student, as he gathers strength from discussion, and takes the measure of the leaders of that day. He is not backward in entering into controversy with, and judging some of them, but he retires at night to be a more rigid censor of himself. There is a sufficient stock of vanity in some of his revelations, but there is a greater diffidence; and he manages to blend the two into a good working union, diligence furnishing the bottom, and vanity being only the spur to his honorable career. There is some vainglory, perhaps, in his writing down, even privately for himself, how he spent his evenings in company with a book at the fireside, while Doctor Gardiner, Billy Belcher, Stephen Cleverly, the Quincys, and other young fellows of the town, are playing cards and drinking punch at the tables: but it is not the less true that he is thereby preparing himself to emerge from poverty, receive fees, bear Parson Smith's daughter as his wife to his home, and in good time support the duties of the State. Having mentioned this marriage, we may here, a little out of date, state that the event occurred in October, 1764; that the lady, the fair Abigail, was the daughter of the Rev. William Smith, of Weymouth, and grand-daughter of Colonel John Quincy, of Mount Wollaston, of colonial fame; that she was young, and possessed accomplishments in intellect and reading, proportioned to his own, as her published letters testify; and that the union, "the source of all his felicity," continued for fifty-three years, having its only pang in absence and the final separation.

We are now to trace Adams' political career. It began with his offering public resolutions at Braintree, and his maintaining an argument in behalf of the town of Boston, addressed to the Colonial Government in opposition to the Stamp Act. He published, about the same date, several papers in the "Boston Gazette," which were reprinted in London by Thomas Hollis, who gave them the not very fortunate title, "A Dissertation on the Canon and the Feudal Law," which has probably prevented many persons looking at the tract, who would be interested by its review of the principles of the New England settlements, and its vigorous appeal to the people in the existing struggle. Notwithstanding he was looked to as a leader for the popular party, he had no sympathy with their acts of violence, and when the disturbance occurred which resulted in the firing upon the people by the British troops, he independently and humanely, a thing which should always be remembered in his honor, gave his services to Preston and the defence. This caused him some unpopularity, but did not hinder his election, immediately after, to the General Court, as the legislative body was called in Massachusetts. When the news of his election was brought to him, he made his first appearance at Faneuil Hall, and accepted the choice. It was the turning point of his career. On one side lay a profitable legal practice, in a routine dear to the legal mind; on the other a troubled sea of opposition and revolt. A popular nominee has seldom accepted an election with less of satisfaction. "I considered the step," he said, "as a devotion of my family to ruin and myself to death." Mrs. Adams burst into tears at the event, but approved the choice; the duty was clear, and the rest was piously left to Providence.

He was now a resident of Boston, but the constant labors of his profession, and the confinement of the city wearing upon his health, he resigned his seat in the Legislature, and again made his residence in Braintree, having his office in Boston. His studies, family cares, and the duties of his profession, had thus far, rather than politics, mainly engaged his attention. The time was come, however, when business was at an end, and home, to be enjoyed, must be protected. If all the leaders of opinion did not speak openly of revolt and revolution, there were probably few of them who did not feel that they were drifting rapidly towards it.

In 1774 he was appointed by the General Court one of the Representatives to the Congress at Philadelphia; his associates being Thomas Cushing, Samuel Adams, and his troublesome old friend, "Bob," now Robert Treat Paine. They journeyed together in one coach, through Hartford and New Haven to New York. At New York Adams is much taken with McDougall, particularly his open manners. The delegates are received with hospitality, so that Adams complains of not being able to see the objects of interest in the town. What were they at that time? The college, the churches, printing offices, and booksellers' shops; few indeed to be compared with the present lions, yet relatively great to the people of that day.

Passing on to Princeton, his patriotism is refreshed by a conference with President Witherspoon, "as high a son of liberty as any man in America." One of the first persons he is introduced to at Philadelphia is Charles Thomson,

the perpetual Secretary of Congress, whom he understands is "the Sam Adams of Philadelphia, the life of the cause of liberty;" a valuable testimony this, by the way, if he needed such, to the popular estimate of his associate. The business of the Congress at once engages his attention. He has to study "the characters and tempers, the principles and views of fifty gentlemen, total strangers, and the trade, policy and whole interest of a dozen provinces; to learn and practise reserve in the communication of his plans and wishes." The discussions are tedious. "Every man is a great man, an orator, a critic, a statesman; and therefore every man, upon every question, must show his oratory, his criticism, and his political abilities." Yet this Congress held Washington, Jay, Patrick Henry, Samuel Adams, John Dickinson, Richard Henry Lee, Rutledge, Gadsden, and other notables, and men learnt to sigh a few years afterwards, when the representation fell into neglect, at the thought of these early deliberative giants. In fact, all great efforts have their weariness; of all things human, there is none great enough to satisfy the wants of the soul. Adams, with the rest, did his good day's work discussing a Declaration of Rights, confronting Galloway, the projector of a plan for union with England, debating the non-importation resolutions, consulting with Patrick Henry on the Petition to the King, and when the long morning work is over, dining and feasting with the wealthy citizens of Philadelphia, in admiration at the costly entertainments, and a little surprised that he is not affected by the unusual libations of Madeira.

Returning home to Massachusetts after the short session of this body, he is chosen to the Provincial Congress, already quite busy with revolt, and when this duty is discharged, turns his pen to answer the annoying Tory arguments of Massachusettensis, Daniel Leonard, as it afterwards appeared, who was greatly cheering the hearts of the administration men in the colonies by his logical efforts in the "Gazette and Postboy." The replies of Adams, signed Novanglus, covering the old legal and historical issues, twelve in number, accomplished something of a diversion, or as the author afterwards expressed it, "had the effect of an antidote to the poison." There were several unpublished in the printer's hands, when the Battle of Lexington "changed the instruments of warfare from the pen to the sword." Three weeks afterwards he was at Philadelphia at the Second Congress, in 1775. Before his departure from Boston, he had visited the camp at Cambridge, and observed its necessities. Early on the assembling of Congress, he proposed Washington for Commander-in-Chief; "the modest and virtuous, the amiable, generous and brave," as he calls him in a letter to his wife, and has the satisfaction of accompanying him a little way out of Philadelphia towards his distant command. Franklin, who had recently bid farewell to England, was also a member of this body.

During the first session of this Congress, Adams was diligently employed in the preparatory measures which led to the Declaration of Independence and Confederation of the following year. As the time approached, his activity and boldness were displayed as the full grandeur of the scenes rose to his mind. "Objects," he wrote to William Cushing, "of the most stupendous magnitude, and measures in which the lives and liberties of millions yet unborn are intimately interested, are now before us." "Yesterday," he writes to his wife, on the third of July, 1776, on the passage of Lee's Resolution of Independence, "the greatest question was decided which ever was debated in America, and a greater, perhaps, never was nor will be decided among men;" and again the same day, in another letter to Mrs. Adams, a remarkable prophetic passage—"The second day of July, 1776, will be the most memorable epoch in the history of America. I am apt to believe that it will be celebrated by succeeding generations as the great Anniversary Festival. It ought to be commemorated, as the day of deliverance, by solemn acts of devotion to God Almighty. It ought to be solemnized with pomp and parade, with shows, games, sports, guns, bells, bonfires and illuminations, from one end of this continent to the other, from this time forward, forevermore."

Adams was on the committee for preparing the Declaration, and was active in the debate. In the absence of the present system of executive duties of government, the old Congress was compelled to resort to the awkward expedient of boards, in which the honor and efficiency, rather than the toil, were diminished by the division of labor

Adams was made chairman of the Board of War, and was much employed in military affairs till his departure from Congress at the close of the next year.

In November, 1777, Congress, having become dissatisfied with the management of Silas Dean, in France, appointed Adams in his place. He set sail in the frigate Boston in the ensuing February, from Boston, accompanied by his son, John Quincy, then a boy of ten. The voyage was diversified by a chase and a storm, and the usual incidents of navigation. Adams, as we learn from his Diary, employed himself in observations of the discipline, the care of the men, and other points of naval regulation for which he had an eye from his duties in Congress. After a voyage of some six weeks, escaping the dreaded perils of the British cruisers, he was landed safely at Bordeaux. At Paris he took up his residence under the same roof with Dr. Franklin, and was shortly introduced by him to Vergennes and Maurepas. The domestic diplomacy of the commissioners was at first sight more formidable than that of the court. They were quite at odds with one another. Lee with Franklin and Deane, the general mischief-monger of the party. Adams saw the source of the difficulty in the mingling of diplomatic, commercial, and pecuniary transactions, and advised that these duties should be divided. In accordance with his suggestions, Congress made the division, creating Franklin minister at Paris, and sending Arthur Lee to Madrid. Oddly enough, Adams, the mover of the resolution, was left out of the programme entirely. Finding nothing to do in the way of government employ, and indisposed to be an idle observer of the Parisians, though he envies his "venerable colleague," as he calls Franklin, then seventy, his privileges with the ladies, and is readily pleased with the sights about him, he is bent upon returning home, and an opportunity at length offering itself in the departure of the French ambassador, the Chevalier de la Luzerne, he sets sail from Lorient, June 17, 1779.

The frigate Sensible arrived at Boston on the second of August; within a week he was elected by his townspeople, of Braintree, their delegate to the Convention to frame a Constitution for Massachusetts. The honor and responsibility of much of the work fell into his hands; but before it was completed, he was again summoned to the foreign service of his country, as minister to negotiate with Great Britain. Embarking in the Sensible, the French frigate in which he had returned, he was landed in Gallicia, travelled thence through Spain to Bayonne, a journey of which his Diary gives an interesting account, and arrived at Paris in February, 1780. Obstacles were here thrown in the way of his negotiation with England by the minister, Vergennes, who wished to keep the foreign policy of America under his control in subordination to French interests. The influence which the important aid rendered to America by the French government had given to her councils, occasioned much embarrassment in the adjustment of the treaty with England. It is a painful portion of the history of America, this conflict of intrigue and benefits, of love of America and hatred of England; of Lafayette and Vergennes, smoothed over by the gratitude of Congress and the compliments of the monarchy, to break out into insidious plotting and open assault under the Revolution. This French imbroglio is henceforth to give John Adams a vast deal of trouble. Vergennes suspects his fidelity to the French anti-Anglican policy, and Adams, with Jay, thinks the Frenchman will sacrifice the interests of America. The negotiations are finally brought to a close by a body of commissioners charged with the work, embracing Adams, Franklin, Jay, Jefferson, and Laurens. In the meantime, Adams is busy in Holland, cultivating the Dutch capitalists, preparing the way for a loan and a treaty of alliance. That his country may be put upon a proper footing for these negotiations, he employs his pen in John Luzac's "Leyden Gazette," an organ of much service to America in the Revolution, and takes other means of disseminating correct information. That his articles might have more authority, he sent the communication to be first published in an English journal, that they might be thence transferred to the Dutch Gazette. He also drew up a series of replies to the inquiries of a gentleman of Holland touching American affairs, which have been often published, and which now appear in the collection of his writings with the title, "Twenty-six letters upon interesting subjects respecting the Revolution of America." The prospects

of a loan were broken up for a time by the war between Holland and England, in which an alleged alliance with America, which did not exist, was made the pretence of wanton aggression. But Adams, single-handed, persevered. He was presently reinforced by special authority from home, and had the satisfaction at last, not only of procuring a valuable loan, but of securing the recognition of his country by Holland as an independent power. This treaty of alliance was completed in October, 1782.

In the month following the conclusion of the negotiations in Holland, Adams, with Jay and Franklin, signed, at Paris, the preliminary articles of peace with England. He shared with Jay his suspicions of Vergennes; and Franklin, being led by their convictions, the responsibility was taken of carrying on the negotiation independently of France, and even contrary to the orders of Congress. The definitive treaty was not signed till the next September. When Adams had put his signature to this important instrument, he immediately set out for England to regain his health, which had been much impaired by his confinement and labors and a recent severe illness. His visit at this time was unofficial. He appears to have enjoyed with his usual zest the sights of the metropolis, in procuring admission to which he found his countryman, Benjamin West, as influential as a prime minister. In the lobby of the House of Lords he had the gratification of hearing the gentleman usher of the black rod "roar out with a very loud voice, where is Mr. Adams, Lord

6

Mansfield's friend ?" The painter, West, remembering the denunciations of Murray against his country in that same House of Lords, said to Adams, "this is one of the finest finishings in the picture of American Independence."

His next diplomatic employment was as a commissioner with Franklin and Jefferson, to negotiate treaties of peace with the European nations. These engagements abroad having now assumed something of a permanent character, he was joined by Mrs. Adams, whom he hastened from the Continent, on her arrival in England, to conduct to his residence at Auteuil, in the suburb of Paris, in the summer of 1784. In February, 1785, Congress appoints John Adams the first American minister to Great Britain, and in May he is installed in the English capital. Friendly as his reception by the king appears to have been, it was not followed by a fair reciprocity towards America. Peace had indeed been made, and the minister received, but Congress was honored by no British representative calling at her doors. The relations of the two countries were in fact yet of the most unsettled character; questions of commercial intercourse, of a restrictive nature, were pressed against the Americans; the western posts were retained; on the other hand, the unsettled relations of the States to one another at home, were at variance with a just and dignified foreign policy. After weathering for awhile these disheartening conditions, Adams, having rendered such services as he could to his country in a new loan negotiation with Holland and conferences with his fellow-commis-

sioner, Jefferson, at Paris, tired of the ineffectual struggle with difficulties and against prejudice, at the close of 1787, requested his recall. His time, however, had not been altogether taken up with these foreign affairs. His famous work, the "Defence of the Constitutions of Government of the United States of America," was produced at this period. It grew out of some remarks by the French philosopher, Turgot, on 'the Constitutions of the State in which the adoption of English usages was objected to, and preference given to a single authority of the nation or assembly over a balanced system of powers. Adams extended the work to three volumes, in which he brought to bear upon the subject a vast amount of political reading, particularly in reference to the Italian Republics. The effect of this long discussion, like that of its sequel, the Discourses on Davila, is much weakened by its form, for Adams, with much spirit as a writer, is defective in his longer works in manner and method. If his style of writing had been formed in early life, like that of Franklin and Madison, upon the reading of the Spectator instead of the declamations of Bolingbroke, in so far as study can modify the genius of a man, his works would have been better for the training. John Adams loses as much as Franklin gains by his way of putting a thing in his writings.

The spring of 1788 restored him again to his native land. It was the period of the adoption of the Federal Constitution, and when that instrument went fully into effect in the meeting of the first Congress at New York, he was found to be chosen Vice-President, receiving the greatest number of votes of the electors next to Washington. He received thirty-four out of sixty-nine, the vote of Washington being unanimous. He held this office, presiding in the Senate, during both terms of Washington's administration, to which he gave active and often important assistance. In 1797, he succeeded to the Presidency by a vote of seventy-one over the sixty-eight of Jefferson. He found the country in imminent danger of a conflict with France. The principles of an English or French alliance were the tests of the party politics of the times. Jay's Treaty, sanctioning the neutrality policy of Washington, had indeed been adopted by Congress, but after a struggle which left many elements of opposition. The full force of these was directed against the Federal party, of which Adams was now the official representative. He was destined to receive aid, however, from an unexpected quarter. The assumptions and aggressions of the French Directory, on the arrival of Marshall and Gerry, as negotiators, developed a new phase of villainy in a contemptuous effort to bribe the American Commissioners. This insult at length opened the eyes and roused the spirit of the nation. Adams was for awhile exceedingly popular; addresses were poured in upon him, the country armed, commissioned a navy, Washington was again called into the field, and with Hamilton at his side, arranged means of military defence. Thus far he was with the strong anti-Gallican Federal party. He was thought, however, to fall off from it in some of his measures for reconciliation with France, which, however, by the turn which placed Napoleon in authority, had a successful issue; some of the acts of his administration, as the Alien and Sedition laws, were powerful instruments with an unscrupulous opposition, and he had, moreover, to bear the disaffection of Hamilton. There was little liberality or charity for defects of taste and temper. The embarrassments arising from these things clouded his administration, which closed with a single term, and the obstinate struggle which resulted in the election of Jefferson. A private affliction, in the loss of his second son, Charles, came also at this moment, to darken the shades of his retirement. He had no heart to witness the inauguration of his successor, and left Washington abruptly for Quincy.

His biographer tells us, as an index of his privacy, that while the year before his letters could be counted by thousands, those of his first year after were scarcely a hundred. Like Jay's protracted age at Bedford, his was a long retirement, but Adams had not in his disposition the quietude of Jay. The restlessness, the activity of pursuit which had driven the poor New England boy to the thrones of monarchs, and had seated him in the Presidency of the Republic, was not to subside without a murmur. The old statesman enjoyed a vicarious public life in the rapid advancement of his son in the councils of his country to the Presidency; the irritations of controversy lent their aid to agitate the torpor of political neglect, in the series of letters vindicating his course, which he published in the "Boston Patriot;" while he occasionally revived for himself and the eye of posterity, past scenes of his history in an Autobiography. In 1818, in his eighty-third year, his wife, his "dearest friend," the gentle and accomplished, one of the mothers of America, full of the sweetest and grandest memories of the past, was taken from him. His last public service was in occasional attendance at the Convention of Massachusetts for the formation of a new Constitution, when he was eighty-five. He was not able to say, but he made his wish known, that the new instrument should express perfect religious tolerance. It was the liberal creed of his youth; it had been growing stronger with his age. Returning to his early friendship, he corresponded with Jefferson. The two venerable fathers of the Republic, Jefferson at the age of eighty-three, John Adams at that of ninety, died together on the birthday of the nation, July 4th, 1826. A few days before his death, the orator of his native town of Quincy, where he lay in his home, called upon Adams for a toast, to be presented at the approaching anniversary. "Independence forever!" was the reply. As the sentiment was delivered at the banquet, amidst ringing plaudits, the soul of the dying patriot was passing from earth to eternity.

We have brought the long and busy life to a close, from boyhood to fourscore and ten. A nation has been born in that time, and one of its founders, after reaching its summit of authority, has seen his son at its head. We have the fullest revelations of this man. It was his passion not only to be employed in great events, but to write down the least of himself. We have his books, learned tomes, his official and personal Correspondence, his Reminiscences, his Diary, his Autobiography, the domestic letters of his wife. He was bent upon declaring himself in every form. What is the impression? Upon the whole, of a man of active conscientious mind, employed from youth in study and thought; diligent in affairs; lacking some of the judicious arts of the writer and statesman, which might have better set off his fair fame with the world. The formative period of his life, his early professional training, has a better lesson for the youth of his country than that of Franklin, for it has fewer errata. Egotism is sometimes apparent, but it led him to know as well as proclaim himself. His sensibility may occasionally be taken for vanity, but it is oftener the indication of true feeling. Had he been more cautious, he might have possessed less heart. He had his weaknesses. He was passionate, we are told, but forgiving; serious in manner, but capable of genial relaxation; of a disposition answering to his frame and look, with more of solidity than elevation; something of the sensual, relieved by a touch of humor, about him; nothing of the idealist: a broad, capacious head, capable of assertion and action.

THOMAS JEFFERSON.

In his Autobiography, written towards the close of his life, the author of the Declaration of Independence, thinking doubtless his new political career a better passport to fame with posterity than any conditions of ancestry in the old society which he had superseded, while he could not be insensible to the worth of a respectable family history, says of the Randolphs, from whom he was descended on the mother's side, "they trace their pedigree far back in England and Scotland, to which let every one ascribe the faith and merit he chooses." Whatever value may be set by his biographers upon an ancient lineage, they cannot overlook the fact—most important in its influence upon his future history— that he was introduced by his family relationships at birth into a sphere of life in Virginia, which gave him many social advantages. The leveller of the old aristocracy was by no means a self-made man of the people, struggling upward through difficulty and adversity. His father, Peter Jefferson, belonged to a family originally from Wales, which had been among the first settlers of the colony. In 1619, one of the name was seated in the Assembly at Jamestown, the first legislative body of Europeans, it is said, that ever met in the New World. The particular account of the family begins with the grandfather of Thomas Jefferson, who owned some lands in Chesterfield County. His third son, Peter, established himself as a planter on certain lands which he had "patented," or come into possession of by purchase, in Albemarle County, in the vicinity of Carter's Mountain, where the Rivanna makes its way through the Range; and about the time of his settlement married Jane, daughter of Isham Randolph, of Dungeness, in Goochland County, of the eminent old Virginia race, to which allusion has already been made, a stock which has extended its branches through every department of worth and excellence in the State. Isham Randolph was a man of talent and education, as well as noted for the hospitality practised by every gentleman of his wealthy position. His memory is gratefully preserved in the correspondence of the naturalists, Collinson and Bartram. The latter was commended to his care in one of his scientific tours, and enjoyed his hearty welcome. His daughter, Jane, we are told, "possessed a most amiable and affectionate disposition, a lively, cheerful temper, and a great fund of humor," qualities which had their influence upon her son's character. Her marriage to Peter Jefferson took place at the age of nineteen, and the fruit of this union, the third child and first son, was Thomas, the subject of this sketch. He was born at the new family location at Shadwell, April 2 (old style), 1743.

Peter Jefferson, the father, was a model man for a frontier settlement, tall in stature, of extraordinary strength of body, capable of enduring any fatigue in the wilderness, with corresponding health and vigor of mind. He was educated as a surveyor, and in this capacity engaged in a government commission to draw the boundary line between Virginia and North Carolina. Two years before his death, which occurred suddenly in his fiftieth year, in 1757, he was chosen a member of the House of Burgesses. His son was then only fourteen, but he had already derived many impressions from the instructions and example of his father, and considerable resemblance is traced between them. Mr. Randall, in his biography, notices the inheritance of physical strength, of a certain plainness of manners, and honest love of independence, even of a fondness for reading—for the stalwart surveyor was accustomed to solace his leisure with his Spectator and his Shakspeare.

The son was early sent to school, and, before his father's death, was instructed in the elements of Greek, and Latin, and French, by Mr. Douglass, a Scottish clergyman. It was his parent's dying wish that he should receive a good classical education; and the seed proved to be sown in a good soil. The lessons which the youth had already re-ceived, were resumed under the excellent instruction of the Rev. James Maury, at his residence, and thence, in 1760, the pupil passed to William and Mary College. He was now in his eighteenth year, a tall, thin youth, of a ruddy complexion, his hair inclining to red, an adept in manly and rural sports, a good dancer, something of a musician, full of vivacity. It is worth noticing, that the youth of Jefferson was of a hearty, joyous character.

Williamsburg, also, the seat of the college, was then anything but a scholastic hermitage for the mortification of youth. In winter, during the session of the court and the sittings of the colonial legislature, it was the focus of provincial fashion and gaiety; and between study and dissipation the ardent young Jefferson had before him the old problem of good and evil not always leading to the choice of virtue. It is to the credit of his manly perceptions and healthy tastes, even then, that while he freely partook of the amusements incidental to his station and time of life, he kept his eye steadily on loftier things. "It was my great good fortune," he says in his Autobiography, "and what probably fixed the destinies of my life, that Dr. William Small, of Scotland, was then professor of mathematics, a man profound in most of the useful branches of science, with a happy talent of communication, correct and gentlemanly manners, and an enlarged and liberal mind." His instructions, communicated not only in college hours, but in familiar personal intimacy, warmed the young student with his first, as it became his constant, passion for natural science. This happy instructor also gave a course of lectures in ethics and rhetoric, which were doubtless equally profitable to his young pupil in the opening of his mind to knowledge. He had also an especial fondness for mathematics, "reading off its processes with the facility of common discourse." He sometimes studied, in his second year, fifteen hours a day, taking exercise in a brisk walk of a mile at evening.

Jefferson was only two years at college, but his education was happily continued in his immediate entrance upon the study of the law with George Wythe, the memorable chancellor of Virginia, of after days, to whom he was introduced by Dr. Small, and of whose personal qualities—his temperance and suavity, his logic and eloquence, his disinterested public virtue —he wrote a worthy eulogium. The same learned friend also made him acquainted with Governor Fauquier, then in authority, "the ablest man," says Jefferson, "who ever filled the office." At his courtly table the four met together in familiar and liberal conversation. It was a privilege to the youth of the first importance, bringing him, at the outset, into a sphere of public life which he was destined afterwards, in Europe and America, so greatly to adorn. He passed five years in the study of the law at Williamsburg, and, without intermitting his studies, at his home at Shadwell. Nor, diligent as he was, is it to be supposed that his time was altogether spent in study. He yet found leisure, as his early telltale cor-

respondence with his friend Page, afterwards Governor of Virginia, shows, to harbor a fond attachment for a fair "Belinda," as he called her, reversing the letters of the name and writing them in Greek, or playing upon the word in Latin. The character of the young lady, Miss Rebecca Burwell, of an excellent family, does credit to his attachment, for it was marked by its religious enthusiasm, but nothing came of it beyond a boyish disappointment.[1]

In 1767 he was introduced to the bar of the General Court of Virginia by his friend Mr. Wythe, and immediately entered on a successful career of practice, interrupted only by the Revolution. His memorandum books, which he kept minutely and diligently as Washington himself, show how extensively he was employed in these seven years; while the directions which he gave in later life to young students, exhibit a standard of application, which he had no doubt followed himself, of the utmost proficiency. His "sufficient groundwork" for the study of the law includes a liberal course of mathematics, natural philosophy, ethics, rhetoric, politics, and history. His pursuit of the science itself ascended to the antique founts of the profession. He was a well-trained, skillful lawyer, an adept in the casuistry of legal questions—more distinguished, however, for his ability in

---

[1] Mr. John Esten Cooke, of Virginia, author of the eminently judicious biography of Jefferson in Appleton's new Cyclopædia, has sketched this love affair in a pleasant paper on the "Early years of Thomas Jefferson." The "Page" correspondence is printed in Professor Tucker's Life of Jefferson.

argument than for his power as an advocate. He was throughout life little of an orator, and we shall find him hereafter, in scenes where eloquence was peculiarly felt, more powerful in the committee room than in debate.

His first entrance on political life was at the age of twenty-six, in 1769, when he was sent to the House of Burgesses from the county of Albemarle, the entrance on a troublous time in the consideration of national grievances, and we find him engaged at once in preparing the resolutions and address to the governor's message. The House, in reply to the recent declarations of Parliament, reasserted the American principles of taxation and petition, and other questions in jeopardy, and, in consequence, was promptly dissolved by Lord Botetourt. The members, the next day, George Washington among them, met at the Raleigh tavern, and pledged themselves to a non-importation agreement.

The next year, on the conflagration of the house at Shadwell, where he had his home with his mother, he took up his residence at the adjacent "Monticello," also on his own paternal grounds, in a portion of the edifice so famous afterwards as the dwelling-place of his maturer years. Unhappily, many of his early papers, his books and those of his father, were burnt in the destruction of his old home. In 1772, on New Year's Day, he took a step farther in domestic life, in marriage with Mrs. Martha Skelton, a widow of twenty-three, of much beauty and many winning accomplishments, the daughter of

John Wayles, a lawyer of skill and many good qualities, at whose death, the following year, the pair came into possession of a considerable property. In this circumstance, and in the management of his landed estate, we may trace a certain resemblance in the fortunes of the occupants of Monticello and Mount Vernon.

Political affairs were now again calling for legislative attention. The renewed claim of the British to send persons for state offences to England, brought forward in Rhode Island, awakened a strong feeling of resistance among the Virginia delegates, a portion of whom, including Jefferson, met at the Raleigh Tavern, and drew up resolutions creating a Committee of Correspondence to watch the proceedings of Parliament, and keep up a communication with the Colonies. Jefferson was appointed to offer the resolutions in the House, but declined in favor of his brother-in-law, Dabney Carr. They were passed, and a committee—all notable men of the Revolution—was appointed, including Peyton Randolph, Richard Henry Lee, Patrick Henry, and others, ending with Thomas Jefferson. The Earl of Dunmore then, following the example of his predecessor, dissolved the House.

We may here pause, with Mr. Jefferson's latest biographer, to notice the friendship of Jefferson with Carr. It belonged to their school-boy days, and had gained strength during their period of legal study, when they had kept company together in the shades of Monticello, and made nature the companion of their thoughts. They had their favorite rustic seat there beneath an oak, and there, each promised the other he would bury the survivor. The time soon came, a month after the scene at the Raleigh Tavern we have just narrated, when Carr, at the age of thirty, was fatally stricken by fever. The friends now rest together in the spot where their youthful summer days were passed. Carr had been eight years married to Jefferson's sister, and he left her with a family of six children. His brother-in-law took them all to his home. The sons, Peter and Dabney, who rose high in the Virginia judiciary, have an honored place in the Jefferson Correspondence, calling forth many of the statesmen's best letters. The whole family was educated and provided for by him; and here again, in these adopted children, we may recognize a resemblance to Mount Vernon with its young Custises.

The new Legislature met, as usual, the next year, and, roused by the passage of the Boston Port Bill, a few members, says Jefferson, including Henry and himself, resolved to place the Assembly "in the line with Massachusetts." The expedient they hit upon was a fast day, which, by the help of some old Puritan precedents, they "cooked up" and placed in the hands of a grave member to lay before the House. It was passed, and the Governor, "as usual," dissolved the Assembly. The fast was appointed for the first of June, the day on which the obnoxious bill was to take effect, and there was one man in Virginia, at least, who kept it. We may read in the Diary of George Washington, of that date,

"Went to church, and fasted all day."[1]

The dissolved Assembly again met at the Raleigh, and decided upon a Convention, to be elected by the people of the several counties, and held at Williamsburg, so that two bodies had to be chosen, one to assemble in the new House of Burgesses, the other out of the reach of government control. The same members, those of the previous House, were sent for both. Jefferson again represented the freeholders of Albemarle. The instructions which the county gave, supposed from his pen, assert the radical doctrine of the independence of the Colonial Legislatures, as the sole fount of authority in new laws. The Williamsburg Convention met and appointed delegates to the first General Congress. Jefferson was detained from the Assembly by illness, but he forwarded a draught of instructions for the delegates, which was not adopted, but ordered to be printed by the members. It bore the title, "A Summary View of the Rights of British America," reached England, was taken up by the opposition, and, with some interpolations from Burke, passed through several editions.[2] Though in

---

[1] Mrs. Kirkland's Memoirs of Washington, p. 220.

[2] The pamphlet took the ground, that the relation between Great Britain and her Colonies was exactly the same as that of England and Scotland after the accession of James, and until the Union, or as Hanover then stood, linked only by the crown. An illustration was also drawn from the Saxon settlement of Britain, " that mother country " never having asserted any claim of authority over her emigrants. The trading and manufacturing repressions of England in particular were dwelt upon, with other pertinent topics of reform. The whole was expressed in terse and pointed language. He would remind George III. that " Kings are the servants, not the propri-

advance of the judgment of the people, who are slow in coming up to the principles of great reforms, this "View" undoubtedly assisted to form that judgment. But so slow was the progress of opinion at the outset, that, at the moment when this paper was written, only a few leaders, such as Samuel Adams and Patrick Henry, were capable of appreciating it. A few years afterwards, and it would have been accepted as a truism. The country was not yet ready to receive its virtual Declaration of Independence. The people had to be pricked on by further outrages. Theoretical rebellion they had no eye for; they must feel to be convinced. Jefferson's paper was in advance of them, by the boldness of its historical positions, and the plainness of its language to His Majesty—yet its array of grievances must have enlightened many minds.

The Congress of 1774 met but adopted milder forms of petition, better adapted to the moderation of their sentiments. Meanwhile committees of safety are organizing in Virginia, and Jefferson heads the list in his county. He is also in the second Virginia Convention at Richmond, listening to Patrick Henry's ardent appeal to the God of Battles—"I repeat it, sir, we must fight!" The Assembly adopted the view so far as preparing means of defence, and that the students of events in Massachusetts began to think meant war. The delegates to the first Congress were elected to the second, and in case Peyton Randolph should be called to preside over the House of Burgesses, Thomas Jefferson was to be his successor at Philadelphia. The House met, Randolph was elected, and Jefferson departed to fill his place, bearing with him to Congress the spirited Resolutions of the Assembly, which he had written and driven through, in reply to the conciliatory propositions of Lord North. It was a characteristic introduction, immediately followed up by his appointment on the committee charged to prepare a declaration of the causes of taking up arms, Congress having just chosen Washington Commander-in-Chief of a national army. He was associated in this task with John Dickinson, to whose timidity and caution, respected as they were by his fellow members, he deferred in the report, in which, however, a few ringing sentences of Jefferson are readily distinguishable, among them the famous watchwords of political struggle—"Our cause is just; our union is perfect." "With hearts," the document proceeds, "fortified with these animating affections, we most solemnly, before God and the world, declare, that, exerting the utmost energy of those powers which our beneficent Creator hath graciously bestowed upon us, the arms which we have been compelled by our enemies to assume, we will, in defiance of every hazard, with unabated firmness and perseverance, employ for the preservation of our liberties, being with one mind resolved to die freemen rather than to live slaves."

This was the era of masterly state papers; and talent in composition was

etors of the people." "The whole art of government," he maintains, "consists in the art of being honest."

in demand. The reputation of Jefferson in this line had preceded him, in the ability of his "Summary View," presented to the Virginia Convention, and was confirmed by his presence. Nearly a year passed—a year commencing with Lexington and Bunker Hill, and including the military scenes of Washington's command around Boston, before Congress was fully ready to pronounce its final Declaration of Independence. When the time came, Jefferson was again a member of that body. The famous Resolutions of Independence, in accordance with previous instructions from Virginia, were moved by Richard Henry Lee, on the seventh of June. They were debated in committee of the whole, and pending the deliberations, not to lose time, a special committee was appointed by ballot on the eleventh, to prepare a Declaration of Independence. Jefferson had the highest vote, and stood at the head of the committee, with John Adams, Benjamin Franklin, Roger Sherman, and Robert R. Livingston. The preparation of the instrument was entrusted to Jefferson. "The committee desired me to do it, it was accordingly done," says his Autobiography. The draft thus prepared, with a few verbal corrections from Franklin and Adams, was submitted to the House on the twenty-eighth. On the second of July, it was taken up in debate, and earnestly battled for three days, when on the evening of the last—the ever-memorable fourth of July—it was finally reported, agreed to, and signed by every member except Mr. Dickinson. Some alterations were made in the original draft—a phrase, here and there, which seemed superfluous, was lopped off; the King of Great Britain was spared some additional severities, and a stirring passage arraigning his Majesty for his complicity in the slave trade then carried on, a "piratical warfare, the opprobrium of infidel powers," was entirely exscinded—the denunciation being thought to strike at home as well as abroad. The people of England were also relieved of the censure cast upon them for electing tyrannical Parliaments. With these omissions, the paper stands substantially as first reported by Jefferson. It is intimately related to his previous resolutions and reports in Virginia and Congress, and whatever merit may be attached to it, alike in its spirit and language, belongs to him.

Mr. Jefferson was elected to the next session of Congress; but, pleading the state of his family affairs, and desirous of taking part in the formative measures of government now arising in Virginia, he was permitted to resign. He declined, also, immediately after, an appointment by Congress as fellow-minister to France with Dr. Franklin. In October, he took his seat in the Virginia House of Delegates, and commenced those efforts of reform with which his name will always be identified in his native State, and which did not end till its social condition was thoroughly revolutionized. His first great blow was the introduction of a bill abolishing entails, which, with one subsequently brought in, cutting off the right of primogeniture, levelled the great landed aristocracy which had hitherto governed in the country. He was also, about the time of the passage of this act, created one of the committee for the general revision of the laws, his active associates being Edmund Pendleton and George Wythe. This vast work was not completed by the committee till June, 1779, an interval of more than two years. Among the one hundred and sixteen new bills reported, perhaps the most important was one, the work of Jefferson, that for Establishing Religious Freedom, which abolished tythes, and left all men free "to profess, and by argument to maintain, their opinions in matters of religion, and that the same shall in no wise diminish, enlarge, or affect their civil capacities." A concurrent act provided for the preservation of the glebe lands to church members. Jefferson was not, therefore, in this instance the originator of the after spoliation of the ecclesiastical property. Of this matter Mr. Randall says: "Whether Mr. Jefferson changed his mind, and kept up with the demands of popular feeling in that particular, we have no means of knowing. We remember no utterance of his on that subject, after reporting the bills we have described."[1] Another important subject fell to his charge in the statutes affecting education. He proposed a system of free common school education, planned in the minutest details; a method of reorganization for William and Mary College, and provision for a free State Library. There was also a bill limiting the death penalty to murder and treason. In his

account of the reception of this "Revision," Mr. Jefferson records: "Some bills were taken out, occasionally, from time to time, and passed; but the main body of the work was not entered on by the Legislature until after the general peace, in 1785, when, by the unwearied exertions of Mr. Madison, in opposition to the endless quibbles, chicaneries, perversions, vexations, and delays of lawyers and demi-lawyers, most of the bills were passed by the Legislature, with little alteration."

In 1779, Mr. Jefferson succeeded Patrick Henry as Governor of Virginia, falling upon a period of administration requiring the military defence of the State, less suited to his talents than the reforming legislation in which he had been recently engaged. Indeed, he modestly confesses this in the few words he devotes to the subject in his Autobiography, where he says, referring to history for this portion of his career: "From a belief that, under the pressure of the invasion under which we were then laboring, the public would have more confidence in a military chief, and that the military commander, being invested with the civil power also, both might be wielded with more energy, promptitude and effect for the defence of the State, I resigned the administration at the end of my second year, and General Nelson was appointed to succeed me." His disposition to the arts of peace, in mitigation of the calamities of war, had been previously shown in his treatment of the Saratoga prisoners of war, who were quartered in his neighborhood, near Charlottesville. He added to the comforts of the men,

---

[1] Life of Jefferson, I. 222.

and entertained the officers at his table, and when it was proposed to remove them to less advantageous quarters, he remonstrated with Governor Henry in their favor. The early part of Jefferson's administration was occupied with various duties connected with the war, and it was only at the end, in the invasions by Arnold and Phillips, in 1780, that he felt its pressure. When Richmond was invaded and plundered, he was obliged to reconnoitre the attack, in his movements about the vicinity, without ability of resistance. The finances and resources of defence of the State were in the most lamentable condition, and it remains a question for the historian to conjecture what degree of military energy, in a Governor, would have been effectual to create an army on the spur of the moment, and extort means for its support. The depredations of Arnold continued till the arrival of Cornwallis, and before his exit from the scene of these operations at Yorktown, an incident occurred which has been sometimes told to Jefferson's disadvantage, though without any apparent reason. The famous Colonel Tarleton, celebrated for the rapidity of his movements, was dispatched to secure the members of the Legislature, then assembled at Charlottesville. Warning was given, and the honorable gentlemen escaped, when it was proposed to capture the Governor at his neighboring residence at Monticello. He however, also had intelligence, perceiving the approach of the enemy from his mountain height, and sending his wife and children in advance to a place of safety, rode off himself as the troopers approached to Carter's Mountain. At this time his term of service as Governor had expired a few days. Happily, the officer who thus visited his house was a gentleman, and his papers, books, and other property, were spared. His estate at Elk Hill, on James River, did not fare so well. Its crops were destroyed, its stock taken, and the slaves driven off to perish, almost to a man, of fever and suffering in the British camp.

Losses like these he could bear with equanimity; not so the inquiry which received some countenance from the legislature into his conduct during the invasion. He was grieved that such an implied censure should be even thought of, and prepared himself to meet it in person; but when he presented himself at the next session, consenting to an election for the express purpose, there was no one to oppose him, and resolutions of respect and confidence took the place of the threatened attack. He had another cause of despondence at this time, which no act of the legislature could cure. His wife, to whom he was always tenderly attached, was daily growing more feeble in health, and gradually approaching her grave. She died in September, 1782—"torn from him by death," is the expressive language he placed on her simple monument.

The illness of his wife had prevented his acceptance of an appointment in Europe, to negotiate terms of peace immediately after the termination of his duties as governor. A similar office was now tendered him—the third proffer of the kind by Congress—and, look ing upon it as a relief to his distracted mind as well as a duty to the State, he accepted it. Before, however, the preparations for his departure were complete, arising from the difficulties then existing of crossing the ocean, intelligence was received of the progress of the peace negotiations, and the voyage was abandoned.

He was then returned to Congress, taking his seat in November, 1783, at Trenton, the day of the adjournment to Annapolis, where one of his first duties, the following month, was as chairman of the Committee which provided the arrangements for the reception of Washington on his resignation of his command. The ceremony took place in public, "the representatives of the sovereignty of the Union" remaining seated and covered while the company in the gallery were standing and uncovered. After Washington's address and delivery of his commission, the President replied in an answer attributed to Jefferson.[1] Eulogy of Washington always fell happily from his pen. "Having defended the standard of liberty in this new world," was one of its sentences; "having taught a lesson useful to those who inflict and those who feel oppression, you retire from the great theatre of action with the blessings of your fellow-citizens: but the glory of your virtues will not terminate with your military command; it will continue to animate remotest ages." Jefferson was accustomed to speak of Washington with eloquence and admiration, suffering no political

disagreements to diminish his historic greatness. Probably the best character ever drawn of the Father of his Country, was written by him, in a letter from Monticello, addressed to Dr. Walter Jones, in 1814.

The presence of Jefferson in any legislative body was always soon felt, and we accordingly find him in the Congress of 1784, making his mark in the debates on the ratification of the treaty of peace, his suggestions on the establishment of a money unit and a national coinage, which were subsequently adopted—he gave us the decimal system and the denomination of the cent; the cession of the Northwestern Territory by Virginia, with his report for its government, proposing names for its new States, and the exclusion of slavery after the year 1800: and taking an active part in the arrangements for commercial treaties with foreign nations. In the last, he was destined to be an actor as well as designer—Congress, on the seventh of May, appointing him to act in Europe with Adams and Franklin, in accomplishing these negotiations. This time he was enabled to enter upon the scene abroad, which had always invited his imagination by its prospects of new observations in art and science, society and government, and intimacy with learned and distinguished men. A visit to Europe to an ordinary American in those days, was like passing from a school to a university; but Jefferson, though he found the means of knowledge unfailing wherever he went, being no ordinary man but a very extraordinary one, carried with him to Europe

---

[1] Randall's Life of Jefferson, I. 392.

more than he could receive there. In the science of government he was the instructor of the most learned; and, in that matter, the relations of the old world and the new were reversed. America, even then, with much to learn before her system was perfected, was the educator of Europe.

Jefferson took with him his oldest daughter, Martha—his family consisting, since the death of his wife, of three young daughters and the adopted children of his friend, Carr—with whom he reached Paris, by the way of England, in August. There he found Dr. Franklin, with whom he entered on the duties of his mission, and whose friendship he experienced in an introduction to the brilliant philosophical society of the capital. His position, also, at the outset, was much strengthened with these savans by a small edition which he printed and privately circulated of his "Notes on Virginia." This work had for some time existed in manuscript, having been written in Virginia, in 1781, during a period of confinement, when he was disabled from active exertion in consequence of a fall from his horse, in reply to certain queries which had been addressed to him by the French minister, M. Marbois, who had been instructed by his government to procure various statistical information in regard to the country. As it had always been a custom of Jefferson to note everything that came to his knowledge relating to topics of national welfare, it was an easy task to supply the required answers from his note-books. In this way, the "Notes" were written and communicated to the minister; and, as these queries were of constant recurrence, relating, as they did, to a new state of things which provoked inquiry, the author kept a copy of the replies for his own use and for that of his friends. He would have printed the little work in America, but was deterred by the expense. Finding this could be done at a fourth of the cost in Paris, he now carried the intention out. The volume was carefully distributed—the writer thinking its opinions on the subject of slavery and of the American Constitution might irritate the minds of his countrymen—but a year or two later, a copy, on the death of its owner, got into the hands of a bookseller, who caused it to be hastily translated by the Abbé Morellet, into French, and in this state sent it to Jefferson on the eve of publication. He could correct only its worst blunders, and the work being now before the world, he thought it but an act of justice to himself to yield to the request of a London publisher, to issue the original. This is the history of the famous "Notes on Virginia." The book itself, as a valuable original contribution to the knowledge of an interesting portion of the country, at a transition period, has been always treasured. Its observations on natural history, and descriptions of scenery, are of value; it has much which would now be called ethnological, particularly in reference to the Indian and the black man; while, in style and treatment, it may be studied as a suggestive index of the mind and tastes of the author.

In the summer of 1785, Dr. Franklin took his departure homeward, retiring from the embassy he had so long and honorably filled, and Jefferson remained as his successor. He was four years in this position, covering the important opening era of the Revolution, including the assembly of the States General, of all the movements connected with which he was a diligent observer and friendly sympathizer with the reformers. His official duties embraced various regulations of trade and commerce, the admission of American products into France on favorable terms; a fruitless attempt with Adams at negotiations with England, which left an unfavorable impression of the mother country on his mind, and the consideration of the Barbary question, for which he proposed, as a remedy to the constant aggressions, active naval coercion. His private correspondence, during this residence abroad, is of the most interesting character. It is not merely well written, with the accuracy of a mind accustomed to reflection, but its topics have, for the most part, an historic value. It is in turn political, scientific, philosophical, or moral, as it is addressed to Washington, Jay, Madison, with whom he keeps up his ideas on American state developments; John Adams; the astronomer Rittenhouse; the ingenious Francis Hopkinson; his nephew, Peter Carr; or his lady friends, Mrs. Cosway, and Mrs. Bingham. To Carr, he lays down a code of precepts, in which we may read the reflection of his own life. "Give up. money, give up fame," he writes, "give up science, give up the earth itself and all it contains, rather than do an immoral act. . . . An honest heart being the first blessing, a knowing head is the second. . . . A strong body makes the mind strong."

A tour which he performed in the provinces of France, and which was extended into northern Italy, was made as subservient to his friends as to his own interest. It was his humor on this journey to study the ways and habits of the common people, and he took as great delight in rambling through the fields with the peasantry and inspecting their cottages, as in visiting palaces and churches. He advised Lafayette to travel in his path, "and to do it effectually," he wrote, "you must be absolutely *incognito;* you must ferret the people out of their hovels, as I have done, look into their kettles, eat their bread, loll on their beds, under pretence of resting yourself, but in fact to find if they are soft. You will feel a sublime pleasure in the course of this investigation, and a sublimer one hereafter, when you shall be able to apply your knowledge to the softening of their beds, or the throwing a morsel of meat into their kettle of vegetables."

The return of Jefferson to the United States in the autumn of 1789, grew out of his desire to restore his daughters—a second one had joined him in Europe, the third died during his absence—to education in America, and to look after his private affairs. A leave of absence was accordingly granted him, with the expectation of a return to the French capital. Before reaching home, he found a letter from President Washington awaiting him, tendering him the office of Secretary of State in the new government. The proposition was received with manifest reluctance, but with a candid reference to the will of the President. The latter smoothed the way, by representing the duties of the office as less laborious than had been conceived, and it was accepted. At the end of March, 1790, he joined the other members of the administration at New York. Then began that separation in politics, which, gradually rising to the dignity of party organization, became known as Federalism and Republicanism. At the present day, it is difficult to appreciate the state of Jefferson's mind towards Hamilton and other members of the administration; his distrust of their movements, and apparently fixed belief that some monarchical designs were entertained by them. If there were any offenders in this way, they were Hamilton and Jay; but it is difficult to credit that either of them entertained any serious intentions of the kind, however naturally they might distrust theories of self-government. In fact, there were "fears of the brave," if not "follies of the wise," on both sides. Each party had much to learn, which experience in the practical working of the government only could teach. It was easy then to exaggerate trifles, as it is unprofitable now, in the face of broad results, to revive them. There was a practical question also before Congress, which seems to have affected the equanimity of Jefferson, that namely of the assumption of the State debts. Hamilton was the advocate of this measure, which met with serious opposition. Jefferson was inclined to oppose it, as

8

an addition to the financial power of the Secretary of the Treasury; which rose in his eyes as an evil of still greater magnitude when Hamilton's proposition came up of a national bank. This institution, in his distrust of paper money, he considered a fountain of demoralization. To these causes of separation in opinion was in no long time added the pregnant controversy of the good or evil, the wisdom or folly of the French Revolution, drawing with it a train of conduct at home, when the neutrality question became the subject of practical discussion. Jefferson is thought to have lent some support to the annoyances of the time under which Washington suffered, in his patronage of the poet Freneau, who irritated the President by sending him his newspaper filled with attacks on the supposed monarchical tendencies of the day. When the insolence, however, of Genet and his advocates reached its height, the case was so clear that Jefferson employed himself in his office in the State Department in the most vigorous protests and denunciation. Whatever opinions he might entertain of men or measures, on a question of practical conduct, he regarded only the honor and welfare of his country. He retired at the end of 1793, with the friendship and respect of Washington unbroken. The public questions which arose during his secretaryship, which we have alluded to, though the noisiest on the page of history, are perhaps not the most significant of Jefferson's career. His services, in many laborious matters of investigation and negotiation, were constant; with England, in regard to conditions of the treaty of peace; with Spain, in reference to her claims at the South, and the navigation of the Mississippi—a question which he was so happily to bring to a termination in his Presidential administration; at home, in his efforts for trade and commerce, exhibited in his various industrial reports.

The simplicity of his retirement at Monticello has been questioned by those who have been accustomed to look upon the man too exclusively in the light of a politician; but the evidence brought forward by his latest biographer, Mr. Randall, shows that the passion, while it lasted, was genuine. Jefferson, with all his coolness and external command, had a peculiar sensitiveness. In fact, it is only a superficial view of his character which could overlook this element lying beneath. A speculative moralist must feel as well as think, and the world can no more get such reflections on life and conduct —whatever we may think of their absolute value—as are thickly sown in his writings, without inner emotion, than fruit can be gathered without the delicate organization of the plant which bears it. Such grapes are not plucked from thorns. In Jefferson's heart there was a fund of sensibility, freely exhibited in his private intercourse with his family. He was unwearied in the cares and solicitudes of his daughters, his adopted children, and their alliances. In reading the letters which passed between them, the politician is forgotten: we see only the man and the father. Besides these pleasing anxieties, he had the responsibilities and resources of several considerable plantations; his five thousand acres about Monticello alone, as he managed them with their novel improvements and home manufacturing operations, affording occupation enough for a single mind. He had, too, his books and favorite studies in science and literature. There were, probably, few public men in the country who like him read the Greek dramatists in the original with pleasure. What wonder, then, that he honestly sought retirement from the labors and struggles of political life, becoming every day more embittered by the rising spirit of party? That the retirement was really such, we have the best proof in an incidental remark in one of his letters written in 1802— the recluse was at the time in the Presidency—to his daughter Maria, then married to Mr. Eppes. Fancying he saw in her a reluctance to society, he rebukes the feeling, adding, "I can speak from experience on this subject. From 1793 to 1797, I remained closely at home, saw none but those who came there, and at length became very sensible of the ill effect it had upon my own mind, and of its direct and irresistible tendency to render me unfit for society and uneasy when necessarily engaged in it. I felt enough of the effect of withdrawing from the world then, to see that it led to an anti-social and misanthropic state of mind, which severely punishes him who gives into it; and it will be a lesson I shall never forget as to myself." But the law of Jefferson's mind was activity, and it was no long time before he mingled again in the political arena. His first decided symptom of returning animation is found by his biographer in his subscription, at the close of 1795, to "Bache's Aurora." He was no longer content with "his solitary Richmond newspaper." After this, there is no more thorough "working politician" in the country than Thomas Jefferson.[1]

It is not necessary here to trace his influence on every passing event. We may proceed rapidly to his reappearance in public life as Vice-President in 1797, on the election of John Adams, soon followed by the storm of party, attendant upon the obnoxious measures of the President in the Alien and Sedition Laws, the rapid disintegration of the Federal party and the rise of the Republicans. Out of the stormy conflict, Jefferson, at the next election, was elevated to the Presidency. The vote stood seventy-three alike for himself and Burr, and sixty-five and sixty-four respectively for Mr. Adams and Mr. Pinckney. As the Presidency was then given to the one who had the highest vote and the Vice-Presidency to the one next below him, neither being named for the offices, this equality threw the election into the House of Representatives. A close contest then ensued between Jefferson and Burr for the Presidency, which was protracted for six days and thirty-six ballotings, when the former was chosen by ten out of the sixteen votes of the States.

His Inaugural Address was an appeal for harmony. After a brief sketch in vivid language, of which no one had a better mastery, of the country, whose laws he was appointed to administer— "a rising nation, spread over a wide and fruitful land, traversing all the seas with the rich productions of their industry, engaged in commerce with nations who feel power and forget right, advancing rapidly to destinies beyond the reach of mortal eye"—he proceeded to assuage the agitations of party. "Every difference of opinion," he said, "is not a difference of principle. We have called by different names brethren of the same principle. We are all Republicans—we are all Federalists. If there be any among us who would wish to dissolve this Union, or to change its republican form, let them stand undisturbed as monuments of the safety with which error of opinion may be tolerated where reason is left free to combat it."

One of the early measures of Jefferson's administration, and the most important of his eight years of office, was the acquisition of Louisiana by purchase from France. It was a work upon which he had peculiarly set his heart. From the first moment of hearing that the territory was passing from Spain to France, he dropped all political sympathy for the latter, and saw in her possession of the region only a pregnant source of war and hostility. Not content with the usual channel of diplomacy through the State department, he wrote himself at once to Mr.

---

[1] The close of his retirement was marked by an honor which he valued, his election as President of the American Philosophical Society. In his letter of acceptance, always mindful of his practical democracy, he wrote, "I feel no qualification for this distinguished post, but a sincere zeal for all the objects of our institution, and an ardent desire to see knowledge so disseminated through the mass of mankind, that it may at length reach the extremes of society, beggars and kings."

Livingston, the minister in France, urging considerations of national policy not so much that the United States should hold the country, as that the European powers should relinquish it. From his own previous discussions with Spain, he understood the topic well, and his zeal was now equal to the occasion. An active European nation of the first class in possession of the mouth of the Mississippi, was utterly inadmissible to his sagacious mind; he saw and felt the fact in all its consequences. The rapidity of his conclusions, his patriotic insight were happily seconded by the necessities of Napoleon at the time, and Louisiana became an integral part of the Republic, with the least expenditure of money and political negotiation. The turn of European events had much to do with it—but had the difficulty been prolonged, the prescience and energy of Jefferson would, there is every reason to believe, have been prepared to cope with the issue. The expedition of Lewis and Clarke, in exploration of the western territory, parallel with this new acquisition, was planned by Jefferson, and must be placed to the credit, alike of his love of science and patriotic insight into the future of his country. The brilliant acts of the navy in the Mediterranean, in conflict with the Barbary powers, came also to swell the triumphs of the administration, and Jefferson, at the next Presidential election, was borne into office, spite of a vigorous opposition, by a vote of one hundred and sixty-two in the electoral college to fourteen given to Charles Cotesworth Pinckney.

The main events of this second administration were the trial of Burr for his alleged western conspiracy, in which the President took a deep interest in the prosecution, and the measures adopted against the naval aggressions of England, which culminated in the famous "Embargo," by which the foreign trade of the country was annihilated at a blow, that Great Britain might be reached in her commercial interests. The state of things was peculiar. America had been grievously wronged in her unsettled relations with England, and not only assailed, but insulted in the attack on the Chesapeake and seizure of her men. What was to be done? The question was not ripe for war. The Embargo was accepted as an alternative, but its immediate pressure at home was even greater than war. The disasters of the latter in the injuries inflicted on our commerce, would have been vast; but they would have been casual, and might have been escaped. Not so this self-denying ordinance of the Embargo, which prohibited American vessels from sailing from foreign ports, and all foreign vessels from taking out cargoes: it was a constant force, acting to the destruction of all commerce. It, moreover, directed the course of trade from our own shores to others, whence it might not easily be recalled. All this must have been seen by the Administration which resorted to the measure as a temporary expedient. It, of course, called down a storm of opposition from the remnants of Federalism in the commercial States, which ended in its repeal early in 1809, after it had been in operation something more than a year. Immediately after, the Presidency of its author closed with his second term, leaving the country, indeed, in an agitated, unsettled state in reference to its foreign policy, but with many elements at home of enduring prosperity and grandeur. The territory of the nation had been enlarged, its resources developed, and its financial system conducted with economy and masterly ability; time had been gained for the inevitable coming struggle with England, and though the navy was not looked to as it should have been, it had more than given a pledge of its future prowess in its achievements in the Mediterranean.

He was now sixty-six, nearly the full allotment of human life, but he was destined to yet seventeen years of honorable exertion—an interval marked by his popular designation, "the sage of Monticello," in which asperities might die out, and a new generation learn to reverence him as a father of the State. He had been too much of a reformer not to suffer more than most men the obloquy of party, and he died without the true Thomas Jefferson being fully known to the public. In his last days he spoke of the calumny to which he had been subjected with mingled pride and charitable feeling. He had not considered, he said, in words worthy of remembrance, "his enemies as abusing him; they had never known *him*. They had created an imaginary being clothed with odious attributes, to whom they had given his name; and it was against that creature of their imaginations they had levelled their anathemas."[1] We may now penetrate within that home, even, in the intimacy of his domestic correspondence, within that breast, and learn something of the man Thomas Jefferson. His questioning turn of mind, and, to a certain extent, his unimaginative temperament, led him to certain views, particularly in matters of religion, which were thought at war with the welfare of society. But whatever the extent of his departure, in these things, from the majority of the Christian world, he does not appear, even in his own family, to have influenced the opinion of others. His views are described, by those who have studied them, to resemble those held by the Unitarians. He was not averse, however, on occasion, to the services of the Episcopal Church, which, says Mr. Randall, "he generally attended, and when he did so, always carried his prayer-book, and joined in the responses and prayers of the congregation." Of the Bible he was a great student, and, we fancy, derived much of his Saxon strength of expression from familiarity with its language.

If any subject was dearer to his heart than another, in his latter days, it was the course of education in the organization and government of his favorite University of Virginia. The topic had long been a favorite one, dating as far back with him as his report to the Legislature in 1779. It was revived in some efforts made in his county in 1814, which resulted in the establishment of a college that in 1818

---

[1] Letter from Colonel T. J. Randolph to Henry S. Randall. Randall's Life of Jefferson, III. 544.

gave place to the projected University. Its courses of instruction reflected his tastes, its government was of his contrivance, he looked abroad for its first professors, and its architectural plans, in which he took great interest, were mainly arranged by him. He was chosen by the Board of Visitors, appointed by the Governor, its Rector, and died holding the office. An inscription for his monument, which was found among his papers at his death, reads: " Here lies buried, Thomas Jefferson, author of the Declaration of American Independence, of the Statute of Virginia for Religious Freedom, and Father of the University of Virginia."

The time was approaching for its employment, as the old statesman lingered with some of the physical infirmities, few of the mental inconveniences of advanced life. His fondness for riding blood horses was kept up almost to the last, and he had always his family, his friends, his books—faithful to the end to the sublimities of Æschylus, the passion of his younger days. He was much more of a classical, even, than of a scientific scholar, we have heard it said by one well qualified to form an opinion; but this was a taste which he did not boast of, and which, happily for his enjoyment of it, his political enemies did not find out. In the decline of life, when debt, growing out of old encumbrances and new expenses on his estates, was pressing upon him, these resources were unfailing and exacted no repayments. His pen, too, ever ready to give wings to his thought, was with him. Even in those last days, preceding the national anniversary which marked his death, he wrote with his wonted strength and fervor: "All eyes are opened or opening to the rights of man. The general spread of the light of science has already laid open to every view the palpable truth, that the mass of mankind have not been born with saddles on their backs, nor a favored few booted and spurred, ready to ride them legitimately, by the grace of God." This was the last echo of the fire which was wont to inspire senates, which had breathed in the early councils of liberty, which had kept pace with the progress of the nation to a third generation. A few days after, at noon of the day which had given the Republic birth, to the music of his own brave words, exactly fifty years after the event; in full consciousness of his ebbing moments, with tranquillity and equanimity, passed from earth the soul of Thomas Jefferson. His old comrade, John Adams, lingered at Braintree a few hours longer, thinking of his friend in his dying moments, as he uttered his last words: "Thomas Jefferson still survives." They were too late for fact, but they have been accepted for prophecy, and in this spirit they are inscribed as the motto to the latest memorial of him of whom they were spoken. Thus, on the fourth of July, 1826, passed away the two great apostles of American liberty; the voice which, louder, perhaps, than any other, had called for the Declaration of Independence, and the hand that penned it.

James Madison

JAMES MADISON.

JAMES MADISON, the fourth President of the United States, was descended from an old family of Virginia planters, which is traced to the first annals of the country, in the records of the great pioneer, Captain John Smith. A branch of the family is distinguished in the history of western settlement beyond the Alleghanies. The first bishop of the Protestant Episcopal Church of Virginia bore the same name with the President, and was related to him.

The family seat of the branch of the Madisons, which gave birth to the subject of our sketch, was Montpelier, in Orange County, Virginia. It was the home of his father and grandfather, and became celebrated as his own residence when years and public services brought pilgrims to the spot. His birthplace, however, was some fifty miles distant, on the banks of the Rappahannock, near Port Royal, at the estate belonging to his maternal grandmother, where his mother was then on a visit.

Mr. Rives, the latest biographer of Madison, speaks of the ancient seat of hospitality, Montpelier, and "the picturesque grandeur of its mountain scenery," enhanced by "the heartiness and cordiality of its possessors. The mother of Mr. Madison, Eleanor Conway," he continues, "must in her day have added largely to the attractions of the social, as she undoubtedly did in the highest degree, to the happiness, comfort and usefulness of the domestic scene. Nothing is more touching and beautiful in the life of her illustrious son, than the devoted tenderness for his mother, with which her virtues and character inspired him—ever recurring with anxious thoughtfulness, in the midst of his most important occupations, to her delicate health, and after the close of his public labors, personally watching over and nursing her old age with such pious care, that her life was protracted to within a few years of the term of his own. His father was, no less, the object of his dutiful and affectionate attachment and respect. The correspondence between them, from the period of young Madison's being sent to Princeton College in 1769, to the installation of the matured and honored statesman in the office of Secretary of State in 1801, when the father died, has been carefully preserved, and shows how much they were bound to each other by sentiments of mutual confidence and respect, even more than by ties of natural affection."[1]

---

[1] History of the Life and Times of James Madison, by William C. Rives, I. 8-9.

Such influences of the beauties of nature and of domestic life, are favorable to a happy development of the youthful faculties, and have much to do with the man's future career. The young Madison was a well disposed, teachable youth. He received his education at a boarding-school kept in the neighboring King and Queen County, by Donald Robertson, a learned Scotchman, with whom he was placed for a few years, at the age of twelve. Returning to his home, he was prepared for college by the clergyman of the parish, the Rev. Thomas Martin, who had his home under the paternal roof. Princeton College, New Jersey, had then risen into distinction by the acquisition of a President of great acuteness of mind and fine literary and philosophical attainments, John Witherspoon, who bore a prominent part in the Revolution, and whose name adorns the Declaration of Independence. To Princeton, then, at this time, flocked the youth, who were to be emphatically the men of the new generation. Madison was foremost among the number, and by his side were Samuel Stanhope Smith, the future accomplished divine, Hugh Henry Brackenridge, the stalwart author of "Modern Chivalry," Philip Freneau, a man of great talent, the verse-maker of the Revolution, who was his classmate, William Bradford, Aaron Burr, and four future governors of States—John Henry, of Maryland, Morgan Lewis, of New York, Aaron Ogden, of New Jersey, and Henry Lee, of Virginia.[1]

[1] We are indebted to Mr. Rives for this enumeration, with the exception of Freneau, whom he has omitted.

Madison was an ardent student, stealing hours from sleep for his books, and compressing the labors of the four years' College course into three. This devotion enabled him to graduate in 1771, a year earlier than he would otherwise have done; but it cost him an illness which he sought to repair by a continued residence at Princeton, which was not without its advantages in the counsel of Witherspoon, who greatly admired the sagacity and prudence of his pupil, and in the opportunity of watching the opening movements of the Revolution at New York. Madison left Princeton with a mind imbued with literature, a polished style of composition, and religious convictions strengthened by much thought and extensive reading.

He now for a while employed his time at home in liberal studies, and assisted in the education of his younger brothers. His correspondence with his friend, William Bradford, at this time, shows an ardent, ingenuous, opening manhood, kindling at the evils of the times, the union of poverty and luxury, the prevalence of vice and wickedness, and the defects of the clergy, and especially the persecutions which were then rife in his neighborhood, under the church and State legislation, directed against some unfortunate Baptist dissenters.

The sentiment of opposition to British authority, which had sprung up simultaneously from foregone conclusions in the minds of the intelligent patriots of the country, was now to assume form in active services. Madison was among the earliest to give expression to it. He anticipated the famous resolutions of Henry in 1775, and upon that popular leader's success in the affair of the powder with Dunmore, drew up, in May of that year, an address of thanks for the Orange County committee. In the first General Convention of the State of Virginia, which organized its independence the following year at Williamsburg, Madison was a delegate from his district. He was one of the committee appointed to frame a Constitution, and, under the leadership of George Mason, rendered valuable services to that instrument. He was the author, in particular, of an important amendment of the original draft of the Declaration of Rights, which substituted for the word "toleration," in matters of religion, a full expression of the absolute right to the exercise of freedom. Madison sat with Jefferson in the first Legislative Assembly under the Constitution at Williamsburg, but lost his election to the next session by his resistance to the popular custom, inherited from the Anglican colonial times, of treating the electors. His opponents were not so scrupulous, and he was defeated. To make amends for this turn of affairs, the legislative body chose him a member of its Council of State. He held this position till he was sent by the Assembly to the National Congress of 1780, at Philadelphia, in which he served till the conclusion of peace. The services rendered by him during this period were rather those of a counsellor and committee man than of a debater. Indeed, a constitutional modesty and diffidence long withheld

him from public displays of the kind, and it was only by degrees that he conquered the inability or reluctance. "So extreme," we are told, "was his diffidence, that it was Mr. Jefferson's opinion that if his first public appearance had taken place in such an assembly as the House of Representatives of the United States, Mr. Madison would never have been able to overcome his aversion to display. But by practice, first in the Executive Council of Virginia, and afterwards in the Old Congress, which was likewise a small body, he was gradually habituated to speech-making in public, in which he became so powerful."[1]

But if we hear little of the oratory of Madison, there is much to be said of his services to the Old Congress. They were those of the statesman continually employed in eking out the resources, sustaining the credit, and adjusting the irregular machinery of an imperfect system of government. After the first glow of patriotism, and the ardor of remonstrance, in the early scenes of the Revolution, there was more of toil than of glory in the later labors of Congress. Its feeble powers, even under the Articles of Confederation, its unsettled authority, the divided allegiance of the people of the States, its shifts in the government of the army, its failures in finance, its unequal foreign diplomacy, all productive of jarring and discord, had, indeed, one compensation. They were well calculated to discipline the statesmen who engaged in them, and enlighten the

[1] Biographical Sketch of Madison. Democratic Review, March, 1839.

public on the necessities and claims of a just government. Out of the troubled strife and confusion came forth, with others, Jay, Hamilton, and Madison, and the nation, after being long in pain, brought forth the Constitution.

We may refer Madison's chief labors to one or other of these trials which we have enumerated. We find him, for instance, at one time discharging, with consummate ability, what would now fall to a Secretary of State, namely, the preparation of a paper to be sent to the minister in Spain, enforcing the claim to the free navigation of the Mississippi; and when the force of his argument had established his positions to the admiration of all men, he is compelled to combat the opposition of his own State, and witness a degrading withdrawal by Congress of the proud instructions he had forwarded to the plenipotentiary at Madrid.

At another time, he is engaged in advocating a simple and necessary revenue system of duties, to discharge the obligations of the war and sustain public credit, a measure which is thwarted by State opposition, when his own Virginia falls away from her resolves, but which he returns to, and again works upon till it is brought, with increased authority, before Congress, and submitted to the States, accompanied by a masterly appeal from his pen. And yet the work is not done. It is left as a legacy to the Government to come.

During his residence in Philadelphia, Madison formed an unrequited attachment for the daughter of General Floyd, a New York delegate, which drew forth from Jefferson a philosophical letter of consolation under his disappointment, which may relieve these rather dry details of political duties. "I sincerely lament," writes Jefferson, who was an acquaintance of the lady, "the misadventure which has happened, from whatever cause it may have happened. Should it be final, however, the world still presents the same and many other resources of happiness, and you possess many within yourself. Firmness of mind and unintermitting occupation will not long leave you in pain. No event has been more contrary to my expectations, and these were founded on what I thought a good knowledge of the ground. But of all machines ours is the most complicated and inexplicable."[1]

Upon his return to Montpelier from Congress, Madison directed his attention again to the study of the law, which, like Richard Henry Lee, he pursued rather with a view to statesmanship, than with any intention to engage in the ordinary conflicts of the profession. From 1784 to 1786, he was in the State legislature, which he reentered with the full intention to bring to the service of Virginia and the country the lessons of experience which he had derived from his labors in the Congress. In his own words, "I acceded to the desire of my fellow citizens of the county, that I should be one of its representatives in the Legislature hoping that I might there best contribute to inculcate the critical posture to which the Revolutionary cause was

---

[1] MS. letter cited in Rives' Life of Madison, I. 523.

reduced, and the merit of a leading agency of the State in bringing about a rescue of the Union and the blessings of liberty staked on it, from an impending catastrophe."[1] The most important of his employments in this capacity, relate to the internal improvements of the State and its commercial condition, in which he seconded the plans of Washington; the proposed mode of supporting the clergy by assessment, advocated by Patrick Henry, which he defeated; and the adjustment of the British debts, which he sought to bring about in furtherance of the treaty obligation of the General Government. His measures were especially directed to the support of the confederacy, in the regulation of trade and commerce. For this purpose, he drafted the resolution of Jan. 21, 1786, appointing Commissioners to assemble at a time and place to be agreed on with the delegates of other States who should accept the invitation, to take into consideration the commercial questions at issue. The representatives of five States—New York, New Jersey, Pennsylvania, Delaware and Virginia—assembled, in September, at Annapolis, Maryland, which was chosen for its remoteness from the seat of Congress and the large cities. The attendance was inadequate to the intended object, but the meeting had one memorable result. It brought together Alexander Hamilton and James Madison, and by its emphatic recommendation drawn up by Hamilton, enlarging the objects

of the meeting, led directly to the Federal Convention of the ensuing year. Madison urged upon the Virginia Assembly compliance with the suggestions at Annapolis, and he was himself chosen as one of the delegates to the new body, having among his colleagues from his native State, Washington, Mason and Wythe. Virginia thus stood foremost in the work of the Convention. Madison approached his great work—the great work of his life—with a solemn sense of its importance and responsibility. No one knew better than himself the absolute necessity of national union, to be expressed in a system of law comprehending the whole and protecting the several parts. No one worked more faithfully in the Convention, which made a mighty nation out of jarring and discordant States. Madison was so impressed with the future import of the work in which he was engaged, that he added to the labors of debate the Herculean task of preparing, day by day, a report of the proceedings of the Convention, embracing all the speeches and discussions. "The curiosity I had felt," he says, in a preliminary essay prefixed to this manuscript history, which he left unpublished at his death as a legacy to his country, " during my researches into the history of the most distinguished confederacies, particularly those of antiquity, and the deficiency I found in the means of satisfying it, more especially in what related to the process, the principles, the reasons and the anticipations which prevailed in the formation of them, determined me to preserve, as far as I

---

[1] Introduction to the Debates in the Convention. The Madison Papers, II. 693.

could, an exact account of what might pass in the Convention whilst executing its trust, with the magnitude of which I was duly impressed, as I was by the gratification promised to future curiosity by an authentic exhibition of the objects, the opinions and the reasonings from which the new system of government was to receive its peculiar structure and organization. Nor was I unaware of the value of such a contribution to the fund of materials for the history of a Constitution, on which would be staked the happiness of a people great even in its infancy, and possibly the cause of liberty throughout the world."

The pains taken by Madison in the preparation of this work was extrordinary. He selected a seat near the chairman, where nothing that passed would escape him; made abbreviated notes of all that was read and said; not a little, he tells us, aided by practice and familiarity with the style and train of observation and reasoning of the principal speakers; wrote out these notes when the Convention was not in session; in a very few instances being aided by the revisions or supervision of the speakers. So important were these private labors of Madison, that when Congress, in 1819, undertook the publication of the Journal of the Convention, Madison was called upon to complete its imperfect official outline. He left the Debates, at his death, carefully prepared for the press, with directions in his will for their publication. Failing to secure satisfactory arrangements with publishers, his widow submitted the affair to President Jackson.

He brought it before Congress, the publication was provided for by that body, and thirty thousand dollars were appropriated to Mrs. Madison for the copyright. The work finally appeared more than half a century after the discussions which it recorded, in 1840, when the public learnt, for the first time, the full history of the Convention. The Madison Papers also include another series of Debates in the Congress of the Confederation, taken in the years 1782–3, and 1787; for, reappointed in 1786, Madison was also a member of the old Congress at its final adjournment.

The work of the Convention being now completed in the formation of the Constitution, it was next to be submitted to the States. Madison, in conjunction with Jay and Hamilton, paved the way for its adoption in the Papers of the Federalist, originally published in a New York journal. The contributions written by him, in whole or in part, are twenty-nine in number, exhibiting, among other points, the utility of the Union as a safeguard against domestic faction and insurrection, the anarchical tendencies of mere confederacies, the nature of the proposed powers, and the law of their distribution. The paper "Concerning the difficulties which the Convention must have experienced in the formation of a proper plan," rises into a philosophical comment; and certainly no one could write with more feeling on this theme than Madison.

Madison was a member of the Ratifying Convention in Virginia, where its adoption met with considerable opposition, headed by Patrick Henry, who looked upon the new government as a sacrifice of State interests. So decided was his antagonism to Madison, as its prominent defender, that he defeated his election as Senator to the first Congress.

He was, however, chosen by the electors of his district a member of the House of Representatives, in which body he continued to serve for eight years. In the interpretation of the powers of the Constitution, and in regard to the policy of several measures of government, he differed from the Administration. He opposed the financial adjustments of Hamilton, and in the course of the French agitations, led the debate in opposition to the British treaty.

This period of Congressional life was relieved by the marriage of Madison, in 1794, to a young widow of Philadelphia, Mrs. Todd, better known by her maiden name, Dolly Payne. This lady was a Virginian by birth, of Quaker parentage. The marriage was a most happy one. The vivacity and amiable disposition of Mrs. Madison have left their gentle recollections alike in the retirement of Montpelier, and the gay salons of Washington. Her feminine grace softened the asperities and relieved the burden of political life. After soothing the protracted age of her husband, his feebleness and his languors, she survived many years, to be honored in herself and in his memory.

After the close of his Congressional life, Madison retired with his wife to his books and home pursuits at Montpelier. He was soon, however to be called forth again into the arena by the agitations of the times. The extraordinary measures of Adams, the Alien and Sedition laws, which grew out of the attacks upon government in the French excitement, were violently assailed in Virginia. Mr. Madison drafted the famous resolutions of the Legislature of 1798, condemning these acts of the Administration, and to extend their influence with the public, issued his Report.

On the election of Jefferson to the Presidency, in 1801, Madison became Secretary of State, and discharged the duties of the office till he was called to succeed his friend at the head of the government, in 1809. It was a period of embarrassing foreign diplomacy, of vexed international relations, of protracted discussions of the rights of neutrals, of restrictions, and that measure of incipient war, the embargo. The contest with England, was the chief event of Madison's administrations. He was a man of peace, not of the sword, and needed not the terror and indecorum of the flight from Washington, and the burning of the capitol, to impress upon him its unsatisfactory necessities. Public opinion was divided as to the wisdom of the contest. The embarrassments of the question have been covered by a flood of glory, but little perhaps was gained besides the victories, which might not have been secured a little later by diplomacy. The war, however established one fact, that America would fight, at whatever cost, in defence of her violated rights, and the lesson may have assisted, and may yet be destined to assist, other deliberations. At any rate, it is to the credit of Madison, that he entered upon the apparently inevitable hostilities with reluctance, that he maintained the struggle firmly, and brought it to an early close.

Montpelier, again, in 1817, gave its friendly welcome to the wearied states-man. With the exception of his participation as a member of the Convention, at Richmond, of 1829, in the revision of the Constitution of Virginia, he is said never to have left his district for the remainder of his life, which, solaced by the entertainment of books and natural history, the comforts of domestic life, and the attentions of his countrymen to the aged patriot, was protracted at his mountain residence, to the advanced term of eighty-five years—an extraordinary period for a constitution feeble from youth, afflicted with various disorders, and exposed to the pressure of harassing occupation. He died at Montpelier, June 28, 1836, the last survivor of that second noble band of signers, the signers of the Constitution.

An interesting article, contributed by Professor George Tucker, of the University of Virginia, of which, after the death of Jefferson, Madison became rector, to the "London Penny Encyclopedia," supplies us with a few personal anecdotes of the man. "In person Mr. Madison was below the middle size; though his face was ordinarily homely, when he smiled it was so pleasing as to be almost handsome. His manner with strangers was reserved, which some regarded as pride, and others as coldness; but, on further acquaintance, these impressions were completely effaced. His temper seemed to be naturally a very sweet one, and to have been brought under complete control. When excited, he seldom showed any stronger indication of anger than a slight flush on the check. As a hus-band, Mr. Madison was without reproach. He never had a child. He was an excellent master, and though he might have relieved himself from debt, and secured an easy income, he could never be induced to sell his slaves, except for their own accommodation, to be with their wives or husbands. The writer has sometimes been struck with the conferences between him and some trusty servant in his sick chamber, the black seeming to identify himself with his master as to plans of management, and giving his opinions as freely, though not offensively, as if conversing with a brother. . . . . With great powers of argument, he had a fine vein of humor he abounded in anecdote, told his stories very well, and they had the advantage of being such as were never heard before, except perhaps from him-self. Such were his conversational powers, that to the last his house was one of the most pleasant to visit, and his society the most delightful that can be imagined. Yet more than half his time he suffered bodily pain, and some-times very acute pain."

"Purity, modesty, decorum—a moderation, temperance, and virtue in everything," said the late Senator Benton, "were the characteristics of Mr. Madison's life and manners."

JAMES MONROE.

James Monroe, the fifth President of the United States, was born in April, 1758, in Westmoreland County, Virginia, on the Potomac, a region remarkable in the history of the country as the birth-place of Washington, Madison, and of the distinguished family of the Lees. Monroe's ancestors had been long settled on the spot. The names of his parents were Spence Monroe and Elizabeth Jones; and, to our regret, the scant biographies of the President tell us nothing more of them. Their son was educated at the college of William and Mary, which he left to take part in the early struggles of the army of Washington,—a cause which in the breasts of Virginians superseded all ordinary occupation. Like Marshall and others, the future civilian began his career in the pursuits of war. He joined the forces of Washington at New York, in time to participate in the courageous retreat after the battle of Long Island. He was in the action at Harlem Heights, and the subsequent battle of White Plains, and was in the retreat through the Jerseys. He led a company in the van of the battle of Trenton, and was severely wounded, a service in the field which procured him a captaincy. He was with Lord Stirling, acting as his aid in the campaigns of 1777 and 1778, and distinguished himself at the Brandywine, Germantown and Monmouth. Being thrown out of the regular line of promotion by accepting his staff appointment, he was anxious to regain his position in the line, and for this purpose was sent by Washington to raise a regiment in Virginia. Failing to accomplish this object he remained in the State and directed his attention to the study of the law, under the direction of Jefferson, then recently elected Governor. He took no further part with the army at the north, but was active as a volunteer when Virginia became the theatre of the war in the successive invasions of Arnold, Phillips and Cornwallis. He was specially employed by Governor Jefferson in 1780, to visit the southern army as a military commissioner, to report on its conditions and prospects, a duty which he performed to the full satisfaction of the Executive.

In 1782 he was elected a member of the Virginia Legislature, and shortly promoted by that body to a seat in its executive council. In June of the next year he was chosen member of Congress and sat in that body at its meeting at Annapolis when Washington resigned his military commission at the close of the war. The immediate pressure of the necessary steps for self-defence, which gave a kind of cohesion to the loose authority of the old Congress, being now removed, attention was drawn in the most forcible manner to its defects and weaknesses. A poor instrument for war, it was utterly incapable of managing the responsibilities of peace. In foreign and domestic regulations, in the discharge of its obligations, in raising a revenue, in giving uniformity to trade, in every species of judicial determination, it was lamentably inefficient. Monroe, though a young legislator—he was only twenty-four when he entered Congress, and consequently had not the dearly-purchased experience of some of the older members who had exhausted every art of labor and ingenuity in holding the disjointed fabric together—yet was sagacious enough to see the difficulties of the confederacy, and was judged of sufficient importance in council to apply a remedy. He took part in the prominent discussions, and in 1785 introduced a report as chairman of a committee intrusted with certain resolutions of Congress regarding the levying of an impost, and a call upon the State legislatures to grant the power of regulating commerce. He reported in favor of an alteration of the Articles of Confederation to meet both objects. The necessity of some provision for these objects led first to the convention at Annapolis, where the initial steps were taken to bring together the convention of 1787, at Philadelphia, which originated the Constitution. Another mark of confidence in the abilities of Monroe was his selection as one of the commis-

sioners to decide upon the controverted boundary between New York and Massachusetts, in 1784. He accepted the appointment, but delays arising in the composition of the board, resigned the office before the case came to a hearing. Indeed it was settled without resort to the court at all. Mr. Monroe also took part in the discussions touching the assumptions of Spain in her attempts to close the navigation of the Mississippi to inland American commerce, opposing the concession of a right which at that time began to be resolutely claimed, and was fortunately at no very distant day established by treaty. We shall find his name prominently associated with this important measure. "It was the qualities of judgment and perseverance which he displayed on that occasion," says Senator Benton, "which brought him those calls to diplomacy, in which he was afterwards so much employed with three of the then greatest European powers—France, Spain and Great Britain; and it was in allusion to this circumstance that President Jefferson afterwards, when the right of deposit at New Orleans had been violated by Spain, and when a minister was wanted to recover it, said, ' Monroe is the man : the defence of the Mississippi belongs to him.' "[1]

The feeling excited by the discussion of the negotiation between the North and South in the old Congress, led him to abandon his appointment as commissioner in the boundary dispute between New York and Massachusetts.[2]

<hr>

[1] Benton's Thirty Years' View, I. 680.
[2] Address on the Life and Character of James Monroe, by John Quincy Adams.

The three years' service of Mr. Monroe in Congress closed in 1786. During that term he married Miss Kortright, a lady of New York, of an old and respectable family of the State, of whose personal merits we may willingly accept the eulogy of President John Quincy Adams. "Of her attractions and accomplishments," says he, " it were impossible to speak in terms of exaggeration. She was, for a period little short of half a century, the cherished and affectionate partner of her husband's life and fortunes. She accompanied him in all his journeyings through this world of care, from which, by the dispensations of Providence, she had been removed only a few months before himself. The companion of his youth was the solace of his declining years, and to the close of life enjoyed the testimonial of his affection, that with the external beauty and elegance of deportment, conspicuous to all who were honored with her acquaintance, she united the more precious and endearing qualities which mark the fulfilment of all the social duties, and adorn with grace and fill with enjoyment the tender relations of domestic life."

At the close of this Congressional term, Mr. Monroe made his residence at Fredericksburg, with a view to the practice of the law, and was presently, in 1787, returned to the Assembly of Virginia. In the following year ne was chosen a member of the Convention of the State, called to decide upon the acceptance of the Constitution. We have seen the part which he bore in the discussions of the old Congress of the Confederacy on his first admission to that body in reference to the increase of its powers. When the new instrument was before the country and under deliberation in the State Convention, he was opposed to its adoption, holding that certain restrictions, afterwards embraced in the amendments, should precede its acceptance. Notwithstanding, however, his opposition to its provisions, he was early appointed to an important office of its creation, that of United States senator, to which he was elected in 1789, on the decease of William Grayson, one of the first members chosen. He continued in the Senate till 1794, when he was appointed by Washington minister plenipotentiary to France, contemporaneously with Chief Justice Jay to the court of Great Britain. Gouverneur Morris, from his sympathies with royalty and his undisguised declarations of his sentiments, had become unpopular with the French court. Moreover, his recall was requested as a compensation to the wounded honor of France in the American rejection of Genet, which was on the point of being consummated, when he was withdrawn. As a measure of reconciliation, Washington chose a successor from the party supposed particularly to favor French ideas, in contradistinction to the admirers of England. In the two divisions of the country between France and Great Britain, the Republican party was of the former, the Federalists of the latter. In sending Jay to England and Monroe to France, the President was conciliating the nations to whom they were commissioned, and parties at home. The policy of Washington was neutrality, and he endeavored, as far as was consistent with the public welfare, to treat both sides with strict impartiality. There were more popular grounds of leaning to France; that nation had assisted us to the final triumph which gave America independence, and so had the better claim upon our sympathies in comparison with an enemy who had not yet learnt to respect a successful rebel. But familiar, spontaneous France was felt to be more exacting than cold and distant England. The continental nation had attempted to play the part of a dictator in American affairs, and she had not shown the virtue at home to command respect to her interference abroad. She represented, beside, dangerous political theories, while our conservative system was essentially based on the authority of English precedents. For all this, it was natural that the administration of Washington should incline to England when a decision was to be made between the two nations.

Mr. Monroe arrived in Paris August 2, 1794, and was well received by the National Convention, when he brought himself to the notice of that body. His reception in fact was enthusiastic. It was public, in the Convention, and as the minister delivered his credentials it was decreed "that the flag of the American and French republics should be united together and suspended in the hall of the Convention, in testimony of eternal union and friendship between the two peoples. To evince the impression made on his mind by this act, and the grateful sense of his consti-

tuents, Mr. Monroe presented to the Convention the flag of the United States, which he prayed them to accept as a proof of the sensibility with which his country received every act of friendship from its ally, and of the pleasure with which it cherished every incident which tended to cement and consolidate the union between the two nations."[1] These congratulations were reciprocated in kind by the transmission of a French flag to the United States by the hands of the new minister, M. Adet, who delivered it to the President at his reception. Words, however, do not always express deeds. The Government continued not only jealous of any diplomatic movements of the United States in England, but pursued a system of aggression upon American commerce and trade, little if anything short of actual hostilities. It was Mr. Monroe's duty to negotiate and protest; his efforts were ineffectual to control the agencies at work, and after something more than two years of diplomacy he received his letters of recall, brought by his successor, General Charles Cotesworth Pinckney. The mission of Monroe was officially closed on the first of January, 1797, when he took leave of the Executive Directory in an audience specially assigned for the purpose.

It was no doubt the impression of Washington, in appointing a successor to Monroe, that the latter had in some way failed properly to urge the views of his Government. In the language of his cabinet, of which Timothy Pick-

---

[1] Marshall's Life of Washington, V. 726.

ering was now at the head, "whether this dangerous omission arose from such an attachment to the cause of France as rendered him too little mindful of the interests of his own country, or from mistaken views of the latter, or from any other cause, the evil is the same;" they therefore advised his recall. It may be mentioned that Washington at first thought of sending a minister extraordinary to negotiate by his side; but this he was unable to do without the action of Congress, and that body was not now in session.

On his return to the United States, Mr. Monroe thought fit to meet what he conceived an unfair judgment of his course by the publication of a volume entitled "A View of the Conduct of the Executive in the Foreign Affairs of the United States, connected with the Mission to the French Republic during the Years 1794–5–6, illustrated by his Instructions and Correspondence, and other Authentic Documents." The book, from which the author expressly refused to receive any profit, was published "by and for" Benjamin Franklin Bache, at the office of the "Aurora," in Philadelphia. The impression it made upon Washington, now retired from public office to the shades of Mount Vernon, is expressed in a letter dated March, 1798, addressed to John Nicholas. "With respect to Mr. Monroe's 'View of the Conduct of the Executive of the United States,' " he writes, "I shall say but little, because, as he has *called* it a 'view' thereof, I shall leave it to the tribunal to which he himself has appealed to decide, first, how far a correspondence with one of its agents is entitled to the unqualified term he has employed; secondly, how, if it is not, it is to exhibit a view thereof; thirdly, how far his instructions, and the letters he has received from that Executive, through the constitutional organ, and to which he refers, can be made to embrace the *great points* which he and his party are evidently aiming at, namely, to impress upon the public mind that favoritism towards Great Britain has produced a dereliction, in the Administration, of good will toward France." Of "the propriety of exposing to public view his private instructions and correspondence with his own government," the censure is still more emphatic. That Washington read the book carefully, is witnessed by his copy of it left in the library at Mount Vernon, copiously annotated by his own hand, with critical marginal comments.[1] It is to the credit of Monroe, that when the immediate occasion of his remonstrance was over he took the opportunity to express his regard for the character and genius of both Washington and Jay. His eulogist, President John Quincy Adams, does justice to this fair-mindedness. After commending the saying of the great orator, statesman and moralist of antiquity, when reproached for reconciliation with a bitter antagonist, that he wished his enmities to be transient, and his friendships immortal, he adds, " thus it was that the genial mind of James Monroe, at the zenith of his public honors, and in the retirement of his latest days, cast off, like the suppura-

---

[1] Many of them are given by Mr. Sparks, in Appendix X. to his eleventh volume of Washington's Writings.

tion of a wound, all the feelings of unkindness, and the severities of judgment which might have intruded upon his better nature, in the ardor of civil discussion." It would have been a rancorous nature indeed to carry into the Presidential chair, when Washington was in the grave, the memory of an acerbity obliterated not only by time, but which originally grew out of a policy that had been sanctioned by experience.

Immediately after his recall, Mr. Monroe was returned to the Virginia Legislature, and speedily elected Governor of the State, holding the office for the constitutional term of three years. In the beginning of 1803 he was again called upon by the President to proceed to France as minister extraordinary to take part in the negotiations already commenced by the resident minister, Robert R. Livingston, for the purchase or cession of Louisiana, which in the turn of European fortunes had been yielded by Spain to France. The province was likely to prove a new instrument of power, or plaything in the hands of the successful soldier of fortune who directed the movements of armies at his will. It was something more than a mere speculation that he would turn a portion of his force to the New World. The troops were assembled to embark for his American possessions on the Mississippi, and there was a prospect of far greater difficulties as to the navigation of that river than had ever presented themselves in the feeble diplomacy and scant authority of the former Spanish owners. Livingston warned his government at home of the

danger, and advised preparation to meet the emergency, while he exerted every nerve to bring his negotiation to a successful issue. The ear of the First Consul would probably have proved deaf to all his appeals of argument, his demonstrations of political economy and geography, and his proffers of payment, had not the short peace of Amiens been suddenly interrupted by symptoms of the renewal of the European struggle. Napoleon wanted his men at home, and wished to put money in his purse. At this opportune moment of affairs, Monroe arrived in Paris in the spring of 1803, in time to share in the lucky negotiation already commenced by Livingston, and on the eve of proving successful. When the will of a nation reposes in the breast of one man, the slow progress of diplomacy may sometimes be greatly shortened. Within a month of Monroe's arrival, on the 30th April, the treaty was concluded ceding Louisiana to the United States. Having already, in our account of the life of Livingston, given some notice of the most important details of the negotiation, it is unnecessary to repeat them here. Suffice it that a more advantageous purchase has seldom if ever been made by any nation; for it was not only an important acquisition in itself, larger than the country had any reason to expect—not only did it include a vast present possession, but it contained within it, to vary the expression of Dr Johnson, "the potentialities of power beyond the dreams of ambition," while for those whose insight did not extend to posterity, an immediate obstacle to commerce, cause of peril, and even possible danger of dismemberment, was removed. The purchase of Louisiana was the glory of the administration of Jefferson. The statesman who in our day should procure the cession of Lower Canada from England, would not secure a parallel advantage.

The treaty having thus been promptly negotiated at Paris, Mr. Monroe passed over to London, the successor to Rufus King as minister plenipotentiary to Great Britain. He entered immediately upon his duties, and was busy with the open maritime questions between the two nations, when he was called off by President Jefferson, to proceed to Spain to assist Charles Pinckney, the American minister at that court, in the negotiations respecting claims for damages and the settlement of the disputed Louisiana boundary question. Though little resulted at the time from the discussions, the diplomatic papers of Monroe remain, in the language of President Adams, "solid monuments of intellectual power applied to national claims of right, deserving the close and scrutinizing attention of every American statesman."

Mr. Monroe resumed his duties in London in 1805—a period of growing difficulty for an American minister in Great Britain, bent as that nation was upon the destruction of the rights of neutral nations upon the seas. In this era of embarrassed diplomacy, he gained what admissions could be gained from the reluctant ministry of Pitt and the partial liberality of Fox, when, the aggressions of England upon the high seas pressing heavily upon American commerce, William Pinkney, the eminent lawyer of Maryland, of great fame in diplomacy, was sent out in the summer of 1806, as his coadjutor, or joint commissioner in the negotiation. Lords Auckland and Howick were appointed by Fox plenipotentiaries, and a treaty was in the beginning of 1807 concluded, by no means what was desired on the part of America, but, as in the case of Jay, the best which could be obtained under the complicated difficulties of the times, when England had her war interests to maintain, and the United States had not the means of enforcing her positions. The special effort at the outset was to induce England to waive her pretensions to the impressment of seamen, an abandonment of her assumed rights which she was unwilling to make; for this and other defects President Jefferson sent back the treaty for revisal; but Mr. Canning having succeeded to the ministry, with less favorable dispositions than his predecessor, the negotiation was not resumed.

Monroe's next public office was as Governor of Virginia for the second time, in 1810; and towards the close of the following year, he was called by Madison to the Secretaryship of State, a position in direct line to the Presidency. He continued in this relation to the Government during the remainder of Madison's two terms, discharging at the close of the contest with Great Britain, the additional duties of the war department. His efficiency in these relations, in which he displayed force and activity, marked him out as the successor to Madison in the Presidential office. Indeed he had been prominent as a candidate upon his return from his English mission; and his spirited and energetic conduct in furthering the operations of the war in Congress, had greatly added to his hold upon the public. He was the advocate of a national policy, and when funds were needed in the embarrassed financial condition of the times, pledged his own fortune, not without future embarrasment, for the public welfare. All this was not forgotten. He was now to reap the fruits of a long course of exertion in public life, stretching backward to his early days with Washington at the Declaration of Independence, and the first campaign of the Revolutionary war. All questions were at rest, time and the change of events having removed them from the national arena. The struggle over, the powers of the Constitution had in a great measure subsided, as the working of the instrument had been proved and precedents established; there was no longer a French and English party to agitate the country. We can hardly, at the present day, estimate the value of emancipation from the latter embarrassment of the days of Washington and the elder Adams. In the words of an eminent statesman, whose experience covered both eras, John Quincy Adams, "We have now, neither in the hearts of personal rivals, nor upon the lips of political adversaries, the reproach of a devotion to a French or a British faction. If we rejoice in the triumph of European arms, it is in the victories of the Cross over the Crescent. If we gladden with the native countrymen of Lafayette, or sadden with those of Pulaski and Kosciusko, it is the gratulation of freedom rescued from oppression, and the mourning of kindred spirits over the martyrs to their country's independence. We have no sympathies, but with the joys and sorrows of patriotism; no attachments, but to the cause of liberty and of man."

Monroe was raised to the Presidency, in 1819, by a large majority of the electoral votes. His Inaugural, which was well received by the public, introduced the topics of a new era; he urged measures for the national defence, and favored the elements of national prosperity in internal improvements and home manufactures. His conciliatory policy looking to the welfare of the country was evident. He followed up his declarations by an early Presidential tour through the Eastern States of which, says Mr. Hildreth, the historian, "embittered and hot-tempered leaders of parties, who for the last seven years had hardly deigned to speak to each other, or even to walk on the same side of the street, met now with smiling faces, vying in extravagance of official adoration. The 'era of good feeling' having thus begun, the way was rapidly paved for that complete amalgamation of parties, which took place a few years after."[1]

The chief events of Mr. Monroe's first term were the admission of Mississippi, Illinois and Alabama as new States into the Union, and the important cession of Florida by Spain, in

---

[1] History of the United States, 2d series III. 623.

1819, completing the work of annexation commenced in the purchase of Louisiana. When the time for reëlection came round, so entire was the subsidence of party, that President Monroe was again chosen with but one dissenting vote, that of New Hampshire, which was given to John Quincy Adams. He continued to pursue a liberal policy of internal improvements within the limits of the Constitution, to forward the military defences on land, and the growth and employment of the navy at sea. The revolutionary movements in the Spanish provinces, in which he took an earnest interest, engaged much of his attention. The close of his administration was marked by the progress of Lafayette through the country, a subject to which he made special allusion in his last annual message. "A more interesting spectacle," he. said, with some reference perhaps to his own recollections, "it is believed was never witnessed, because none could be founded on purer principles, none proceed from higher or more disinterested motives. That the feelings of those who had fought and bled with him in a common cause should have been much excited was natural. But the circumstance which was most sensibly felt, and which his presence brought to the mind of all, was the great cause in which we were engaged, and the blessings which we have derived from our success in it. The struggle was for independence and liberty, public and personal, and in this we succeeded." President Monroe was a plain writer, not at all given to the graces of rhetoric; had he been at all a man of eloquence, or trained in its liberal art, he could hardly have failed to impress some striking images of his past life in a retrospect of his memorable career. But this was not the nature or talent of the man. In the simplest words, he takes leave of the public; but to those who were acquainted with his life, as to himself, they were pregnant with meaning. "I cannot conclude this communication," ends his eighth annual message, "the last of the kind which I shall have to make, without recollecting, with great sensibility and heartfelt gratitude, the many instances of public confidence and the generous support which I have received from my fellow citizens in the various trusts with which I have been honored. Having commenced my service in early youth, and continued it since with few and short intervals, I have witnessed the great difficulties to which our Union has been exposed, and admired the virtue and courage with which they were surmounted."

Mr. Monroe retired from Washington to a temporary residence in Loudon County, where, true to a policy of usefulness which had governed him through life, he discharged the duties of Justice of the Peace. He was also one of the Board of Visitors of the University of Virginia, a body of nine appointed by the Governor every fourth year, who with the Rector have the entire direction of that important State institution. He was also chosen President of the Convention which sat to revise the Constitution of Virginia, in the winter of 1829–30; but ill health, and the infirmities of advanced life, compelled him to retire from his seat before the adjournment of that body. The death of his wife was now added to his affliction, and his home in Virginia being thus broken up, he removed to New York to dwell with his son-in-law, Mr. Samuel L. Gouverneur. His death happened shortly after in this new home, on the Fourth of July, 1831, "the flickering lamp of life holding its lingering flame as if to await the day of the nation's birth and glory."[1] He was buried with public honors in the Marble Cemetery, in Second street, where his remains reposed till the summer of 1858, when they were removed at the instance of the State of Virginia to the rural cemetery of Hollywood, on the banks of James River, overlooking the city of Richmond. They again received public honors from New York, and were escorted to their final resting-place by the Seventh Regiment of New York State troops, generally known as the National Guard. The time chosen for the new interment was the anniversary of his death, but as that day fell on Sunday, the funeral celebration at Richmond took place on the fifth of July. An address was delivered at the grave by Governor Wise of Virginia, in which, after enumerating the events of the long and honorable public career of the departed, he dwelt upon the circumstances of his burial. "Venerable patriot!" was his language, "he found his rest soon after he retired. On the Fourth of July, 1831,

____

[1] John Quincy Adams.

twenty-seven years ago, he departed, like Jefferson and Adams, on the anniversary of Independence. His spirit was caught up to heaven, and his ashes were enshrined in the soil of his adopted State, whose daughter he had married; of that grand and prosperous Commonwealth whose motto is 'Excelsior,' our sister New York, the Empire State of the United States of America. Virginia was the natural mother of Monroe, and New York was his mother-in-law; Virginia by birth and baptism, New York by marriage and burial. This was well, for he gave to her invaders the glaived hand of 'bloody welcome' at Trenton, and New York gave to him a 'hospitable grave.' Virginia respectfully allowed his ashes to lie long enough to consecrate her sister's soil, and now has dutifully taken them to be 'earth to her earth and ashes to her ashes,' at home in the land of his cradle."

In person President Monroe was tall and well formed, of light complexion and blue eyes. His long and acceptable public life bears witness to his personal and intellectual qualities. In the words of the sketch of the late Senator Benton just quoted, "his parts were not shining but solid. He lacked genius, but he possessed judgment; and it was the remark of Dean Swift, that genius was not necessary to the conducting of the affairs of State; that judgment, diligence, knowledge, good intentions and will were sufficient. Mr. Monroe was an instance of the soundness of this remark."

J. Q. Adams

JOHN QUINCY ADAMS.

WE have already traced the lineage of John Quincy Adams. He comes nobly heralded upon the scene of our Revolutionary annals. His stirring relative, the zealous and always consistent Samuel Adams, the very front and seed-plot of obstinate rebellion, had taught the mechanics of Boston to resist, and his eloquence had reached the ears of men of influence throughout the colony and nation. His father, John Adams, thirty-two years old at the time of his birth, deeply grounded in the history of constitutional liberty and with the generous flame of freedom burning brightly in his bosom from boyhood, was already prepared for that warm, enlightened, steady career of patriotism — never swerving, always true to his land—which bore him aloft, the chosen representative of New England to the Congress of his country, and ultimately to her highest authority; while the nation in turn adopted him her express image in the important negotiations at three of the great courts of Europe.

Nor should we forget the tender, heroic mother, the child of sensibility and genius, hardened into the maturity and perfection of the female character by the fire of the Revolution, the gentle Abigail, in whose fair friendship and sympathies and feminine gracefulness posterity has an ever-living participation through the delightful pages of her " Correspondence."

Of that family, in a house adjoining the old paternal Braintree home, in the present town of Quincy, at this imminent moment of the Revolution, John Quincy Adams, the eldest son, was born July 11, 1767. He derived his baptismal name from his great-grand father, John Quincy, the time-honored representative of Quincy in the Colonial Legislature. The name was given by his grandmother, as her husband was dying. The incident was not forgotten by the man. He recurred to it with emotion, fortified by a sense of duty. In a sentence cited by his recent biographer, the venerable Josiah Quincy, he says: "This fact, recorded by my father at the time, is not without a moral to my heart, and has connected with that portion of my name a charm of mingled sensibility and devotion. It was filial tenderness that gave the name—it was the name of one passing from earth to immortality. These have been through life, perpetual admonitions to do nothing unworthy of it."

It is interesting to trace the progress of the child in his mother's correspondence, from the infant lullaby which she prattles to her husband, when " our daughter rocks him to sleep with the song, ' Come, papa, come home to brother Johnny.' The boy has just entered his eighth year, and his father is on his way to the Continental Congress at Philadelphia, when she writes : " I have taken a very great fondness for reading Rollin's ' Ancient History,' since you left me. I am determined to go through with it if possible, in these my days of solitude. I find great pleasure and entertainment from it, and I have persuaded Johnny to read me a page or two every day, and hope he will, from his desire to oblige me, entertain a fondness for it." The child had some instruction at the village school, but he was especially taught by his father's law students, in the house. As the pressure of war increases, this resource is broken up. The anxious mother writes, " I feel somewhat lonely. Mr. Thaxter is gone home. Mr. Rice is going into the army as captain of a company. We have no school. I know not what to do with John." In the summer of this year, 1775, " standing," we are told, " with her on the summit of Penn's Hill, he heard the cannon booming from the battle of Bunker's Hill, and saw the flames and smoke of burning Charlestown. During the siege of Boston he often climbed the same eminence alone, to watch the shells and rockets thrown by the American army." [1] A letter from the boy himself, two years later, then at the age of ten, exhibits his youthful precocity. " I love," he writes to his father, " to receive letters very well—much better than I love to write them. I make but a poor figure at composition ; my head is much too fickle. My thoughts are running after birds' eggs, play and trifles, till I get vexed with myself. Mamma has a troublesome task to keep me steady, and I own I am ashamed of myself. I have but just entered the third volume of Smollett, though I had designed to have got half through it by this time. I have determined this week to be more diligent, as Mr. Thaxter will be absent at court, and I cannot pursue my other studies. I have set myself a stint, and determined to read the third volume half out." He asks for directions to proportion his time between play and writing, and in a postscript says, " Sir, if you will be so good as to favor me with a blank book, I will transcribe the most remarkable occurrences I meet with in my reading, which will serve to fix them upon my mind." [1]

In this letter we may read the aged man backward, from his steadfast, methodical desk in the House of Representatives, to the little boy at his mother's side in Braintree. The " childhood shows the man as morning shows the day." He was an old-fashioned, studious youth, nurtured amidst grave scenes of duty, early in harness, a resolute worker from his cradle to his grave.

The next year the boy is taken with his father, on board the frigate Boston, on his first mission to France ; followed, in her first letter after the separation,

---

[1] Quincy's Memoir, p. 8.

[1] This letter appears from the manuscript in Mr. Edward Everett's eloquent Faneuil Hall eulogy on Adams.

by this noble injunction of the mother: " Enjoin it upon him never to disgrace his mother, and to behave worthily of his father." The boy is a little man on the voyage, securing the favor of the French gentlemen on board, who teach him their language. In a perilous storm which arose, his father records his inexpressible satisfaction at his behavior, " bearing it with a manly patience, very attentive to me, and his thoughts constantly running in a serious strain." When they arrive in France, and take up their lodgings with Benjamin Franklin at Passy, he is put to school with the sage's grandson, Benjamin Franklin Bache, in the neighborhood. At the close of this short sojourn abroad, his father sums up his advantages: " My son has had a great opportunity to see this country ; but this has unavoidably retarded his education in some other things. He has enjoyed perfect health from first to last, and is respected wherever he goes for his vigor and vivacity, both of mind and body, for his constant good humor and for his rapid progress in French as well as his general knowledge, which, for his age, is uncommon." [1] On the return voyage, in the Sensible, the Chevalier de la Luzerne, the minister to the United States, and his secretary, M. Marbois, " are in raptures with my son. They get him to teach them the language. I found, this morning, the ambassador seated on the cushion in our state-room, M. Marbois in his cot, at his left hand, and my son stretched out in his, at his right ; the ambassador reading out

loud in Blackstone's Discourse at his entrance on his professorship of the common law at the University, and my son correcting the pronunciation of every word and syllable and letter." [1]

In November, father and son are at sea again in the Sensible, on their return to France. This time they are landed in Gallicia, and pursue their way through the northern provinces of Spain to the French frontier. When the boy's Diary shall be published, that gigantic work which we are told he commenced on this second voyage, and continued, with few interruptions, through life, the world will doubtless get some picturesque notices of these foreign scenes, so happily sketched in his father's note-book. The boy was again at school in France, and on his father's mission to Amsterdam, in the summer, was placed with an instructor under the wing of the venerable university of Leyden, where in January, 1781, with Franklin's correspondent, Benjamin Waterhouse, then a student of medicine, he went before the Rector Magnificus and was duly matriculated. His father's object in taking him to Leyden was to escape " the mean-spirited wretches," as he describes them, the teachers of the public schools at Amsterdam.

The youth, however, was not long at the University. His father's secretary, Francis Dana, having received the appointment of minister to St. Petersburg, in July, took the boy of fourteen with him as *his* secretary. " In this capacity," says Mr. Everett, " he was recog-

<hr>

[1] Letters of John Adams to his wife, II. 54.

[1] John Adams' Sea Diary, June 19, 1779. Works, III. 214.

nized by Congress; and there is, perhaps, no other case of a person so young being employed in a civil office of trust, under the government of the United States. But in Mr. Adams' career there was no boyhood." His knowledge of French, indeed, appears to have been of real service in interpreting between his chief and the French minister, the Marquis de Verac, with whom the negotiations were conducted at the Russian capital. In the autumn of the succeeding year he left St. Petersburg for a winter in Stockholm, and in the spring travelled alone through Sweden, Denmark and Germany to the Hague, where in May, 1773, we hear of him in his father's correspondence, as again "pursuing his studies with great ardor." He was present with his father at the concluding peace negotiations at Paris, where he witnessed the signing of the memorable final treaty. The greater part of the next two years was passed in London and Paris, where he had now the society of his mother. He is still the same vigilant student, while he assists his father as his secretary. "He is a noble fellow," writes John Adams from Auteuil to Francis Dana at the close of 1784, "and will make a good Greek or Roman, I hope, for he spends his whole time in their company, when he is not writing for me."[1]

When his father was appointed the first minister plenipotentiary to England, it was but natural to suppose that the secretary who had shared his humbler labors would have desired to participate in the full-blown honors of the royal court. There is not one youth in a thousand who would have resisted the temptation. For what does John Quincy Adams, at the age of eighteen, after his responsible duties in Russia, his independent sojourn in Stockholm, and intercourse with the brilliant American circles in Paris, with Franklin at the centre, exchange the splendid prospect of life in the British metropolis? For the leading-strings and restraints of Harvard, and a toilsome pupilage at the bar. The choice between inclination and duty never was more temptingly presented. His own expression of the resolve is too memorable to be omitted. "I have been seven years travelling in Europe," he writes, "seeing the world and in its society. If I return to the United States, I must be subject, one or two years, to the rules of a college, pass three more in the tedious study of the law, before I can hope to bring myself into professional notice. The prospect is discouraging. If I accompany my father to London, my satisfaction would probably be greater than by returning to the United States; but I shall loiter away my precious time, and not go home until I am forced to it. My father has been all his lifetime occupied by the interests of the public. His own fortune has suffered. His children must provide for themselves. I am determined to get my own living, and to be dependent upon no one. With a tolerable share of common sense, I hope in America to be independent and free. Rather than live otherwise, I would wish to die before my time."[1]

---

[1] John Adams' Works, IX. 527.

[1] Quincy's Memoir, p. 6.

With this creditable resolve he bore with him from his father a letter to Benjamin Waterhouse, touching his examination at Harvard. The solicitous parent, who had read some of the classics with his son, and forsaking the card-table, attempted even an introduction to the higher mathematics, in which he failed, candidly admitting that these abstruse studies had quite departed from him in thirty years' utter unconsciousness of them, is anxious to impress upon his friend those general acquisitions which might be obscured at an examination for want of some of the technicalities of instruction. Thus, while he had steadily pursued his studies, and made written translations of the Æneid, Suetonius. Sallust, Tacitus' Agricola and Germany, and portions of the Annals, with a good part of Horace, he might be defective in quantities and parsing. Harvard, however, was not likely to be too inexorable in her demands; nor was the pupil likely to fall short of them. After a few months' reading with the Rev. Mr. Shaw of Haverhill, he was admitted to the junior class in March, 1786, and continuing in the University long enough to leave a fragrant memory of his scholarship and good principles, received his degree the following year. His commencement oration, which was published, was on "The Importance and Necessity of Public Faith to the Well-being of a Community."

He now engaged in a three years' course of the study of the law, with Theophilus Parsons, at Newburyport, in which he must have heard much from his vigorous-minded preceptor, who afterwards became chief justice of the State, of the struggle then going on for the adoption of the Constitution. Adams was admitted to the bar in 1790, and at once, as he long afterwards expressed it, " commenced what I can hardly call the practice of the law in the city of Boston." For the first three years he had the usual opportunity of young lawyers for further study; and unlike many of them, he availed himself of it. A portion of his leisure was spent in the discussion of the important political questions of the day. He answered the plausible sophistries on government, of Paine's " Rights of Man," in a series of essays published in Russell's " Columbian Centinel," signed Publicola; and in 1793, in the same journal, urged neutrality upon the country in the contest between England and France, and attacked the insolent Genet in terms of wholesome indignation. This service, and doubtless his father's great successes in Holland, led Washington's administration to appoint him, in 1794, minister to the Netherlands. His acceptance of this honorable position was at the cost of a rapidly developing legal practice. Arriving in London in time to confer with Jay, whose British treaty was then getting adjusted, he reached Holland in season to witness the occupation of the country by the French propagandists. He remained at the Hague, availing himself of the opportunities and leisure of the place to add to those stores of knowledge already considerable, which he had accumulated, with the exception of a few months passed in diplomatic business in England till the summer of 1797, when he received the appointment of minister to Portugal. On his father's occupancy of the Presidency this was changed to the mission to Berlin. Before proceeding to his new post he passed over to England to claim the hand of a lady to whom he had become engaged on a former visit, Miss Louisa Catharine Johnson, the daughter of the American consul at London.

Adams felt at first a natural reluctance to accept an important office at the hands of his father; but his independence was reconciled to the step when he learned that it had been urged by Washington himself, who considered him fully entitled by his previous services, to diplomatic promotion. He now took up his residence at Berlin. He was engaged in this mission to the close of his father's administration. During this time he negotiated a treaty of commerce with Prussia, and in the summer of 1800 made a considerable tour in Silesia. A number of letters' addressed to his brother in America, descriptive of this country, were published without his advice in the "Port Folio," and a few years after were issued in a volume by a London publisher. In this collection they form a methodically written work, descriptive of the industry and resources of an interesting country with a comprehensive account of its history and geography.

Adams also, during his residence at Berlin, employed himself in several literary compositions, of which the most important was a poetical version of Wieland's "Oberon." He intended this for publication, but found that Sotheby, the English translator, had anticipated him. Several satires of Juvenal were also among his translations. He moreover prepared for publication in America, a treatise of Frederick de Gentz, "On the Origin and Principles of the American Revolution,' which interested him by its appreciation of American principles of liberty, as contradistinguished from the license of the French Revolution.

On his return to Boston, he turned his attention again to the study and resumed the practice of the law. He was not, however, suffered to remain long free from official employment. A few months after his arrival he was called to the Senate of Massachusetts, and almost immediately chosen to the Senate of the United States. It was at that period of the disintegration of the federal party when the old order of things was fast going out, and the new was not fully established. Adams, who was always inclined to think for himself, chose an independent position. In some things, as the constitutionality of taking possession of Louisiana, in the way in which it was done, he opposed the administration; in voting for the appropriation of the purchase money, he was with it. When the prominent measures of Jefferson's administration in reference to England began to take shape in the Embargo, he was at variance with his colleague, Mr. Pickering. He was of opinion that submission to British aggression was no longer a virtue. His course, which was considered a renunciation of federalism, created a storm in Massachusetts, where the legislature, in anticipation of the usual period, elected a successor to his senatorial term. Upon this censure he immediately resigned.

His retirement was characteristic enough. He had been some time before, in 1805, chosen professor of rhetoric and oratory on the Boylston foundation at Harvard, and had delivered his Inaugural the following year. The preparation of these lectures, in the delivery of which he now continued to be employed, called for fresh classical studies; but to study he was never averse, and it is the memorable lesson of his career, that the pursuits of literature are not only the ornament of political life, but the best safeguards of the personal dignity of the politician, when, as must sometimes happen with an independent man, he is temporarily thrown out of office by party distractions. If he is then found, as Adams always was, making new acquisitions of learning, and preparing anew for public usefulness, he must and will be respected, whichever way the popular favor of the moment may blow. Mr. Adams continued his duties at Harvard, reading lectures and presiding over the exercises in elocution till the summer of 1809. In the following year, his " Lectures on Oratory, delivered to the Senior and Junior Sophisters in Harvard University," were published at Cambridge. Mr. Edward Everett, who was at the time one of the younger students, bears witness to the interest with which these discourses were received, not merely by the collegians but by various voluntary listeners from the neighborhood. " They formed," he says, " an era in the University, and

were," he thinks, " the first successful attempt in the country at this form of instruction in any department of literature."

Immediately upon the entrance of Madison upon the Presidency, Adams received the appointment of minister to Russia, the court which he had approached, in his boyish secretaryship, during the Revolution, with Dana. He sailed from Boston early in August, 1809, in a merchant ship, for St. Petersburg; but from various detentions, a rough passage, and the vexatious examinations of the British cruisers in the Baltic, then blockading Denmark, he did not arrive in Russia till October. The commercial embarrassments, in the complicated relations of the great Napoleonic wars of the time, witnessed on the voyage, in the detention and oppression of American ships, furnished his chief diplomatic business at the imperial court. As much as any man, perhaps, he aided in solving these international difficulties. He had a cordial reception at court on his first arrival, and as time wore on, having prepared the way by his interviews with Count Romanzoff, the chancellor of the empire, received a proffer of mediation from the Emperor Alexander, between Great Britain and the United States, in the war which had now broken out. The offer was accepted at home, and in the summer of 1813, he was joined at St. Petersburg by his fellow commissioners, Bayard and Gallatin, appointed for the negotiation. The mediation was not, however, accepted by Great Britain, though it proved a step forward to the final con ferences and adjustment at Ghent. England proposed to treat directly at Gottenburg or London. The American government chose the former, and Adams was placed on the commission with Bayard, Clay, Russell and Gallatin, to negotiate. Before his arrival on the spot, he learnt that the conference was appointed at Ghent, whither he proceeded in the summer of 1814; and, after a protracted round of diplomacy, had the satisfaction of signing the Treaty of Peace the day before Christmas of that year. The scene of this event in that region which had witnessed his father's successes, and his early entrance upon the world, and above all, the event itself closing the gates of war, as his father again had signed the great pacification of 1783, must have been peculiarly gratifying, not merely to his patriotic pride, but to the love of method which characterized his life. He may readily have recognized in it that courteous fate which so often marked the career of his family. If there is a political as well as a poetical justice, it was certainly exhibited in the history of John Quincy Adams, and his illustrious father. The coincidences are most striking.

Adams having now closed his mission to St. Petersburg, and having been appointed minister to Great Britain, was joined by his family from Russia, in Paris, where he witnessed the return of Napoleon from Elba, and the commencement of the Hundred Days. It was one of those dramatic surprises of Parisian life, which we may expect to be faithfully represented in Mr. Adams'

Diary, when it shall be given to the world. We get, perhaps, a glimpse of his record in his biographer, Mr. Quincy's narrative. Napoleon, we are told "alighted so silently, that Mr. Adams who was at the Théâtre Français, not a quarter of a mile distant, was unaware of the fact till the next day, when the gazettes of Paris, which had showered execrations upon him, announced 'the arrival of his majesty, the emperor, at *his* palace of the Tuileries.' In the Place du Carousel, Mr. Adams, in his morning walk, saw regiments of cavalry belonging to the garrison of Paris, which had been sent out to oppose Napoleon, pass in review before him, their helmets and the clasps of their belts yet glowing with the arms of the Bourbons. The theatres assumed the title of Imperial, and at the opera in the evening, the arms of the Emperor were placed on the curtain, and on the royal box."

Adams, again respecting his father's precedents, took up his residence with his family in London. He was the American representative at the court of St. James for two years, when he was called by President Monroe to his cabinet as Secretary of State. His time in England was passed in the best society of books, things and men. After concluding the commercial relations of the treaty, he removed from London to a retired residence, at Boston House, Ealing, nine miles distant, where he found time—he could always make time—for his liberal studies.

The year 1817 saw him again in America, at Washington, the leading member of the new administration, in the direct line of promotion to the Presidency. Old party lines were becoming, or had already become extinct. It was a period of fusion, "an era of good feeling," as it came to be called on the quiet reëlection of Monroe. The chief diplomatic measures of Adams' secretaryship, had reference to Spain. He was always spirited in his assertions of the foreign policy of the country, and on this occasion was greatly instrumental in the negotiations which ended in the cession of Florida. One of his special services was the preparation of an elaborate Report on Weights and Measures, at the call of Congress. He devoted six months of continuous labor to this production, entering into the subject philosophically, and in its historical and practical relations. The report was made to Congress in February, 1821.

Adams continued to hold his secretaryship through both terms of Monroe's administration. At its close, he was chosen by the House of Representatives his successor in the Presidency, the vote being divided between Jackson, himself, Crawford and Clay, who decided the choice by throwing the vote of Kentucky in his favor. His administration, says Mr. Everett, in the address already cited, "was, in its principles and policy, a continuation of Mr. Monroe's. The special object which he proposed to himself was to bind the distant parts of the country together, and promote their mutual prosperity by increased facilities of communication." There were many elements of opposition at work against a reëlection, in the complicated struggles of the

12

times. Adams encountered a full measure of unpopularity and retired—in political disaster, as well as in diplomatic triumph, like his father—to the shades of Quincy—that long retirement which had only recently ended in death. The departure from the world of the elder Adams, occurred in the second year of his son's Presidency.

Unlike the father, however, he was not to sit brooding over the past. Work, persistent work, was the secret of John Quincy Adams' life. Of a tough mental fibre, there was no such thing as defeat, while he had a mind to contrive, a tongue to utter, or a hand to hold the pen. He was sixty-two at his retirement from the Presidency, within a few years of the age when his father was succeeded by Jefferson. Both felt the storm of unprecedented party spirit and annoyance, and both yielded to great popular heroes.

Literature again offered her hand to her assiduous son. "His active, energetic spirit," we are told, "required neither indulgence nor rest, and he immediately directed his attention to those philosophical, literary and religious researches, in which he took unceasing delight. The works of Cicero became the object of study, analysis and criticism. Commentaries on that master-mind of antiquity were among his daily labors. The translation of the Psalms of David into English verse was a frequent exercise; and his study of the Scriptures was accompanied by critical remarks, pursued in the spirit of free inquiry, chastened by a solemn reference to their origin and influence on the conduct and hopes of human life. His favorite science, astronomy, led to the frequent observation of the planets and stars; and his attention was also called to agriculture and horticulture. He collected and planted the seeds of forest trees, and kept a record of their development; and, in the summer season, labored two or three hours daily in his garden. With these pursuits were combined sketches preparatory to a full biography of his father, which he then contemplated as one of his chief future employments."[1]

He was, however, again soon called into action, being elected, in November, 1830, by his district, to the House of Representatives. It was a novel spectacle—an ex-president of the United States sitting in the lower house, but it was fully in accordance with the spirit of our institutions, which honor all faithful servants of the public. Nor is it to be denied that at least equal talent may be called for, and equal influence exerted in the discharge of duties of public life, which to the eye of the world have a comparative inferiority of position. Power may be wielded by a representative which may govern the administration itself. There are many acts of our legislative bodies more potential than the simple acquiescence of the Executive; as the originator of a measure or line of policy must be of more consequence than the instrument which gives it effect. For more than sixteen years Adams labored at his seat in the House. He was the most punctual man of the assembly, always on the alert; cool, resolute, even

pugnacious. There was scarcely a question, involving a point of morality, of national honor, or of literary and philosophical culture, on which his voice was not heard. He supported the demands of Jackson upon France; he asserted and successfully maintained the right of petition against vast obloquy and opposition; he was especially instrumental in the establishment of the National Observatory, and the Smithsonian Institution. A bare enumeration of his speeches, writings and addresses, would fill the space assigned to this sketch—lectures and addresses on points of law, government, history, biography and science, moral and social, local and national, before senators and before youths, on anniversaries of towns, on eras of the State, eulogies on the illustrious dead, on Madison, Monroe, Lafayette, the oration at the Jubilee of the Constitution.

As he had lived, so he died in harness. Death found him where he could have wished its approach, in the halls of Congress. His robust powers of body and mind had held out surprisingly, as his vigor, no less than his venerable appearance in the House, enforced an authority not always readily conceded to the persistence in unpopular appeals of "the old man eloquent." He was approaching eighty: still in the exercise of his extraordinary faculties, when, in a recess of Congress, walking in the streets of Boston, in November, 1846, he was stricken by paralysis, from which, nevertheless, he recovered in time to take his seat in Congress early in the year. The House rose to greet him, and he was conducted

---

[1] Josiah Quincy's Biography, p. 175–6.

to his chair with marked honors. He felt, however, his approach to the grave. There is a most touching evidence of this in the anecdote related by Mr. Everett. His journal, the diary of his long life, interrupted the day of his attack, was resumed after an interval of nearly four months, with the title, "Posthumous Memoir." Writing in its now darkened pages, he says of the day when it was interrupted, "From that hour I date my decease, and consider myself, for every useful purpose to myself and fellow creatures, dead; and hence I call this, and what I may hereafter write, a posthumous memoir."

He continued in the House another year, when the final messenger came, on Monday morning, the twenty-first of February, 1848. After passing a Sunday in harmony with his elevated religious life, he was observed to ascend the steps of the Capitol with his accustomed alacrity. As he rose, with a paper in his hand, to address the Speaker in the House, he was seized by a return of paralysis, and fell, uttering, "this is the last of earth— I am content." He was taken, as the House adjourned, to an adjacent room, where he lingered over Washington's birthday till the twenty-third, when he died in the speaker' apartment, under the roof of the Capitol. His remains were taken to Boston, reposed in state in old Faneuil Hall, and were quietly laid by the side of his parents, in a grave at Quincy.

The lesson of such a life is plain. Labor, conscientiousness, religious duty; talent borne out to its utmost stretch of performance by the industrious improvement of every opportunity; the self-rewarding pursuits of letters and science, in the gratification of an insatiable desire for knowledge; a constant invigoration of the moral powers by the strenuous discharge of duty; independence bought by self-denial and prudence, enjoying its wealth—the calm temper, the untroubled life—in the very means of acquiring it. How noble an illustration of the powers of life! When the correspondence and Diary, which Adams maintained through his long life, shall be published—when his writings shall be collected from the stray sheets in which they have been given to the winds, when the literary aids, due to his memory, shall be gathered in the library about his fair fame, there will be seen an enduring monument of a most honorable life of public service and mental activity.

ANDREW JACKSON.

Few of the eminent men of America, whose acts are recorded in these pages, entered upon the public stage so early and continued on it so late, as the subject of this sketch. To no one but himself was it reserved to bridge over so completely the era of the Revolution with the latest phase of political life in our day. The youth who had suffered wounds and imprisonment at the hands of a British officer in the war of Independence, was destined long after, when a whole generation had left the stage, to close a second war with that powerful nation by a triumphant victory; and when the fresh memory of that had passed away, and men were reading the record in history, the same hero, raised to the highest honor of the State, was to stand forth, not simply President of the United States, but the active representative of a new order of politics, reaping a new harvest of favor in civil administration, which would throw his military glory into the shade. Nor was this all. These comprehensive associations, much as they include, leave out of view an entirely distinct phase of the wonderful career of this extraordinary man. A rude pioneer of the wilderness, he opened the pathway of civilization to his countrymen, and by his valor in a series of bloody Indian wars, made the terrors of that formidable race a matter of tradition in lands which he lived to see blooming with culture and refinement. A hero in his boyhood, when Greene was leading his southern army to the relief of the Carolinas, he was in Congress the first representative of a new State, when Washington was President; and when the successors of that chieftain, Adams and Jefferson, had at length disappeared from the earthly scene in extreme old age, he, a man more of the future than the past, sat in the same great seat of authority, with an influence not inferior to theirs. Surrounded by these circumstances, in the rapid development of national life, in the infancy and progress of the country, if he had been a common man he would have acquired distinction from his position; but it was his character to form circumstances as well as profit by them. There are few cases in all history where, under adverse conditions, the man was so master of fortune. The simplest recital of his life carries with it an air almost of romance; his success mocked the wisdom of his contemporaries, and will tax the best powers of the future historians of America in its analysis.

Andrew Jackson was of Irish parentage. His father, of the same name, bo

Andrew Jackson

longed to a Protestant family in humble life, which had been long settled at Carrickfergus, in the north of Ireland, whence he brought his wife and two children to America, in 1765. They were landed at Charleston, South Carolina, and proceeded at once to the upper region of the country, on the Catawba, known as the Waxhaw settlement. They came as poor emigrants to share the labors of their friends and countrymen who were settled in the district. Andrew Jackson, the elder, began his toilsome work in clearing the land on his plot at Twelve Mile Creek, a branch of the Catawba, in what is now known as Union County, North Carolina, but had barely established himself by two years' labor when he died, leaving his widow to seek a refuge with her brother-in-law in the neighborhood. A few days after her husband's death, on the 15th March, 1767, she brought forth a third son, Andrew, of whose life we are to give an account. The father having left little, if any, means of support for his family, the mother found a permanent home with another brother-in-law named Crawford, who resided on a farm just over the border in South Carolina. There the boyhood of Jackson was passed in the pursuits incident to youth, in frontier agricultural life. His physical powers were developed by healthy sports and exercise, and his mind received some culture in the humble rudiments of education in the limited schooling of the region. It is probable that something better was intended for him than for most of the boys in his position, since we hear of his being at

an Academy at Charlotte, and of his mother's design to prepare him for the calling of a Presbyterian clergyman. Such, indeed, might well have been his prospects, for he had a nature capable of the service, had not the war of the Revolution, now breaking out afresh in the South, carried him in quite a different direction.

In 1779 came the invasion of South Carolina, the ruthless expedition of Prevost along the seaboard preceding the arrival of Clinton, and the fall of Charleston. The latter event occurred in May of the following year, and Cornwallis was free to carry out his plan for the subjugation of the country. Sending Tarleton before him, the very month of the surrender of the city, the war of devastation was carried to the border of the State, to the very home of Jackson. The action at the Waxhaws was one of the bloodiest in a series of bloody campaigns, which ended only with the final termination of hostilities. It was a massacre rather than a battle, as American blood was poured forth like water. The mangled bodies of the wounded were brought into the church of the settlement, where the mother of the young Jackson, then a boy of thirteen, with himself and brother—he had but one now, Hugh having already joined the patriots and fallen in the affair at Stono—attended the sick and dying. That "gory bed" of war, consecrated by the spot where his father had worshipped, and near which he reposed in lasting sleep, summoned the boy to his baptism of blood. He was not the one to shrink from the encounter. We accordingly find him on hand at Sumter's attack, in the following August, on the enemy's post at Hanging Rock, accompanying Major Davies' North Carolina troop to the fight, though he does not appear to have engaged in the battle. A few days after, Gates was defeated at Camden, and Mrs. Jackson and her children fled before the storm of war to a refuge in the northern part of the district. The escape was but temporary, for, on her return in the spring, her boys were entangled, as they could not well fail to be in that region, in the desultory, seldom long intermitted partisan warfare which afflicted the Carolinas. In the preparation for one of the frequent skirmishes between Whig and Tory, the two brothers were surprised, escaped in flight, were betrayed and captured. It was on this occasion that the scene, often narrated, occurred, of the indignity offered by the British officer, met by the spirited resistance of the youth. Andrew was ordered by the officer, in no gentle tone, to clean his boots. He refused peremptorily, pleading his rights as a prisoner of war, an argument which brought down a rejoinder in a sword-thrust on head and arm raised for protection, the marks of which the old hero bore to his last day. A similar wound, at the same time, for a like offence, was the cause of his brother's death. Their imprisonment at Camden was most cruel; severely wounded, without medicine or care, with but little food, exposed to contagion, they were brought forth by their mother, who followed them and managed their exchange. Few scenes of war can be fancied, more truly heroic

and pitiful than the picture presented by Mr. Parton, in his faithful biography of this earnest, afflicted, patriotic mother receiving her boys from the dungeon, " astonished and horrified " at their worn, wasted appearance. The elder was so ill as not to be able to sit on horseback without help, and there was no place for them in those troubled times but their distant home. It was forty miles away. Two horses, with difficulty we may suppose, were procured. "One she rode herself. Robert was placed on the other, and held in his seat by the returning prisoners, to whom his devoted mother had just given liberty. Behind the sad procession, poor Andrew dragged his weak and weary limbs, bareheaded, barefooted, without a jacket." Before the long journey was thus painfully accomplished, " a chilly, drenching, merciless rain " set in, to add to its hardships. Two days after, Robert died, and Andrew was, happily, perhaps, insensible to the event in the delirium of the small pox, which he had contracted in prison. What will not woman undertake of heroic charity? This mother of Andrew Jackson had no sooner seen her surviving boy recovered by her care, than she set off with two other matrons, on foot, traversing the long distance to Charleston to carry aid and consolation to her nephews and friends immured in the deadly prison-ships in the harbor. She accomplished her errand, but died almost in its execution, falling ill of the ship fever at the house of a relative in the vicinity of the city. Thus sank into her martyr's grave, this woman, worthy to be the mother of a hero, leaving her son Andrew, " before reaching his fifteenth birth-day, an orphan ; a sick and sorrowful orphan, a homeless and dependent orphan, an orphan of the Revolution." [1]

The youth remained with one of the Crawfords till a quarrel with an American commissary in the house—this lad of spirit would take indignity neither from friend nor foe—drove him to another relative, whose son being in the saddler's trade, led him to some six months' engagement in this mechanical pursuit. This was followed by a somewhat eager enlistment in the wild youthful sports or dissipations of the day, such as cockfighting, racing and gambling, which might have wrecked a less resolute victim ; but his strength to get out of this dangerous current was happily superior to the force which impelled him into it, and he escaped. He even took to study and became a schoolmaster, not over competent in some respects, but fully capable of imparting what he had learnt in the rude old field schools of the time. We doubt not he put energy into the vocables, as the row of urchins stood before him, and energy, like the orator's action, is more than books to a schoolmaster.

A year or two spent in this way, not without some pecuniary profit, put him on the track of the law, for which there is always an opening in the business arising from the unsettled land titles of a new country, to say no-

thing of those personal strifes and traditions which follow man wherever he goes. The youth—he was yet hardly eighteen—accordingly offered himself to the most eminent counsel in the region—that is, within a hundred miles or so—alighting at the law office of Mr. Spence McCay, a man of note at Salisbury, North Carolina. There he passed 1785 and the following year, studying probably more than he has had credit for, his reputation as a gay young fellow of the town being better remembered, as is natural, than his ordinary office routine. He had also the legal instructions of an old warrior of the Revolution, brave Colonel Stokes, a good lawyer and mixture of the soldier and civilian, who must have been quite to Andrew Jackson's taste. Thus fortified, with the moderate amount of learning due his profession in those days, he was licensed and began the practice of the law.

His biographer, Mr. Parton, pleased with having brought him thus far successfully on the stage of life, stops to contemplate his subject at full length. His points may be thus summed up : " A tall fellow, six feet and an inch in his stockings ; slender, but graceful ; far from handsome, with a long, thin, fair face, a high and narrow forehead, abundant, reddish-sandy hair, falling low over it— hair not yet elevated to the bristling aspect of later days—eyes of a deep blue, brilliant when aroused, a bold rider, a capital shot."

As for the moral qualities which he adds to these physical traits, the prudence associated with courage and

---

[1] Parton's Life of Jackson, I 95. We may here make a general acknowledgment for the aid we have received in this sketch from Mr. Parton's exhaustive narrative. He has far exceeded all previous biographers in the diligence of his investigations, and those who write after him of Jackson must needs follow in his steps.

"that omnipotent something which we call a presence," which faithful Kent saw in his old discrowned monarch Lear, as an appeal to service and named "authority,"—it is time enough to make these reflections when the man shall have proved them by his actions. He will have opportunity enough.

After getting his "law," the young advocate took a turn in the miscellaneous pursuits of the West, as a store-keeper at Martinsville, in Guildford County, keeping up his connection with his profession, it is reported, by performing the executive duties of a constable. He has now reached the age of twenty-one, when he may be said fairly to have entered upon his career, as he received the appointment of solicitor or public prosecutor in the western district of North Carolina, the present Tennessee. This carried him to Nashville, then a perilous journey through an unsettled country, filled with hostile Indians. He arrived at this seat of his future home, whence his country was often to summon him in her hour of need, in October, 1788, and entered at once vigorously on the practice of his profession, which was very much an off-hand, extempore affair, requiring activity and resolution more than learning, especially in the main duties of his office as collector of debts. A large extent of country was to be traversed in his circuits of the wilderness, on which it was quite as important to be a good woodman as a well-informed jurist. Indeed, there was more fear of the Indian than of the Opposite Counsel. Jackson had the confidence of the mercantile community behind him, and

discharged his duties so efficiently, and withal was so provident of the future which his keen eye foresaw, that he prospered in his fortunes, and in a few years became a considerable landed proprietor.

In 1791 an event occurred which became subsequently a matter of frequent discussion, and which certainly required some explanation. Andrew Jackson married at Natchez, on the Mississippi, Mrs. Robards, at the time not fully divorced from her husband, though both Jackson and the lady believed the divorce had been pronounced. The error, after the sifting which the affair received when it became a ground of party attack, and the blazing light of a Presidential canvass was thrown upon it, is easily accounted for. The circumstances of the case may be thus briefly narrated : A Colonel Donelson, one of the founders of Nashville, brought with him to that settlement, not many years before, his daughter Rachel, who at the time of Jackson's arrival was married to a Mr. Robards, of Kentucky. The young "solicitor" found the pair living with the lady's mother, Mrs. Donelson, in whose house Jackson became an inmate. Robards appears to have been of a jealous temperament, and moreover of unsettled habits of living. At any rate, he had his home apart from his wife, and we presently find him, in the second winter after Jackson's arrival, applying as a Kentuckian, to the Virginia legislature for a divorce. He procured an order for the preliminary proceedings, which were understood, or rather misunderstood by the people of Tennessee, as an authoritative separation. With this view of the matter, as the explanation is given, the marriage took place. The divorce was legally completed in 1793. When Jackson then learnt the true state of the case he had the marriage ceremony performed a second time. During the whole of the affair from the beginning, though he acted as a friend of the lady, he appears to have conducted himself toward her with the greatest propriety. Indeed, a certain innate sense of delicacy and pure chivalrous feeling toward woman, was always a distinctive trait of his character. It was constantly noticed by those most intimate with him, as a remarkable characteristic, in a man roughly taking his share in the wild pursuits and dissipations of the day. He was no doubt early an admirer of the lady, whose gay, spirited qualities and adventurous pioneer life were likely to fascinate such a man, and made no secret of his contempt for the husband, threatening on one occasion, when he was pestered by his jealousies, to cut out his ears. The story of his marriage was of course variously interpreted, but he allowed no doubtful intimations of the matter in his presence. It was a duel or war to the knife when any hesitation on that subject was brought to his hearing.

The region into which Jackson had emigrated, having passed through its territorial period, when the solicitor became attorney general, reached its majority in a State name and government of its own in 1796. He was one of the delegates to the convention at Knoxville, which formed the consti-

tution of Tennessee, and one of the two members of each county, to whom was intrusted the drafting of that instrument. When the State was admitted into the Union, Andrew Jackson was chosen its first, and, at that time, only representative to Congress. He took his seat at the beginning of the session, at the close of the year, and was consequently present to receive the last opening message of George Washington, it being usual in those days for the President to meet both houses together at the commencement of their sitting, and deliver his speech in person—what is now the President's message. In like manner, according to the usage of the English Parliament, a reply was prepared and voted upon by each house, which was carried in person by the members to the President's mansion. The reply, in this instance, proposed in the House of Representatives by the Federalist committee, was thought too full an indorsement of the policy of the administration, and met with some opposition from the Republican minority, Andrew Jackson appearing as one of twelve, by the side of Edward Livingston, and William B. Giles, of Virginia, voting against it. He did not speak on the question, and his vote may be regarded simply as an indication of his party sentiments, though, had he been an ardent admirer of Washington, he might, spite of his Tennessee politics, have voted with Gallatin for the original address. That he did not, does not imply necessarily any disaffection to Washington; but there was probably little of personal feeling in the matter to be looked for from him. The independent life of the South and West had never leaned, as the heart of the Eastern and Atlantic regions, upon the right arm of Washington. The only question upon which he spoke during the session was in favor of assuming certain expenses incurred in an Indian expedition in his adopted State; and the resolution which he advocated was adopted. His votes are recorded in favor of appropriations for the navy, and against the black mail paid to Algiers. His success in the Indian bill was well calculated to please his constituents, and he was accordingly returned the next year to the Senate. It was the first session of the new administration, and all that is told of his appearance on the floor is the remark of Jefferson in his old age to Daniel Webster, that he had often seen him, from his Vice President's chair, attempt to speak, and "as often choke with rage." Mr. Parton adds to this recollection the bare fact that he made the acquaintance of Duane of the "Aurora," Aaron Burr and Edward Livingston. He retired before the end of the session, and resigned his seat. Private affairs called him home; but he could not have been well adapted to senatorial life, or he did not like the position, else he would have managed to retain it. It was an honor not to be thrown away lightly by an ambitious young man.

We next behold him chosen by the legislature a judge of the Supreme Court of Tennessee—a post, one would think, of severer requisitions than that of United States senator, since a member of a legislative body may give a silent vote or be relieved of an onerous committee, while the occupant of the bench is continually called upon to exercise the best faculties of the mind. It is to Jackson's credit that he held the position for six years, during which, as population flowed into the State and interests became more involved, the requisitions of the office must have been continually becoming more exacting. Its duties carried him to the chief towns of the State, where he was exposed to the observation of better read lawyers than himself. As no record was kept of his decisions, we have to infer the manner in which he acquitted himself from what we know of his qualifications. He no doubt made himself intelligible enough on simple questions and decided courageously and honestly what he understood; but in any nice matter he must have been at fault from want of skill in statement, if we may judge of his talents in this respect by his printed correspondence, which is ill spelt, ungrammatical and confused.

His personal energy, however, doubtless helped him on occasion, as in the famous anecdote of his arrest of Russell Bean. This strong villain, infuriated by his personal wrongs, was at war with society, and bade defiance to justice. It was necessary that he should be brought before the court where Jackson presided, but it was pronounced impossible to arrest him. The sheriff and his posse had alike failed, when the difficulty was solved by the most extraordinary edict which ever issued from the bench. "Summon me," said the judge to the law officer. It was done and the arrest was made. It is curious to read of a judge of the Supreme Court planning duels and rough personal encounter with the governor of the State, as we do of Judge Jackson in his quarrel with Governor Sevier. No stronger evidence could be afforded of the imperfect social condition of the country. It was a rude, unfinished time, when life was passed in a fierce personal contest for supremacy, and wrongs real and imaginary were righted at sight by the pistol. This period of Jackson's career, including the ten years following the retirement from the bench, are filled with prodigious strife and altercation. The duelling pistols are always in sight, and dreary are the details of wretched personal quarrels preliminary to their use.

The first of these encounters in which Jackson was a principal occurred as early as 1795, when he was engaged in court and challenged the opposite counsel on the spot for some scathing remark, writing his message on the blank leaf of a law book. Shots were exchanged before the parties slept. The most prominent of Jackson's altercations, however, was his duel with Dickinson, a meeting noted among narratives of its class for the equality of the combat, and the fierce hostility of the parties. It was fought in 1806, on the banks of Red River in Kentucky. Charles Dickinson was a thriving young lawyer of Nashville, who had used some invidious expressions regarding Mrs. Jackson. These were apologized for and overlooked when a roundabout quarrel arose out of the terms of a horse race, which, after involving Jackson in a caning of one of the parties, and his friend Coffee in a duel with another, ended in bringing the former in direct collision with Dickinson. A duel was arranged. The principals were to be twenty-four feet apart, and take their time to fire after the word was given. Both were excellent shots, and Dickinson, in particular, was sure of his man. So certain was Jackson of being struck, that he made up his mind to let his antagonist have the first fire, a deliberate conclusion of great courage and resolution, based on a very nice calculation. He knew that his antagonist would be quicker than himself at any rate, and that if they fired together his own shot would probably be lost in consequence of the stroke he must undoubtedly receive from the coming bullet. He consequently received the fire, and was hit as he expected to be. The ball, aimed at his heart, broke a rib and grazed the breast bone. His shoes were filling with blood as he raised his pistol, took deliberate aim, re-adjusted the trigger as it stopped at half cock, and shot his adversary through the body. Dickinson fell, to bleed to death in a long day of agony. Jackson desired his own wound to be concealed, that his opponent might not have the gratification of knowing that he had hit him at all. Such was the courage and such the revenge of the man.[1]

After leaving the judgeship, Jackson —he was now called General Jackson,

[1] The details of this affair with all its preliminaries, occupy forty octavo pages of Mr. Parton's narrative—a curious and most instructive picture of the times.

having been chosen by the field officers major general of the State militia in 1801, gaining the distinction by a single vote—employed himself on his plantation, the Hermitage, near Nashville, and the storekeeping in which he had been more or less engaged since his arrival in the country. In partnership with his relative, Coffee, he was a large exchanger of the goods of the West for the native produce, which he shipped to New Orleans; and it was for his opportunities of aiding him in procuring provisions, as well as for his general influence, that Colonel Burr cultivated his acquaintance in his western schemes in 1805, and the following year. General Jackson, at first fascinated by the man, who stood well with the people of the country as a republican, introduced him into society and entertained him at his house; but when suspicion was excited by his measures, he was guarded in his intercourse, and stood clearly forth on any issue which might arise, involving the preservation of the integrity of the Union. On that point no friendship could bribe him. Accordingly he offered his services to President Jefferson, and, receiving orders to hold his command in readiness, there was great military bustle of the major general in Nashville, raising and reviewing companies, to interrupt the alarming proceedings of Colonel Burr on the Ohio. When it was found that there was nothing formidable to arrest, Jackson's feeling of regard for Burr revived, he acquitted him of any treasonable intent, and resolutely took his part during the trial at Richmond.

On the breaking out of the war with England, in 1812, General Jackson was one of the first to tender his services to the President. He called together twenty-five hundred volunteers and placed them at the disposal of the Government. The proffer was accepted, and in December Jackson was set in motion at the head of two thousand men to join General Wilkinson, then in command at New Orleans. The season was unusually cold and inclement; but the troops, the best men of the State, came together with alacrity, and by the middle of February were at Natchez, on the Mississippi. Jackson's friend and relative, Colonel Coffee, led a mounted regiment overland, while the rest descended the river. Colonel Thomas H. Benton also appears on the scene as General Jackson's aid. At Natchez, the party was arrested by an order from Wilkinson, and remained in inaction for a month, when a missive came from the War Department disbanding the force. Thus was nipped in the bud the ardent longing of the general, and the promise of one of the finest bodies of men ever raised in the country. Jackson, taking the responsibility, resolved that they should not be dismissed till, as in duty bound, he had returned them home. He accordingly led them back by land, and so solicitous was he for their welfare by the way, so jealous of their rights, carelessly invaded by the government, that his popularity with the men was unbounded. The fiery duellist, "sudden and quick in quarrel," gained by his patient kindness and endurance on that march, the endearing appellation, destined to be of world-wide fame—Old Hickory.

He had taken, as we have said, the responsibility in bringing home the troops. This involved an assumption of their debts by the way, for it was not certain, though to be presumed, that the government would honor his drafts for the expenses of transportation. It did not. The paper was protested and returned upon his hands. In this strait, Colonel Benton, going to Washington, undertook the management of the affair, and by a politic appeal to the fears of the administration, lest it should lose the vote of the State, secured the payment. As he was about returning to Nashville, warmed by this act of friendship, he received word from his brother that General Jackson had acted as second in a duel to that brother's adversary—a most ungracious act, as it appeared, at a moment when the claims of gratitude should have been uppermost. The explanation was that Carroll, who received the challenge, was unfairly assailed, and appealed, as a friend, to the generosity of Jackson to protect him. Taking a duel very much as an everyday affair, the latter probably thought little of the absent Benton. The meeting came off, and Jesse Benton was wounded. An angry letter was written to Jackson by his brother, who came on to Nashville, venting his wrath in the most denunciatory terms —for Benton's vocabulary of abuse, though not more condensed, was more richly furnished with expletives than that of his general. This coming to the hearing of Jackson, he swore his big oath, " by the Eternal, that he would horsewhip Tom Benton the first time he met him." The Bentons knew the man, did not despise the threat, but waited armed for the onset. It came off one day at the door of the City Hotel in Nashville. There were several persons actors and victims in the affair. These are the items of the miserable business. The two Bentons are in the doorway as Jackson and his friend Colonel Coffee approach. Jackson, with a word of warning to Benton, brandishes his riding-whip; the Colonel fumbles for a pistol; the General presents his own, and at the instant receives in his arm and shoulder a slug and bullet from the barrel of Jesse Benton, who stands behind. Jackson is thus dropped, weltering in his blood with a desperate wound. Coffee thereupon thinking Tom Benton's pistol had done the work, takes aim at him, misses fire, and is making for his victim with the butt end, when an opportune cellar stairway opens to the retreating Colonel, who is precipitated to the bottom. Meanwhile Stokely Hays arrives, intent on plunging the sword, which he drew from his cane, into the body of Jesse Benton. He deals the thrust with unction, but striking a button, its force is lost and the weapon shivered. A struggle on the floor then ensues between the parties, the fatal dagger of Hays being raised to transfix his wounded victim, when it is intercepted by a bystander, and the murderous and bloody work is over. Such was the famous Benton feud. It laid Jackson ingloriously up for several weeks, and drove Colonel Benton to Missouri. There was a long interval of mutual hostile feeling, to be succeeded by a devoted friendship of no ordinary intensity.

This Benton affray took place on the 4th of September, 1813. A few days before, on the 30th of August, occurred the massacre by the Creek Indians of the garrison and inhabitants at Fort Mimms, a frontier post in the southern part of Alabama. A large number of neighboring settlers, anxious for their safety, had taken refuge within the stockade. The assailants took it by surprise, and though the defenders fought with courage, but few of its inhabitants escaped the terrible carnage. The Indians were led by a redoubtable chieftain, named Weathersford, the son of a white man and a Seminole mother, a leader of sagacity, of great bravery and heroism, and of no ordinary magnanimity. He was unable, however, to arrest, as he would, the fiendish atrocities committed at the fort. Women and children were sacrificed in the horrible rage for slaughter, and the bloody deed was aggravated by the most indecent mutilations. A cry was spread through the Southwest similar to that raised in our own day in India, at the Sepoy brutalities. Vengeance was demanded alike for safety and retribution. On the 18th of September the news had reached Nashville, four hundred miles distant, and General Jackson was called into consultation as he sat, utterly disabled with his Benton wounds, in his sick-room. It was resolved that a large body of volunteers should be summoned, and, ill as he was, he promised to take command of them when they were collected. Still suffering severely, before they were ready to move he joined them at Fayetteville, the place of meeting. He arrived in camp the seventh of October, and began his work of organizing the companies. Everything was to be done in drill and preparation for the advance into a wilderness where no supplies were to be had; yet in four days, a report having reached him that the enemy were approaching, he led his troops, about a thousand men, an afternoon march of thirty-two miles in six hours to Huntsville. The Indians, however, were not yet at hand, and joining Colonel Coffee, whom he had sent forward with a cavalry command, on the banks of the Tennessee, he was reluctantly compelled to wait there too long a time for his impatience, till something could be done in providing stores, in which the army was lamentably deficient. A post was established on the river named Fort Deposit, whence Jackson, still inadequately provided, set out, on the twenty-fifth of the month, on his southward march, and carried his force to an encampment at Ten Islands, on the Coosa River. There Coffee was detached to attack a body of Indians at their town of Talluschatches. He performed the service with equal skill and gallantry; and though the Creeks, as they did throughout the war, fought with extraordinary valor, urged on by religious fanaticism, he gained a brilliant victory. One of the incidents of the bloody field was the accidental slaughter of an Indian mother clasping her infant to her breast. The child was carried to Jackson, who had it tenderly cared for, and finally taken to his home. The boy, named Lincoyer, was brought up at the Hermitage, and suitably provided for by the general.

The next adventure of the campaign was an expedition led by Jackson himself to relieve a camp of friendly Indians at Talladega, invested by a large band of hostile Creeks. The very night on which he received the message asking aid, brought by a runner who had escaped from the beleaguered fort in disguise, he started with a force of two thousand men, eight hundred of whom were mounted, and in a long day's march through the wilderness traversed the intervening distance, some thirty miles, to the neighborhood of the fort. The dawn of the next morning saw him approaching the enemy—a thousand picked warriors. Disposing the infantry in three lines, he placed the cavalry on the extreme wings, to advance in a curve and inclose the foe in a circle. A guard was sent forward to challenge an engagement. The Indians received its fire and followed in pursuit, when the front line was ordered up to the combat. There was some misunderstanding, and a portion of the militia composing it retreated, when the general promptly supplied their place by dismounting a corps of cavalry kept as a reserve. The militia then rallied, the fire became general, and the enemy were repulsed in every direction. They were pursued by the cavalry and slaughtered in great numbers, two hundred and ninety being left dead on the field and many more bore the marks of the engagement.

The American loss was fifteen killed and eighty-five wounded. The friendly Creeks came forth from the fort to thank their deliverers, and share with them their small supply of food.

This was emphatically, contrary to all the rules of war, a hungry campaign. On his return to his camp, to which, having been fortified, the name Fort Strother was given, Jackson found the supplies which he had urgently demanded, and which he so much needed, not yet arrived. His private stores, which had been bought and forwarded at his expense, were exhausted to relieve the wants of his men. He himself, with his officers, subsisted on unseasoned tripe, like the poor and proud Spanish grandee in the Adventure of Lazarillo de Tormes, eulogizing the horse's foot, maintaining that he liked nothing better. The story is told of a starving soldier approaching him at this time with a request for food. "I will give you," said the general, "what I have," and with that he drew from his pocket a few acorns, "my best and only fare."[1]

Food, food, was the constant cry of Jackson in his messages to the rulers in the adjoining States. It was long in coming, and in the meanwhile the commander, eager to follow up his successes and close the war, was condemned to remain in inactivity—the hardest trial for a man of his temper. Scant subsistence and the hardships common to all encampments brought discontent. The men longed to be at home, and symptoms of revolt began to appear. The militia actually com-

---

[1] Eaton's Life of Jackson, p. 66.

menced their march backward; but they had reckoned without their leader. On starting they found the volunteers drawn up to oppose their progress, and abandoned their design. Such was the force of Jackson's authority in the camp, that when these volunteers, who were in reality disappointed that the movement did not succeed, attempted in their turn to escape, they were in like manner met by the militia.. The occasion required all Jackson's ingenuity and resolution, and both were freely expended. His iron will had to yield something in the way of compromise. Appealing to his men, he secured a band of the most impressible to remain at Fort Strother, while he led the rest in quest of provisions toward Fort Deposit. The understanding was that they were to return with him when food was obtained. They had not gone far when they met a drove of cattle on their way to the camp. A feast was enjoyed on the spot; but the men were still intent on going homeward. Nearly the whole brigade was ready for motion, when Jackson, who had ordered their return, was informed of their intention. His resolution was taken on the instant. He summoned his staff, and gave the command to fire on the mutineers if they attempted to proceed. One company, already on the way, was thus turned back, when, going forth alone among the men, he found the movement likely to become general. There was no choice in his mind but resistance at the peril of his life, for the men once gone, the whole campaign was at an end. Seizing a musket, he rested the barrel on the neck of his horse—he was unable, from his wound, to use his left arm—and threatened to shoot the first who should attempt to advance. An intimation of this kind from Jackson was never to be despised. The men knew it, and returned to their post. They yielded to the energy of a superior mind, but they were not content. Their next resource was, an assertion of the termination of their year's enlistment, which they said would expire on the tenth of December; but here they were met by the astute lawyer, who reminded them that they were pledged to serve one year out of two, and that the year must be an actual service in the field of three hundred and sixty-five days. The argument, however, failed to convince, and as the day approached the men were more resolute for their departure. They addressed a courteous letter to their commander, to which he replied in an earnest expostulatory address. "I know not," he said, "what scenes will be exhibited on the tenth instant, nor what consequences are to flow from them here or elsewhere; but as I shall have the consciousness that they are not imputable to any misconduct of mine, I trust I shall have the firmness not to shrink from a discharge of my duty." The appeal was not heeded, and on the evening of the ninth the signs of mutiny were not to be mistaken. The general took his measures accordingly. He ordered all officers and soldiers to their duty, and stationed the artillery company with their two pieces in front and rear, while he posted the militia on an eminence in advance. He himself rode along the line and addressed the men, in their companies, with great earnestness. He talked of the disgrace their conduct would bring upon themselves, their families and country; that they would succeed only by passing over his dead body: while he held out to them the prospect of reinforcements. "I am too," he said, "in daily expectation of receiving information whether you may be discharged or not; until then, you must not and shall not retire. I have done with entreaty; it has been used long enough. I will attempt it no more. You must now determine whether you will go, or peaceably remain: if you still persist in your determination to move forcibly off, the point between us shall soon be decided." There was hesitation. He demanded a positive answer. Again a slight delay. The artillerist was ordered to prepare the match. The word of surrender passed along the line, and a second time the rebellious volunteers succumbed to the will of their master. These, it should be stated, were the very men, the original company, whom Jackson had carried to Natchez, and for whose welfare on their return he had pledged his property. But in vain he reminded them of the fact, and appealed to their sense of generosity to remain in the service. He gave them finally the choice to proceed to Tennessee or remain with him. They chose the former, and he let them go.

The men he had left with him were enlisted for short periods, or so understood it. There was little to build upon for the campaign, and he was even advised by the Governor of Ten-

14

nessee, to abandon the prosecution of the war, at least for the present, or till the administration at Washington should provide better means for carrying it on. This was not advice, desperate as appeared the situation, to be accepted by Jackson. His reply was eminently characteristic—charged with a determined self-reliance which he sought to infuse into his correspondent. "Take the responsibility" is written all over it. "If you would preserve your reputation," he writes, "or that of the State over which you preside, you must take a straightforward, determined course; regardless of the applause or censure of the populace, and of the forebodings of that dastardly and designing crew, who, at a time like this, may be expected to clamor continually in your ears. The very wretches who now beset you with evil counsel, will be the first, should the measures which they recommend eventuate in disaster, to call down imprecations on your head, and load you with reproaches. Your country is in danger: apply its resources to its defence! Can any course be more plain? Do you, my friend, at such a moment as the present, sit with your arms folded and your heart at ease, waiting a solution of your doubts and a definition of your powers? Do you wait for special instruction from the Secretary of War, which it is impossible for you to receive in time for the danger that threatens?" The governor had said that his power ceased with the call for troops. "Widely different," replies Jackson, "is my opinion. You are to see that they come when they are called. Of what avail is it," he urges with an earnestness savoring of sarcasm, " to give an order if it be never executed, and may be disobeyed with impunity? Is it by empty mandates that we can hope to conquer our enemies and save our defenceless frontiers from butchery and devastation? Believe me, my valued friend, there are times when it is highly criminal to shrink from responsibility or scruple about the exercise of our powers. There are times when we must disregard punctilious etiquette and think only of serving our country." He also presented, in like forcible terms, the injurious effects of abandoning the frontiers to the mercy of the savage. The governor took the advice to heart, pointedly as it was given; he ordered a fresh force of twenty-five hundred militia into the field, and seconded General Jackson's call upon General Cocke for the troops of East Tennessee. Meantime, however, Jackson's force at Fort Strother was reduced to a minimum; the militia, enlisted for short terms, would go, and there was great difficulty in getting new recruits on to supply their places. The brave Coffee failed to reënlist his old regiment of cavalry. There was a strange want of alacrity through the early period of this war, in raising and disciplining the militia. With a proper force at his command, duly equipped and supplied, Jackson would have brought the savages to terms in a month. As it was, nearly a year elapsed; but the fighting period, when he was once ready to move, was of short duration.

While he was waiting for the new Tennessee enlistments. he determined to have one brush with the enemy with such troops as he had. He accordingly set in motion his little force of eight hundred raw recruits on the fifteenth of January, on an excursion into the Indian territory. At Talladega he was joined by between two and three hundred friendly Cherokees and Creeks, with whom he advanced against the foe, who were assembled on the banks of the Tallapoosa, near Emuckfau. He reached their neighborhood on the night of the twenty-first, and prepared his camp for an attack before morning. The Indians came, as was expected, about dawn; were repulsed, and when daylight afforded the opportunity, were pursued with slaughter. There was another sharp conflict about the middle of the day, which ended in a victory for the Americans, at some cost to the conquerors, who, ill prepared to keep the field, moved back toward the fort. Enotochopco Creek was reached and crossed by a part of the force, when the Indians fell upon the rear guard, who turned and fled; the artillery, however, still left on that side of the river, gave the savages a warm reception, when they were pursued by the cavalry, which had recrossed the stream.

By this time the country was roused to some adequate support of its general in the field. At the end of February, Jackson was reinforced by the arrival at Fort Strother of a force from East and West Tennessee of about five thousand men. By the middle of the next month he was in motion, terribly in earnest for a short and summary extirpation of the savages. The execution of John Woods, a Tennessee youth who had shown some insubordination in camp, was a prelude to the approaching tempest. The commander thought it necessary to the unity and integrity of the service. Fortunately for the purposes of this new invasion, the chief warriors of the nation assembled themselves at a place convenient enough for defence, but where defeat was ruin. It was at Tohopeka, an Indian name for the horse-shoe bend of the Tallapoosa, an area of a hundred acres inclosed by the deep waters of the river and protected at its junction with the land by a heavy breastwork of logs pierced for musketry and skillfully arranged for defence. Within this inclosure, at the time of Jackson's arrival, on the twenty-seventh of March, with less than three thousand men, including a regiment of regulars under Colonel Williams, were assembled some eight or nine hundred warriors of the Creeks. The plan of attack was thus arranged. Sending General Coffee to the opposite side of the river to effect a diversion in that quarter, Jackson himself directed the assault on the works at the neck. He had two field pieces, which were advantageously planted on a neighboring eminence. His main reliance, however, was at close quarters with his musketry. On the river side General Coffee succeeded in inclosing the bend and cutting off escape by the canoes, which he captured by the aid of his friendly Indians, and used as a means of landing in the rear of the enemy's position. This success was the signal for the as-

sault in front. Regulars and volunteers, eager for the contest, advanced boldly up. Reaching the rampart, the struggle was for the port-holes, through which to fire, musket meeting musket in the close encounter. "Many of the enemy's balls," says Eaton, "were welded between the muskets and bayonets of our soldiers. Major Montgomery, of Williams's regiment, led the way on the rampart, and fell dead summoning his men to follow. Others succeeded and the fort was taken. In vain was the fight kept up within, from the shelter of the fallen trees, and equally hopeless was the attempt at escape by the river. No quarter was asked, and none given, for none would be received. Women and children were the only prisoners. It was a desperate slaughter. Nearly the whole band of Indians perished, selling their lives as dearly as possible. The American loss was fifty-five killed and about thrice the number wounded; but the Cherokee dead were to be counted by hundreds. Having struck this fearful blow, Jackson retired to Fort Williams, which he had built on his march, and issued, as was his wont—he was quite equal to Napoleon in this respect—an inspiriting address to his troops. If the words are not always his, the sentiment, as his biographer suggests, is ever Jacksonian. Somebody or other was always found to give expression to his ardent ejaculations, which need only the broad theatre of a European battlefield to vie with the thrilling manifestoes of Bonaparte. "The fiends of the Tallapoosa will no longer murder our women and children, or disturb the quiet of our borders. Their midnight flambeaux will no more illumine their council-house, or shine upon the victim of their infernal orgies." The gratifying event was nearer even than the general anticipated. He looked for a further struggle, but the spirit of the nation was broken. Advancing southward, he joined the troops from the south at the junction of the Coosa and Tallapoosa, the "Holy Ground" of the Indians, where he received their offers of submission. The brave chieftain, Weathersford, voluntarily surrendered himself. A portion of the Indians fled to Florida. Those who were left were ordered to the northern parts of Alabama, Fort Jackson being established at the confluence of the rivers to cut off their communication with foreign enemies on the seaboard. The war had originally grown out of the first English successes and the movements of Tecumseh on the northern frontier, and was assisted by Spanish sympathy on the Gulf.

Jackson was now at liberty to return to Nashville with the troops who had shared his victories. He had of course a triumphant reception in Tennessee, and his services were rewarded at Washington by the appointment of major general in the army of the United States, the resignation of General Harrison at the moment placing this high honor at the disposal of the government. It was an honor well deserved, earned by long and patient service under no ordinary difficulties—difficulties inherent to the position, aggravated by the delays of others, and some, formidable enough to most

men, which he carried with him bound up in his own frame. We so naturally associate health and bodily vigor with brilliant military achievements that it requires an effort of the mind to figure Jackson as he really was in these campaigns. We have seen him carrying his arm in a sling, unable to handle a musket when he confronted his retiring army; but that was a slight inconvenience of his wound compared with the gnawing disease which was preying upon his system. "Chronic diarrhœa," says his biographer, "was the form which his complaint assumed. The slightest imprudence in eating or drinking brought on an attack, during which he suffered intensely. While the paroxysm lasted he could obtain relief only by sitting on a chair with his chest against th back of it and his arms dangling forward. In this position he was sometimes compelled to remain for hours. It often happened that he was seized with the familiar pain while on the march through the woods at the head of the troops. In the absence of other means of relief he would have a sapling half severed and bent over, upon which he would hang with his arms downward, till the agony subsided."[1]

In July, General Jackson was again at the South on the Alabama, presiding at the treaty conference with the Indians. The terms he proposed were thought hard, but he was inexorable in requiring them. The treaty of Fort Jackson, signed on the tenth of August, stripped the Creeks of more than

[1] Parton's Jackson, I. 547-8.

half of their possessions, confining them to a region least inconvenient to the peaceful enjoyment of the neighboring States. "As a national mark of gratitude," the friendly Creeks bestowed upon General Jackson and his associate in the treaty, Colonel Hawkins, three miles square of land to each, with a request that the United States Government would ratify the gift: but this, though recommended to Congress by President Madison, was never carried into effect.

While the treaty was still under negotiation, Jackson was intent on the next movement of the war, which he foresaw would carry him to the shores of the Gulf. He knew the sympathy of the Spaniards in Florida with the English, and was prepared for the designs of the latter against the southern country. Having obtained information that British muskets were distributed among the Indians, and that English troops had been landed in Florida, he applied to the Secretary of War, General Armstrong, for permission to call out the militia and reduce Pensacola at once. The matter was left to the discretion of the commander, but the letter conferring the authority did not reach him for six months. In the mean time he felt compelled to take the management of the war into his own hands. Fully aware of the impending struggle, he was in correspondence with Governor Claiborne of Louisiana, putting him on his guard, and with Maurequez, the Spanish governor of Pensacola, calling him to a strict account for his tampering with the enemy. To be nearer the scene of operations, he removed, immediately after the conclusion of the treaty, to Mobile, where he could gain the earliest intelligence of the movements of the British. Learning there, in September, of a threatened visit of the fleet under the orders of Colonel Nichols to Mobile, he called loudly upon the governors of the adjoining States for aid, and gave the word to his adjutant, Colonel Butler, in Tennessee, to enlist and bring on his forces. They responded eagerly to the call, for the name of Jackson was now identified with glory and victory, which they were ambitious to share. His old friend, General Coffee, was their leader. Before they arrived, the fort at the mouth of the bay was put in a state of defence under the command of Major Lawrence, of the United States infantry. In the after noon of the fifteenth of September it was his fortune to maintain the post against a bombardment by the British fleet of Captain Percy which recalls both the attack and success of the defenders at Fort Sullivan, in the war of the Revolution. What Moultrie and his brave men did on that day in repelling the assault of Sir Peter Parker and his ships was now done by Lawrence at Fort Bowyer. "Don't give up the fort" was his motto, as "Don't give up the ship" had been uttered by his namesake on "the dying deck" of the Chesapeake, the year before. The fort was not given up. Percy's flagship, the Hermes, was destroyed, and the remainder of his command returned, seriously injured, to Pensacola.

General Jackson rejoiced in this victory at Mobile, and waited only the arrival of his forces to carry the war home to the British in Florida. At the end of October, General Coffee arrived with twenty-eight hundred men on the Mobile River, where Jackson joined him, and mustering his forces to the number of three thousand, marched on the third of November against Pensacola. Owing to the difficulty of obtaining forage on the way, the cavalry was dismounted. The troops had rations for eight days. On his arrival before the town, being desirous as far as possible of presenting his movements in a peaceful light, General Jackson sent a messenger forward to demand possession of the forts to be held by the United States " until Spain, by furnishing a sufficient force, might be able to protect the province and preserve unimpaired her neutral character." On approaching the fort the bearer of the flag was fired on and compelled to retire. Aware of the delicacy of his self-imposed undertaking, before proceeding to extremities he sent a second message to the governor, by a Spanish corporal who had been captured on his route. This time, word was brought back that the governor was ready to listen to his proposals. He accordingly sent Major Piere a second time with his demands. A council was held, and they were refused. Nothing was then left but to proceed. The town was gained by a simple stratagem. Arranging a portion of his troops as if to advance directly on his road, he drew the British shipping to a position on that side, when, by a rapid march, he suddenly presented his main force on the other.

He consequently entered the town before the movement could be met. A street fight ensued, and a barrier was taken, when the governor appeared with a flag of truce. General Jackson met him and demanded the surrender of the military defences, which was conceded. Some delay, however, occurred, which ended in the delivery of the fortifications, of the town, and the blowing up of the fort at the mouth of the harbor. Having accomplished this feat, the British fleet sailed away before morning. Whither were they bound? To Fort Bowyer and Mobile in all probability, and thither Jackson, leaving the Spanish governor on friendly terms behind him, hastened his steps. Tarrying a few days for the British, who did not come, he took his departure for New Orleans, with his staff, and in a journey of nine days reached the city on the first of December.

If ever the force of a single will, the safety which may be provided for an imperilled people by the confidence of one strong right arm, were fully illustrated, it would seem to be in the military drama which was enacted in this and the following month on the banks of the Mississippi. Andrew Jackson was the chief actor. Louisiana had brave men in her midst, numerous in proportion to her mixed population and still unsettled condition, but whom had she, at once with experience and authority, to summon on the instant out of the discordant materials a band strong enough for her preservation? At the time of General Jackson's arrival a large fleet of the enemy was hovering on the coast amply provided with every resource of naval and military art, bearing a host of the veteran troops of England, experienced in the bloody contests under Wellington—an expedition compared with which the best means of defence at hand for the inhabitants of New Orleans resembled the resistance of the reeds on the river bank to Behemoth. It was the genius of Andrew Jackson which made those reeds a rampart of iron. He infused his indomitable courage and resolution in the whole mass of citizens. A few troops of hunters, a handful of militia, a band of smugglers, a company of negroes, a group of peaceful citizens stiffened under his inspiration into an army. Without Jackson, irresolution, divided counsels, and surrender, might, with little reproach to the inhabitants, under the circumstances, have been the history of one fatal fortnight. With Jackson all was union, confidence and victory.

The instant of his arrival he set about the work of organization, reviewing the military companies of the city, selecting his staff, personally examining the approaches from the sea and arranging means of defence. He was determined that the first step of the enemy on landing should be resisted. This was the inspiration of the military movements which followed, and the secret of his success. He did not get behind intrenchments and wait for the foe to come up, but determined to go forth and meet him on the way. He was not there so much to defend New Orleans as to attack an army of insolent intruders and drive them into the sea. They might be thousands, and his force might be only hundreds, but he knew of but one resolve, to fight to the uttermost, and he pursued the resolution as if he were revenging a personal insult.

Events came rapidly on as was anticipated, an attack was made from the fleet upon the gunboats on Lake Borgne. They were gallantry defended, but compelled to surrender. This action took place on the fourteenth of December. Now was the time, if ever, to meet the invading host. The spirit of Jackson rose, if possible, yet higher with the occasion. Well knowing that not a man in the city could be spared, and the inefficiency, in such emergencies, of the civil authority, he resolve to take the whole power in his own hands. On the sixteenth, he proclaimed martial law. Its effect was to concentrate every energy of the people with a single aim to their deliverance. Two days after, a review was held of the State militia, the volunteer companies, and the battalion of free men of color, when a stirring address was read, penned by the general's secretary, Edward Livingston—a little smoother than Old Hickory's bulletins in the Alabama wilderness, but not at all uncertain. The Tennessee, Mississippi and Kentucky recruits had not yet arrived; but they were on their way, straining every nerve in forced marches to meet the coming danger. Had the British moved with the same energy, the city might have fallen to them. It was not till the twenty-first, a week after their victory on the lake, that they began their advance, and pushed a portion of their force through the swamps, reaching a plantation on the river bank, six miles below the city, on the forenoon of the twenty-third. It was past mid-day when word was brought to Jackson of their arrival, and within three hours a force of some two thousand men was on the way to meet them. No attack was expected by the enemy that night; their comrades were below in numbers, and they anticipated an easy advance to the city the next morning. They little knew the commander with whom they had to deal. That very night they must be assailed in their position. Intrusting an important portion of his command to General Coffee, who was on hand with his brave Tennesseans, charged with surrounding the enemy on the land side, Jackson himself took position in front on the road, while the Carolina, a war schooner, dropped down on the river opposite the British station. Her cannonade, at half-past seven, throwing a deadly shower of grape-shot into the encampment, was the signal for the commencement of this night struggle. It was a fearful contest in the darkness, frequently of hand to hand individual prowess, particularly where Coffee's riflemen were employed. The forces actually engaged are estimated on the part of the British, including a reinforcement which they received, at more than twenty-three hundred; about fifteen hundred Americans took part in the fight. The result, after an engagement of nearly two hours, was a loss to the latter of twenty-four killed, and one hundred and eighty-nine wounded and missing. The British loss was much larger, sustaining as they did the additional fire of the schooner.

Before daylight, Jackson took up his position at a canal two miles distant from the camp of the enemy, and consequently within four of the city. The canal was deepened into a trench, and the earth thrown back formed an embankment, which was assisted by the famous cotton bales, a device that proved of much less value than has been generally supposed. A fortnight was yet to elapse before the final and conclusive engagement. Its main incidents were the arrival of General Sir Edward Pakenham, the commander-in-chief, with General Gibbs, in the British camp, on the twenty-fifth, bringing reinforcements from Europe; the occupation by the Americans of a position on the opposite side of the river protecting their camp; the destruction of the Carolina by red hot shot on the twenty-seventh; an advance of the British, with fearful preparation of artillery, to storm the works the following day, which was defeated by the Louisiana sloop advantageously posted in the river, and the fire from the American batteries, which were every day gaining strength of men and munitions; the renewal of the attack with like ill success on the first of January; the simultaneous accession to the American force of over two thousand Kentucky riflemen, mostly without rifles; a corresponding addition to the enemy on the sixth, and a general accumulation of resources on both sides, in preparation for the final encounter. On the eighth of January, a last attempt was made on the American front, which extended about a mile in a straight line from the river along the canal into the wood. The plan of attack, which was well conceived, was to take possession of the American work upon the opposite bank of the river, turn its guns upon Camp Jackson, and under cover of this diversion scale the embankment, and gain possession of the battery. The first was defeated by the want of means, and loss of time in getting the necessary troops across the river; the main attack, owing to some neglect, was inadequately supplied with scaling ladders, and the troops were marched up to slaughter from the murderous fire of the artillerymen and riflemen from behind the embankment. Throughout the whole series of engagements, the American batteries, mounting twelve guns of various calibre, were most skilfully served. The loss on that day of death was to the defenders but eight killed and thirteen wounded; that of the assailants in killed, wounded and missing exceeded, in their official returns, two thousand.[1] A monument in Westminster Abbey attests the regret of the British public for the death of the commander-in-chief, a hero of the Peninsular war, the lamented Pakenham.

Ten days after, having endured various hardships in the meantime, the British army, under the direction of General Lambert, took its departure. On the twenty-first, Jackson broke up his camp with an address to his troops, and returned to New Orleans in triumph. On the twenty-third, at his request, a *Te Deum* was celebrated at the cathedral, when he was received at the door, in a pleasant ceremonial, by a group of young ladies, representing the States of the Union.

The conduct of Jackson throughout the month of peril, whilst the enemy was on the land, was such as to secure him the highest fame of a commander. He had not been called upon to make any extensive manœuvres in the field, but he had taken his dispositions on new ground with a rapid and profound calculation of the resources at hand. His employment of Lafitte and his men of Barrataria, the smugglers whom he had denounced from Mobile as "hellish banditti," is proof of the sagacity with which he accommodated himself to circumstances, and his superiority to prejudice. They had a character to gain, and turned their wild experience of gunnery to most profitable account at his battery. His personal exertions and influence may be said to have won the field; and it should be remembered in what broken health he passed his sleepless nights, and days of constant anxiety.

The departure of the British did not relax the vigilance of the energetic Jackson. Like the English Strafford, his motto was "thorough," as the good people of New Orleans learnt before this affair was at an end. He did not abate, in the least, his strict military rule, till the last possible occasion for its exercise had gone by. It was continued when the enemy had left, and through days and weeks when assurance of the peace news was established to every mind but his own. He

---

[1] Dawson's Battles of the United States; II. 419.

chose to have certainty, and the "rigor of the game." In the midst of the ovations and thanksgivings, in the first moments of exultation, he signed the death warrant of six mutineers, deserters, who as long before as September, had construed a service of the old legal term of three months as a release from their six months' engagement; and the severe order was executed at Mobile. In a like spirit of military exactitude, New Orleans being still held under martial law, to the chafing of the citizens, he silenced a newspaper editor who had published a premature, incorrect bulletin of peace; banished the French citizens who were disposed to take refuge from his jurisdiction in their nationality; arrested an important personage, M. Louaillier, a member of the Legislature, who argued the question in print; and when Judge Hall, of the United States Court, granted a writ of habeas corpus, to bring the affair to a judicial investigation, he was promptly seized and imprisoned along with the petitioner. The last affair occurred on the fifth of March. A week later, the official news of the peace treaty was received from Washington, and the iron grasp of the general at length relaxed its hold of the city. The civil authority succeeded to the military, when wounded justice asserted its power, in turn, by summoning the victorious general to her bar, to answer for his recent contempt of court. He was unwilling to be entangled in legal pleadings, and cheerfully paid the imposed fine of one thousand dollars. He was as ready in submitting to the civil authority now that the

war was over, as he had been decided in exacting its obedience when the safety of the State seemed to him the chief consideration. Thirty years after, the amount of the fine, principal and interest was repaid him by Congress.

The reception of the victorious defender of New Orleans, on his return to Nashville, and subsequent visit, in autumn, to the seat of government, was a continual ovation. On his route, at Lynchburgh, in Virginia, he was met by the venerable Thomas Jefferson, who toasted him at a banquet of citizens. The administration, organizing anew the military defence of the country, created him major general of the southern division of the army, the whole force being arranged in two departments, of which the northern was assigned to General Brown.

It was not long before the name of Jackson was again to fill the public ear, and impart its terrors alike to the enemy and to his own government. The speck of war arose in Florida, which, what with runaway negroes, hostile Indians, filibustering adventurers, and the imbecility of the Spanish rule, became a constant source of irritation to the adjoining American States. There were various warlike preliminaries, and at last, towards the end of 1817, a murderous attack by the Seminoles upon a United States boat's crew ascending the Appalachicola. General Jackson was called into the field, charged with the suppression of the war. Eager for the service, he sprang to the work, and conducted it in his own fashion, "taking the responsibility" throughout, summoning volunteers to accompany him from Tennessee without the formality of the civil authority, advancing rapidly into Florida after his arrival at the frontier, capturing the Spanish fort of St. Marks, and pushing thence to the Suwanee. General M'Intosh, the half-breed who accompanied his march, performed feats of valor in the destruction of the Seminoles. At the former of these places, a trader from New Providence, a Scotchman named Arbuthnot, a superior member of his class, and a pacific man, fell into his hands; and in the latter, a vagrant English military adventurer, one Ambrister. Both of these men were held under arrest, charged with complicity with the Indian aggressions, and though entirely irresponsible to the American commander of this military raid, were summarily tried under his order by a court-martial on Spanish territory, at St. Marks, found guilty, and executed by his order on the spot. He even refused to receive the reconsideration of the court of its sentence of Ambrister, substituting stripes and imprisonment for death. Ambrister was shot, and Arbuthnot hung from the yard-arm of his own vessel in the harbor. During the remainder of Jackson's life, these names rang through the country with a fearful emphasis in the strife of parties. Of the many difficulties in the way of his eulogists, this is, perhaps, the most considerable. His own explanation, that he was performing a simple act of justice, would seem, with his previous execution of the six mutineers, to rest upon a partial study of the testimony; but this responsibility should of course be divided with the members of his court-martial. The chief remaining events of the campaign were an angry correspondence with the governor of Georgia, in respect to an encroachment on his authority in ordering an attack on an Indian village, and the capture of Pensacola, in which he left a garrison.

Reckoning day with the government was next in order. The debate in Congress on the Florida transactions was long and animated, Henry Clay bearing a conspicuous part in the opposition. The resolutions of censure were lost by a large majority in the House. The failure to convict was a virtual vote of thanks. Fortified by the result, the general, who had been in Washington during the debate, made a triumphal visit to Philadelphia and New York. At the latter place he was presented with the freedom of the city in a gold box, which, a topic for one of the poets of the "croakers" at the time, has become a matter of interest since, in the discussion growing out of a provision of the general's will. He left the gift to the bravest of the New York officers in the next war. It was finally bestowed, in 1850, upon General Ward B. Burnett, the colonel of a New York regiment distinguished in the Mexican war. The original presentation took place at the City Hall, in February 1819.

The protracted negotiations with Spain for the purchase of Florida being now brought to an end by the acquisition of the country, General Jackson was appointed by President Monroe the first governor of the Territory. He was present at the formal cession at

Pensacola, on the 17th of July, 1821, and entered upon his new duties with his usual vigor—a vigor in one instance, at least, humorously disproportioned to the scene, in a notable dispute with the Spanish governor, in the course of which there was a fresh imbroglio with a United States judge, and the foreign functionary was ludicrously locked up in the calaboose—all about the delivery of certain unimportant papers. On a question of authority, it was Jackson's habit to go straight forward without looking to see what important modifying circumstances there might be to the right or left. It was a military trait which served him very well on important occasions in war, and subsequently in one great struggle, that of the Bank, in peace; but in smaller mixed matters, it might easily lead him astray. For this Don Callava's comedy, we must refer the reader to Mr. Parton's full and entertaining narrative—not the most imposing, but certainly not the least instructive portion of his book. The Florida governorship was not suited to the demands of Jackson's nature; his powers were too limited and restricted; the irritation of the Spanish quarrel was not calculated to lighten his disease, and Mrs. Jackson was at his side to plead the superior claims of home. Thither, after a few months' absence, he returned, doubtless greatly to the relief of the Secretary of State, Mr. Adams, who said at the time to a friend, "he dreaded the arrival of a mail from Florida, not knowing what General Jackson might do next."[1] The

remainder of General Jackson's life may be regarded as chiefly political; it is rather as a man of action in politics than as a theoretical statesman, in any sense, that he is to be considered. H had certain views in public affairs apar' from the army, which were more mat ters of instinct than of reflection or argument. The two great trophies of his administrations, his course towards South Carolina in the preservation of the Union, and his victory over the interests of the United States Bank, were of this character. They were both questions likely to present themselves strongly to his mind. He had an old republican antagonism to paper money, and the corruptions of a large moneyed corporation allied to the government, and having once formed this idea, his military energy came in to carry it out through every availabl means at his disposal.

His availability for the Presidency was based upon his popularity with the people wherever they had fairly come in contact with him. The people, above all other qualities, esteem those of a strong, earnest, truthful, straightforward character. They admire force and unity of purpose, and require honesty. Jackson had these requisites in perfection. There was no mistaking his single aim. It had been displayed on a field where nothing is hidden from the popular eye, where it is even disposed to exaggeration of what it fairly takes in. In producing a candidate for popular favor in an ordinary election, a great deal is to be done, in common cases, in bringing the public to an understanding of his claims. His reputa-

---

[1] Parton's Jackson, II. 639.

tion has, in a measure, to be manufactured. Voters have to be schooled to his appreciation. But Jackson's fame was already made—made by himself. Various things of great importance to the nation were, at different times, to be done, and Jackson had accomplished them. He had freed the land from the savage, and swept the invader from the soil. He had been charged with some errors, but, granting the worst, they had no taint of selfishness or fraud. If he was over rigorous in punishing deserters, and punctilious in his military authority, it was a public necessity which nerved his resolution. A few might be sufferers by his ill-directed zeal, but the masses saw only the splendor of a righteous indignation. It was for them the work was done, and the penalty incurred. His worst private vice was that of a duellist, which is always more apt to be associated with principles of honor, than its frequent incentive, unworthy self-assertion.

It is not at all surprising that such a man should be summoned to the Presidency. He was nominated by the legislature of his own State in 1823, which sent him again to the Senate, and he was highest on the list of the candidates voted for the following year—he had ninety-nine out of two hundred and sixty-one votes—when the election was carried into the House of Representatives, and Adams was chosen by the influence of Henry Clay. At the next election, he was borne triumphantly into the office, receiving more than double the number of votes of his antagonist, Mr. Adams. The vote was one hundred and seventy-

eight to eighty-three. At the election of 1832, the third time Jackson's popularity was tested in this way, the vote stood for Clay forty-nine, for Jackson two hundred and thirty-nine.

The record of these eight years of his Presidential service, from 1829 to 1837, is the modern history of the democratic party, of the exertions of its most distinguished representatives, of the establishment of its most cherished principles—its anti-bank creed in the overthrow of the national bank, and origination of the subtreasury system, which went into operation with his successor—the reduction of the tariff—the opposition to internal improvements—the payment of the national debt. In addition to the settlement of these long agitated questions, his administration was signalized by the removal of the Cherokees from Georgia, and the Creeks from Florida while its foreign policy was candid and vigorous, bringing to a satisfactory adjustment the outstanding claims on France and other nations, and maintaining friendly relations with England. In all these measures, his energetic hand was felt, but particularly was his peculiar character manifested in his veto of 1832, and general conduct of the bank question, the collection of the French indemnity, and his enforcement of the national authority in South Carolina. The censure of the Senate on the 28th March 1834, for his removal of the deposits of the public money from the bank as " an assumption of authority and power not conferred by the Constitution and laws, but in derogation of both "—a censure supported by the ex traordinary coalition of Calhoun, Clay and Webster, measures the extent of the opposition his course encountered in Congress; while the Expunging Resolution of 1837, blotting out that condemnation, indicates the reception and progress of his opinions with the several States in the brief interim. The personal attack made upon him in 1835, by a poor lunatic at the door of the Capitol, "a diseased mind acted upon by a general outcry against a public man,"[1] may show the sentiment with which a large portion of the press and a considerable popular party habitually treated him.

The love of Andrew Jackson for the Union deserves at this time more than a passing mention. It was emphatically the creed of his head and heart. He had no toleration for those who sought to weaken this great instinct of nationality. No sophism could divert his understanding from the plainest obligations of duty to his whole country. He saw as clearly as the subtlest logician in the Senate the inevitable tendencies of any argument which would impair the allegiance of the people of the States to the central authority. He could not make such a speech as Webster delivered on the subject, but he knew as well as Webster the abyss into which nullification would plunge its advocates. His vigorous policy saved his own generation the trials to which ours has been subjected. Had his spirit still ruled at the proper moment in the national administration,

we too might have been spared the untold evils of a gigantic rebellion. It is remarkable that it was predicted by him—not in its extent, for his patriotism and the ardor of his temperament would not have allowed him to imagine a defection so wide-spread, or so lamentable a lack of energy in giving encouragement to its growth—but in its motive and pretences. When nullification was laid at rest, his keen insight saw that the rebellious spirit which gave the doctrine birth was not extinguished. He pronounced the tariff only the pretext of factious and malignant disturbers of the public peace, "who would involve their country in a civil war and all the evils in its train, that they might reign and ride on its whirlwinds, and direct the storm." Disunion and a southern confederacy, and not the tariff, he said, were the real objects of the conspirators, adding, with singular sagacity, "the next pretext will be the negro or the slavery question."[1]

Eight years of honorable repose remained to the victor in so many battles, military and political, after his retirement from the Presidency. They were passed in his seat near Nashville, the home of his happy married life, but no longer cheered by the warm-hearted, sincere, devout sharer of his many trials. That excellent wife had been taken from him on the eve of his first occupation of the Presidential chair, and her memory only was left, with its inviting lessons of piety, to temper the passions of the true-hearted old man as

---

[1] Benton's Thirty Years' View, I. 523.

[1] Letter to the Rev. Andrew J. Crawford. Washington, May 1, 1833.

he resigned himself to religion and the cares of another and better world. He had early adopted, as his own son, a nephew of his wife, and the child grew up always fondly cherished by him, bore his name and inherited his estate. "The Hermitage," the seat of a liberal hospitality, never lacked intimates dear to him. He had the good heart of Dr. Johnson in taking to his home and attaching to himself friends who grew strong again in his manly confidence. Thus, in the enjoyment of a tranquil old age, looking back upon a career which belonged to history, he met the increasing infirmities of ill health with pious equanimity, a member of the Presbyterian church, where his wife had so fondly worshipped—life slowly ebbing from him in the progress of his dropsical complaint—till one summer day, the eighth of June, 1845, the child of the Revolution, an old man of seventy-eight, closed his eyes in lasting repose at his beloved Hermitage.

The genius and peculiarities of Andrew Jackson afford a tempting subject for the pen of the essayist. His resolute will, strong, fierce and irresistible, resting upon a broad honesty of nature, was paramount. It was directed more by feeling and impulse than by education and reflection; consequently there was a spice of egotism even in its purest resolves, and it sometimes took harsh ways to good ends. Somehow or other it generally had the sanction of success. The integrity of his public life, the great national measures with which his name is identified, will throw into obscurity, on the page of history, his personal weaknesses—the violence of his temper, his oaths, his quarrels and occasional seeming want of magnanimity. Strange that so finished and courteous a gentleman should at times have been so rude!

An apology has been found in the struggles of his early life, the rough frontier society into which he was introduced, and the lifelong irritations of disease. That in despite of these tangible defects, he should, through so great a variety of circumstances, civil and military, have controlled so many strong and subtle elements, and have found so many learned and able men to do his work and assist him in his upward path, is the highest proof of his genius.

MARTIN VAN BUREN.

Martin Van Buren, the eighth President of the United States, was born at Kinderhook, Columbia County, New York, December 5th, 1782. His name imports his Dutch descent, his family being among the early settlers who came from Holland to the New Netherlands. Abraham Van Buren, the father of Martin, is spoken of as a farmer in moderate circumstances, "an upright, amiable, and intelligent man, of strong common sense, and distinguished for his pacific disposition." He had little opportunity to bestow upon his son a costly classical education; but the boy had the benefit of such instruction as the village school and academy afforded, and its course included "some knowledge of Latin." His quickness and intelligence marked him out for the profession of the law, the study of which he commenced at the early age of fourteen, in the office of Mr. Francis Sylvester, a highly respectable practitioner at Kinderhook. This apparently premature entrance in the training of the profession is accounted for by a former regulation of the bar, which required a seven years' course of instruction, except in the case of those who had received a collegiate degree, when an allowance was made for the usual four years of the undergraduate course.

The young Van Buren was early set to try cases in the Justices' Courts, and as it is always in America but a single step from the lawyer's office to the political arena, he found his way when he was but eighteen to a nominating convention of the Republican party, of a candidate for the State legislature. These and similar employments marked the young man while he was yet a student, for future activity and employment in public affairs. This tendency was increased by his engagement in the last year of his preparatory course in the office of Mr. William P. Van Ness, a distinguished leader of the Republican party in the city of New York, and friend of Aaron Burr. The latter is said to have cultivated the society of the young student at law from Columbia County, and impressed upon him much of his political sagacity in the organization and government of party. In 1803, in his twenty-first year, Mr. Van Buren was admitted to the bar of the Supreme Court of the State, and returned to Kinderhook to begin practice at the law. His half-brother, his mother's son by a first marriage, Mr. James I. Van Alen, afterward a member of Congress, was there established as a lawyer, and the two formed at once a business connection. This part

ner, who was somewhat of a politician, was attached to the Federal party, which was the ruling influence in the county, and many considerations were urged upon young Van Buren to adopt the prevalent creed. He had, however, chosen his path. "Firmly fixed," says his biographer, Mr. Holland, " by reflection and observation in the political faith of his father, who was a Whig in the Revolution, an anti-Federalist in 1788, and an early supporter of Jefferson, he shrunk not from the severe tests which were applied to the strength and integrity of his convictions. Without patronage, comparatively poor, a plebeian by birth, and not furnished with the advantages of a superior education, he refused to worship either at the shrine of wealth or power, but followed the dictates of his native judgment and benevolent feelings, and hesitated not, in behalf of the cause which he thus adopted, to encounter the utmost violence of his political enemies. That violence soon burst upon his head with concentrated fury. His character was traduced, his person ridiculed, his principles branded as infamous, his integrity questioned, and his abilities sneered at." This is one side of the picture— the opposition of the Federalists; it has another, the partisan friendship of the Republicans. The latter gave the young lawyer and politician their support; he throve in his profession; was married happily, in 1806, to Miss Hannah Hoes, a distant relative on the mother's side; and in 1808 had his first party reward from the Republican state administration of Governor Tompkins, which he had assisted into office. He

received the appointment of surrogate of Columbia County, which induced him to remove to the county seat at Hudson, where he devoted himself assiduously to the bar.

In politics, as we have seen, Mr. Van Buren was an active participant from the start as an ardent supporter of the Jeffersonian politics of the day. In the State divisions he attached himself to the fortunes of Governor Tompkins, and was prominent in sustaining his anti-bank policy. It was on the latter issue, in opposition to Edward P. Livingston, a bank-democrat supported by the Federalists, that Mr. Van Buren was chosen a State senator from the counties comprising the Middle District. It was a closely contested election, the successful candidate having a majority of only about two hundred in an aggregate vote of twenty thousand.

It was the season of a new Presidential election, the first term of Mr. Madison being about to expire. As it was the custom at that time to nominate the State electors by a caucus of the political parties in the legislature, Mr. Van Buren was, of course, called upon to participate in their decision. The Republican members had already, in their spring session, nominated De Witt Clinton for that high office, a nomination to which Mr. Van Buren now gave his support. This brought him in a quasi union with the Federalists, who gave their support to Mr. Clinton, and has led his biographers to take particular pains to exhibit his adherence to the war policy of the administration at Washington, toward which, at the outset at least, Mr. Clinton had been opposed. But whatever doubts may have been thrown over his views by this accidental party relation, seeming to compromise his thorough-going republicanism, his adherence to war measures was made explicit enough in the Address which he prepared as chairman of the committee nominating Governor Tompkins for reëlection in 1813, and by his subsequent advocacy in the legislature of the most stringent war measures, particularly in an act to encourage privateering, and another which was known as the "classification law," of the nature of a conscription, authorizing the governor to place at the disposal of the President twelve thousand men of the militia—a measure which, though adopted, peace intervening, was not required to be put in practice. The acts just alluded to were violently opposed by the Federalists, and submitted to a severe scrutiny after their passage, in the Council of Revision, a body which then sat as an integral part of the legislature in confirming its laws. Chancellor Kent there delivered an opinion against them. It was published, and replied to by Samuel Young, then Speaker of the Assembly, in several newspaper articles signed "*Juris Consultus*," which were answered by the chancellor under the signature "*Amicus Curiæ.*" Upon this Mr. Van Buren met the latter, directing his attention especially to the assault upon the morality of the privateering law, in a series of articles signed "*Amicus Juris Consultus.*"

After peace was concluded, in the words of his eulogist, Colonel Benton, ' to complete his course in support of the war, and to crown his meritorious labors to bring it to a happy conclusion, it became Mr. Van Buren's fortune to draw up the vote of thanks of the greatest State of the Union, to the greatest general which the war had produced—'the thanks of the New York legislature to Major-General Jackson, his gallant officers and troops, for their wonderful and heroic victory, in defence of the grand emporium of the West.'"

The ability displayed by Mr. Van Buren in the Senate indicated him as a worthy incumbent of the office of attorney-general of the State, an appointment which he received in 1815. He was also in this year created a Regent of the University, and in the following was reëlected for another term of four years to the Senate. He then took up his residence at Albany, where he continued his practice at the bar, which had steadily increased, and formed a partnership with his pupil, the late Benjamin F. Butler, to whom, as the political relations of Mr. Van Buren became more engrossing, the business of the office was gradually relinquished.

It is not necessary here to attempt to follow Mr. Van Buren through the intricate windings of New York political history. It is a story of cross purposes, which can be fully understood only by a minute study of the history of the times, if, indeed, we are as yet supplied with the full materials for its comprehension. It may be sufficient to say that much in those days, by a politician bent upon advancement, had to be accomplished by management and intrigue. The ship was to be assisted in its course by side winds and under currents. Thus we find Mr. Van Buren with his party at one time, by some process of fusion of Republicans and Federalists, supporting De Witt Clinton; at another, leading in his overthrow. It became a question of party existence. What is called the Albany Regency, a body of practised politicians who combined their resources in office and through the press in establishing and cementing democratic authority, was called into being. Clinton had the prestige of a great name in the State, and the influence of commanding talents, sustained by the most indomitable usefulness and industry; he was the great supporter of the Canal policy, which was at length triumphantly carried through, but which had, meanwhile, to bear the brunt of a ruthless opposition; in his personal bearing he was charged with haughtiness, which was, probably, nothing more than the dignity and reserve of a superior nature, exclusively engrossed in honorable ends, requiring the devotion of the whole man. At any rate, a party struggle ensued between the friends of the governor and of Mr. Van Buren, which was conducted with great acrimony. One of its results was the removal of the latter from his office of attorney-general, by that political machine of the old constitution, the Council of Appointment, in 1819, at a moment when he had become obnoxious to the Clintonians by his efforts to oppose the re-election of their chieftain. The decapitation caused some stir at the time, which is commemorated in one of the poetical effusions of the Croakers, with a prophetic hint of the victim's higher destiny.

'Tis vain to win a great man's name,
  Without some proof of having been one,
And *killing*'s a sure path to fame,
  Vide Jack Ketch and Mr. Clinton!
Our Council well this path have trod,
  Honor's immortal wreath securing,
They've dipped their hatchets in the blood,
  The patriot blood of Mat. Van Buren.

He bears, as every hero ought,
  The mandate of the powers that rule,
He's higher game in view, 'tis thought,
  All in good time; (the man's no fool),
With him, some dozens prostrate fall,
  No friend to mourn, nor foe to flout them,
They die unsung, unwept by all,
  For no one cares a *sous* about them.

It was about this time that the democrats, including Mr. Van Buren, engaged in one of those party compromise manœuvres to which we have alluded, in the election of Mr. Rufus King, an old federalist, to the Senate. In support of this measure, Mr. Van Buren wrote and published, in conjunction with the late Governor Marcy, a pamphlet entitled "Considerations in favor of the appointment of Rufus King to the Senate of the United States." In the great question of the day, in which Mr. King bore so prominent a part, the admission of Missouri into the Union, Mr. Van Buren concurred with the Senate in its instructions to the State representatives at Washington, to insist upon the prohibition of slavery. His service in this body ended with the expiration of his second term, in 1820, when he was not a candidate for reëlection. In February of the following year he was chosen by the legislature Senator of the United States. In the same year he was also elected a mem ber of the convention to revise the constitution of the State, from Otsego County, his party not being strong enough to return him from his own district. When this important body met he took an active part in its deliberations, advocating generally a medium course of reform. On one of the prominent subjects under discussion, the extension of the right of suffrage, he was in favor of a relaxation of the old system, but stopped short of universal suffrage. That was a measure of an after day. He was opposed to the continuance of the Council of Revision, and in favor of the substitute for its check upon hasty legislation, of the veto power of the governor. He favored the direct choice of officers of government by the people, with some reservations, however, which, adopted at the time, have been subsequently removed. His course was thus politic, and, in a measure, conservative.

The convention concluded its sittings in time for Mr. Van Buren to take his seat, at the opening of the winter session of the Senate at Washington, by the side of his colleague Rufus King. His reputation being now well established, he was at once charged with important duties as a member of the committees of finance and the judiciary. One of the topics which early engaged his attention was the abolition of imprisonment for debt in the process of the United States Courts, unless in certain cases of fraud—an amelioration of the statutes of the olden time, which he had already advocated in the State jurisprudence at Albany. He also proposed amendments to the judiciary sys-

tem, and was a prominent speaker in the discussion of a bill establishing a uniform system of bankruptcy.

On the occession of Mr. Adams in 1825 Mr. Van Buren, who had already attached himself to the fortunes of Jackson, was enrolled in the number of the President's opponents. Among other measures of the Administration, the proposed Panama mission drew forth his determined opposition.

In 1827 he was reëlected to the Senate by a decisive vote of the New York State Legislature, but he had little more than entered on the new term, when he was chosen, on the death of De Witt Clinton, who expired suddenly while in office, Governor of New York. He consequently resigned his seat in the Senate and began his new course of duties in January, 1829.

Mr. Van Buren had not been long at Albany, in his seat as governor, when, on the entrance of Jackson upon the Presidency in 1829, he was called to the high office, directly, according to the old precedents in the line of succession, of Secretary of State. He held this for two years, when political hostilities having grown rife in the cabinet, a dissolution seemed inevitable, and, " convinced that the success of the administration, and his own prospects for the future, demanded his retirement from a position so unpleasant, he led the way by a voluntary resignation of the office which he held." [1]

Mr. Van Buren retired during the recess of Congress in April, 1831, and was immediately appointed by the

---

[1] Jenkins' Van Buren. Governors of New York, p. 414.

President Minister Plenipotentiary to Great Britain. He accepted the position, the duties of which were not altogether disconnected from those of his late office, so far as they related to the settlement of open questions with England, which he had already had in hand. He reached London in September, and was received with every attention by the government. Before, however, he was well seated, his appointment, on being submitted to the Senate, was rejected by that body, on the ostensible ground of certain instructions, in reference to the trade with the West Indies, which he had forwarded, when Secretary of State, to the previous minister, Mr. McLane. The political constitution of the Senate, which was now arraying its forces, may be presumed to have had more to do with the rejection, which was decided against the appointment by the casting vote of the Vice-President, Mr. Calhoun.

That act, it was often said, made Mr. Van Buren President. He was the victim of an opposition vote, and was ruthlessly thrown out from an honorable office which he was well qualified to discharge. This, at least, was the view of the Democratic party, and the friends of the President, who continued to give him his support. Consequently when General Jackson was nominated for reëlection, it was with Martin Van Buren on the ticket for Vice-President. Both were chosen by a decided majority, the vote being the same, with the exception of that of Pennsylvania, which, in consequence of Mr. Van Buren's anti-protectionist views, was withheld from him.

As the presiding officer of the Senate, during the stormy period of Jackson's second term, the new Vice-President, by his parliamentary experience, unwearied attention, and that polished courtesy which always characterized his bearing, won golden opinions from all parties. He was the devoted supporter of the measures of the President in this active period, which witnessed the overthrow of the United States Bank, the decided stand taken with regard to nullification in South Carolina, and the indemnity negotiation with Louis Philippe. The reign of Jacksonism, as it was sometimes called, became fully established, and Mr. Van Buren succeeded to the retiring chieftain as his rightful political heir. He was nominated to the Presidency at Baltimore, in May, 1835, and in the ensuing election of the following year was chosen by a majority of forty-six votes over all other candidates.

His inauguration, on the 4th of March, 1837, was duly celebrated according to custom, by the delivery of an address, and administration of the oath at the portico of the Capitol. The day was a very fine one, as the new President was driven to the spot, seated alongside of the retiring incumbent, in a phæton made of the wood of the frigate Constitution, which had been presented to General Jackson by the democracy of New York. The address was chiefly a eulogy on the success of the Government in its triumph over all previous obstacles. The agitation of the slavery question was pointedly alluded to and deprecated in earnest terms. The speaker renewed his pledge as "the inflexible and uncompromising opponent of every attempt on the part of Congress to abolish slavery in the District of Columbia, against the wishes of the slaveholding States; and also his determination, equally decided, to resist the slightest interference with it in the States where it exists."

In the selection of his Cabinet, Mr. Van Buren retained those who held office under the late administration, including John Forsyth, of Georgia, in the State Department; Levi Woodbury, of New Hampshire, in the Treasury; Amos Kendall in the Post Office, and Benjamin F. Butler as Attorney-General. Mr. Poinsett, of South Carolina, was appointed in the War Department to succeed General Cass, who proceeded as Minister to France. The bureau of administration thus organized, the government with an established, recognized policy, appeared to have an easy course before it. There was, however, a cloud rising which soon burst upon the country. The difficulty arose from the banks out of the plethora of the public treasury. A large surplus had accumulated in the State banks, which were the substitutes of the former national institution, which was now to be divided among the States. Credit had been stimulated, paper money had been expanded, and the result was now the contraction, memorable in our commercial annals, of the year 1837. The banks suspended specie payments, millions of value were depreciated, and the whole system of trade and industry seemed in utter wreck and ruin. An extra session of Congress was called in September, to take into consideration the state of affairs in relation to the public credit. A message from the President proposed the remedy which, known under the name of the Sub-Treasury, has passed into an established feature of the government unquestioned in party conflicts. The Independent Treasury Bill, which thus separated the financial affairs of the State from all banks whatsoever, making the care of the gold and silver paid for duties, a simple matter of safe keeping, under the charge of certain officers, met at the outset with considerable opposition. It passed the Senate in this extra session but was defeated in the House of Representatives. The same fate attended it in the next regular session. It did not become a law till the last year of Mr. Van Buren's Presidential term, in 1840. It was undoubtedly the most important event of his administration.

The foreign policy of the country was conducted with ability during this period. Two questions of some importance arose in these connections, one in relation to Texas, the other regarding the management of the frontier difficulties with Great Britain. In respect to the former, which came up on the proposition for the annexation of Texas to the Union, the President was opposed to the measure. He thought the independence of that State had not been fully recognized by the United States, and that to enter upon annexation would be, as the event proved, to encounter hostilities with Mexico, with which country he desired to maintain peace. In the Maine Boundary Question and the Niagara frontier disturbances he pursued a firm and equable policy, protecting the rights of the country and checking the lawless spirit which had been aroused within our own borders.

In the election of 1840 Mr. Van Buren was again the candidate of his party, in a canvass in which he suffered an overwhelming defeat. The country, depressed by the financial crisis from which it had not yet recovered, was bent upon political change. General Harrison, a popular hero of the West was nominated by the Whigs and borne into office by a triumphant vote. He received two hundred and thirty-four electoral votes against the sixty of President Van Buren. The administration of the latter being thus ended, he retired from Washington on the accession of the new President, to his old home at Kinderhook, where he had purchased an estate which had belonged to the late Judge Van Ness, to which he gave the name Lindenwold. In 1844 his friends again brought him forward as a candidate for the Presidency, and an earnest effort was made for his nomination in the national convention of his party at Baltimore. It might have been obtained for him but for a letter which he wrote in favor of deferring the annexation of Texas till the consent of Mexico should be obtained. Something more decided was required by the convention on this point, and the nomination was given to Mr. Polk, who was less scrupulous in regard to the measure. Mr. Van Buren, true to the party organization, which he had done so much to aid in previous days, gave an influential support to the democratic candidate, and on his election, was tendered the mission to England, which he declined. Four years now elapsed, and 1848 brought round again the recurring struggle for the Presidency. A division had arisen in the ranks of the democracy in the State of New York, involving the question of the introduction of slavery into the new territory acquired from Mexico. Two delegations were sent from rival factions to the nominating convention of the party at Baltimore. In the political nomenclature of the day one bore the name of Hunkers, the other of Barnburners. The latter, which represented the interests of Mr. Van Buren, was in favor of freedom in the territories. Resolutions were passed in the convention admitting both delegations, upon which the Barnburners retired. The faction of the latter then held a convention of their own at Utica, at which Mr. Van Buren was nominated as an independent democratic candidate of the Free Soil party, as it began to be called. General Cass was the regular nominee at Baltimore, and General Taylor of the Whigs. The result of the election was a Free Soil popular vote for Van Buren, chiefly drawn from New York, which gave him over 120,000; Massachusetts, 38,058; Ohio, over 35,000; Illinois, nearly 16,000; Pennsylvania, about 11,000—an aggregate of 291,378. General Cass received 1,233,795 votes; General Taylor's votes exceeded this by 138,447. Mr. Van Buren did not receive the electoral vote of a single State.

Mr. Van Buren, " a passive instrument in the hands of his old and do voted friends," appears to have been little concerned at the result. It was not his humor or his character. He had seen enough of party not to be greatly affected by its decisions, and he had, moreover, reached an age of honorable, well-earned repose, which his habits of study and reflection, a certain philosophic temper, and his happy family relations disposed him to enjoy.

The retirement of Mr. Van Buren's latter days was varied by a visit to Europe, undertaken for his health in 1853. There he remained for more than a year, visiting various countries and enjoying such attention as befitted the elevated career in which he had moved. On his return his time was chiefly passed at his estate of Lindenwold, among the scenes of his childhood, in Columbia County, varied by an occasional visit to New York. An asthmatic affection was gradually growing upon him, which increased in intensity, and finally brought him to his end. His death occurred on the 24th of July, 1862, in the midst of the great political and social revolution, which in the storm of civil war was shaking the land to its foundations. In the public honors which were paid to his memory the association was not forgotten. President Lincoln, in a national tribute of respect, announced his death to the country. "This event," was the language of his Proclamation, "will occasion mourning in the nation for the loss of a citizen and a public servant whose memory will be gratefully cherished. Although it has occurred at a time when his country is afflicted with division and civil war, the grief of his patri-

otic friends will measurably be assuaged by the consciousness that, while suffering with disease, and seeing his end approaching, his prayers were for the restoration of the authority of the Government of which he had been the head, and for peace and good-will among his fellow-citizens. As a mark of respect for his memory, it is ordered that the Executive Mansion and the several Executive Departments, excepting those of the War and Navy, be immediately placed in mourning, and all business be suspended during to-morrow. It is further ordered that the War and Navy Departments cause suitable military and naval honors to be paid on this occasion to the memory of the illustrious dead." The courts of New York paid their eulogies to the man and his active influential life.

The funeral services were performed at the Dutch Church, in the village of Kinderhook, in the presence of a large gathering of friends and neighbors, when a discourse befitting the occasion was delivered by a friend of the deceased, the Rev. Dr. J. Romeyn Berry, in which a stirring incentive to patriotism, rendered doubly impressive by the national crisis, was a prominent topic.

Mr. Van Buren had been long a widower, his wife having died in 1818, twelve years after their marriage, leaving him a family of four sons, Abraham, John, Martin, and Smith Thompson. Mr. John Van Buren is well known as an eminent legal practitioner in New York, and more widely of late by his active participation in the political movements of the day.

The more prominent characteristics

of Mr. Van Buren have been delicately touched by a son of one of his most devoted friends, Mr. William Allen Butler, in an interesting obituary sketch of the "Lawyer, Statesman and Man." "In his personal traits," says he, "Mr. Van Buren was marked by a rare individuality. He was a gentleman, and he cultivated the society of gentlemen. He never had any associates who were vulgar or vicious. He affected the companionship of men of letters, though I think his conclusion was that they are apt to make poor politicians and not the best of friends. Where he acquired that peculiar neatness and polish of manners which he wore so lightly, and which served every turn of domestic, social, and public intercourse, I do not know. It could hardly be called natural, although it seemed so natural in him. It was not put on, for it never was put off. As you saw him once you saw him always—always punctilious, always polite, always cheerful, always self-possessed. It seemed to any one who studied this phase of his character as if, in some early moment of destiny, his whole nature had been bathed in a cool, clear and unruffled depth, from which it drew this life-long serenity and self-control. It was another of the charges against him that he was no Democrat. He dressed too well, he lived too well, the company he kept was too good, his tastes were too refined, his tone was too elegant. So far as democracy is supposed to have an elective affinity for dirt, this was all true; he was no Democrat in taste or feeling, and he never pretended to be. . . . As to the elements of the widest popularity, they were not in him. He never inspired enthusiasm, as Jackson did, or Henry Clay. The masses accepted him as a leader, but they never worshipped him as a hero. . . . Mr. Van Buren has left memoirs, partly finished. If his reminiscences can be given to the world as he was in the habit of giving them to his friends, in all the freshness of familiar intercourse, they will be most attractive. There was a charm about his conversation when it turned on the incidents of his personal experience which could hardly be transferred to the printed page, so much of its interest depended on manner and expression. Mr. Van Buren had no wit, but he had humor, and a keen sense for the humorous, and he could reproduce with rare fidelity whatever in the actions or the character of men he had thought worth remembering."

17

WILLIAM HENRY HARRISON.

THE Virginia Harrison family, of which the President of the United States was descended, is traced to a colonial ancestor in the middle of the seventeenth century. A son of this early inhabitant gave birth to Benjamin Harrison, who established the line at the family seat at Berkeley, Charles City County, on James River. He was a lawyer, speaker of the House of Burgesses, and much esteemed in the colony, where he exercised a liberal influence by his virtues and hospitality. His grandson of the same name was the signer of the Declaration of Independence, and father of the President.

The family had always taken an active part in public affairs, proportioned to its growing wealth and importance, and the young Benjamin, who was early left to the care of the estate, was not disposed to avoid this responsibility. He took his seat in the House of Burgesses, before he reached the legal age, and became at once marked out by his firmness and ability as a political leader. He was one of the committee appointed in 1764 to prepare an address to the king, and memorials to parliament on the resolutions of the House of Commons, preparatory to the Stamp Act. When the first independent convention of delegates met at Williamsburgh, ten years afterward, when the mismanagement of parliament had ripened the country for revolt, he was sent a member of the first Continental Congress, which met in Philadelphia. He was also a member of the second Virginia assembly of delegates at Richmond in 1775, which took the active measures placing the county in a state of self-defence and resistance. He at first regarded these steps as premature, but speedily acquiesced in the vote of the House. He was again returned to the second and more important General Congress at Philadelphia. An anecdote is related of him at this time in connection with John Hancock. When the spirited Boston leader showed some reluctance or diffidence in accepting the Presidency on the retirement of Peyton Randolph, Harrison, who was standing by him, is said to have seized him in his arms and placed him bodily in the chair, with the exclamation, "We will show Mother Britain how little we care for her, by making a Massachusetts man our president, whom she has excluded from pardon by a public proclamation."[1] Another story

---

[1] Life of Harrison. Sanderson's Biography of the Signers.

is narrated involving a similar allusion to his powerful figure, in his remark to Elbridge Gerry, his very opposite, in a slender, spare person, at the signing of the Declaration. "When the hanging scene comes to be exhibited," said Harrison, as he raised his pen from the instrument, "I shall have all the advantage over you. It will be over with me in a minute, but you will be kicking in the air half an hour after I am gone." Anecdotes like these, of such a man, show no levity of disposition in conflict with the serious duties in which he was employed, but they do show an animation and good heart in the cause which needed every support of physical temperament as well as mental resolve. Our fathers fought with cheerfulness as well as resolution.

Harrison continued in Congress actively employed in its various employments till the close of 1777, when he only transferred his political duties to his native State. He was speaker of the House of Burgesses till 1782, including the disastrous period of the invasion of Virginia, and was then twice elected governor. He was again called from private life to sit in the State Convention, of the Constitution, to which he gave his influential support, and was more or less engaged in public life to his death, in 1791.

William Henry Harrison was his third son. He was born at Berkeley, the family residence, February 9, 1773; so that he came into the field of active life with the new generation which succeeded the Revolutionary era. His education was well provided for under the care of the family friend, the finan-cier Robert Morris, and at Hampden Sidney College in Virginia, whence he turned to the study of medicine. He had acquired some knowledge of the profession in the office of a physician of Richmond, and was about to pursue his studies with the celebrated Doctor Rush, at Philadelphia, when his father's death occurred, and, with some reluctance on the part of his family, he chose for himself a military life. He was aided by General Henry Lee in obtaining a commission as ensign in the 1st regiment of United States infantry, and as the government had then an Indian war on its hands in the Western Territory, he at once, at the age of nineteen, found himself engaged in active service. Passing but a few days in Philadelphia, he hastened to his regiment, stationed at fort Washington, the site of the present Cincinnati, where he joined the remains of the broken forces of St. Clair, just escaped from the disastrous engagement at the Miami villages. It was thus that he was introduced to a region with which he became thoroughly identified, and his popularity in which, long after the scenes of war were over, carried him triumphantly into the Presidential chair.

The ill fortune which had befallen St. Clair was calculated to rouse the warlike spirit of the generous youth; and it had its lesson of caution and preparation in dealing with the Indians, which was not lost upon subsequent campaigns. When Major-General Wayne took the field, in the summer of 1793, Harrison, now holding the rank of lieutenant in his regiment, was appointed his aid. In the brilliant engagement at the Rapids of the Miami, he distinguished himself by his valor, and secured from Wayne special mention in his dispatch of the victory, as "one who rendered the most essential service, by communicating my orders in every direction, and by his conduct and bravery exciting the troops to press for victory." The battle on the Miamis was fought August 20, 1794, and a year afterward, with various intermediate demonstrations and negotiations brought forth its peaceable fruits in Wayne's treaty of Greenville, which closed the war.

Harrison was then, at the age of twenty-three, with the rank of Captain, placed in command of Fort Washington, where he about the same time was married to the daughter of John Cleves Symmes, whose name is so honorably distinguished in the history of the western settlements, and particularly as the founder of Cincinnati. The young officer held this post till 1797, when he sent in his resignation, with the intention thereafter, says his biographer, Montgomery, "of devoting his time to the peaceful and more congenial pursuits of agriculture." He was speedily, however, withdrawn from these quiet anticipations to public duties, in his appointment by President Adams as secretary of the Northwest Territory, then under the government of St. Clair. When the Territory became organized, and was qualified to send a delegate to Congress, Harrison was chosen its first representative in 1799. He distinguished himself in this body by his activity and success in securing to settlers the privilege of purchasing the public lands in small quantities, and in measures favoring their preëmption rights and modes of payment.

On the division of the Territory, Harrison was withdrawn from Congress to discharge the duties of the first governor of the newly formed Territory of Indiana, which included the present States of Indiana, Illinois, Michigan, and Wisconsin. This was in 1801, and the whole region now so populous numbered only five thousand people, scattered over the whole country, exposed to the dangers of frontier life and the unsettled relations with the Indians. "With such difficulties," says his biographer, "it was no less a matter of duty than of necessity that he should be clothed with the amplest independent powers. Amongst those of a civil as well as political nature conferred upon him were those jointly with those of the judges, of the legislative functions of the Territory, the appointment of all the civil officers within the Territory, and all the military officers of a grade inferior in rank to that of general; commander-in-chief of the militia; the absolute and uncontrolled power of pardoning all offences; sole commissioner of treaties with the Indians with unlimited powers, and the power of conferring, at his option, all grants of lands." Harrison held this proconsular office for sixteen years, during which he saw the country steadily increasing in strength and prosperity; though his career, experienced and prudent as it was, proved not without difficulties with the Indians, rising at length to open warfare.

The struggle, known as the battle of Tippecanoe, which took place on the seventh of November, 1811, involved various elements of preparation on the part of the savages, some of which impart to their conduct of the war an interest with which there will always be a certain degree of sympathy. The effort of a falling race to regain its authority under a leader like Tecumseh, assisted by the fanaticism of his brother the Prophet, is raised out of the rank of the ordinary Indian fighting propensities. The Indian chief was a hero of no ordinary class. To the virtues of the warrior in arms, he united many of those moral qualities so powerful in strengthening the courage of the soldier. He was self-denying, forbearing, and even compassionate. Born in the centre of Ohio, he represented the races immediately west of the Alleghanies, whom he appears early to have sought to unite against the whites. Consistently with his character for sincerity he declined to attend Wayne's council of peace at Greenville. His great effort was to bring the scattered tribes to act in concert. For this purpose he established, in 1808, an Indian settlement at the Tippecanoe River, a tributary of the Wabash, in Indiana, whither, with the aid of the Prophet, he brought together a considerable number of recruits to his mingled political and superstitious teaching.

The "Wabash Prophet," as he was called, was at first considered a simple visionary. Jefferson, then in the Presidency, took this view of him, and thought little harm would come of his preaching the simple austerities of their forefathers to a race not remarkably disposed to abstinence and self-denial. His success, however, and the activity and declarations of Tecumseh, with the imminent English war at hand, aroused the anxieties of the people of the Territory, and when positive ground was taken by the Indian leader at the conference of Vincennes against the progress of the treaties by which Harrison was extending the authority of the whites, it was found necessary to assume a decided military stand. The governor therefore at length, in October, 1811, advanced his forces, composed of regulars and militia, officered by experienced western leaders, toward the Indian settlement presided over by the prophet on the Tippecanoe. Moving forward cautiously with a force of nine hundred men, he reached a station about a mile and a half from the town, where a military encampment was formed, when some conferences were commenced with the foe. It was evident that the purposes of the Prophet were hostile. Harrison arranged his men in order to receive the assault, which was made by the Indians early on the morning of the seventh of November. It was in fact a night attack, though commenced after four o'clock, a drizzling rain, and the season of the year favoring the darkness. The onset was made with vigor, on all sides of the encampment, which was gallantly defended, with considerable loss of life by the rifle companies at their several stations. The camp was thus resolutely held, and kept unbroken, till daybreak, when new military dispositions were made, and a charge at the point of the bayonet, put the Indians to the rout.

"With this success," says Mr. Dawson, in his account of the battle,[1] "the engagement was ended; both parties appeared to have satisfied the expectations of their friends. The steady, undeviating courage of the American troops elicited great commendation; while Governor Harrison, speaking of his savage enemy, says 'the Indians manifested a ferocity uncommon even with them.' In this, however, they were inspirited by the religious fanaticism under which they acted—the Prophet, during the action, being posted on a neighboring eminence, singing a war-song; and in faint imitation of Moses in the wilderness, directing his people by the movements of his rod." The forces engaged in this battle were probably about equal. The Americans lost some sixty officers and men killed, or who died of their wounds, beside the wounded survivors, and the Indian loss was supposed to have been greater.

The attack upon the American camp was urged and directed in the absence of Tecumseh, by the Prophet, who promised in virtue of his soothsaying insight, an easy victory. The result was that he altogether lost credit with the tribes whom he had inveigled to his town by his necromantic appeals. When the battle was fought, Tecumseh was on a journey to the Southern Indians, whom he was stirring up to his warlike enterprises. He reached the Wabash on his return in time to witness the first effects of the discomfiture of his followers, and it is said, so great was his indignation toward his brother,

the Prophet, that on his attempting to palliate his fool-hardy conduct, he seized him by the hair and threatened his life. The disaster had broken up his long entertained hope of an Indian confederacy against the white man. The game, however, was not quite up yet. The desperation of the Indians was taken advantage of by the British authorities on the frontier, to engage them in the war with America. In May, 1812, Tecumseh openly joined the British standard at Malden. On the eighteenth of the following month war against Great Britain was formally declared by Congress.

The campaign of Hull in Canada, opened with brilliant promise in his invasion of the country, speedily to be checked by his inefficiency and to terminate in his ignominious surrender of Detroit. This disaster, of a sufficiently afflictive character, so far however, from intimidating the western defenders, called them to new exertions, and volunteer forces were raised in large numbers in Ohio and Kentucky. There was at first some conflict of authority as to the command of the troops of the latter State, which, for the purpose of placing Harrison at their head, conferred upon him the brevet commission of Major-General, while the Secretary of War, ignorant of this movement, assigned the command to General Winchester. The difficulty, however, was speedily solved by the appointment of General Harrison by the President, in September, commander-in-chief of the Western Department, when the left wing of the army was assigned to General Winchester. Harrison himself took

---

[1] Battles of the United States, II. 73–81.

his position in what the British conquests had now made the frontier, the
northerly portion of Ohio bordering on
Michigan, and made his headquarters
at Upper Sandusky.

The new year 1813, opened with a
movement on the part of Winchester,
now established at the rapids of the
Maumee to protect the outlying settlements in Michigan on the Raisin River,
a territory virtually in possession of
the British. For this purpose Colonel
Lewis was dispatched with a force over
the frozen waters of the adjacent portion of Lake Erie to Frenchtown, from
which the enemy were driven with
great gallantry. This action occurred
on the eighteenth of January. On the
twenty-second, the victors in the meantime having been joined by Winchester
with a small body of troops, an attack
was made upon the American position
by Colonel Proctor, who had issued
forth from the neighboring Malden,
only eighteen miles distant, with a considerable party of royal troops, several
pieces of artillery, and a formidable
band of six hundred Indians. The
camp was taken unprepared; such resistance as could be offered at the moment was made, but the American
defeat was complete. Such was the
cruelty of the Indian allies and the
merciless conduct of the British commander, that the action, an indelible
disgrace to the British arms, passes
in history as the massacre at the River
Raisin. Both the officers, Lewis and
Winchester were captured; of about
a thousand American troops engaged,
but thirty-three escaped, nearly four
hundred were killed or missing, and

the rest taken prisoners. General Harrison, though he disapproved of the
more than questionable attempt at holding a position like Frenchtown in the
face of the superior foe, did all that he
could to save the fortunes of the army
by hastening thither with recruits; but
the action was fought and the disaster
completed before he reached the scene.
All further onward movements were of
course, for the time, unavailing, and
the commander-in-chief intrenched his
forces at the Rapids of the Maumee,
constructing there a fort, named in
honor of Governor Meigs, of Ohio.

The next important event of the war
in this quarter was the attack on this
fort in the spring, by a force led by
General Proctor, of over two thousand
men, more than one half of whom were
Indians, and of the rest above five hundred were regulars. He made good his
landing on the river two miles below
the fort; but he had this time a more
diligent commander than Winchester to
encounter. Harrison, who anticipated
an attack, had hastened from a recruit-
ing mission to Cincinnati, to superintend
the defence. The fort was defended by
its elevated position and the usual protection of works of that kind, of pickets and block houses. As a further
protection against the pieces of artillery
which the besiegers were bringing to
bear upon it, a heavy embankment was
carried across the works which sheltered
the troops from the enemy's fire. The
batteries of the assailants were opened
on the first of May, and continued with
energy for four days with little effect,
when the arrival in the vicinity of Kentucky reinforcements under General

Clay, which Harrison had originally sent for, gave the commander the opportunity to plan a concerted attack upon the besiegers. It was made by a sally from the fort and two divisions of Clay's troops at different points with various success; but the result was the virtual discomfiture or defeat of the British. The fighting of that fifth of May, proved the superiority of the Americans and a few days after the seige was abandoned.

We here meet again with the Indian leader, Tecumseh, who proved himself a skillful combatant in the day's work, and who, we may mention, had exhibited his prowess in the campaign in Michigan at the expense of a detachment of Hull's command previous to his surrender. A story of this chieftain's interposition in saving some of the prisoners taken by the British in this action before Fort Meigs, is creditable to his humanity, while the necessity for such interposition adds another item to the fearful account against Proctor for his treachery and cruelty at the River Raisin. While a dispute was raging between the Potawatamies and the more merciful Miamis and Wyandots, as to the fate of the captives, the work of scalping and slaughter having been already wreaked on some twenty defenceless victims, Tecumseh came upon the spot flourishing his hatchet, and it is said burying it in the head of a chief engaged in the bloody work, commanded them, for shame to desist. "It is a disgrace," said he, "to kill a defenceless prisoner:" and his order was obeyed.[1]

____

[1] Dawson's Seige of Fort Meigs. Battles of the United States.

The loss of the Americans in the seige and the action was greater than that of the British; but we are to consider in the number of the slain those perfidiously murdered by the savage allies of the enemy. Proctor, at any rate, was unable to stand before the American forces now thickening around him.

Thus relieved of the presence of the enemy, General Harrison waited the effects of Perry's movements on the lake below. Once in command of Lake Erie, the British occupation of Michigan he felt would now be abandoned. The interim between this time and Perry's victory which opened the way to the expected conquests was honorably marked by Major Croghan's gallant defence of Fort Stephenson, against another attack of Proctor. That action was fought on the first of August; on the tenth of September, Perry defeated and captured the whole British squadron. Harrison who had been impatiently waiting this result, now rapidly matured his measures for the reconquest of the country overrun by the British. Employing the smaller vessels taken from the enemy to transport a portion of his forces, now powerfully recruited by the Kentucky volunteers, Harrison effected a landing on the Canadian shore, on the twenty-seventh of the month, and advancing to Malden, found it abandoned by the British and its fort and storehouses destroyed. Proctor, with all his royal forces accompanied by Tecumseh with his Indians, had retreated within the peninsula along the line of the Thames, which empties into Lake St. Clair. General Harrison, leaving detachments of his force at Sandwich and Detroit, now regained, pushed on with a company of about a hundred and forty regulars, Colonel Richard M. Johnson's mounted Kentuckians, and Governor Shelby's volunteers, also Kentuckians, after the retreating foe. Lewis Cass and Commodore Perry were with him as volunteer aids. The whole force amounted to about three thousand five hundred men. For some distance along the river the troops were accompanied by the smaller vessels of the fleet.

The progress of the Americans along the route was of the most exciting character as they drove in the enemy from the defence of the bridges which lay in their way. On the fifth of October they came up with the British forces of Proctor drawn up in the vicinity of the Moravian town. He had some eight hundred regular troops and about two thousand Indians. They were posted in front of the road and in an open wood flanked by the river on one hand and a swamp on the other. The Indians adjoined the swamp on the enemy's right. The attack was made on the front by the mounted Kentuckians, whose charge at once threw that portion of the foe into utter confusion, driving through their ranks and assailing them from the rear. Colonel Johnson, meanwhile, was engaged in a stubborn conflict with the Indians, who, directed by the skill of Tecumseh, reserved their fire to tell with deadly effect upon the advancing column. Johnson was wounded, but his Kentuckians were not to be dismayed. Dismounting from their horses they plied their rifles with great effect against the Indians who stood their ground well, but being un-

supported by their British employers, were soon compelled to retreat. Proctor himself had already taken to flight. Tecumseh was slain in the battle, the most illustrious victim of the day. The number of chivalrous leaders engaged in the American ranks, men who were then or afterward became greatly celebrated, Johnson, Cass, Perry, Shelby, is noticeable, while more than a quarter of a century later, "The battle of the Thames" was to be one of the watchwords of victory for its General in a great political contest.

The effect of this successful termination of the contest following upon Perry's naval triumph—a success enhanced by the embarrassments and failures of the early part of the struggle—upon the West, can hardly be appreciated at the present day. It was a release from danger and from fear, from a remorseless foe and the scalping knife of the savage. With Tecumseh fell the last Indian enemy known to a great region of the West. Henceforth we are to follow his successful adversary through the paths of civil life. General Harrison was not engaged in the later occupations of the army. He was in effect driven to retirement by the arrangements of General Armstrong, the Secretary of War, by whom he was, under some adverse influence or other, virtually suspended in his command. When he was omitted in the plan of the next year's campaign, he resigned the commission which he held as major-general, and its accompanying emoluments.

He now resided at his farm at North Bend, on the Ohio, near Cincinnati, which henceforth, in the intervals of public occupation to which he was frequently called, continued his residence. He was in Congress from 1816 to 1818, a member of the House of Representatives, and from 1824 to 1828 a member of the Senate. Between these dates he sat in the Ohio Senate. In 1828 we find him appointed by President John Quincy Adams, Minister Plenipotentiary to the Republic of Columbia. He reached Bogota, the seat of his duties, in February of the next year, and was received with favor, but he had hardly entered upon the mission when President Jackson coming into office, he was recalled. Resuming again his agricultural pursuits at North Bend upon his return, he was occasionally called upon to deliver public addresses and speeches, of which several were printed. One of these, which was republished during his canvass for the presidency, was a discourse before the Philosophical and Historical Society of Ohio, in 1837, in which he took the aborigines of the State for his text. He had some talent for composition and was fond of illustrations drawn from ancient history.

In 1836, General Harrison was a candidate for the presidency in opposition to Van Buren. Though the strength of the Whig party which he represented, was somewhat divided, he received seventy-three electoral votes, a sufficient test of his popularity to bring him into the field again at the next election. The elements of opposition had in the meantime gained force; the country was suffering under an extraordinary financial depression; there was discontent on all sides. General Harrison received the nomination of twenty-two states at Harrisburg, and was triumphantly borne into the presidential chair. A peculiarity of the canvass was the popular good will, which eagerly seizing hold of the "log cabin" and "hard cider" as emblems of the simplicity of his early western life, turned them to political account. "Log cabins" were set up in villages and towns throughout the country, at which hard cider or its more comfortable equivalents were freely dispensed. Carried rapidly onward in the popular enthusiasm, he received the electoral vote of twenty of the twenty-six States, and two hundred and thirty-four electoral votes against only sixty given to Mr Van Buren.

The inauguration of President Harrison at Washington, took place on the 4th of March, 1841; on the same day of the following month he breathed his last. The active duties of his responsible station, the exacting pretensions of office seekers who beset a new president, the pressure of the previous canvass, may have all contributed to the severity of the shock which deprived him of life. He was sixty-eight years old, a time of life when any great change of habit may easily destroy the constitution; when a simple cause may shake a wearied frame. A slight cold which he took by exposure to the rain was followed by sudden prostration; a diarrhœa set in, and after an illness of but a few days he expired. His last words, heard by his physician, Dr. Worthington, were as if addressing his successor, "Sir, I wish you to understand the true principles of the government. I wish them carried out. I ask nothing more." In announcing the event to the public, the members of the Cabinet, of which Daniel Webster was at the head, wrote: "The people of the United States, overwhelmed like ourselves, by an event so unexpected and so melancholy, will derive consolation from knowing that his death was calm and resigned as his life had been patriotic, useful, and distinguished; and that the last utterance from his lips expressed a fervent desire for the perpetuity of the constitution and the preservation of its true principles. In death, as in life, the happiness of his country was uppermost in his thoughts."

The personal qualities of General Harrison had much to do with his elevation to the presidency. His life was marked by a union of moderation with good fortune and substantial success in public affairs. He was prosperous as a commander where others failed; he was identified with the growth and prosperity of a powerful region of the republic; he had made few enemies though he had been the subject of hostility, and he had been too long retired from public life to awaken any new prejudices. His military reputation, after the precedent of Jackson, was doubtless in his favor; but a belief in his good sense and his integrity, with the expectations of the times, in a change of policy, were the elements of his success.

JOHN TYLER.

THE family of John Tyler was of an old English stock, established in Virginia from the early days of the settlement. He is said, in fact, by one of his biographers, to be descended from that redoubtable Walter or Watt Tyler, the man of Kent who offered such brave resistance to the tax-gatherers of the second Richard, and who had for his associate the famous John Ball, a reverend itinerant, to whom is attributed the wholesome democratic inquiry

> When Adam delved and Eve span
> Who was then the gentleman?

Be all this, however, as it may, the grandfather of the President was a respectable landholder in the colony of Virginia, in the vicinity of Williamsburgh, enjoying the office of marshal in the ante-revolutionary period. His son, John Tyler, born in time to take part in the new era, was a member of the House of Delegates from Charles City County when Patrick Henry and his associates sounded the first notes of revolt. As the cause advanced he devoted his fortunes and energies to the patriotic work, and was rewarded by the suffrages of the people with the highest honors of the State. He rose to be speaker of the House of Delegates, Governor of the State, Judge of the United States District Court, and in his last days, in the period of the second war with England, was created by President Madison, Judge of the Federal Court of Admiralty. He died at the age of sixty-five. He was the intimate friend and correspondent of Patrick Henry, for whom he entertained an ardent admiration. No one was more esteemed or better thought of in the State.

This revolutionary patriot left three sons, the first of whom appears to have been called Watt, after the old Englishman of the people, the stout rebel of the fourteenth century. The second, destined to occupy the chair of the President of the United States, named after his father and grandfather, John, was born in Charles City County, March 29, 1790. The youth had the education and training of the son of a Virginia gentleman. At the age of twelve he entered the college of William and Mary, at Williamsburg, and enjoyed the particular friendship of the venerable Bishop Madison, who had then presided over the institution for a quarter of a century. He graduated with credit, his commencement address on "Female Education" gaining more than the usual plaudits of such occasions, and next occupied himself with the

John Tyler

study of the law, partly with his father the judge, partly with the eminent lawyer Edmund Randolph, who was at one time Governor of the State, and who was conspicuous in the affairs of the nation as a member of the old Congress, the Convention of the Constitution, and the cabinet of President Washington. At nineteen, we are told, he was permitted to practice at the bar, no question being made as to his age; and his success was decided. On arriving at twenty-one he was unanimously elected a member of the House of Delegates. It was at the season when the war with Great Britain, long imminent was on the eve of actual outbreak. The topic was an attractive one for many a nascent orator throughout the country, and was not neglected by the youthful Tyler. By education and tradition he belonged to the democratic party, and his voice was raised in favor of a vigorous prosecution of hostilities by the government. When the war had been entered upon and the British forces in Chesapeake Bay threatened an attack on Norfolk and Richmond, the young legislator turned his attention to the more active preparation for the field. He occupied himself in raising a company of militia in his county, whose services happily were not called for. This slight flavor of warfare in comparison with the important military deeds of many of the occupants of the Presidential chair, gave him the familiar title, during his canvass for the Presidency, of Captain Tyler; a title by which he is yet occasionally named.

We must not, however, anticipate this portion of his career. He continued for five years a member of the House of Delegates in Virginia, in the last of which he was raised to a seat in the executive council. He had hardly, however, entered upon this new honor when another awaited him, at the close of 1816, in his election to the House of Representatives, to fill a vacancy caused by the death of the incumbent. His rival in the canvass was a gentleman, Mr. Andrew Stevenson, afterward distinguished at Washington, whom he defeated by a majority of some thirty votes. At the next regular election his triumph over the same candidate was more decided. In his course in the House he pursued generally the career, so plainly marked out under the rigid party discipline in that State, of a state-rights or strict constructional Virginia politician. He was opposed to internal improvements, and to that great evil in the eyes of all thoroughly-trained democrats, a national bank. He opposed Mr. Clay in his attempt to gain the recognition of the independence of the South American Republics, but was with him in the censure of General Jackson's assumptions of responsibility in the Seminole wars. A third time elected to Congress, he voted in 1820 for the unrestricted admission of Missouri into the Union. Before his new term of office had expired he was compelled to seek retirement in consequence of ill health. He returned to his farm in Charles City County, and continued the practice of his profession.

According to a custom which does honor to American politics, he thought it no indignity after occupying a seat in the national councils, to return again to the humbler duties, with which he had commenced life, of service in the legislature of his state. He was for three years, from 1823 in the House of Delegates, applying his best efforts to the welfare of Virginia. It is an example which might be more generally imitated. Our state legislatures embrace a variety of interests unknown to the national representatives at Washington, and the maturity of years and experience might be brought to them with effect. Mr. Tyler in this capacity applied his efforts to the improvement of Virginia, and many of the finest roads in the state, it is said, are due to his exertions.

In 1825 he was chosen Governor of the State, and in the following year was taken from that office to succeed John Randolph in the Senate of the United States. It was the third year of the administration of John Quincy Adams when he took his seat and he at once engaged on the side of the opposition, that is in support of the inevitable nomination of General Jackson as the succeeding President. In the late election he had been in favor of the Southern candidate, Mr. Crawford, and on the decision being carried into the House, had cheerfully acquiesced in Mr. Clay's casting vote for Mr. Adams. The latter soon lost ground and every means was taken for his defeat.

When General Jackson was elected, Mr. Tyler was one of his supporters in the Senate, at least on such questions as his rejection of internal improvements and veto of the Bank. He opposed a tariff for protection. On one important measure, however, he was in opposition to the President. He took part with the South Carolinians in their nullification doctrines, and spoke against the Force Bill introduced into the Senate to aid General Jackson in their overthrow. When Mr. Clay introduced his compromise bill, modifying the obnoxious tariff, Mr. Tyler gave it his support.

On the close of his term in 1833, he was again elected to the Senate. It was the beginning of that second term of Jackson's administration memorable in the annals of the country for the accomplishment of his warfare against that political giant, the Bank of the United States. To these measures Mr. Tyler in conjunction with Mr. Calhoun and other members of his party stood opposed. He voted in favor of Mr. Clay's resolutions of censure, standing on his old Virginia ground as a strict constructionist, hostile to all undue assumptions of power on the part of the Executive. He did this at the time no less in accordance with his own feelings than with the views of the Virginia legislature which had elected him. Time passed on, and the President, gaining ground throughout the country and in the Senate, the pertinacious resolution of Mr. Benton to expunge the obnoxious resolution was pressed to a final issue. Mr. Tyler now received instructions to vote for it. What should he do? The right of instruction and the duty of the Representative to obey it had always been a maxim of his political creed, which it so happened that he had on more than one occasion in his career, brought conspicuously before the public. Could he now disavow his cherished convictions? One choice was left him—to resign, and he cheerfully met the issue, resigning his seat in the Senate rather than take part in the mutilation of the sacred record. In his letter of resignation to the Legislature of Virginia he wrote: "I dare not touch the Journal of the Senate. The Constitution forbids it. In the midst of all the agitations of party, I have heretofore stood by that sacred instrument. It is the only post of honor and of safety. A seat in the Senate is sufficiently elevated to fill the measure of any man's ambition; and as an evidence of the sincerity of my convictions that your resolutions cannot be executed, without violating my oath, I surrender into your hands three unexpired years of my term. I shall carry with me into retirement the principles which I brought with me into public life, and by the surrender of the high station to which I was called by the voice of the people of Virginia, I shall set an example to my children which shall teach them to regard as nothing, place and office, when to be either obtained or held at the sacrifice of honor." In the excited state of the political world at the time, when the attention of the whole community was fastened upon the scene in the Senate, such an act could not escape notice. It met with the general plaudits of the country.

Mr. Tyler now became a resident at Williamsburg, the early residence of his father, and passed his time in comparative retirement. In the presidential canvass of 1836 he was placed on the ticket for Vice President in several of the states, receiving forty-seven votes in all. His support was derived from the Southern State Rights Party in opposition to Jackson and Van Buren. Two years later, in 1838, we find him once more seated in the Virginia House of Delegates "acting with the Whig Party, under which name the different sections of the opposition to Mr. Van Buren's administration gradually became amalgamated in Virginia." This connexion introduced him to the Whig nominating convention of 1839, which sat at Harrisburg where he made his appearance as a friend of Henry Clay. Upon the vote being taken in favor of General Harrison, Mr. Tyler was adopted on the ticket as Vice President. In the election which ensued he was chosen by the same overwhelming vote with the President.

The fourth of March, 1841, saw the inauguration of President Harrison at Washington, and barely one month after, Vice President Tyler was himself summoned from his home at Williamsburg to enter upon the duties of that high office. It was the first time death had seized an occupant of the presidential chair. President Harrison died on the fourth of April, at Washington. Congress was not in session. The officers of the cabinet, of whom Daniel Webster was at the head, took charge of the government for the moment, immediately sending a special messenger with an announcement to Vice President Tyler of the melancholy fact. On the morning of the second day, the sixth of April, Mr. Tyler arrived in Washington, and the same day, before Judge Cranch, of the District of Columbia, took the oath, " faithfully to execute the office of President of the United States, and to the best of his ability, preserve, protect and defend the Constitution of the United States." He did not think it necessary to make this oath after that which he had taken on entering upon his duties as Vice President but as a measure of prudence and "for greater caution as doubts may arise." On receiving the members of the cabinet he expressed his wish that they should remain in office. The funeral of the late president took place on the seventh and was attended by President Tyler.

There was no public ceremonial of an inauguration on his taking the oath before Justice Cranch and consequently no public address, but two days after the funeral, on the ninth of April, an "inaugural address" was issued by the President which was read with much interest. It was expected to solve the question which began to be much agitated of the degree of conformity of the views of the new incumbent to the Whig principles of his predecessor. He had, as we have seen, been led on various occasions to coöperate with the Whig party, but many of his antecedents were directly hostile to their views. His name had been placed on the ticket in the Southern interest and as a friend of Mr. Clay, without any distinct pledges on his part to serve the doctrines of the party. In fact the probability of his being placed in the authoritative position of President had not been very seriously if at all entertained, by the convention which, somewhat hastily, put him in nomination. The address, however, was upon the whole, acceptable to the Whigs; it certainly

gave little satisfaction to the opposite party which saw in it a lurking condemnation of the "assumptions" of President Jackson, and an inclination at least, toward a national bank.[1]

A few days after this address President Tyler issued "a recommendation" to the people of the United States, of a day of fasting and prayer, in recognition of the solemn bereavement in the death of the late president.

An extra session of Congress had been already summoned by President Harrison, to meet the last day of May. It sat from that date till September. As its main object was to take into consideration the financial condition of the country, and, if possible, provide ways and means for its relief, the question of the creation of a new United State Bank became a paramount subject of discussion. The President was apparently in favor of such an institution In his message he reviewed the previous course of legislation in this matter, and admitted the last substitute, the subtreasury, to be condemned by the people. "To you, then," he concluded, addressing Congress, "who have come more directly from the body of our common constituents, I submit the entire question, as best qualified to give a full exposition of their wishes and opinions. I shall be ready to concur with you in the adoption of such system as you may propose, reserving to myself the ultimate power of rejecting any measure which may, in my view of it, conflict with the Constitution, or otherwise jeopard the prosperity of the country—

---

[1] Benton's Thirty Years' View, II., 212.

a power which I could not part with if I would, but which I will not believe any act of yours will call into requisition." This sentence foreshadowed the result. Two bills were prepared according to plans more or less adapted to the views of the President, and both, when they had been passed after much discussion in Congress, were vetoed by him. For the plans and devices, the learned political doubts and constitutional arguments on either side we must refer the reader to the debates in Congress and the messages of President Tyler himself. On the side of the Whigs throughout the country there sprung up a great disaffection in consequence, toward the President whom they had created. On the other hand, the Democratic party thanked their unexpected assistant with moderated enthusiasm. It was thought to be the last effort in Congress to establish a National Bank. Other measures of relief, however, were passed at this extra session including the bankrupt act and a national loan.

The defection of President Tyler, as it was considered, from the Whig party caused the resignation of most of the members of his cabinet. Daniel Webster, however, remained in the office of Secretary of State to complete the important negotiation with England in reference to the disputed North Eastern Boundary. This treaty, one of the most important acts of President Tyler's administration, was negotiated between Lord Ashburton who was sent a special minister from England for the purpose, and Mr. Webster as Secretary of State in 1842. Mr. Webster held his office

in the cabinet till May of the following year. His successor was Mr. Abel P Upshur of Virginia, who perished while in office, in February, 1844. by the fatal explosion on board the Princeton, on the Potomac. Mr. Calhoun was afterwards appointed Secretary of State, and in 1844 negotiated a treaty of annexation between the United States and the Republic of Texas, which was rejected by the Senate. In the following year the annexation, which had been recommended by the President, and became a test question with politicians through the country, passed both houses. This was among the last acts of President Tyler's administration. His successor, Mr. Polk, had already been chosen, and a few months after, on the fourth of March, 1845, entered upon the duties of his office. Mr. Tyler then retired to his seat in Virginia, carrying with him to grace his home a lady of New York, a daughter of the late Mr. David Gardner, whom he had married during his Presidency, in 1844. He had been previously married in 1813 to a lady of Virginia, Miss Letitia Christian, who died at Washington, leaving three sons and three daughters. One of the sons, Mr. Robert Tyler, attracted some attention in the literary world as the author of a poem entitled Ahasuerus. After his retirement from the Presidency Mr. Tyler passed his time in honorable leisure, appearing on one or two occasions to deliver public addresses on anniversary and other meetings of historical or other general interest. His first production of this kind was an address which should have been mentioned in the order of our narrative, delivered in July, 1826, at the capitol square in Richmond, in memory of his own and father's friend, the illustrious Jefferson.

The agitation arising out of the Presidential election of 1860 brought Mr. Tyler again before the public. When the success of the Republican party in the election of Mr. Lincoln was followed by threats and active measures of disunion on the part of the South, he was sent by the legislature of Virginia to Washington, a member of the notable Peace Convention of delegates from the northern and border States, a measure originally proposed in Virginia with the view of warding off impending hostilities between the two portions of the country by some adjustment or compromise of the questions in dispute. The convention met at Washington on the 4th of February, 1861, and Mr. Tyler was chosen its President. In an opening address he declared the object of the assembly "to snatch from ruin a great and glorious confederation, to preserve the government, and to renew and invigorate the Constitution." In the course of his remarks he observed that "our ancestors probably committed a blunder in not having fixed upon every fifth decade for a call of a general convention to amend and reform the Constitution." The convention, in which twenty-one States were represented, debated for three weeks various propositions, and finally determined upon the recommendation of a plan, extending the line of the Missouri Compromise to the Pacific, and proposing additional securities for the "peculiar institution" by limitation of the legislation of Congress, and other measures. The whole was submitted to the consideration of the national Congress then in session, and the convention adjourned.

Congress was not disposed to accept this and the like palliatives of the national difficulties which were proposed in that body. The crisis rapidly approached. The acts of secession of the Southern States were followed by the attack on Sumter. Virginia, no longer neutral, cast in her lot with the Confederacy, and Mr. Tyler followed the fortunes of his State, and became an active Secessionist. He was chosen a senator in the Confederate Congress, and held this position at the time of his death, which occurred suddenly at Richmond, January 18, 1862.

JAMES KNOX POLK.

The eleventh President of the United States was born in Mecklenburg county, North Carolina, in the vicinity of the county town of Charlotte, November 2, 1795. He was of Scoto-Irish descent, the name being said to have been originally Pollock in Scotland. Robert Polk, the first American ancestor of the family, emigrated from Ireland about the middle of the eighteenth century. He came to Maryland, and was temporarily established, with his children, on the eastern shore; thence his sons removed first to the interior of Pennsylvania, and afterward to the more permanent settlement in North Carolina. In this frontier district, in the western part of the State, bordering on South Carolina, in the region bounded by the parallel streams of the Yadkin and the Catawba, the three sons of Thomas Polk, Thomas, Ezekiel and Charles, found a home, in the midst of a sturdy, independent population, who carried the virtues of order, sobriety, and secular and religious education to the borders of what was then the Indian wilderness. Two of these brothers, Thomas and Ezekiel, became distinguished in the early annals of the Revolution, in those measures of protest and resistance which placed North Carolina in the foremost rank of State patriotism. Thomas Polk was put forward as the leader of these independent mountaineers. He was colonel of the militia, and had been a surveyor and member of the colonial assembly. It was at his call that a convention of the citizens of the region, delegates of the militia districts, assembled at Charlotte on the 19th of May, 1775, to deliberate on the crisis at hand. While they were assembled, it is said, news was brought by a post rider of the bloody day at Lexington. The meeting was stimulated to action, and expressed its resolve in the famous Mecklenburgh Declaration of Independence, which curiously anticipated, in its spirit and even a portion of its language, the words of the great national instrument from the pen of Jefferson. Thomas Polk was a master-spirit in these transactions.

His nephew Samuel, son of Ezekiel, was the father of the future President. He was a farmer "of unassuming pretensions, but of enterprising character." His wife, who gave her family name to her son, was the daughter of James Knox, who became captain in the military service of the Revolution. In 1806, when their son James was about eleven years old, the family, tempted by the accounts of western lands, removed across the mountains into the adjoining state of Tennessee, and settled on the banks of Duck river. In this region, the boyhood of the future President was passed in the hardy pursuits of a farmer's life, spent in subduing the land to the purposes of cultivation. His health, however, was not robust, and his father, thinking perhaps that less demand would be made upon his physical powers, procured him employment at first with a store-keeper. The occupation was not to the youth's taste; he was of a reflective turn, fond of reading, and his mind had been led to study by witnessing his father's occupations as a surveyor. He desired to leave merchandize—his wish was granted—and at the age of eighteen, he applied himself regularly to study, at first under the care of the Rev. Dr. Henderson, and afterward at the academy of Murfreesborough in the State, in charge of Mr. Samuel P. Black, a man of valuable classical acquirements. With these advantages and diligent application, the pupil in 1815 entered the Sophomore Class of the University of North Carolina, at Chapel Hill.

He distinguished himself in his college course by his punctual, earnest application and proficiency in his studies. He became the foremost scholar both in mathematics, for which he had a natural liking, and in the classics. He graduated in 1818 with the highest honors, delivering the Latin salutatory oration. He was then twenty-three, some two or three years older than the great majority of the crowd who are sent out annually as bachelors of arts;

but the later preparation was doubtless an advantage to him in the greater maturity of his powers. Our college studies, in fact, would be far better pursued by older students, more thoroughly grounded in the introductory apprenticeship to learning. The work of education, if accomplished at all, is in most cases, we are persuaded, to be begun over again by the pupil himself after the so called university course is ended. Mr. Polk carried his duties with him into active life; they were always self-imposed, and were with him a living reality.

After taking his degree, though ill health pleaded for a relaxation from his diligent application to books, we find him soon commencing the study of the law with Felix Grundy, the eminent legal pioneer of the west, then established in the fullness of his professional career at Nashville, with the additional eclat of successful statesmanship at Washington, as a member of the committee of Foreign Relations in the war administration of Madison. Association with such a preceptor, a man of vigorous mind, who had achieved distinction by the force of his own character, must doubtless have exercised a leading influence upon a young man who had already given proof of his triumph over ordinarily adverse fortunes. Pursuing his legal studies for two years, he was in 1820 admitted to the bar, and returned from Nashville to pursue the profession in the region of his home at Columbia. His success, based upon his thorough acquisitions and the influence of his family associations, for there were numerous emigrants of his stock to the district, was so rapid that in less than a year he was acknowledged as a leading practitioner. He had already acquired fame and profit at the bar, when, in 1823, he had his first introduction to political life, or rather office, as a member from his county of Maury in the State legislature. A lawyer in the west at that time, and the remark may be applied more or less to the present day, was of necessity something of a politician, and we hear of Mr. Polk assisting the traditionary tendencies and conduct of his family by his earnest advocacy of the democratic policy. He was often called upon to address political gatherings, and acquitted himself, we are told, with credit and favor by a plain use of argument, without resort to the tawdry and meretricious ornaments in which popular speakers so often feel themselves called upon to indulge. The success, in fact, of his life was due to quite other qualities—to his simple, sincere, straightforward character, and the confidence those who knew him derived from his manners and conduct.

Mr. Polk remained two years in the Tennessee legislature, in the course of which he had the opportunity of rendering important service to his early friend, Andrew Jackson, in his election to the senate of the United States. Mr. Polk, at this time, was married to the daughter of Joel Childress, a merchant of Tennessee, a lady whose virtues and graces, in public and private life, in the prominent social theatre at Washington, are gratefully held in esteem by the nation. In 1825, Mr. Polk was elected a member of congress, took his seat in December, and was continued a member of that body for fourteen years. No one during this period was more completely identified with its proceedings. It embraced the vigorous period of his life, from thirty to forty-four. He appeared on the floor of the House of Representatives, the representative, in all their integrity and severity, of the creed of strict construction which had grown out of the doctrines of the old Republican Jeffersonian party. He was opposed to the recharter of the Bank of the United States, to a protective tariff, to wasteful expenditures in internal improvements; he advocated economy in the government. In all questions arising from the discussions, he was a zealous, persistent supporter of his party. In 1827, he was placed on the committee of foreign affairs; and during the administration of General Jackson, as head of the committee of ways and means, rendered the President the most important assistance in his vigorously conducted war against the United States Bank. His other more prominent position in the House was as speaker, to which he was elected at the opening of the session in 1835, and again at the session of 1837, with the conclusion of which he retired from congress, declining a reëlection.

The four years, during which he presided over the deliberations of the House, were marked by strong political excitement, and the duties of the office had grown, with the increase of congress, to be of a more arduous character. Through all discussions, however,

Mr. Polk pursued his steady, calm, inflexible course, always present, the most punctual man in the House, tasking his powers, it seemed to the stranger looking on the excited scene, beyond his strength, educing order out of chaos, dividing the knotty questions of debate with the skill and impartiality of an acute mind well practised in parliamentary logic. The importance of the position has been more than once shown, since Mr. Polk's discharge of the office, in the protracted struggles at the commencement of new sessions of the House in the equal division of parties. It must always be regarded as a most distinguishing honor for any man, and the ability and energy of Mr. Polk will be honorably remembered in its annals.

That Mr. Polk himself held a no less high sense of the dignity of his position may be gathered from the language in which he took leave of the House on the adjournment of that body in 1839. His brief review of his duties presents an extraordinary picture of duty faithfully performed and as honorably appreciated. "When I look back to the period," was his language, "when I first took my seat in this House, and then look around me for those who were at that time my associates here, I find but few, very few, remaining. But five members who were here with me fourteen years ago, continue to be members of this body. My service here has been constant and laborious. I can perhaps say what but what few others, if any, can, that I have not failed to attend the daily sittings of this House a single day since I have been a member of it, save on a single occasion, when prevented for a short time by indisposition. In my intercourse with the members of this body, when I occupied a place upon the floor, though occasionally engaged in debates upon interesting public questions and of an exciting character, it is a source of unmingled gratification to me to recur to the fact, that on no occasion was there the slightest personal or unpleasant collision with any of its members. Maintaining, and at all times expressing, my own opinions firmly, the same right was fully conceded to others. For four years past, the station I have occupied, and a sense of propriety, in the divided and unusually exciting state of public opinion and feeling, which has existed both in this House and the country, have precluded me from participating in your debates. Other duties were assigned me.

"The high office of Speaker, to which it has been twice the pleasure of the House to elevate me, has been at all times one of labor and high responsibility. It has been made my duty to decide more questions of parliamentary law and order, many of them of a complex and difficult character, arising often in the midst of high excitement, in the course of our proceedings, than had been decided, it is believed, by all my predecessors, from the foundation of the government. This House has uniformly sustained me, without distinction of the political parties of which it has been composed. I return them my thanks for their constant support in the discharge of the duties I have had to perform. . . . I trust this high office may in future times be filled, as doubtless it will be, by abler men. It cannot, I know, be filled by any one who will devote himself with more zeal and untiring industry to do his whole duty, than I have done."

Mr. Polk had hardly reached his home in Tennessee after his retirement from Congress, when he engaged in a diligent canvassing of the State as a candidate for governor at the approaching election. He was untiring in his devotion to his object, and so successful was his energy, that he gained the election over his opponent, the incumbent of the office. His inaugural address, delivered at Nashville in October, 1839, a remarkably clear and well-written composition, reviewed the leading distinctive principles of his party—the strict interpretation of the Constitution, in reference to express and implied powers; the unconstitutionality and dangers of a national bank; the evil of a surplus Federal revenue; the inviolability of slavery by Congress in the slave-holding States, and other well known positions. In his own State he encouraged and assisted a "well regulated system of internal improvement." His administration was generally well received; but when the time came for reëlection, he shared the fortunes of his party and suffered a defeat. It was the moment of the popular whig triumph of General Harrison; two years later his rival, Governor James C. Jones, was again successful in the contest.

The next turn of the political wheel carried ex-Governor Polk to the Presidency. A decided letter, written by him in favor of the annexation of Texas, brought him favorably before the Baltimore Convention of May, 1844, when that nominating body had exhausted the roll of prior candidates. On the ninth ballot, after Van Buren, Cass and others had been set aside, he received the requisite two-thirds vote and became the candidate of the party. In accepting the nomination, he avowed his intention, in the event of his election, not to be a candidate for a second term. The contest between the two tickets, Polk and Dallas, Clay and Frelinghuysen, resulted in the electoral college in a majority for the former ticket of sixty-five. Fifteen States voted for Polk; eleven, and among them Tennessee, by a small majority, for Clay. The successful candidate was duly inaugurated at Washington in March, 1845.

The leading measures, or rather the chief events, of Polk's administration of the Presidency were the adjustment of the Oregon question with England, and the War with Mexico. In the former he took ground in his inaugural and annual message, in accordance with the resolutions of the Baltimore nominating convention, in favor of the claim to the whole of the territory, a position which, while maintaining his view of the matter, he in a measure yielded to the will of the Senate in their acceptance of the terms of the British government. The treaty was signed in June, 1846. A month before this, Congress officially recognized, by its declaration, the existence of war with Mexico. Of the events of that war, of which President Polk must be considered the influential agent, it is not necessary here to speak in detail. Its progress was, upon the whole, so honorable to the arms of the country, as victory after victory was chronicled in the movements of the great campaigns of Taylor and Scott, and the conduct of the war, at its termination, was so moderate in imposing the conditions of peace at an early moment, that much of the opposition to its commencement was happily neutralized. The immediate settlement of California, and its brilliant progress in civilization, under the stimulus of the gold discovery, have also thrown a halo over the war. Its ulterior effects are yet to be read in history; but, whatever be the result, the date of the acquisition of so wide a region of territory bordering upon the great ocean of the West, and so rounding the world to the fabled regions of the East, and its influence upon the welfare of countless numbers of the human race, will always mark the period of the administration of President Polk. Of the unexpected results of the war, probably the least looked for was the development of one of its least known officers at the outset, into his successor in the presidential chair. President Polk, having accompanied General Taylor to the inaugural ceremonies at the capitol on the fifth of March, 1849, retired to his home at Nashville, taking Charleston and New Orleans by the way. He made the journey in safety, though an attack of diarrhœa, in his ascent of the Mississippi, and the inevitable fatigue of travel, probably somewhat enfeebled his powers. He reached home to occupy the mansion and grounds in the heart of the city, formerly occupied by Senator Grundy, of which he had become the purchaser; but he was not destined to enjoy them long. An attack of the chronic diarrhœa to which he was subject proved unmanageable by his physicians, and after a few days' illness his powers of life were exhausted. His death took place on the fifteenth of June, 1849, in his fifty-fourth year, little more than three months after his retirement from the Presidency.

In person Mr. Polk was spare, of the middle height, with a bright, expressive eye, and ample, angular forehead. Of his personal character we may cite the words of his biographer: "He was simple and plain in all his habits. His private life was upright and blameless. Honesty and integrity characterized his intercourse with his fellow men; fidelity and affection his relations to his family. In his friendships he was frank and sincere; and courteous and affable in his disposition. He was generous and benevolent; but his charities, like his character, were unostentatious. He was pious, too, sincerely; his wife was a member of the Presbyterian church, but he never united with any denomination, though on his dying bed he received the rite of baptism at the hands of a Methodist clergyman, an old neighbor and friend."[1]

____

[1] The Life of James Knox Polk, by John S. Jenkins.

Zachary Taylor

ZACHARY TAYLOR.

Of the modern heroes of America, few stand out so simply and distinctly, so "clear in their great office," as General Zachary Taylor. His character was of remarkable purity, distinguished by equal worth and modesty. When he suddenly became celebrated in the Mexican war, it was found that, though unknown to fame, he had deserved reputation by his gallant conduct in 1812, and subsequently in Florida. He was known and respected in the army; but there had been no blazon of his deeds in the newspapers. He was content with the performance of his duty. This was a motto and reward all sufficient to his mind. The type of character which distinguishes him is that of the elder worthies of the Revolution, the Schuylers, Moultries and Pinckneys.

Zachary Taylor was born in Orange county, Virginia, November 24, 1784, of a family, English in its origin, which had long been settled in the colony. His father, a man of a brave, adventurous turn, familiarly known among his brother pioneers as Captain Dick Taylor, emigrated when the child was not a year old, to the western part of the State, what was then known as "the dark and bloody ground" of Indian strife—the present Kentucky. There

the boy had his training in the rude, hearty, independent pursuits of frontier life. We hear something of his schoolmaster, the approved migratory New England pedagogue, who, when his pupil became celebrated, remembered him as "a very active and sensible boy." Of his good sense we have no doubt, for it was a quality which marked him through life; while, of his activity, there is a story related of his younger days, of his swimming across the Ohio, from the Kentucky to the Indiana shore, stemming a freezing flood in March.

His entry in the army dates from that memorable period of the attack of the Shannon upon the Chesapeake, the fountain of many woes and glories in the national annals. His father, who was something of a politician, procured him the appointment from Jefferson's administration in 1808 of lieutenant in the Seventh United States infantry. He thus commenced his career in the regular service. Two years later the young man is married to Miss Margaret Smith of Maryland. Immediately upon the declaration of war with England in 1812, we find him engaged under General Harrison in the protection of the northwestern territory against the attacks of the Indians. His defence, in that year, of Fort Harrison, on the Wabash, in the territory of Indiana, against an attack of the Miamis, is one of the memorable incidents of the war. This fort, built by the general whose name it bears, was situated on the upper part of the river, above the present town of Terre Haute. It was defended by pickets on three sides, with a row of barracks and a block-house at either end on the fourth. Captain Taylor was left in charge of the work with a small company of men, in the words of his dispatch to General Harrison, "not more than ten or fifteen able to do a great deal, the others being either sick or convalescent." He had warning of the threatened approach of a party of the Prophet's men—the attack belonging to that series of movements instigated by Tecumseh and his brother—and though for some time he had not considered the post tenable against a large force, he prepared to defend it to the best of his ability. On the third of September, two young men, making hay in the neighborhood of the fort, were picked off by the Indians, and the next night they came in numbers to the assault. They began by firing one of the block-houses, which endangered the whole line of barracks. Captain Taylor, almost disabled from a severe fever, rallied his little force of invalids to extinguish it, but the fire having communicated to a stock of whisky in the building, soon ascended to the roof, and his efforts had to be directed to the adjoining houses. The situation was desperate. In his own simple words, "Sir, what from the raging of the fire, the yelling and howling of several hundred Indians, the cries of nine women and children, part soldiers' and part citizens' wives, who had taken refuge in the fort, and the desponding of so many men, which was worse than all, I can assure you that my feelings were unpleasant." But, by his own energy, and the assistance of Surgeon Clark, the only one to aid him in the command, the roof was stripped from the next building and water from the well applied to the exposed portions. The line was saved, and the open space of the fire defended by a temporary breastwork. All this was done under the enemy's fire of bullets and arrows, lasting for seven hours, the flames lighting up the men at work as marks for the hostile missiles. When daylight came the fire was returned with effect, and the Indians took their departure, slaughtering the horses in the vicinity, and driving off a large stock of cattle; what with this and the stores lost in the conflagration, leaving the garrison to a diet of green corn. For this spirited defence, President Madison conferred upon Taylor the brevet rank of major.

On the reorganization of the army after the peace, it was proposed to deprive him of this rank, which he resented, and would have retired to an agricultural life had not the government, by yielding, retained him in the army. He was employed in the Indian service in various ways, and in the Black Hawk war of 1832 appears in the field, taking an active part as colonel in the concluding battle of the Bad Axe river. His next scene of operations was the Florida war, a field of greater difficulty than glory. He was ordered to this service in 1836, and in December of the following year led an expedition of about a thousand men, a few volunteers and the rest regulars, from Fort Gardiner toward Lake Okechobee, in the immediate neighborhood of which the enemy, some seven hundred strong, were encamped in a hammock. As the place was approached, it was found to be protected in front by a swamp three quarters of a mile in breadth. It was "totally impassable for horses, and nearly so for foot, covered with a thick growth of saw-grass five feet high, and about knee deep in mud and water." This was to be crossed to get within range of the foe, who fought from behind trees with every advantage of position. In the arrangement of the attack, the volunteers were sent forward with directions to fall back, if necessary, while the regulars would sustain them. They advanced, were fired upon, their commander Colonel Gentry of Missouri slain, when they retreated. The regulars then made their way through the high, stiff grass, suffering heavy losses; the place of the fallen was succeeded by others, and the enemy finally driven to the lake in confusion. The action lasted from half-past twelve till three P.M. It was one of the important victories of the war, it being exceedingly difficult to get the Indians to stand in battle in any numbers. Here nothing but the most tried valor could prevail against them. Colonel Taylor's loss was very heavy, both in officers, as was usual in this war, and in men. In his

dispatch, he stops to express his feeling for the wounded. "Here," says he, "I trust I may be permitted to say that I experienced one of the most trying scenes of my life, and he who could have looked on it with indifference, his nerves must have been differently organized from my own."

His management of this affair and general efficiency in the campaign were rewarded with the brevet rank of brigadier-general, and shortly after with the chief command in the State, which he held till the arrival of General Macomb. General Taylor's plan was to divide the whole region into a series of military districts, each presided over by a fort or stockade, whence the troops might take the aggressive on occasion. He was employed in Florida two years later till 1840, when he was assigned to the command of the southwestern division of the army, and had his head quarters at Fort Jesup, Louisiana. This brought him within the line of employment in Texas, when, on the annexation of that country to the United States, it became necessary to protect her western frontier from Mexican invasion. He was consequently ordered to the district in June, 1845, and immediately established his headquarters at Corpus Christi, on the west bank of the Nueces, at its mouth. There the "army of observation" gradually augmented, with the progress of war alarms, to a force of nearly four thousand men, the "army of occupation," remained many months, till March of the following year, when its commander received directions to advance to the ultimate boundary, the Rio Grande. The march of seventeen days was made across the intervening desert, meeting with no opposition of consequence up to the time of arrival at the point of the river opposite Mata-moras, on the twenty-eighth of the month. A flag-staff was immediately erected on the spot, and the American ensign raised, as the bands played the national airs "Yankee Doodle" and "The Star-spangled Banner." This vicinity was destined to be the scene of several formidable conflicts. We shall not trench upon the province of history to pursue the movements here with any great minuteness; but shall touch lightly upon the main incidents of the campaign, which leads us over the battlefields of Palo Alto, Resaca de la Palma, to the storming of Monterey and the great struggle at Buena Vista.

The place at which the army first rested was within sight of the enemy's headquarters at Matamoras, separated only by the intervening river. There having taken his station, and, as he told the Mexican authorities, in accordance with the instructions of his government, being determined to remain, the first employment of General Taylor, of course, was to provide some adequate defences—the more as he was in face of a considerable body of the foe, to whom large reinforcements, commanded by experienced generals, were already on the way, and war was no longer a matter of uncertainty. A camp was established, and the extensive work, Fort Brown, on the bank of the river, commanding the opposite town, commenced. Point Isabel, a day's march distant in the rear, on the coast, the first harbor to the north of the Rio

Grande, was the depot for supplies General Taylor in his advance had taken possession of this place, and left a small garrison for its protection. On the twelfth of April, General Ampudia, having arrived at Matamoras with reinforcements, and taken the command, addressed a communication to General Taylor, requiring him within twenty-four hours to retire to the Nueces while the Texas question was under discussion between the two governments, or accept the alternative of a resort to arms. To this the American commander replied, that he had been ordered to occupy the country to the left bank of the Rio Grande till the boundary should be definitely settled; that in discharging this duty, he had carefully abstained from all acts of hostility, and that the instructions under which he was acting would not permit him to retrograde from the position he occupied; and as for war, while he regretted the alternative, he should not avoid it, but "leave the responsibility with those who rashly commence hostilities."

After this the military proceedings thickened apace. The right bank of the river, above and below the camp, swarmed with the irregular troops of the enemy. Colonel Trueman Cross, assistant quartermaster-general, already, on the tenth, had been murdered, as he was taking his usual ride in the neighborhood of the camp. On the twenty-fourth a communication came from General Arista, who had succeeded Ampudia in the command, conveying a further declaration of hostilities; and simultaneously word reached the camp of the crossing of the enemy in considerable numbers. Captain Thornton, sent above to reconnoitre, was surprised in a plantation inclosure, and his little force captured. Below, Point Isabel was in danger of being cut off, an obvious movement of the enemy, which required all the vigilance of General Taylor to counteract. Leaving, accordingly, a sufficient garrison for the defence of Fort Brown, he set out, on the first of May, with the main body of his troops, for the relief of that important station. He arrived at the place without interruption, accomplished his purpose in adding to its strength, and, on the seventh, invited by the signal guns of Fort Brown, which was suffering a bombardment, began his return, with about twenty-two hundred men, bringing with him two eighteen-pounders, in addition to the artillery he had taken with him, and a large train of wagons. About noon on the following day, the Mexican troops were reported in front, and were soon found occupying the road, on an open prairie skirted by a growth of chaparral.

This was the field of Palo Alto, so named from the thickets rising above the general level. The Mexicans, six thousand in number, commanded by General Arista, were drawn up in a single line, " artillery, infantry and cavalry placed alternately, forming a living wall more than a mile in extent, of physical strength, of steel and latent fire." [1] The American force was disposed by General Taylor with less regularity, but mostly in a parallel outline. The right wing, comprising the

larger part of the force, including Ringgold's artillery and the eighteen-pounders, was under the orders of Colonel Twiggs; the left was commanded by Lieutenant-Colonel Belknap. The train was protected by a squadron of dragoons in the rear. Having made these arrangements, General Taylor coolly directed the men to stack their arms, march in companies, and supply themselves with the fresh water of the adjoining ponds in place of the brackish water with which they had been furnished at Point Isabel. The columns then advanced, when the engagement was commenced, shortly after two in the afternoon, by the Mexican batteries. This fire was promptly met by the whole American artillery, the eighteen-pounders, drawn up in the road, and Ringgold's pieces doing eminent execution. An important movement of the enemy's cavalry, fifteen hundred strong, led by General Torrejon, on the right, threatening the flank, was defeated by the fifth infantry, the flying artillery and Captain Walker's Texan volunteers. While this was proceeding, the dry grass of the prairie took fire and swept a volume of smoke over the field, partially concealing the armies from one another. Under cover of this obscuration, the line of the enemy, which had suffered from the artillery, was reformed in the rear of its first position, and the American correspondingly advanced. After a pause of about an hour, the fire was reopened, the action being confined chiefly to the artillery on both sides. The superiority of the American fire was undoubted; but it was dearly purchased,

---

[1] Thorpe's " Our Army on the Rio Grande," p. 74.

by the loss of the gallant Major Ringgold, whose name is identified with this effective arm of the service. The day closed with a brilliant attack from the enemy's right, which was met with great spirit by Captain Duncan's artillery In the darkness of the evening the enemy retired to a new position, and the wearied Americans slept on their battle-field, their general spreading his blanket on the grass in the midst of the troops. The loss of the Mexicans was much heavier than that of our own forces; the commander of the former reporting two hundred and fifty-two killed, wounded and missing, while General Taylor's dispatch numbers only seven killed, including three officers, and thirty-nine wounded—an apparently small number of either army, considering the strength on both sides of the artillery and the skill with which it was served on a level plain.

The next day brought the battle of Resaca de la Palma. Early in the morning the enemy had retired toward Matamoras, to a strong position at a ravine, crossed by the road and surrounded by a thick growth of chaparral. The approach on the highway was defended by a strongly posted force of artillery. Thither the foe were pursued by General Taylor, who, spite of the superiority of numbers confronting him, expressed his determination to be at Fort Brown before night. Having provided for the safety of the supply-train, he commenced the attack about three in the afternoon, by advancing a large body of skirmishers and the battery of Lieutenant Ridgely. The latter took up a position on the road. Owing to the nature of the ground, the engagement which ensued was of an entirely different character from that of the preceding day. The enemy were sheltered by the ravine on both its sides. The growth in front, beside the protection of the rising ground, impeded the free play of the American artillery. As the enemy's cannon commanded the only accessible approach by the road, it became evident to General Taylor, after sending forward his infantry, that however the latter might discharge their duty—and they did make, in his own language, "resistless progress"—nothing decisive could be accomplished till that fire was silenced. He consequently sent to the rear for the gallant Captain May and his dragoons, and committed to them the work. "You must charge the enemies' batteries, and take them," was the general' language. "I will do it," was May' response. And, ardent as the onset of the six hundred at Balaclava, "into the jaws of death," but not so purposeless, sped the brave captain and his troop. Waiting a few moments for Ridgely at his battery, three hundred yards distant, to draw the fire of the enemy's artillery, he galloped furiously over the road, followed by his company, to receive the fire of the inner battery, which levelled at one discharge eighteen horses and seven men of his troop, Lieutenant Inge, one of the number, at his side But the battery was swept of its defenders; and though May, unsupported by infantry, exposed as he was to a shower of grape and musketry, was compelled to retire, he fought his way out of the mass of the foe, bringing with him to the camp an eminent prisoner of war, General La Vega, a brave officer, whom he had found the last at the guns, rallying his flying soldiers to their duty. Infantry were meanwhile ordered up, and the advantage of the charge secured in driving the enemy from their artillery on the left. On the right a breastwork was stormed, its gun taken, and other successes achieved, completing the rout in this quarter, including the capture of the general's camp, with all his official correspondence. The artillery battalion left to guard the train, with other forces, were now ordered in pursuit, and the flying army was driven to the river, where many perished in the attempt to escape. " In the camp of the army," says an interesting narrator of these scenes, " were found the preparations for a great festival, no doubt to follow the expected victory. The camp-kettles were simmering over the fires, filled with savory viands, off of which our troops made a plentiful evening meal. In the road were carcasses of half-skinned oxen. The hangers-on of the camp, while the battle was raging, were busy in their feast-preparing work, unconscious of dangers, when, on an instant, a sudden panic must have seized them, and they fled, leaving their half-completed labors to be consummated by our own troops."[1]

Seventeen hundred was the number of General Taylor's force engaged with the Mexicans. His loss was three officers, Lieutenants Inge, Cochrane and Chadbourne, and thirty-six men killed;

twelve officers and seventy men wounded. General Taylor, in his dispatch, estimated the Mexican loss, killed, wounded and missing, during the two days, at not less than one thousand men. In a dispatch from the field that night, he wrote with characteristic simplicity: " The affair of to-day may be regarded as a proper supplement to the cannonade of yesterday; and the two taken together exhibit the coolness and gallantry of our officers and men in the most favorable light. All have done their duty, and done it nobly." A few days, in a fuller report, he added: " Our victory has been decisive. A small force has overcome immense odds of the best troops that Mexico can furnish—veteran regiments, perfectly equipped and appointed. Eight pieces of artillery, several colors and standards, a great number of prisoners, including fourteen officers, and a large amount of baggage and public property, have fallen into our hands."

This decided success established the fortunes of General Taylor's Mexican campaign. Everything had been put to the hazard, and everything gained. The force which he commanded, large enough for resistance, too small, apparently, for conquest, invited the attack of the superior hosts. Victory appeared an easy matter to the Mexican general, who had the choice of the ground, and who was enabled to divide the little American army between the field and the fort. His supplies were at hand in a considerable city with a chain of towns in its rear, reaching into the heart of the country. He had made every calculation for success. While he

---

[1] Thorpe's " Our Army on the Rio Grande," p. 104.

was attacking the Americans on their march by a well-planned military movement, the batteries of Matamoras were at work on Fort Brown. One thing only was wanting to his forces, the desperate courage for an assault. If this nerve of the bayonet had been supplied, Arista might, with his numbers and resources, have done with ease what Jackson and his defenders at New Orleans so bravely accomplished, and swept his enemies into the sea. But he had other stuff in his ranks.

If the Mexicans at the outset were naturally confident of success, the Americans at home trembled for the fate of General Taylor's expedition, and the moral effect of his victory, in the same proportion, disheartened the one and elevated the other. The brave troops on the Rio Grande, it was felt, had repaired the over confidence of the administration at Washington. General Taylor had achieved not only a military success, but he had rescued the country from the risk of disgrace. Nothing could have been better contrived than the unintentional conduct of the government, for the creation of a hero. The American general was placed in a position where the greatest glory was to be reached with the smallest command.

The Mexican army was completely disorganized at Matamoras. Their cannonading of Fort Brown had ceased with the defeat of their army, and little was to be thought of but surrender. General Taylor was soon on hand to hasten the movement. After the duty to the dead and wounded had been performed, he proceeded to Point Isa-

bel to confer with Commodore Conner, who had brought up his fleet to the assistance of the imperilled little army. The story is, that the etiquette of this meeting severely taxed the resources of the brave general's wardrobe. Long accustomed to frontier warfare and protracted Indian campaigns, where there was more rough labor to be performed than military pomp to be indulged, Old Zach, as he was affectionately and familiarly called, had adapted his dress to the exigency of the climate and service. His linen roundabout was far better known in the camp than his uniform. Thinking, however, that something was due from the commander-in-chief of the army to the head of the navy, who was understood to be punctilious in dress, he painfully arrayed himself in the regulation coat, fished from the depths of his chest; while the gallant commodore knowing the habits of the general, in an equally generous spirit of concession, clothed himself for the interview in a simple suit of drilling. After this, it is said, Old Zach returned more sedulously than ever to his wonted simplicity of attire. All his habits, indeed, partook of the same plain convenience. Hardy and unostentatious in his mode of living, he was accustomed to the rough fare of the camp and an unpretending tent sufficed for the dignity of his headquarters.

The proper arrangements having been made at Point Isabel, General Taylor hastened again to the camp over a road no longer interrupted by Arista and his host. His next movement was to take possession of Matamoras, peaceably if he could, forcibly if he must. Upon his making his preparations for the latter, the discreet course appeared preferable to the Mexicans, and the town was given up, on the eighteenth of the month, to the army of occupation. Arista had fled, with such of his troops as were in a condition to travel, leaving the place to the hostilities of the Americans, which proved much kinder than the tender mercies of the defenders.

The summer was passed by General Taylor at Matamoras, receiving the recruits, who, summoned by the first signal of danger, were now pouring to the Rio Grande. The means of advance had also to be collected, and the force organized to pursue the enemy in the interior. Monterey to the west, at the foot of the Sierra Madre, where General Ampudia, who had succeeded Arista in the command, had established himself with a considerable body of troops, was the first object of attack. Sending forward his forces by the Rio Grande to Camargo, General Taylor thence pursued his way across the desert, reaching the San Juan, in the immediate neighborhood of Monterey, on the nineteenth of September. From that moment the brave and toilsome operations of the attack, which was continued for five days, may be said to have commenced. The town, thoroughly capable of defence, was manned by a garrison of ten thousand men, more than two-thirds of whom were regular troops, with a defence of forty-two pieces of cannon; its outworks were important, and the most extensive preparations of barricades and batteries were made within. The entire force General Tay-

21

lor brought against it, numbered six thousand, six hundred and seventy-five. He had no siege train, which might be thought indispensable to the work he was about to undertake, and an artillery force of only one ten-inch mortar, two twenty-four pounder howitzers, and four light field batteries of four guns each.

The first observation of the town convinced General Taylor that it might be turned on its westerly side, where the only means of escape to its occupants lay in the road to Saltillo. There were important detached works on that side, but the main defences were in the citadel on the north, the river and a series of redoubts on the southerly and easterly approaches. The reconnaisance was made after General Taylor's arrival on the nineteenth; on the twentieth, General Worth moved with his command toward the Saltillo road to carry out the plan of the commander-in-chief. The latter himself directed the proceedings on the east. The main points, and they were highly important ones, accomplished by General Worth on that day of hard fighting, the twenty-first, were the occupation of the road, and the storming of the works at the heights, adjacent to the city on the west. Turning to General Taylor's special command, we find him at the same time directing an attack on the opposite side of the town, which was conducted with such gallantry, in the face of a murderous cross-fire from the forts, that the streets of the city were gained, and the roof of one of its buildings taken advantage of to assail with musketry the defenders of the fort commanding this approach, which was also attacked from the outer side. Under this combination the fort fell. It was the important success of the day.

In General Taylor's words, "the main object proposed in the morning had been effected. A powerful diversion had been made to favor the operations of the second division (General Worth's); one of the enemy's advanced works had been carried, and we now had a strong foothold in the town." The loss in achieving this result, may indicate the gallantry with which it was accomplished. The number killed and wounded, in these operations in the lower part of the city that day, was three hundred and ninety-four. The next, the twenty-second, saw the completion of General Worth's design in the capture of the Bishop's Palace on Independence Hill, that work being commanded by the position he had stormed the day before. General Taylor employed the day in relieving his troops who had passed the night on the lower side of the town, and maintaining his advantages in that quarter. It was now evident that the city, being commanded from either end, must in due time surrender. The military event of the twenty-third, the third great day of the siege, was the advance into the town of the volunteers under Generals Quitman and Henderson, supported by Captain Bragg's battery. From house to house, from square to square, the advance against the strong barriers was gained by musketry from the roofs, by grape-shot in the streets, to a position but a single square dis-tant from the principal plaza, where the enemy's force was mainly concentrated.

A similar advance was made into the city from the opposite side by General Worth. The work of the next day, had it been necessary to continue the assault, would have been a last, short, bloody, decisive struggle. Fortunately, it was spared by a capitulation. The outcries of the townspeople, no less than the necessities of the garrison, compelled the surrender. On the morning of the twenty-fourth. a communication was received by General Taylor from General Ampudia, stating that having made the defence of which he thought the city susceptible, he had "fulfilled his duty, and satisfied that military honor which, in a certain manner, is common to all armies of the civilized world." To continue the defence, he said, would only be further to distress the population which had suffered enough already: he, therefore, proposed to evacuate the city and fort, carrying with him the *personnel* and *matériel* of war. In answer to this, a complete surrender of the town and garrison as prisoners of war was demanded; but such surrender, it was added, would be upon terms recognizing by their liberality "the gallant defence of the place, creditable alike to the Mexican troops and nation." The hour of twelve was appointed to determine the question. At that time the two chiefs met to arrange the terms of surrender. General Ampudia, not satisfied with the proposition offered, insisted upon his original conditions; and General Tay lor, who had made up his mind, was in consequence on the point of breaking up the conference, when a suggestion was offered and reluctantly accepted by him, to refer the negotiation to a body of commissioners on both sides. General Worth, General Henderson, and Colonel Jefferson Davis acted for the Americans. With some difficulty the terms were arranged. The town and citadel, with the arms and munitions of war were surrendered, the Mexican forces to retire—the officers with their side arms, the cavalry with their arms and accoutrements, the artillery with one field battery—within seven days beyond the line formed by the pass of Linconada, the city of Linares and San Fernando de Preras; and an armistice of eight weeks to be entered upon. The Mexican flag, when struck at the citadel, was to be saluted by its own battery. That ceremony was performed on the morning of the twenty-fifth. The American flag was unfolded, and the Mexican troops took their departure. It was a brilliant success in the taking of a town. Its cost, as summed up by General Taylor in his dispatch, was twelve officers and one hundred and eight men killed; thirty-one officers and three hundred and thirty-seven men wounded.

It was thought by the government at Washington that too favorable terms had been allowed the enemy in the capitulation, that their surrender should have been unconditional, and that the armistice should not have been granted. But those who made the negotiation were governed by sound motives, both of policy and humanity. They might,

indeed, have completed the conquest at the plaza and taken the citadel; but it would have been at an enormous cost of life, both to victors and vanquished much property would have been destroyed which was saved by the negotiation; nor had General Taylor a force sufficient to guard all the avenues of escape to so great a body of men. Moreover, the prospect of peace was urged by the Mexican General in consequence of the return of Santa Anna, which had been more than winked at, with this view, by the American government itself, which had indeed previously proffered peace negotiations. As for the armistice, the little army at Monterey was at any rate unable to move for some time, until reinforcements should arrive, upon any further considerable expedition into the interior. It had but ten days' rations at the time of the capitulation, and had been all along deficient in wagons. So that, on many grounds, the negotiation of General Taylor was to be justified.

These military successes, however brilliant as they were, were unproductive of the desirable result of "conquering a peace" from the enemy. The very humiliation which they inflicted, only roused the spirit of the country to greater resistance, and whatever peace intentions General Santa Anna, now placed at the head of affairs, had when he landed at Vera Cruz, he was clearly unable to carry them out while the Americans were thus constantly victorious. For the purposes of the war, it might have been good policy of the invaders to have suffered a defeat, to humor national pride, and smooth the way to negotiation and concession. Defeat was not, however, a word to be found in the military vocabulary of Old Zach. He had an indomitable, unreasoning soldier's logic, which led him by a very short path to one single conclusion, that victory was the business of war; and well or ill provided with such resources as he had, in the face of whatever obstacles might be in the way, he went straight forward to that result. He made no noisy demonstrations, but took his ground boldly and fought to the end. His last battle was to crown the whole.

The circumstances under which the engagement at Buena Vista was fought, render it the most memorable of the whole campaign. The government at Washington having come to the conclusion that their system of border attack, however well pursued, would not end the war, determined to strike at the heart of the country, its capital, by its great avenue of approach, the line of Vera Cruz. In the month of November, General Scott was ordered to the Gulf of Mexico to take such measures, as in his judgment he might think proper, to carry the resolution into effect. General Taylor, in this arrangement, was to be left on the Rio Grande, with a force barely sufficient to maintain a defensive position, while he yielded to Scott, for his more brilliant service, the best part of his troops, the tried regulars who had fought with him from Corpus Christi along the line of battles to Monterey. General Scott arrived at the Rio Grande about the first of January, 1847, and began to collect the forces for his expedition. The important divisions of General Worth, Twiggs, Quitman, and other choice troops, artillery and volunteers, were stripped from General Taylor's command, and his plan of operations at Victoria and other advanced places in the interior entirely broken up. Nothing further was expected of him than to defend himself at Monterey, should Santa Anna, who was in great force at San Luis Potosi, extend his movements in that direction. The Mexican General, who had become aware of the plans of his foe by an intercepted dispatch, was thought more likely to turn his attention to the intended landing at Vera Cruz. He determined, however, to strike a blow with his large army, which seemed quite sufficient to sweep every American from the neighborhood of the Rio Grande. He accordingly marched with his twenty thousand men toward the position, in the vicinity of Saltillo, of General Taylor and his bands of volunteers.

Among the latter was the new and important command of General Wool, which had just reached the scene of action from an overland march through Texas. To this officer belongs the credit of the selection of the pass where the Americans so well defended themselves: it was his fortune, being left in command at the point, to open the battle; and to him were specially entrusted some of the most important movements of the day. It was an admirably chosen ground for defence, a narrow valley enclosed on either hand by lofty mountains, with seamed and broken ground, with the passage on the road additionally protected by a river course and deep ravine at its side. The best naturally guarded ground of the whole, where the mountain on one side and the ravine on the other approached nearest each other, the Pass of Angostura, was that taken for the American stand. There, on the morning of the twenty-second of February, Washington's birthday, as the enemy made his appearance, the road was defended by a battery of eight guns, supported on either hand by companies of infantry. The remaining troops were placed, in advantageous positions, on a plateau and amidst the ravines, across the whole breadth of the valley. These dispositions were made by General Wool, General Taylor having been during the night at Saltillo, to provide against a threatened attack in that quarter. He presently came up, bringing with him additional troops, and assumed the command.

At eleven o'clock, a summons was received from Santa Anna to surrender. "You are surrounded," was the language of this communication, "by twenty thousand men, and cannot, in any human probability, avoid suffering a rout and being cut to pieces with your troops; but as you deserve consideration and particular esteem, I wish to save you from a catastrophe, and for that purpose give you this notice, in order that you may surrender at discretion, under the assurance that you will be treated with the consideration belonging to the Mexican character to which end you will be granted an hour's time to make up your mind, to commence from the moment when my flag of truce arrives in your camp;" to all which considerate attention, Zachary Taylor sent the following brief sentence—"Sir: In reply to your note of this date, summoning me to surrender my forces at discretion, I beg leave to say that I decline acceding to your request." So the battle was inaugurated. There was some skirmishing in the afternoon, as the Mexicans felt their way preparatory to the action of the twenty-third. General Taylor again passed the night at Saltillo, his presence there being necessary to assure the defence of the place which was now more seriously threatened. Before his return to the pass, the enemy, at daylight, had commenced their attack. It was made with great force, and with varying success. There was danger of the American position being completely turned, but by a series of skillful manœuvres, admirably executed, and sustained by the artillery and companies of volunteers, the enemy was driven back.

An incident occurred in this repulse, which for its bearing upon the personal character of General Taylor, may be separated from the mass of details of this engagement lying before us. "It was during this retreat," says Mr. Dawson in his account of the action, "that two thousand Mexicans, anxious to escape the fire in their rear, as well as a destructive fire on their flank from the troops on the plateau, had sought shelter in the recesses of the mountains, and were huddled together in a helpless, disorderly mass. At this moment the good ness of General Taylor's heart interceded in their behalf, notwithstanding they were enemies; and he hesitated before sacrificing a single life—even that of an enemy—unnecessarily. With the merciful desire of saving life, therefore, he dispatched Lieutenant Crittenden, his aid-de-camp, with a flag, and demanded the surrender of the party; but instead of complying with the demand, the Mexicans availed themselves of the opportunity afforded them, and marched out of the gorge, while the troops under General Wool, under orders from General Taylor, silently looked on, without being permitted to fire a shot, or take a step to prevent their escape."[1]

One last effort was left to be directed by Santa Anna himself. Rallying his forces for an overwhelming attack on the central plateau, he would have gained that important position had he not been met by the American artillery, the Mississippi rifles, and other companies suddenly brought into position against him. It was on this occasion that General Taylor, as the fortune of the day stood in the balance, coolly uttered his memorable advice to his artillerist, "A little more grape, Captain Bragg!" Let him tell the story in the usual simple words of his own dispatch, where we may be sure we shall hear nothing of this dramatic point. "The moment was most critical. Captain O'Brien, with two pieces, had sustained the heavy charge to the last, and was finally obliged to leave his guns on the field—his infantry

support being entirely routed. Captain Bragg, who had just arrived from the left, was ordered at once into battery. Without any infantry to support him, and at the imminent risk of losing his guns, this officer came rapidly into action, the Mexican line being but a few yards from the muzzle of his pieces. The first discharge of canister caused the enemy to hesitate; the second and third drove him back in disorder and saved the day." There were other services rendered in the final repulse, but for them and the merits of particular officers and companies in the battle, we must refer the reader to the various dispatches and military narratives of the day.

Let one brief passage from General Taylor's narrative declare the spirit which ruled the gallant bands of volunteers, nearly all for the first time under fire on that occasion. "No further attempt," he writes in his official account, "was made by the enemy to force our position, and the approach of night gave an opportunity to pay proper attention to the wounded, and also to refresh the soldiers, who had been exhausted by incessant watchfulness and combat. Though the night was severely cold, the troops were compelled for the most to bivouac without fires, expecting that morning would renew the conflict. During the night the wounded were removed to Saltillo, and every preparation made to receive the enemy, should he again attack our position." The enemy, however, made no such attempt. Leaving his wounded on the way, he made good his retreat to San Luis Potosi. The few figures with

---

[1] Battles of the United States, II. 496.

which the stories of all battles end will tell better than aught else the heroism of the brave encounter. The American force engaged was three hundred and thirty-four officers and four thousand four hundred and twenty-five men, of which two squadrons of cavalry and three batteries of light artillery, making not more than four hundred and fifty-three men, composed the only force of regular troops. The Mexican forces, we have seen stated by Santa Anna himself, at twenty thousand, an estimate confirmed by all subsequent information. The American loss was two hundred and sixty-seven killed, four hundred and fifty-six wounded and twenty-three missing. The Mexican loss was computed by General Taylor at between fifteen hundred and two thousand. At least five hundred killed were left on the field of battle.

Thus closed General Taylor's connection with the active operations of the Mexican War. He was for some time engaged in camp duties, when he requested leave of absence to attend to the duties of his plantations on the Mississippi. His home was at Baton Rouge, Louisiana, the residence also of his estimable son-in-law the late Colonel Bliss, a member of his staff during his Mexican campaigns.

The battle of Buena Vista, was, as we have seen, fought at the end of February, 1847. Just two years from that time, March 4, 1849, its brave and modest commander was installed as President of the United States at Washington. The two events may safely be put in conjunction, for one proceeded directly out of the other. General Tay-

lor, as Senator Benton remarked, was the first President elected upon a reputation purely military. He had been in the army from his youth, and, according to the custom of officers of the army, had not even voted at an election. He was selected, of course, on account of his availability; yet it was an availability which did not rest altogether on his purely military character. "It will be a great mistake," said Daniel Webster to the Senate, "to suppose that he owed his advancement to high civil trust, or his great acceptableness with the people to military talent or ability alone. Associated with the highest admiration for those qualities possessed by him, there was spread throughout the community a high degree of confidence and faith in his integrity, and honor, and uprightness as a man. I believe he was especially regarded as both a firm and a mild man in the exercise of authority; and I have observed more than once, in this and in other popular governments, that the prevalent motive with the masses of mankind for conferring high honors on individuals is a confidence in their mildness, their paternal, protecting, prudent and safe character." This was well said. Every word is in harmony with the popular appreciation of General Taylor; and there are doubtless many living in Mexico, as well as in his own country, who would respond to the sentiment. The soldier who could pause in the midst of such a day as that of Buena Vista to arrest the tide of slaughter, when slaughter was self-preservation, with the deed of mercy we have recorded, must be entitled to no common meed of praise on the ground of humanity. But something more was added by his eminent eulogist. "I suppose," said Mr. Webster, "that no case ever happened, in the very best days of the Roman republic, when a man found himself clothed with the highest authority in the state under circumstances more repelling all suspicion of personal application, of pursuing any crooked path in politics, or of having been actuated by sinister views and purposes, than in the case of this worthy, and eminent, and distinguished, and good man."[1]

The circumstance that Mr. Webster was himself a candidate before the Whig convention, which nominated General Taylor for the Presidency, adds weight to these assertions. Mr. Cass was the opposing democratic candidate. The vote of the electors was one hundred and sixty-three to one hundred and twenty-seven.

. Of the qualities of his short administration of the office, let a member of the party opposed to his election speak. The late Senator Benton says: "His brief career showed no deficiency of political wisdom for want of previous political training. He came into the administration at a time of great difficulty, and acted up to the emergency of his position. . . . His death was a public calamity. No man could have been more devoted to the Union, or more opposed to the slavery agitation; and his position as a Southern man, and a slaveholder—his military reputation and his election by a majority of the people and of the States—would have given him a power in the settlement of these questions which no President without these qualifications could have possessed. In the political division he classed with the Whig party; but his administration, as far as it went, was applauded by the democracy, and promised to be so to the end of his official term. Dying at the head of the government, a national lamentation bewailed his departure from life and power, and embalmed his memory in the affections of his country."[1]

General Taylor died at Washington, at the Presidential mansion, July 9, 1850, of a fever contracted by exposure to the intense heat of the sun, in attendance upon the ceremonies of the Day of Independence.

---

[1] Remarks in the Senate on the death of General Taylor.—Webster's Works, p. 409.

[1] Benton's Thirty Years' View, II. 765-6.

MILLARD FILLMORE.

The family of Millard Fillmore has an honorable descent in American history. Its records are diversified by remarkable incidents of war and adventure. John Fillmore, the great-grandfather of the President of the United States, and the common ancestor of all of that name in the United States, was born at Ipswich, Massachusetts, about the beginning of the eighteenth century. He is recollected as the hero of a brave and successful struggle with certain pirates into whose hands it was his luck to fall in a sailing venture out of Boston. He was about nineteen when he sailed in a fishing vessel from that port, and had been but a few days at sea when the craft was captured by a noted pirate ship commanded by one Captain Phillips. Fillmore became a prisoner, and so continued on board the ship for nine months, steadily refusing his liberty on the only condition on which it would be granted, to sign the piratical articles of the vessel and take part in its fortunes. Though threatened with death, he persisted in his denial, till finally, two others having been taken captive, he joined with them in an attack on the crew ; several were killed ; the vessel was rescued and carried safely into Boston. The surviving pirates were tried and executed, and the captors were honored by the thanks of the British government. Young Fillmore afterwards settled in Connecticut, where he died. His son, Nathaniel, was an early settler in the Hampshire Grants, at Bennington, a frontier position in those days which, as a matter of course, made him a soldier in the seven years' war with France. He was also a gallant Whig of the Revolution, serving, when his home became the theatre of hostilities, as lieutenant under General Stark, in the spirited and decisive conflict at Bennington. He died in 1814, leaving a son, Nathaniel, who early in life migrated to what is now called Summer Hill, in Cayuga County, New York, where he followed the life of a farmer. There his son Millard, the future President, was born, January 7, 1800. The family shortly after removed to another place in the same county.

"The narrow means of his father," we are told in a narrative of these early years, published some years since in the "American Review," "deprived Millard of any advantages of education beyond what were afforded by the imperfect and ill-taught common schools of the county. Books were scarce and dear, and at the age of fifteen, when more favored youths are far advanced in their classical studies, or enjoying in colleges the benefit of well-furnished libraries, young Fillmore had read but little except his common-school books and the Bible. At that period he was sent into the then wilds of Livingston County to learn the clothier's trade. He remained there about four months, and was then placed with another person to pursue the same business and wool-carding, in the town of Sempronius, now Niles, where his father lived. A small village library that was formed there soon after, gave him the first means of acquiring general knowledge through books. He improved the opportunity thus offered; the appetite grew by what it fed upon. The thirst for knowledge soon became insatiate, and every leisure moment was spent in reading. Four years were passed in this way, working at his trade and storing his mind, during such hours as he could command, with the contents of books of history, biography, and travels. At the age of nineteen he fortunately made an acquaintance with the late Walter Wood, Esquire, whom many will remember as one of the most estimable citizens of Cayuga County. Judge Wood was a man of wealth and great business capacity; he had an excellent law library, but did little professional business. He soon saw that under the rude exterior of the clothier's boy, were powers that only required proper development to raise the possessor to high distinction and usefulness, and advised him to quit his trade and study law. In reply to the objection of a lack of education, means and friends to aid him in a course of professional study, Judge Wood kindly offered to give him a place in his office, to advance money to defray his expenses, and wait until success in business should furnish the means of repayment. The offer was accepted. The apprentice boy bought his time, entered the office of Judge Wood, and for more than two years applied himself closely to business and study. He read law and general literature and practised surveying."

Not content with entire dependence upon his benefactor for his support, he resorted to that unfailing resource of an American youth making progress from poverty upward to the intellectual professions—he became a schoolmaster for a portion of the year. At the age of twenty-one he removed to Erie County and entered a law office in Buffalo. His legal studies were completed in 1823, when, diffident of success in a city so well stocked with the profession as his late residence, he began the practice of law at Aurora. He shortly after was married to the daughter of the Rev. Lemuel Powers. Success came to him gradually, affording him ample time to develop his studies by patient application. He pursued this path, gaining his ground surely and steadily. In 1828, he was elected a member of the assembly in the State legislature by a Whig constituency of his county, and signalized himself at Albany by his advocacy of the bill for the abolition of imprisonment for debt, a portion of which was prepared by him as a member of the committee. He now had his residence as a member of the bar at Buffalo.

His congressional life commenced in 1833, with his election to the House of Representatives. It was the beginning of the second term of Jackson's administration, that period of conflict which was to test to the uttermost the party strength of the great chieftain, and out of which he was to emerge triumphantly. Mr. Fillmore, a young member of the House of the losing side was there to learn his lesson of political wisdom in the agitation. He secured the respect of his constituents by his course, and made a considerable step onward in his career, without greatly attracting public attention. His term of two years having expired, he was not immediately a candidate for reëlection, but devoted himself to his profession at Buffalo. He was not, however, suffered to rest in private life. In 1836, he was again elected to Congress, taking his seat at the commencement of Mr. Van Buren's administration, and continuing to serve by reëlection through the whole period of his Presidency. He rose with his experience in the national councils, being in this second term, the first session of the twenty-sixth Congress, placed at the head of the committee on elections, which threw into his hands the management of the famous contested New Jersey case. Mr. Fillmore was again elected to the next succeeding Congress of 1841, by a larger majority than he had hitherto received. The Whigs being now in power, he was placed at the head of the important committee on Ways and Means, where he was charged with duties which fully called forth his esources, and placed him at length in a conspicuous position before the public.

At the close of this term, though renominated by his friends in Erie County, he persisted in declining a continuance in office. His profession had claims upon his attention to which he was eager to respond, and his temperament invited repose. His political position, however, was too well established for him to be left in quiet by his party. He was immediately adopted as their candidate for Governor of New York, accepted the nomination, and was defeated in the election of 1844. In 1847 he was chosen comptroller of the State, by a large majority. He commenced his new duties at Albany, at the beginning of 1848, and before the year was closed, was nominated and elected Vice-President of the United States. He had the same vote with his principal, General Taylor, of fifteen States, and a majority of the electoral vote of thirty-six.

The duties of his new office of course involved his resignation of the comptrollership. He entered upon the Presidency of the Senate in March, 1849; it was an office which he was well fitted to discharge, and he left behind him, when he was called to a higher station, an impression of his moderation and urbanity. On the 9th of July, 1850, while Congress was in session, the sudden death of General Taylor, devolved upon him the cares and responsibilities of the Presidency. In deference to the general feeling of regret which was called forth by the departure of this estimable man, and in obedience to his successor's own feelings, his entrance into office was conducted in the simplest manner. The day after the death of the late President, attended by a committee of the two Houses and the members of the late President's cabinet, the oath was administered to him, not in front of the Capitol but in the Hall of the House of Representatives, by the venerable Judge Cranch, of the Circuit Court of the District of Columbia, "which being done, President Fillmore, without any inaugural address, bowed and retired, and the ceremony was at an end." [1]

In his annual message, however, on the reassembling of Congress, in December, he took occasion to supply what may be regarded as the substitute for the usual inaugural address. "Being suddenly called," says he in that document, "in the midst of the last session of Congress, by a painful dispensation of Divine Providence, to the responsible station which I now hold, I contented myself with such communications to the Legislature as the exigency of the moment seemed to require. The country was shrouded in mourning for the loss of its venerated chief magistrate, and all hearts were penetrated with grief. Neither the time nor the occasion appeared to require or to justify, on my part, any general expression of political opinions, or any announcement of the principles which would govern me in the discharge of the duties to the performance of which I had been so unexpectedly called. I trust, therefore, that it may not be deemed inappropriate, if I avail myself of this opportunity of the reassembling of Congress, to make known my sentiments in a general manner, in regard to the policy which ought to be pursued by the government, both in its intercourse with foreign nations, and in its management and administration of internal affairs.

"Nations, like individuals in a state of nature, are equal and independent, possessing certain rights, and owing certain duties to each other, arising from their necessary and unavoidable relations; which rights and duties there is no common human authority to protect and enforce. Still, they are rights and duties, binding in morals, in conscience, and in honor, although there is no tribunal to which an injured party can appeal, but the disinterested judgment of mankind, and ultimately the arbitrament of the sword.

"Among the acknowledged rights of nations is that which each possesses of establishing that form of government which it may deem most conducive to the happiness and prosperity of its own citizens; of changing that form, as circumstances may require; and of managing its internal affairs according to its own will. The people of the United States claim this right for themselves, and they readily concede it to others. Hence it becomes an imperative duty not to interfere in the government or internal policy of other nations; and, although we may sympathize with the unfortunate or the oppressed, everywhere, in their struggles for freedom, our principles forbid us from taking any part in such foreign contests. We make no wars to promote or to prevent successions to thrones; to maintain any theory of a balance of power; or to

---

[1] Benton's Thirty Years' View, II. 767.

suppress the actual government which any country chooses to establish for itself. We instigate no revolutions, nor suffer any hostile military expeditions to be fitted out in the United States to invade the territory or provinces of a friendly nation. The great law of morality ought to have a national, as well as a personal and individual, application. We should act towards other nations as we wish them to act towards us; and justice and conscience should form the rule of conduct between governments, instead of mere power, self-interest, or the desire of aggrandizement. To maintain a strict neutrality in foreign wars, to cultivate friendly relations, to reciprocate every noble and generous act, and to perform punctually and scrupulously every treaty obligation—these are the duties which we owe to other States, and by the performance of which we best entitle ourselves to like treatment from them; or if that, in any case, be refused, we can enforce our own rights with justice and with a clear conscience.

"In our domestic policy, the Constitution will be my guide; and in questions of doubt, I shall look for its interpretation to the judicial decisions of that tribunal which was established to expound it, and to the usage of the government, sanctioned by the acquiescence of the country. I regard all its provisions as equally binding. In all its parts it is the will of the people, expressed in the most solemn form, and the constituted authorities are but agents to carry that will into effect. Every power which it has granted is to be exercised for the public good; but no pretence of utility,

no honest conviction even, of what might be expedient, can justify the assumption of any power not granted. The powers conferred upon the government and their distribution to the several departments, are as clearly expressed in that sacred instrument as the imperfection of human language will allow; and I deem it my first duty, not to question its wisdom, add to its provisions, evade its requirements, or nullify its commands."

The loss of General Taylor was the more felt as the country was at the time agitated with the discussions growing out of the subject of slavery, which had arisen with the question of the disposition of the territory conquered from Mexico; and the late President, of moderate views, and capable of giving great weight to them in the national councils, by his intimate relations with the South, was looked to as the great mediator in effecting a compromise of the conflicting interests. This had already been proposed by Mr. Clay, and found an advocate in the President. Thus, when his aid seemed most needed, he expired, leaving the great work to be accomplished by his successor. It was undertaken by him, so far as the influence of his office extended, in a spirit of conciliation. His choice of Daniel Webster as Secretary of State, and of the other members of his cabinet, from different portions of the Union, was an earnest of his intentions. The boundary between Texas and New Mexico, a matter of some difficulty, was adjusted, California was admitted as a free State, Utah Territory was organized, and the Fugitive Slave Law en acted. In other affairs of social importance, President Fillmore's brief term of office was signalized by several incidents which will always find a place in the history of the country. The reduction of postage on letters to the uniform rate of three cents; the return of the government Arctic expedition of Lieutenant De Haven, sent in quest of Sir John Franklin; the visit of Kossuth to the country in 1851; the sailing of Commodore Perry's expedition to Japan in the following year, are events which will be more lasting in their consequences than many battles which have filled, for the time, a larger space in the public attention.

Mr. Fillmore's term of office closed in the spring of 1853. The following year he made a tour in the South, where he was well received, and in 1855 visited Europe to return in season for the Presidential canvass of 1856. He was put forward in that election as a medium candidate of the American party, between the nominee of the Democratic party, Mr. Buchanan, and Colonel Fremont, of the Republican. In such a contest there was little strength to be wasted by the two great divisions which swallowed up the rest. Mr. Fillmore received the vote only of the single State of Maryland.

Since that period Mr. Fillmore has not been before the public as a candidate for office. He has continued to reside in the western part of the State of New York. He took an active part in the Civil War, but it was believed that his sentiments were on the side of the Union. During the later years of his life, his name seldom attracted public attention except as the president officer of several important commercial conventions, for which his firm yet courteous manner, his knowledge of the management of large assemblies, and his imperturbable temper qualified him perfectly. He died at Buffalo, March 8, 1874.

Franklin Pierce

FRANKLIN PIERCE.

Franklin Pierce, the fourteenth President of the United States, was born at Hillsborough, in the State of New Hampshire, November 23, 1804. His father, Benjamin Pierce, a native of Massachusetts, with many other spirited youths, entered the Revolutionary army at the summons of Lexington, served through the war with credit, and retiring with the rank of captain, a year or two after peace was declared, became the purchaser of a plot of fifty acres in the present town of Hillsborough, then a rough clearing in the wilderness. There he built a log-house and settled down to the clearing of the land, his second wife, to whom he was united in 1789, becoming the mother of the subject of this sketch who was the sixth of her eight children. The captain of the Revolution meanwhile attracted the attention of the people of the region, was made brigade major on the organization of the militia of the county; in 1789 was elected a member of the House of Representatives at Concord, continuing to serve in that capacity for thirteen years till he was chosen a member of the Governor's Council. An eminent member of the Democratic party, he was an ardent supporter of the war of 1812, sending two of his sons to the army. He rose to be Governor of New Hampshire in 1827, and was again elected to that office in 1829. He subsequently lived in retirement, leaving the world in 1839, at the venerable age of eighty-one. The people of New Hampshire have not yet forgotten the shrewd sense and kindliness, the unaffected democratic principles, of the honest, cheerful old soldier of the Revolution and Governor of the State. It is to his memory, doubtless, supported by the popular traits of character inherited from him, that his son has been indebted for much of his advancement.

Franklin had good opportunities of education. He was early sent to the neighboring academies at Hancock and Francestown, enjoying at the latter the advantages of a residence with the family of an old friend of his father, Peter Woodbury, whose son, Judge Woodbury, became afterward so eminent in public affairs. Young Pierce, who was of a warm-hearted, susceptible nature, was much impressed by the superior mind and character of the lady of this household, the mother of Judge Woodbury. Indeed he appears in his boyhood to have won the kindness of those around him by his frank, ingenuous disposition. He was admitted to Bowdoin college in 1820. It is to the credit of young Pierce as a collegian that, having fallen into some indifference during the first years of his course, he more than regained his position in the upper classes, graduating with credit in 1824. It is a fact worth mentioning, though, as his biographer remarks, by no means unusual in the history of the rise of New England statesmen, that in one of the winter vacations Franklin Pierce took a turn at school-keeping.

His college instruction being completed, he began the study of the law as a profession in the office of Judge Woodbury, of Portsmouth, the son of his father's old friend, then Governor of the State, and soon afterward greatly distinguished at Washington as Speaker and senator, and member of the cabinet of Jackson. After a year with this eminent jurist, Mr. Pierce completed his studies in the law school at Northampton and the office of the Hon. Edmund Parker, at Amherst. He was admitted to the bar in 1827, and opened an office opposite to his father's house at Hillsborough. His success, though he had the advantage of the family popularity, was not very decided at the outset. His biographer, indeed, speaks of his first case as a decided failure. He had not yet learned the full command of his resources. It was his fortune to make his position at the bar good by steady effort. Politics, meanwhile, offered him a ready resource, as his father had just been elected Governor. Democratic sentiments were gaining the ascendency under the influence of Jackson, and to this cause young Pierce devoted himself. In 1829, and for three

successive years, he was elected to the legislature of his State, as representative of Hillsborough, filling in 1832 and 1833 the office of Speaker. In the last year he was chosen a member of Congress, taking his seat in the House of Representatives at Washington, in December. He was again elected and served a second term. He was of course a steady, unflinching supporter of the administration, for the democratic rule of those days admitted no other—not a frequent. or long, or eloquent speaker, but a zealous, persistent committee man, giving his vote for the measures of his chief, seconding the views of the South, and, a decided man generally in his party relations.

In 1837 he left the House of Representatives for the Senate of the United States, where he was the youngest member of that body. His term of service embraced the whole of Mr. Van Buren's administration and a portion of that of his successor, during which his services to his party were resolute and unintermitted. They were not forgotten when an opportunity subsequently arose to confer upon him the highest reward. He retired from public life at the end of the period for which he was elected, having his residence now at Concord, in his native State. He had been for some time married to a daughter of the Rev. Dr. Appleton, once President of Bowdoin; his father was now dead; and his domestic affairs required his care at home. Thither he retired to devote himself assiduously to his profession. His success was immediately assured, his practice at the bar yielding him a very handsome income. In proof of his contentment and the sincerity of his wishes for retirement, he declined in 1845 an appointment by the Governor to the United States Senate to fill the place vacated by Judge Woodbury, and a proffer by the Democracy of his State of a nomination as Governor; refusing also in the following year a seat in the cabinet of President Polk as Attorney-General. He held meanwhile the post, at home, of District Attorney of New Hampshire.

His reluctance to engage in public life at Washington partly proceeded from his professional duties in his own State and partly from the health of his wife, to which the climate of the seat of government was unfavorable. In his letter to President Polk, dated September 6, 1846, declining the position of Attorney-General, he made use of this expression: "When I resigned my seat in the senate in 1842, I did it with the fixed purpose never again to be voluntarily separated from my family, for any considerable length of time, except at the call of my country in time of war." The reservation, looking to the date, was not without its significance. General Taylor had in May fought the battles of Palo Alto and Resaca de la Palma, and it was evident that more serious struggles, which would call out a new military force, were impending. Congress was slow to admit the necessity in making provision for the additional force, but when the time came and the bill creating ten new regiments was passed, Franklin Pierce was looked to and created by the President a brigadier-general, his commission being

23

dated March 3, 1847. He had previously enrolled his name on the first list of volunteers at Concord as a private soldier. He considered his acceptance of the duty a fulfillment of his pledge on taking leave of the Senate. The old military spirit of two wars in which his father and brothers had taken part again lived in the family.

The brigade of which he was placed in command consisted of twenty-five hundred men, composed of the ninth regiment of New Englanders, the twelfth from the south-western States, and the fifteenth from the north and west. They were to assemble at Vera Cruz, and join the forces of General Scott on his march to the capital. General Pierce sailed from Newport on the 27th of May, with a portion of the New England regiment; the voyage was calm and consequently long; bringing the passengers to the rendezvous at the most unhealthy season of the year. As the vomito then prevailed at Vera Cruz, the prospect of landing new recruits was anything but a happy one. It was the work before the new general, however, and he courageously faced it. The portions of his Diary published by his biographer, show the full extent of the difficulties which he encountered, and which were met by him with manly resolution. Avoiding the city, he stationed his men on an extensive sand beach in the vicinity, where they would at least have the benefit of a free circulation of air. It was the beginning of July, and no means were at hand to expedite the departure for the interior. A large number of wild mules had been collected. but, inferior as they were for purposes of transportation, they were so ill provided with proper attendants that most of them broke away in a stampede. "The Mexicans fully believe," is the language of the journal of June 28, "that most of my command must die of vomito before I can be prepared to march into the interior." A delay of but a day or two was expected; it was now running into weeks. Then he records the services of Major Woods, a West Point officer "of great intelligence, experience, and coolness, who kindly consented to act as my adjutant-general." There is a serious case of vomito in the camp, Captain Duff, who is sent to the hospital in the city. At length, after three weeks on the shore, the advance is sent off, and a few days after the general himself follows. It is not an easy road to travel. The great battles of the previous expeditions had cleared the road of extensive fortifications, but left it free to be assailed by straggling parties of guerillas, of whom General Pierce and his men are to have a taste as they carry their train of men and munitions to the main army at Puebla. He was twice attacked on the route, on leaving San Juan, when both sides of the road were beset by the Mexicans, and again at the National Bridge, where a formidable effort was made to arrest his progress. The enemy had erected a barricade at the bridge, and manned a temporary breastwork on a high commanding bluff above. General Pierce, looking around for means of annoyance to cover his advance, found a position for several pieces of cannon, but the main advantage was gained by a portion of his command in charging the defences at the bridge and gaining the enemy's works from the rear. In this engagement, which seems to have been well managed in securing the speedy retreat of the Mexicans, General Pierce was under fire, and received an escopette ball through the rim of his hat, without, however, other damage, as he adds in his journal, "than leaving my head for a short time without protection from the sun." The train thus relieved advanced to the Plan del Rio, where the bridge, a work of the old Spaniards, was found to be destroyed. Its main arch, a span of about sixty feet, was blown up. Below yawned a gulf of a hundred feet. The bank in the neighborhood appeared impassable for wagons. In this emergency General Pierce called upon one of his New England officers, Captain Bodfish, of the Ninth Infantry, who "had been engaged for many years in the lumber business, and accustomed to the construction of roads in the wild and mountainous districts of Maine, and was, withal, a man not lightly to be checked by slight obstacles in the accomplishment of an enterprise." This enterprising officer had by no means the resources of Maine at his command, for there was no timber in the vicinity; but the road was constructed, nevertheless, and the train passed in safety over it. After this there were no extraordinary difficulties to be overcome, and General Pierce, on the seventh of August, reached the head quarters of General Scott at Puebla, with his brigade, which, after undergoing some changes on the way at Perote, consisted of some twenty-four hundred men. The guerillas who infested his path had not succeeded in capturing a single wagon.

With this reënforcement General Scott immediately began his advance to the valley of Mexico. In the first action, that at the heights of Contreras, where the enemy's works, having been approached with difficulty, were successfully stormed with great gallantry, General Pierce was in command at the outset in the attack upon the front of the intrenchments. It was a duty of peculiar toil and hazard. The ground, the famous pedregal, was a broken, rocky surface, impracticable for cavalry and harassing for infantry. General Pierce was the only mounted officer in the brigade, and, as he was pressing to the head of his column, after addressing the colonels and captains of his regiment as they passed by him, his horse slipped among the rocks and fell, crushing his rider in the fall. This was the first of a series of disasters which weighed heavily upon General Pierce through the remainder of the brief campaign, but which his energy and spirit enabled him in a considerable measure to overcome. He was at first stunned by the fall with the horse, but recovering his consciousness, was hurried on in the battle, having been assisted to a seat in the saddle. When told that he would not be able to keep his seat, "Then," said he, "you must tie me on." He lay that night writhing in pain from his wounded knee, on an ammunition wagon, to be mounted again the next morning, the decisive day at Contreras, and was enabled to hold his position and lead his brigade in pur-

suit. In the course of this duty he was summoned to the commander-in-chief, who perceived at once his shattered condition. "Pierce, my dear fellow," said the veteran kindly, "you are badly injured; you are not fit to be in the saddle." "Yes, general, I am," replied Pierce, "in a case like this." "You cannot touch your foot to the stirrup," said Scott. "One of them I can," answered Pierce. The general, says the authentic narrative before us, looked again at Pierce's almost disabled figure, and seemed on the point of taking his irrevocable resolution. "You are rash, General Pierce," said he; "we shall lose you, and we cannot spare you. It is my duty to order you back to St. Augustin." "For God's sake, general," exclaimed Pierce, "don't say that! This is the last great battle, and I must lead my brigade!" The commander-in-chief made no further remonstrance, but gave the order for Pierce to advance with his brigade. The sequel may best be told in his biographer, Mr. Hawthorne's, interesting narrative. "The way lay through thick, standing corn, and over marshy ground, intercepted with ditches, which were filled, or partially so, with water. Over some of the narrower of these Pierce leaped his horse. When the brigade had advanced about a mile, however, it found itself impeded by a ditch ten or twelve feet wide, and six or eight feet deep. It being impossible to leap it, General Pierce was lifted from his saddle, and in some incomprehensible way, hurt as he was, contrived to wade or scramble across this obstacle, leaving his horse on the hither side. The troops were now under fire. In the excitement of the battle he forgot his injury and hurried forward, leading the brigade a distance of two or three hundred yards. But the exhaustion of his frame, and particularly the anguish of his knee—made more intolerable by such free use of it—was greater than any strength of nerve, or any degree of mental energy could struggle against. He fell, faint and almost insensible, within full range of the enemy's fire. It was proposed to bear him off the field; but, as some of his soldiers approached to lift him, he became aware of their purpose, and was partially revived by his determination to resist it. "No," said he, with all the strength he had left, "don't carry me off! let me lie here!" And there he lay under the tremendous fire of Cherubusco, until the enemy, in total rout, was driven from the field." In the negotiations which immediately ensued, General Pierce was honored by the commander-in-chief with the appointment of one of the commissioners to arrange the terms of the armistice. Jaded and worn out as he was, having been two nights without sleep and unable to move without assistance, he attended to this duty before seeking repose.

In the subsequent action of the campaign, at the battle of Molino del Rey, he rendered an important service to General Worth at the close of that bloody fight, in interposing to receive the fire of the enemy, and, the victory having been gained, occupied the field. He would have been prominently engaged in the sequel to this battle, the storming of Chapultepec, but he had now become so ill as to be compelled to seek relief at the head-quarters of General Worth, where he remained when this concluding action of the war was fought. He rose, however, from his sick couch to report himself to General Quitman, ready to take part in the final assault upon the city; but this perilous duty was happily spared him by the timely capitulation.

On his return to the United States at the close of 1847, General Pierce having resigned his commission at Washington, was received at Concord, in his native State, with the utmost enthusiasm. Welcomed to the town hall in a complimentary speech by General Low, he replied in an address of great propriety, skillfully turning the occasion to the praises of his comrades in the war. He spoke of the New England regiment in general, of its sacrifices and deeds of honor, and particularly of the brave men who had fallen on the field. He also paid a well-deserved compliment to the officers furnished to the war by the Military Academy at West Point, a tribute which came with more emphasis from his lips, as in former days in Congress he had opposed the usual annual appropriation for that institution. In recognition of his services, he was shortly after presented with a sword by the legislature of New Hampshire.

General Pierce now passed into retirement and was again engaged in the practice of his profession. He took part, however, in the political affairs of his party, particularly in the canvass of 1848 when General Cass was a candidate for the Presidency. The Democratic party then suffered a defeat, but rallied again for action in 1852, when General Pierce was put in nomination for that high office. Previously to this election his position was strengthened in New Hampshire by his election as President of the convention for the revision of the State constitution, and as the time for the choice of a new President of the Union approached he was put forward by the democracy of the State as a suitable candidate. The nominating convention of his party met at Baltimore in June, 1852; there was some difficulty in deciding upon a candidate, and several days had passed in the discussion, when General Pierce was brought forward by the Virginia delegation on the thirty-sixth ballot. His strength continued to increase as the contest was carried on, till, on the forty-ninth ballot, he received two hundred and eighty-two out of the two hundred and ninety-three votes cast. In the election which followed, he was chosen over General Scott, the candidate of the Whig party, by a popular majority of two hundred and three thousand, three hundred and six, their joint votes being two millions, nine hundred and eighty-nine thousand, four hundred and eighty-four. He had the electoral votes of all the States excepting Vermont, Massachusetts, Kentucky and Tennessee.

The Presidential administration of General Pierce from 1853 to 1857 when he was succeeded by James Buchanan, was an interval of comparative repose, marked by no extraordinary events of foreign or domestic policy, with the exception of the revival of the slavery agitation in the passage of the Kansas and Nebraska Territorial act in 1854, setting aside the geographical limit imposed by the compromise of 1850. In the late Governor Marcy, President Pierce had the services of a Secretary of State of eminent ability, who conducted the foreign affairs of the government with firmness and discretion. Among the home incidents of the time may be mentioned the erection of a Crystal Palace at New York, following the example of the previous great fair at London, for the exhibition of the industry of all nations. This undertaking, which was brilliantly carried out, was inaugurated by President Pierce in July, 1853, shortly after the commencement of his administration. After the close of his Presidential term, General Pierce visited the island of Madeira and made a prolonged tour in Europe. On his return to America, he again took up his residence in his old home at Concord, New Hampshire.

During the civil war he remained in strict retirement, but his sympathies were understood to be with the South. The death of his wife and of his loved friend Hawthorne depressed his spirits and shattered his health. For several years before his death he had experienced severe attacks of illness. He died in his old home October 8, 1869.

JAMES BUCHANAN.

THE father of James Buchanan, the fifteenth President of the United States, was a native of the county of Donegal, in the north of Ireland, who emigrated to the United States in 1783, the year which closed the War of the Revolution with the declaration of peace. He came to America a poor man, like thousands of others, to establish himself on what was then, as it is in many districts still, the virgin soil of the New World. Making his home in Pennsylvania, he there married Miss Elizabeth Spear, the daughter of a respectable farmer of Adams County. With her he set out for Franklin County, on the borders of Maryland, then a partially cultivated region, built a log hut, and made a clearing at a spot in the mountains in the vicinity of the town of Mercersburg. At this place, called Stony Batter, James Buchanan, the future President, was born April 23, 1791. When he was seven years old, his parents removed to Mercersburg. Being well informed, and appreciating the advantages of a good education, they here carefully provided for their son's instruction. The father had profited by his English schooling, and the mother, we are told, was distinguished by her strong sense and a certain taste for literature, being able to repeat from memory striking passages in Pope, Cowper, Milton and other English poets. Her piety is also spoken of as a noticeable trait of her character.[1] At the age of fourteen, James was sufficiently instructed in English studies, and the elements of the Greek and Latin classics, to enter Dickinson College at Carlisle. There he proved a ready student, acquitted himself with credit, and took a leading part in the literary society connected with the college. After receiving his degree, in 1809, he began the study of the law with Mr. James Hopkins of Lancaster, and three years afterwards, on arriving at age, was admitted to the bar. He applied himself with diligence to the profession, at Lancaster, and early acquired a lucrative practice. In a letter written more than thirty years afterwards, when he had risen to the position of Secretary of State, he recalled the occasion of his first public speech. It was when in the war with Great Britain, Maryland had been invaded, the capital burnt at Washington, and Baltimore was threatened. The country was aroused, and Mr. Buchanan addressed his fellow-citizens at Lancaster, urging upon them the duty of volunteering their services to resist the foe. A volunteer company

---

[1] Horton's Life of Buchanan, p. 15.

James Buchanan

was formed on the spot; he enlisted in it as a private, and proceeded with it to Baltimore, where, the danger having passed over, it was discharged. He little thought that half a century afterwards the region would again be aroused in a similar manner by the approach of a domestic foe, in a civil conflict of which his own administration, while he was President of the United States, was first to feel the shock. In this same year, 1814, Mr. Buchanan made his first entrance on political life, at the age of twenty-three, when he was elected a member of the Pennsylvania Legislature. On taking his seat he became an active supporter of the war measures then in progress, counselling stringent means of defence, and advocating a loan to the General Government to pay the militia of the State called into the public service.

In 1820, Mr. Buchanan took his seat in the House of Representatives, and continued a member by successive re-elections for ten years. This period embraced many important public measures, in which he took a prominent part. He was opposed to a tariff for protection, and to a general bankrupt law; when John Quincy Adams was elected, he opposed his favorite project of the Panama mission, and gave his zealous support to the advancement of General Jackson. On that chieftain's election to the Presidency, which was promoted by his influence in Pennsylvania, he was placed at the head of the Judiciary committee, and was one of the five managers chosen by the House to conduct the prosecution of Judge James H. Peck, of the District Court

of the United States for Missouri, against whom articles of impeachment were passed for an undue exercise of authority, in silencing and imprisoning a lawyer in his court, who had presumed to criticise one of his decisions. Judge Peck was defended before the Senate by William Wirt and Jonathan Merideth. The case was closed by Mr. Buchanan. The result was the passage of a law calculated to prevent a recurrence of the offence.

In 1831, Mr. Buchanan received the appointment from President Jackson of Euvoy Extraordinary and Minister Plenipotentiary to St. Petersburg, and succeeded in the object of his mission in securing a valuable commercial treaty, opening to our merchants important privileges in the Russian waters. On his return, in 1833, he was elected to the United States Senate, where he rendered important partisan services to the administration of General Jackson, then closely pressed in that body by a combination of its greatest political leaders, Clay, Calhoun, and Webster He was always opposed to the agitation of the subject of slavery in Congress, regarding the discussion of the topic at the North as alike injurious to the prospects of the slave and the integrity of the Union. These were his views when the right of petition brought the discussion before Congress, and he remained steadily on the side of the South in all matters of this nature, where the institution was concerned. An ardent supporter of President Jackson, he, of course, gave his influence in favor of the expunging resolutions of Senator Benton, which crowned the long list of

Congressional triumphs of the retiring President. To the administration of his successor, Mr. Van Buren, Mr. Buchanan gave important aid in his advocacy of the establishment of an independent treasury, and when that measure was temporarily set aside under the presidency of General Harrison and Tyler, he was urgent in his efforts to defeat the banks, or fiscal institutions, proposed in its place. On all the test questions of the Democratic party, Mr. Buchanan preserved political consistency. With one, in particular, he especially identified himself—the Annexation of Texas. He was for immediate action on its first introduction into the Senate, and when it was afterwards adopted, at the close of Tyler's administration, he stood alone in the committee on foreign relations in favor of the measure.

Mr. Polk succeeded to the Presidency in 1845, when Mr. Buchanan was called to his cabinet as Secretary of State. It was an important era in the foreign relations of the country, when the office was no sinecure. The North-western Boundary question was to be settled with England, and on the South-western frontier another difficulty of no ordinary magnitude existed, in the threatened conflict with Mexico. The former was settled on a compromise basis, adopting the parallel of latitude of 49° instead of the ultra demand, insisted upon by certain members of the party, and advocated in an elaborate state paper by Mr. Buchanan himself, of 54° 40'. The Government, in fact, had become pledged to the latter, but the difficulty was solved by referring the matter to the Senate, where the compromise line was accepted. The Mexican question was of graver responsibility. It was met by the administration as a war measure, and by the spirit and energy of the army of the country, and the volunteers called to the field, was successfully carried through, while efforts were constantly made to bring the contest to an end by negotiations for peace. When the enemy was thoroughly humbled, and his capital gained possession of, the latter finally prevailed. It is to the credit of our government that the war was conducted in no sanguinary spirit of cruelty, and that its terms of reconciliation, though they proved in the end highly advantageous to the victors, were, all things considered neither exacting nor humiliating to the conquered.

To the war with Mexico succeeded the political struggle at home on the slavery question, growing out of the new increase of territory. Mr. Buchanan, at the close of Mr. Polk's presidency and the breaking up of the cabinet, had retired to his home in Pennsylvania, in the neighborhood of Lancaster. Though out of office, however, his interest in politics was not diminished. When the contest over the Wilmot Proviso came up, setting bounds to the extension of slavery, he opposed its principles, and in his "Harvest-Home Letter," as it was called, recommended as a settlement the basis of the act of 1820, and that the Missouri line be extended to the Pacific. When the Compromise Measures of 1850 were adopted, he gave them his approval, urging in a letter which he addressed to a political committee in Philadelphia, "as the deliberate conviction of his judgment, the observance of two things as necessary to preserve the Union from danger: first, that agitation in the North on the subject of southern slavery must be rebuked and put down by a strong and enlightened public opinion; and, second, that the Fugitive Slave Law must be enforced in its spirit." There is a passage in this letter of interest in relation to subsequent events and the future position of the writer. "I now say," he wrote, "that the platform of our blessed Union is strong enough and broad enough to sustain all true-hearted Americans. It is an elevated—it is a glorious platform, on which the down-trodden nations of the earth gaze with hope and desire, with admiration and astonishment. Our Union is the star of the West, whose genial and steadily increasing influence will at last, should we remain an united people, dispel the gloom of despotism from the ancient nations of the world. Its moral power will prove to be more potent than millions of armed mercenaries. And shall this glorious star set in darkness before it has accomplished half its mission? Heaven forbid! Let us all exclaim with the heroic Jackson, 'The Union must and shall be preserved.'

"And what a Union has this been! The history of the human race presents no parallel to it. The bit of striped bunting which was to be swept from the ocean by a British navy, according to the predictions of a British statesman, previous to the war of 1812, is now displayed on every sea, and in every port of the habitable globe. Our

glorious stars and stripes, the flag of our country, now protects Americans in every clime. 'I am a Roman citizen!' was once the proud exclamation which everywhere shielded an ancient Roman from insult and injustice. 'I am an American citizen!' is now an exclamation of almost equal potency throughout the civilized world. This is a tribute due to the power and resources of these thirty-one United States. In a just cause, we may defy the world in arms. We have lately presented a spectacle which has astonished the greatest captain of the age. At the call of their country, an irresistible host of armed men, and men, too, skilled in the use of arms, sprung up like the soldiers of Cadmus, from the mountains and valleys of our confederacy. The struggle among them was not who should remain at home, but who should enjoy the privilege of enduring the dangers and privations of a foreign war in defence of their country's rights. Heaven forbid that the question of slavery should ever prove to be the stone thrown into their midst by Cadmus, to make them turn their arms against each other, and die in mutual conflict.

"The common sufferings and common glories of the past, the prosperity of the present, and the brilliant hopes of the future, must impress every patriotic heart with deep love and devotion for the Union. Who that is now a citizen of this vast Republic, extending from the St. Lawrence to the Rio Grande, and from the Atlantic to the Pacific, does not shudder at the idea of being transformed into a citizen of one of its broken, jealous and hostile fragments? What patriot had not rather shed the last drop of his blood, than see the thirty-one brilliant stars that now float proudly upon his country's flag, rudely torn from the national banner, and scattered in confusion over the face of the earth?

"Rest assured that all the patriotic emotions of every true-hearted Pennsylvanian, in favor of the Union and Constitution, are shared by the southern people. What battle-field has not been illustrated by their gallant deeds; and when, in our history, have they ever shrunk from sacrifices and sufferings in the cause of their country? What, then, means the muttering thunder which we hear from the South? The signs of the times are truly portentous. Whilst many in the South openly advocate the cause of secession and disunion, a large majority, as I firmly believe, still fondly cling to the Union, awaiting with deep anxiety the action of the North on the compromise lately effected in Congress. Should this be disregarded and nullified by the citizens of the North, the southern people may become united, and then farewell, a long farewell to our blessed Union. I am no alarmist; but a brave and wise man looks danger steadily in the face. This is the best means of avoiding it. I am deeply impressed with the conviction that the North neither sufficiently understands nor appreciates the danger."

Mr. Buchanan lived in comparative retirement at his Lancaster home till, on Mr. Pierce being chosen President, he was, in 1853, appointed minister to England. He accepted the post, and was occupied, in the course of its duties, in a negotiation of the Central American question, and also, incidentally, in a discussion respecting the possession of the island of Cuba. The latter, known as the Ostend Conference, grew out of the design of the President to purchase the island if possible, from Spain, and for this purpose a consultation was had in Europe between the American Ministers to Spain, France, and England, who might aid the undertaking by mutual counsel. The history of this proceeding is thus given in the recent notice of President Buchanan in "Appleton's Cyclopedia." "Ostend was first selected for the place of meeting; but the conferences were subsequently adjourned to Aix la Chapelle. The American Ministers kept written minutes of their proceedings, and of the conclusions arrived at, for the purpose of future reference, and for the information of their government at home. These minutes were afterwards styled a 'protocol,' though they contained nothing but memoranda to be forwarded for consideration to the authorities in Washington. They were not intended to be submitted to a foreign power. They contained no proposition, laid down no rule of action, and in no manner whatever interfered with our regular diplomatic intercourse. The President desired to know the opinions of our Ministers abroad on a subject which deeply concerned the United States, and the Ministers were bound to furnish it to him. Their minutes exhibited the importance of the island to the United States, in a commercial and strategical point of view; the advantages that would accrue to Spain from the sale of it at a fair price, such as the United States might be willing to pay for it; the difficulty which Spain would encounter in endeavoring to keep possession of it by mere military power; the sympathy of the people of the United States with the inhabitants of the island, and, finally, the possibility that Spain, as a last resort, might endeavor to Africanize Cuba, and become instrumental in the reënacting of the scenes of St. Domingo. The American Ministers believed that in case Cuba was about to be transformed into another St. Domingo, the example might act perniciously on the slave population of the Southern States of our own confederacy, and there excite the blacks to similar deeds of violence. In this case, they held that the instinct of self-preservation would call for the armed intervention of the United States, and we should be justified in wresting the island by force from Spain."

Mr. Buchanan returned home in the spring of 1856, and in the following summer received the nomination for the Presidency from the Democratic convention which met at Cincinnati. In the contest which ensued with Colonel Fremont, the candidate of the new Republican party, he was elected President of the United States by the vote of nineteen out of thirty-one States. The popular vote was, for Buchanan, 1,803,029; for Fremont, 1,342,164; for Fillmore, 874,625. The main interest of Mr. Buchanan's administration centered in the discussion of the control of the territories in reference to the introduction of slavery. The ominous agitations regarding Kansas, itself the the-

atre of bloody conflict, employed much of this period. At the close of Mr. Buchanan's term, the clouds which had been gathering since its commencement broke in the storm of war. The election of his successor, Mr. Lincoln, the candidate of the Republican party, was followed by secession in the Southern States, and there was no weapon in the hands of Mr. Buchanan powerful enough to arrest the rebellion. He spoke entreatingly, persuasively, in favor of the preservation of the Union; but the South, whose interests he had so long served, was deaf to his appeals.

His concluding annual message, at the opening of Congress in December, 1860, was full of despondency, the consciously vain effort of a disappointed statesman to resist the overwhelming tide which was approaching. The South had placed itself in an attitude of threatened opposition to the inauguration of President Lincoln. President Buchanan, with a certain simplicity, reminded the disaffected that "the election of any one of our fellow-citizens to the office of President, does not of itself afford just cause for dissolving the Union;" adding, "this is more especially true if his election has been effected by a mere plurality, and not a majority of the people, and has resulted from transient and temporary causes which may probably never again occur. In order to justify a resort to revolutionary resistance, the Federal Government must be guilty of a deliberate, palpable, and dangerous exercise of powers not granted by the Constitution. The late Presidential election, however, has been held in strict conformity with its express provisions. How, then, can the result justify a revolution to destroy this very Constitution? Reason, justice, a regard for the Constitution, all require that we shall wait for some overt and dangerous act on the part of the President elect, before resorting to such a remedy. * * After all, he is no more than the chief executive officer of the government. His province is not to make, but to execute the laws; and it is a remarkable fact in our history that, notwithstanding the repeated efforts of the anti-slavery party, no single act has ever passed Congress, unless we may possibly except the Missouri Compromise, impairing in the slightest degree the rights of the South to their property in slaves. And it may also be observed, judging from present indications, that no probability exists of the passage of such an act by a majority of both Houses, either in the present or the next Congress. Surely, under these circumstances, we ought to be restrained from present action by the precept of Him who spake as never man spake, that 'sufficient unto the day is the evil thereof.' The day of evil may never come, unless we shall rashly bring it upon ourselves." After presenting other considerations showing how little danger there really existed for apprehension on the part of the South, he turned to an examination of the doctrine of Secession as it was openly advocated by a large class of disaffected politicians. "In order," said he, "to justify secession as a Constitutional remedy, it must be on the principle that the Federal Government is a mere voluntary association of States, to be disolved at pleasure by any one of the contracting parties. If this be so, the confederacy is a rope of sand, to be penetrated and dissolved by the first adverse wave of public opinion in any of the States. In this manner our thirty-three States may resolve themselves into so many petty, jarring, and hostile republics, each one retiring from the Union without responsibility, whenever any sudden excitement might impel them to such a course. By this process, a Union might be entirely broken into fragments in a few weeks, which cost our forefathers many years of toil, privation, and blood to establish." He further supported the obvious doctrine of the paramount authority of the Union by references to the opinions of Madison and Jackson, and a deduction from the express provisions of the Constitution. "This Government," he concluded, "is a great and powerful Government, invested with all the attributes of sovereignty over the special subjects to which its authority extends. Its framers never intended to implant in its bosom the seeds of its own destruction, nor were they at its creation guilty of the absurdity of providing for its own dissolution. It was not intended by its framers to be the baseless fabric of a vision which, at the touch of the enchanter, would vanish into thin air; but a substantial and mighty fabric, capable of resisting the slow decay of time, and of defying the storms of ages. Indeed, well may the jealous patriots of that day have indulged fears that a government of such high powers might violate the reserved rights of the States, and wisely did they adopt the rule of a strict construction of these powers to prevent the danger. But they did not fear, nor had they any reason to imagine, that the Constitution would ever be so interpreted as to enable any State, by her own act, and without the consent of her sister States, to discharge her people from all or any of their Federal obligations. It may be asked, then, are the people of the States without redress against the tyranny and oppression of the Federal Government? By no means. The right of resistance on the part of the governed against the oppression of their governments cannot be denied. It exists independently of all constitutions, and has been exercised at all periods of the world's history. Under it old governments have been destroyed, and new ones have taken their place. It is embodied in strong and express language in our own Declaration of Independence. But the distinction must ever be observed, that this is revolution against established government, and not a voluntary secession from it by virtue of an inherent constitutional right. In short, let us look the danger fairly in the face: secession is neither more nor less than revolution. It may or it may not be a justifiable revolution, but still it is revolution."

Having thus established the legal inability of a State to withdraw from the confederacy at will, he proceeded to discuss the "responsibility and true position of the Executive" under the circumstances. His duty was, according to the words of his oath, "to take care that the laws be faithfully executed." The administration of justice by the Federal judiciary naturally first present-

ed itself; but in South Carolina he found this was now impracticable. The officers of justice in that State had resigned, the whole machinery of the courts had been broken up, and "it would be difficult, if not impossible, to replace it." The revenue, indeed, still continued to be collected in the State, and as for the public property in the forts, magazines, arsenals, etc., the belief was expressed that no attempt would be made to expel the United States from its possession; "but if in this I should prove to be mistaken," said the President, "the officer in command of the forts has received orders to act strictly on the defensive. In such a contingency, the responsibility for consequences would rightfully rest upon the heads of the assailants."

The mere mention of such points was ominous of war, and the President perceived the tendency. He felt the difficulties of his situation and submitted them to Congress. In doing this, however, he added to his argument against secession another, denying to that body the possession of any power under the Constitution "to coerce a State into submission which is attempting to withdraw, or has actually withdrawn from the confederacy." His conclusion on this subject was this:—"The power to make war against a State is at variance with the whole spirit and intent of the Constitution. Suppose (he added), such a war should result in the conquest of a State, how are we to govern it afterwards? Shall we hold it as a province, and govern it by despotic power? . . . The fact is, that our Union rests upon public opinion and can never be cemented by the blood of its citizens shed in civil war. If it cannot live in the affections of the people, it must one day perish. Congress possesses many means of preserving it by conciliation; but the sword was not placed in their hands to preserve it by force."

As an escape from this threatened evil of secession, President Buchanan recommended that an amendment of the Constitution should be adopted, initiated either by Congress or the State Legislatures, according to the provisions of that instrument, "confined to the final settlement of the true construction of the Constitution on three special points :—1st. An express recognition of the right of property in slaves in the States where it now exists or may hereafter exist. 2d. The duty of protecting this right in all the common Territories throughout their territorial existence, and until they shall be admitted as States into the Union, with or without slavery, as their Constitutions may prescribe. 3d. A like recognition of the right of the master to have his slave, who has escaped from one State to another, restored and 'delivered up' to him, and of the validity of the Fugitive Slave Law enacted for this purpose, together with a declaration that all State laws impairing or defeating this right are violations of the Constitution, and are consequently null and void."

Such was the attitude of President Buchanan in sight of the impending revolution, and such the suggestions which he made to resist its progress. The crisis which had arrived, beyond the control of palliatives, was destined to shatter his political creed.

Beset with doubts and difficulties, but true to the plain duty before him, he incurred the censure of the Commissioners sent to Washington from South Carolina, by his resistance to their demand of the withdrawal of Major Anderson and his command from Fort Sumter.

The war which he feared was now inevitable, and preparations, at last, were to be made to meet it. Deserted by his old Southern friends in Congress, and even in his cabinet, President Buchanan summoned to his aid new counsellors like Scott, Dix, Stanton, Holt, and others whose patriotism redeemed the last days of his administration. In weakness, sorrow, almost in despair of the future of his country, he assisted at the inauguration of his successor, and left Washington for the retirement of his home in Pennsylvania.

There his days were passed in comparative seclusion during the four years of the national warfare for the preservation of the Union, while his leisure was employed in the preparation of a work, a review of the rise and progress of the anti-slavery agitation and a vindication of the conduct of his administration of the Presidency. Under the new order of affairs which followed the successful termination of the war, the publication of this book attracted little attention. He did not long survive. After a brief illness he met death with Christian resignation at Wheatland, on the morning of the first day of June, 1868. His funeral at Lancaster was largely attended, without distinction of party, and the usual public honors were paid to his memory.

A. Lincoln

ABRAHAM LINCOLN.

Abraham Lincoln was born February 12th, 1809, in a district of Hardin County, now included in Larue County, Kentucky. His father and grandfather, sprung from a Quaker family in Pennsylvania, were born in Rockingham County, Virginia. Thence the grandfather, Abraham Lincoln, removed to Kentucky, where, encountering the fortunes of the first settlers, he was slain by the Indians, about the year 1784. His third and youngest son, Thomas, brought up to a life of rude country industry, in 1806 married Nancy Hanks, of Kentucky, a native of Virginia, so that the blood of Abraham Lincoln is directly traceable to the Old Dominion—the mother of Presidents.

The parents, it is said, partly on account of slavery, partly on account of the disputed Kentucky land titles, removed to a new forest home, in what is now Spencer County, Indiana, when their son Abraham was in his eighth year. The task before the settlers was the clearing of the farm in the wilderness; and in this labor and its incidents of hunting and agricultural toils the rugged boy grew up to manhood, receiving such elementary instruction as the occasional schoolmasters of the region afforded. Taken altogether, it was very little—for the time which he attended schools of any kind, was in the whole less than a year. His knowledge from books was to be worked out solely by himself; the vigorous life around him and rough experience were to teach him the rest. His first adventure in the world was at the age of nineteen, when hired as an assistant to a son of the owner, the two, without other aid, navigated a flat boat to New Orleans, trading by the way—an excursion on which more might be learnt of human nature than in a year at college. At twenty-one, he followed his father, who had now married a second time, to a new settlement in Macon County, Illinois, where a log cabin was built by the family, and the land fenced in by rails, vigorously and abundantly split by the stalwart Abraham.

The rail-splitter of Illinois was yet to be summoned to a fiercer conflict. To build a flat-boat was no great change of occupation for one so familiar with the axe. He was engaged in this work on the Sangamon River, and in taking the craft afterward to New Orleans, serving on his return as clerk in charge of a store and mill at New Salem, belonging to his employer. The breaking out of the Black-Hawk war in Illinois, in 1832, gave him new and more spirited occupation. He joined a volunteer company, was elected captain, served through a three months' campaign, and was in due time rewarded by his share of bounty lands in Iowa. A popular man in his neighborhood, doubtless from his energy, sagacity, humor, and innate benevolence of disposition, admirably qualifying him as a representative of the West, or of human nature in its better condition anywhere, he was, on return from the war, set up as a Whig candidate for the Legislature, in which he was beaten in the district, though his own precinct, democratic as it too was, gave him 277 out of 284 votes. Unsettled, and on the lookout for occupation in the world, he now again fell in charge of a country store at New Salem, over the counter of which he gained knowledge of men, but little pecuniary profit. The store, in fact, was a failure, but the man was not. He had doubtless chopped logic, as heretofore timber, with his neighbors, and democrats had felt the edge of his argument. Some confidence of this nature led him to think of the law as a profession. Working out his problem of self-education, he would borrow a few books from a lawyer of the village in the evening, read them at night, and return them in the morning. A turn at official surveying in the county meanwhile, by its emoluments, assisted him to live. In 1834, he was elected, by a large vote to the Legislature, and again in 1836, '38, and '40. In 1836, he was admitted to the bar, and the following year commenced practice at Springfield, with his fellow-representative in the Legislature, Major John F. Stuart. He rapidly acquired a reputation by his success in jury trials, in which he cleared up difficulties with a sagacious, ready humor, and a large and growing stock of apposite familiar illustrations. Politics and the bar, as usual in the West, in his case also went together; a staunch supporter of Whig principles in the midst of the democracy, he canvassed the State for Henry Clay in 1844, making numerous speeches of signal ability, and in 1846, was elected to Congress from the central district of Illinois. During his term he was distinguished by his advocacy of free soil principles, voting in favor of the right of petition, and steadily supporting the Wilmot proviso prohibiting slavery in the new territories. He also proposed a plan of compensated emancipation, with the consent of a majority of the owners, for the District of Columbia. A member of the Whig National Convention of 1848, he supported the nomination of General Taylor for the Presidency, in an active canvass of Illinois and Indiana. In 1856, he was recommended by the Illinois delegation as a candidate for the Vice Presidency, on the Republican ticket with Colonel Fremont. In 1858, he was nominated as candidate for United States Senator in opposition to Stephen A. Douglas, and "took the stump" in joint debate with that powerful antagonist of the Democratic party, delivering a series of speeches during the summer and autumn, in the chief towns and cities of the State. In the first of these addresses to the Republican State Convention at Springfield, June 17th, he uttered a memorable declaration on the subject of slavery, much quoted in the stirring controversies which afterwards ensued. "We are now," said he, "far into the fifth year since a policy was initiated with the avowed object, and confident promise of putting an end to slavery agitations. Under the operation of that policy, that agitation has not only not ceased, but has constantly augmented. In my opinion, it will not cease until a crisis shall have been reached and passed. 'A house divided against itself cannot stand.' I believe this government cannot endure permanently, half slave and half free. I do not expect the Union to be dissolved—I do not expect the house to fall; but I do expect it will cease to be divided. It will become all one thing or all the other."

Other opinions expressed by him in this political campaign, while they exhibited him as no friend to slavery, placed him on the ground of a constitutional opposition to the institution. In answer to a series of questions proposed by Mr. Douglas, he replied that he was not in favor of the unconditional repeal of the fugitive slave law; that he was not pledged against the admission of any more slave States into the Union, nor to the admission of a new State into the Union with such a constitution as the people of that State may see fit to make, nor to the abolition of slavery in the District of Columbia, nor to the prohibition of the slave trade between the different States; while he was "impliedly, if not expressly, pledged to a belief in the right and duty of Congress to prohibit slavery in all the United States Territories." With regard to the acquisition of any new territory, unless slavery is first prohibited therein, he answered: "I am not generally opposed to honest acquisition of territory; and in any given case, I would or would not oppose such acquisition, accordingly as I might think it would or would not aggravate the slavery question among ourselves." Mr. Lincoln, in fine, while he held the firmest opinions on the evil of slavery as an institution, and its detriment to the prosperity of the country, was not disposed to transcend the principles or pledges of the Constitution for its suppression. He would not, without regard to circumstances, press even the legitimate powers of Congress. Of the vexed negro question, he said further, on a particular occasion in those debates: "I have no purpose, directly or indirectly, to interfere with the institution of slavery in the States where it now exists. I believe I have no lawful right to do so, and I have no inclination to do so. I have no purpose to introduce political and social equality between the white and the black races. There is a physical difference between the two, which, in my judgment, will probably forever forbid their living together upon the footing of perfect equality, and inasmuch as it becomes a necessity that there must be a difference, I, as well as Judge Douglas, am in favor of the race to which I belong having the superior position. I have never said anything to the contrary; but I hold that, notwithstanding all this, there is no reason in the world why the negro is not entitled to all the natural rights enumerated in the Declaration of Inde pendence—the right to life, liberty, and the pursuit of happiness. I hold that he is as much entitled to these as the white man. I agree with Judge Douglas he is not my equal in many respects—certainly not in color, perhaps not in moral or intellectual endowment. But in the right to eat the bread, without the leave of any one else, which his own hand earns, he is my equal, and the equal of Judge Douglas, and the equal of every living man."

This contested Douglas and Lincoln election in Illinois ended in the choice of a Legislature which sent the former to the United States Senate, though the Republican candidates pledged to Mr. Lincoln received a larger aggregate vote.

Mr. Lincoln, now a prominent man in the West, was looked to by the rapidly developing Republican party as a leading expounder of its principles in that region. In the autumn and winter of 1859, he visited various parts of the country, delivering lectures on the political aspect of the times, and was constantly received with favor. In a speech which he made, addressing a mixed assembly at Leavenworth, in Kansas, in this season, the following passage occurred, which, read by the light of subsequent events, appears strangely prophetic. "But you, Democrats," said he, "are for the Union; and you greatly fear the success of the Republicans would destroy the Union. Why? Do the Republicans declare against the Union? Nothing like it. Your own statement of it is, that if the Black Republicans elect a President, you *won't stand it!* You will break up the Union. That will be your act, not ours. To justify it, you must show that our policy gives you just cause for such desperate action. Can you do that? When you attempt it, you will find that our policy is exactly the policy of the men who made the Union Nothing more and nothing less. Do you really think you are justified to break up the government rather than have it administered as it was by Washington, and other great and good men who made it, and first administered it? If you do, you are very unreasonable, and more reasonable men cannot and will not submit to you. While you elect Presidents we submit, neither breaking nor attempting to break up the Union. If we shall constitutionally elect a President, it will be our duty to see that you also submit. Old John Brown has been executed for treason against a State. We cannot object even though he agreed with us in thinking slavery wrong. That cannot excuse violence, bloodshed, and treason. It could avail him nothing that he might think himself right. So, if constitutionally we elect a President, and, therefore, you undertake to destroy the Union, it will be our duty to deal with you as old John Brown has been dealt with. We shall try to do our duty. We hope and believe that in no section will a majority so act as to render such extreme measures necessary."

In the ensuing nomination, in 1860, for the Presidency, by the National Republican Convention at Chicago, Mr. Lincoln, on the third ballot, was preferred to Mr. Seward by a decided vote, and placed before the country as the candidate of the Republican free-soil party. He had three rivals in the field: Breckinridge, representing the old Southern pro-slavery Democratic party; Douglas, its new, "popular sovereignty" modification; Bell, a respectable, cautious conservatism. In the election, of the entire popular vote, 4,662,170, Mr. Lincoln received 1,857,-610; Mr. Douglas, 1,365,976; Mr. Breckinridge, 847,953; and Mr. Bell, 590,631. Every free State except New Jersey, where the vote was divided, voted for Lincoln, giving him seventeen out of the thirty-three States which then composed the Union. In nine of the slave States, besides South Carolina, he had no electoral ticket. Alabama, Arkansas, Delaware, Florida, Georgia, Louisiana, Maryland, Mississippi, North and South Carolina, Texas, cast their votes for Breckinridge and Lane, 72; for Bell and Everett, 39; for Douglas and Johnson, 12.

The "Platform" or series of resolutions of the Republican Convention by which Mr. Lincoln was nominated for the Presidency, were explicit on the principles and objects of the party. The highest devotion was expressed for the Union, with a political instinct seemingly prescient of the future. It was declared that " to the Union of the States this nation owes its unprecedented increase in population; its surprising development of material resources; its rapid augmentation of wealth; its happiness at home, and its honor abroad; and we hold in abhorrence all schemes for disunion, come from whatever source they may; and we congratulate the country that no Republican member of Congress has uttered or countenanced a threat of disunion, so often made by Democratic members of Congress without rebuke, and with applause from their political associates; and we denounce those threats of disunion, in case of a popular overthrow of their ascendency, as denying the vital principles of a free government, and as an avowal of contemplated treason, which it is the imperative duty of an indignant people strongly to rebuke and forever silence.

The " maintenance inviolate of the rights of the States, and especially of each State to order and control its own domestic institutions according to its own judgment exclusively," was declared to be essential to " that balance of power on which the perfection and endurance of our political faith depends," and " the lawless invasion by armed force of any State or Territory, no matter under what pretext," was denounced " as among the gravest of crimes." The existing Democratic administration was arraigned for its " measureless subserviency to the exactions of a sectional interest, as is especially evident in its desperate exertions to force the infamous Lecompton Constitution upon the protesting people of Kansas—in construing the personal relation between master and servant to involve an unqualified property in persons—in its attempted enforcement everywhere, on land and sea, through the intervention of Congress and the Federal Courts, of the extreme pretensions of a purely local interest."

The principles of the party in regard

to slavery in the Territories, were laid down in the declarations "that the new dogma that the Constitution, of its own force, carries slavery into any or all the Territories of the United States, is a dangerous political heresy, at variance with the explicit provisions of that instrument itself, with contemporaneous expositions, and with legislative and judicial precedent; is revolutionary in its tendency, and subversive of the peace and harmony of the country:" and "that the normal condition of all the territory of the United States is that of freedom; that as our republican fathers, when they had abolished slavery in all our national territory, ordained that no person should be deprived of life, liberty, or property, without the process of law, it becomes our duty, by legislation, whenever such legislation is necessary, to maintain this provision of the Constitution against all attempts to violate it; and we deny the authority of Congress, of a territorial legislature, or of any individuals, to give legal existence to slavery in any territory of the United States."

Such were the declarations under which Mr. Lincoln was elected to the Presidency. The legitimate influence of the Government, it was designed, should be exerted to give every fair opportunity for the development of liberty, and not, as was charged upon the Democrats, for its forced suppression. For the maintenance of these views, it was admitted by all who were acquainted with him, that a man of singular plainness and sincerity of character had been chosen for the chief magistracy. "He is possessed," wrote an intelligent observer who had studied his disposition in his home in Illinois "of all the elements composing a tru' western man, and his purity of character and indubitable integrity of purpose add respect to admiration for his private and public life. His word 'you may believe and pawn your soul upon it.' It is this sterling honesty (with utter fearlessness) even beyond his vast ability and political sagacity, that is to command confidence in his administration."

In February, 1861, Mr. Lincoln left his home at Springfield, on his way, by a circuitous route through the northern States, to Washington. His journey at the start was impressed with the peculiar responsibility of his new position. A defeated party, supported by the haughty pretensions and demands of the South, which even then stood in an attitude of armed rebellion, was determined to place every obstacle in his way which the malignity of disappointed political ambition could suggest. He felt that a crisis was at hand requiring the most consummate prudence and political wisdom in the guidance of the Ship of State. In taking farewell of his friends at the railway station, at Springfield, he said with fervor, "no one not in my position can appreciate the sadness I feel at this parting. To this people I owe all that I am. Here I have lived more than a quarter of a century; here my children were born, and here one of them lies buried. I know not how soon I shall see you again. A duty devolves upon me which is, perhaps, greater than that which has devolved upon any other man since the days of Washington. He never would have succeeded except for the aid of Divine Providence, upon which he at all times relied. I feel that I cannot succeed without the same Divine aid which sustained him; and in the same Almighty Being I place my reliance for support, and I hope you, my friends, will all pray that I may receive that Divine assistance, without which I cannot succeed, but with which success is certain. Again I bid you all an affectionate farewell."

With this feeling of religious earnestness, Mr. Lincoln, who did not over-estimate the importance of his position, set his face towards Washington. At every stage on the journey he took the opportunity, when he was called upon to speak, by the citizens, to express his determination to use his influence and authority equitably for the interests of the nation, without infringement on the rights of any. "We mean to treat you," he said at Cincinnati, to an audience in which, we may suppose, the Democratic party was liberally represented, "as near as we possibly can as Washington, Jefferson, and Madison treated you. We mean to leave you alone, and in no way to interfere with your institutions; to abide by all and every compromise of the Constitution, and in a word, coming back to the original proposition; to treat you so far as degenerate men, if we have degenerated, may, according to the example of those noble fathers, Washington, Jefferson, and Madison." On the same day, the 12th of February, in another speech at Indianapolis, he alluded to the question then pressing upon the country for early solution regarding the maintenance of the national authority in a rebellious State, by force, if it should be necessary. An outcry had been raised against the "coercion" of a State? He saw in the clamor, a specious mask favoring a desperate political intrigue which threatened the life of the nation, and he sought to strip off the disguise that the reality beneath might be seen. Would it be "coercion," he asked, if the United States should retake its own forts, and collect the duties on foreign importations. Do those who would resist coercion resist this? "If so their idea of the means to preserve the object of their great affection would seem to be exceedingly thin and airy. If sick, the little pills of the homœopathist would be much too large for them to swallow. In their view, the Union, as a family relation, would seem to be no regular marriage, but rather a sort of free love arrangement, to be maintained on passional attraction."

Everywhere on his journey he was received with enthusiasm. At New York he was greeted by the Mayor and citizens at the City Hall; and at Philadelphia, on Washington's birthday, he assisted in raising the national flag on Independence Hall. In a few remarks on the latter occasion, he spoke feelingly, with a certain impression of melancholy, of the great American principle at stake, promising to the world "that in due time, the weight should be lifted from the shoulders of all men;" adding, "if the country cannot be saved without giving up that prin ciple, I was about to say, I would rather be assassinated on this spot than surrender it." The word "assassination" was afterwards noticed when, a day or two later, it was found that the President, warned of a plot to take his life on his way to Washington, had felt compelled, by the advice of his friends, to hasten his journey by an extra train at night, to the capital, and thus baffle the conspirators. He had been made acquainted with the scheme on his arrival at Philadelphia, by the police; and it was after this intimation had been received by him that he spoke at Independence Hall. He then proceeded to keep an appointment with the Pennsylvania Legislature, at Harrisburg, whom he met on the afternoon of the same day. At night he quietly returned by rail to Philadelphia, and thence to Washington, arriving there early on the morning of the twenty-third.

Ten days after, his inauguration as President took place at the Capitol. The usual ceremonies were observed; but in addition, General Scott had provided a trained military force which was at hand to suppress any attempt which might be made to interrupt them. Happily its interference was not called for. The inaugural address of the President was every way considerate and conservative. He renewed the declarations he had already made, that he had no intention to interfere with the institution of slavery in the States where it exists, adding, "I believe I have no lawful right to do so, and I have no inclination to do so." In a brief argument he asserted the perpetuity of the Union. "It is safe to assert," he said, "that no government proper ever had a provision in its organic law for its own termination. Continue to execute all the express provisions of our national Constitution, and the Union will endure forever, it being impossible to destroy it, except by some action not provided for in the instrument itself." He therefore announced his intention, as in duty bound by the terms of his oath, to maintain it. "I shall take care," said he, "as the Constitution itself expressly enjoins upon me, that the laws of the Union shall be faithfully executed in all the States. Doing this, which I deem to be only a simple duty on my part, I shall perfectly perform it, so far as is practicable, unless my rightful masters, the American people, shall withhold the requisition, or in some authoritative manner direct the contrary. I trust this will not be regarded as a menace, but only as the declared purpose of the Union, that it will constitutionally defend and maintain itself. In doing this there need be no bloodshed or violence, and there shall be none unless it is forced upon the national authority. The power confided to me will be used to hold, occupy and possess the property and places belonging to the Government, and collect the duties and imposts; but beyond what may be necessary for these objects there will be no invasion, no using of force against or among the people anywhere. Where hostility to the United States shall be so great and so universal as to prevent competent resident citizens from holding the federal offices, there will be no attempt to force obnoxious strangers among the people who object. While the strict legal right may exist of the Government to enforce the exercise of the offices, the attempt to do so would be so irritating, and so nearly impracticable withal, that I deem it better to forego for the time the uses of such offices. The mails, unless repelled, will continue to be furnished in all parts of the Union. So far as possible, the people everywhere shall have that sense of perfect security, which is most favorable to calm thought and reflection. The course here indicated will be followed, unless current events and experience shall show a modification or change to be proper, and in every case and exigency my best discretion will be exercised according to the circumstances actually existing, and with a view and hope of a peaceful solution of the national troubles and the restoration of fraternal sympathies and affections."

This disposition to effect a peaceful settlement of the existing difficulty was further shown in an earnest expostulation or plea for the preservation of the endangered Union, and the admission or declaration that "if a change in the Constitution to secure this result should be thought desirable by the people, he would favor, rather than oppose a fair opportunity to act upon it." He had no objection, he said, that a proposed amendment introduced into Congress "to the effect that the Federal Government shall never interfere with the domestic institutions of States, including that of persons held to service,"

should be made "express and irrevocable."

"My countrymen," he concluded, "my countrymen, one and all, think calmly and well upon this whole subject. Nothing valuable can be lost by taking time. If there be an object to hurry any of you, in hot haste, to a step which you would never take deliberately, that object will be frustrated by taking time; but no good object can be frustrated by it. Such of you as are now dissatisfied still have the old Constitution unimpaired, and on the sensitive point the laws of your own framing under it; while the new administration will have no immediate power, if it would, to change either. If it were admitted that you who are dissatisfied hold the right side in the dispute, there is still no single reason for precipitate action. Intelligence, patriotism, Christianity, and a firm reliance on Him who has never yet forsaken this favored land, are still competent to adjust, in the best way, all our present difficulties. In your hands, my dissatisfied fellow-countrymen, and not in mine, is the momentous issue of civil war. The Government will not assail you. You can have no conflict without being yourselves the aggressors. You have no oath registered in Heaven to destroy the Government; while I shal. have the most solemn one to 'preserve, protect, and defend' it. I am loath to close. We are not enemies, but friends. We must not be enemies. Though passion may have strained, it must not break our bonds of affection. The mystic chords of memory, stretching from every battle-field and patriot grave to every living heart and hearthstone all over this broad land, will yet swell the chorus of the Union, when again touched, as surely they will be, by the better angels of our nature."

In this spirit, the President commenced his administration. In the following month the bombardment of Fort Sumter, by the South Carolinians under General Beauregard, "inaugurated" the war. On receipt of the news of its fall, President Lincoln, on the 15th of April, issued his proclamation calling for seventy-five thousand militia, to suppress the combinations opposing the laws of the United States, and commanding the persons composing the combinations to disperse, and retire peaceably to their respective abodes within twenty days. Congress was, at the same time, summoned to meet in extra session on the ensuing 4th of July. When that body met, the Southern Confederacy had succeeded in arraying large armies in the field for the accomplishment of its revolutionary designs. Various skirmishes and minor battles had occurred in Missouri, Western Virginia, and elsewhere, and the troops which had been raised at the North were about to meet the enemy in the disastrous battle of Bull Run. The President laid the course which he had pursued before Congress, calling upon them for "the legal means to make the contest a short and decisive one." He felt, he said, that he had no moral right to shrink from the issue, though it was "with the deepest regret that he had found the duty of employing the war-power." "Having," he said, in the conclusion of his message, "chosen our course without guile and with pure purpose let

us renew our trust in God, and go forward without fear and with manly hearts.

The story of the conduct of that struggle through four years of unexampled sacrifices by the people, of unprecedented trials to the State, of a controversy of arms and principles testing every fibre of the nation, and ending in the vindication and reëstablishment of the Union, belongs to History rather than to Biography. But the part borne in the struggle by President Lincoln will ever be memorable. He was emphatically the representative of the popular will and loyal spirit of the nation. In his nature eminently a friend of peace, without personal hostilities or sectional prejudices, he patiently sought the welfare of the whole. Accepting war as an inevitable necessity he conducted it with vigor, yet with an evident desire to smooth its asperities and prepare the way for final and friendly reconciliation. Unhappily, the demands of the South for independence, and their continued struggle for the severance of the Union, rendered any settlement short of absolute conquest of the armies in the field impossible. To hasten this end, when the condition appeared inevitable, President Lincoln, after many delays and warnings, issued a proclamation of negro emancipation within the rebellious States, on the twenty-second of September, 1862. It was appointed to go into effect—the States continuing in rebellion —on the first of January ensuing. "All persons," it declared, "held as slaves within any State, or designated part of a State, the people whereof shall then be in rebellion against the United States, shall be thenceforward and forever free; and the Executive Government of the

United States, including the military and naval authority thereof, will recognize and maintain the freedom of such persons, and will do no act or acts to repress such persons, or any of .them, in any efforts they may make for their actual freedom." This proclamation, in general accordance with the action of the Congress, was a war measure; it had grown out of the war as a necessity, was promulgated conditionally with an appeal for the termination of the war, and, if destined to be operative, was dependent upon military success for its efficiency. The war, it was generally admitted, if continued, would put an end to slavery; and as the slave passed under new social relations by the advance of the national armies, by conquest, by services rendered to the national cause, and finally by enlistment in the national armies, this became every day more apparent. The President's proclamation, the great act of his Administration, proved the declaration of an obvious and inevitable result. Two years more of war, after it was issued, of war growing in malignity and intensity, and extending through new regions, confirmed its necessity; while President Lincoln, as the end drew nigh, sought to strengthen the fact of emancipation by recommending to Congress and the people, as an independent measure, the passage of an amendment of the Constitution, finally abolishing the institution of slavery in the United States.

President Lincoln, as we have said, in his conduct of the war, steadily sought the support of the people. Indeed, his measures were fully in accordance with their conviction, his resolutions, waiting the slow development of events, being
26

governed more by facts than theories. He thus became emphatically the executive of the national will; his course wisely guided by a single view for the maintenance of the Union was in accordance with the popular judgment; and in consequence, as the expiration of his term of office approached, it became evident that he would be chosen by the people for a second term of the Presidency. As the canvass proceeded the result was hardly regarded as doubtful, and the actual election in Nov., 1864, confirmed the anticipation. Out of 25 States, in which the vote was taken he received a majority of the popular vote of 23—Delaware, Kentucky, and New Jersey for McClellan..

President Lincoln's second Inaugural Address on the 4th of March, 1865, was one of his most characteristic State papers. It was a remarkable expression of his personal feelings, his modesty and equanimity, his humble reliance on a superior power for light and guidance in the path of duty. Success in his great career, the evident approach of the national triumph, in which he was to share, generated in his mind no vulgar feeling of elation; on the contrary he was impressed, if possible, with a weightier sense of responsibility and a deeper religious obligation. "With malice toward none," was his memorable language, "with charity for all, with firmness in the right—as God gives us to see the right—let us strive on to finish the work we are in—to bind up the nation's wounds—to care for him who shall have borne the battle, and for his widow and orphans—to do all which may achieve and cherish a just and lasting peace among ourselves, and with all nations." The peace so ardently longed for was not far distant. On the 9th of April General Lee surrendered the chief rebel army to General Grant, and with that event the war was virtually ended. President Lincoln had been witness of some of its closing scenes at Richmond, and had returned to Washington in time to receive at the capital news of the surrender. In an address to a gathering of the people who came to the Presidential mansion to congratulate him on the result, he avoided any unseemly expressions of triumph, and turned his thoughts calmly to the great problem of reconstruction, upon which his mind was now fully intent. At the close he declared, in view of some act of amnesty overtures of reconciliation, that it might soon be his duty "to make some new announcement to the people of the South." This speech was made on the evening of the eleventh of April. The fourteenth was the anniversary of Sumter, completing the four years' period of the war. There was no particular observance of the day at Washington, but in the evening the President, accompanied by his wife, a daughter of Senator Harris, and Major Rathbone, of the United States army, attended by invitation the performances at Ford's Theatre, where a large audience was assembled to greet him. When the play had reached the third act, about nine o'clock, as the President was sitting at the front of the private box near the stage, he was deliberately shot from behind by an assassin, John Wilkes Booth, the leader of a gang of conspirators, who had been for some time intent, in concert with the rebellion, upon taking his life. The ball entered the back part of the President's head, penetrated the brain, and rendered him, on the instant, totally insensible. He was removed by his friends to a house opposite the theatre, lingered in a state of unconsciousness during the night and expired at twenty-two minutes past seven o'clock on the morning of the 15th.

Thus fell, cruelly murdered by a vulgar assassin, at the moment of national victory, with his mind intent upon the happier future of the Republic, with thoughts of kindness and reconciliation toward the vanquished enemies of the State, the President who had just been placed by the sober judgment of the people a second time as their representative in the seat of executive authority. The blow was a fearful one. It created in the mind of the nation a feeling of horror and pity, which was witnessed in the firmest resolves and tenderest sense of commiseration. All parties throughout the loyal States united in demonstrations of respect and affection. Acts of mourning were spontaneous and universal. Business was everywhere suspended, while the people assembled to express their admiration and love of the President so foully slain, and to devote themselves anew to the cause— their own cause—for the assertion of which he had been stricken down. When the funeral took place, the long procession, as it took its way from Washington through Pennsylvania, New York, Ohio and Indiana, to the President's home in Illinois was attended, at every step, with unprecedented funeral honors; orations were delivered in the large cities, crowds of mourners by night and day witnessed the solemn passage of the train on the long lines of railway; a half million of persons it was estimated, looked upon the face of their departed President and friend.

Andrew Johnson

ANDREW JOHNSON.

Among the many public men in the United States who have risen to distinction from humble circumstances by industry and natural force of character, Andrew Johnson of Tennessee, by fortune and position, is certainly not the least noticeable. Born of poor parents, in Raleigh, North Carolina, December 29th, 1808, he was apprenticed in his boyhood to a tailor, and was engaged in this occupation in South Carolina till the age of seventeen. He subsequently crossed the mountains bordering his State on the west, travelling, it is said, on foot with his wife, and established himself at Greenville, Tennessee. Pursuing there a life of industry, working out, meanwhile, by his own exertions the problem of education—for he had never attended school—he prospered in the world, and having a disposition to public life, with a talent for speaking, he soon became known as a politician. He was elected Mayor of Greenville in 1830, was chosen a member of the State Legislature in 1835, and of the State Senate in 1841. For ten years, from 1843 to 1853, he represented his district in the national House of Representatives; in the last-mentioned year being elected Governor of the State of Tennessee, and again in 1855. In 1857, crowning this rapid series of honorable political promotions, he took his seat as United States Senator for the full term ending in 1863.

A man of the people, he represented in the Senate the strongly-nurtured democratic energy and instincts of the West, identifying himself with its welfare, distinguishing himself particularly by his advocacy of the Homestead Bill, which opened the unsettled territory virtually to free occupancy by th settler. It was not to be supposed that such a man, the representative of the free mountain region of East Tennessee, where his home lay, would have much sympathy with the great Southern Rebellion. On the contrary, he was, in his seat in the Senate, one of the foremost to oppose its first manifestations. In that memorable session, in the closing months of President Buchanan's administration, when the Southern members were abandoning their posts, preparatory to their work of treason, he stood unmoved, strenuously opposing every exhibition of disloyalty, and calling resolutely on all to maintain the Constitution and the integrity of the Union as the secure and only basis of popular rights. His course was known and marked by the disloyal in his own State and else where. The mob of Memphis, during this period, in proof of their hostility, burnt his effigy, and at the close of the session he was directly insulted and threatened with violence at the railway station, at Lynchburg, Virginia, while on his way homeward from Washington. Arrived in East Tennessee, he took part in the Union Convention at Greenville, at the end of May, supporting the declaration of grievances which, in an emphatic manner, bore witness to the loyalty of that portion of the State. On the 19th of June he made a memorable speech at Cincinnati, denouncing, in unmeasured terms, the iniquity of the Tennessee Legislature, in procuring, contrary to the expressed will of the people, an alliance with the Southern Confederacy. In glowing language he summoned all, without regard to old party considerations, to come to the support of their common country, and "crush, destroy, and totally annihilate" the spirit of secession, as an influence utterly hostile to all religious, moral, or social organization. "It is," said he, "disintegration, universal dissolvement, making war upon everything that has a tendency to promote and ameliorate the condition of the mass of mankind."

In the extra session of Congress in July, he reiterated these sentiments in an eloquent speech in the Senate, characterizing the war upon which the country had entered as a struggle for the very existence of the Government against internal foes and traitors. "It is a contest," said he, "whether a people are capable of governing themselves or not. We have reached that crisis in our country's history, and the time has arrived when, if the Government has the power, if the people are capable of self-government, and can establish this great truth, that it should be done." Nothing discouraged by the recent disaster to the national army at Bull Run, he exclaimed on this occasion, at the close of a masterly review of the political situation of the country, after calling on the Government to redouble its energies in the field, "We must succeed. This Government must not, cannot fall. Though your flag may have trailed in the dust let it still be borne onward; and if for the prosecution of this war in behalf of the Government and the Constitution, it is necessary to cleanse and purify the banner, let it be baptized in fire from the sun and bathed in a nation's blood. The nation must be redeemed; it must be triumphant."

In the months which followed, Senator Johnson rendered eminent service by his speeches and influence to the national cause. At length, in the spring of 1862, the Union victories in Tennessee having resulted in the military occupation of Nashville, his patriotism was rewarded by the appointment, with the rank of brigadier-general of volunteers, of military Governor of Tennessee. He immediately, in March, 1862, entered upon the duties of this office, which he has continued to discharge, through many vicissitudes of public affairs, with firmness and discretion.

At the meeting of the National Convention of the Republican party, which assembled at Baltimore on the 7th of June, 1864, Andrew Johnson was nominated for Vice President on the ticket with President Lincoln. The nomination was well received by the party—for the principles and steadfastness of Governor Johnson had been fully tried in his private station and in office during the war; and the success of the ticket, as the canvass proceeded, was regarded as a matter of certainty previously to the election in November. Simultaneously with the inauguration of President Lincoln, at his entrance on his second term of office on the 4th of March 1865, the oath of office was administered to Vice-President Johnson, in the Senate Chamber. He remained in Washington, and was one of the eminent heads of the Government marked out by the assassin Booth and his fellow conspirators to be murdered at the development of their fiendish plot in April, on the anniversary, of the attack upon Fort Sumter. Narrowly escaping this fate by the timidity or reluctance of the person to whom his murder was assigned, he was, on the instant, at the immediate fatal termination of the wound inflicted upon President Lincoln, called to be his successor in office. Notified of this event, and summoned to the performance of his new duties by the members of the Cabinet, the oath of office as President was administered to him by Chief Justice Chase, in the forenoon of the fourteenth of April, a few hours after President Lincoln's decease, at his rooms at the Kirkwood House, in Washington. After receiving the oath, and being declared President of the United States, Mr. Johnson remarked to the members of the Cabinet and others present: " I must be permitted to say that I have been almost overwhelmed by the announcement of the sad event which has so recently occurred. I feel incompetent to perform duties so important and responsible as those which have been so unexpectedly thrown upon me. As to an indication of any policy which may be pursued by me in the administration of the Government, I have to say that that must be left for development as the Administration progresses. The message or declaration must be made by the acts as they transpire. The only assurance that I can now give of the future is reference to the past. The course which I have taken in the past in connection with this rebellion must be regarded as a guarantee of the future. My past public life, which has been long and laborious, has been founded, as I in good conscience believe, upon a great principle of right, which lies at the basis of all things. The best energies of my life have been spent in endeavoring to establish and perpetuate the principles of free Government, and I believe that the Government, in passing through its present perils, will settle down upon principles consonant with popular right, more permanent and enduring than heretofore. I must be permitted to say, if I understand the feelings of my own heart, I have long labored to ameliorate and elevate the condition of the great mass of the American people. Toil, and an honest advocacy of the great principles of free government, have been my lot. The duties have been mine—the consequences are God's. This has been the foundation of my political creed. I feel that in the end the Government will triumph, and that these great principles will be permanently established. In conclusion, gentlemen, let me say that I want your encouragement and countenance. I shall ask and rely upon you and others in carrying the Government through its present perils. I feel in making this request that it will be heartily responded to by you and all other patriots and lovers of the rights and interest of a free people."

At this moment, as an indication of his views, a recent speech of Johnson was recalled which he delivered in Washington at the beginning of April, when news of the capture of Richmond was received at the capital. "You must indulge me," said he on that occasion, "in making one single remark in connection with myself. At the time the traitors in the Senate of the United States plotted against the Government, and entered into a conspiracy more foul, more execrable and more odious than that of Cataline against the Romans, I happened to be a member of that body, and, as to loyalty, stood solitary and alone among the Senators from the Southern States. I was then and there called upon to know what I would do with such traitors, and I want to repeat my reply here. I said, if we had an Andrew Jackson he would hang them as high as Haman. But as he is no more, and sleeps in his grave in his own beloved State, where traitors and treason have even insulted his tomb and the very earth that covers his remains, humble as I am, when you ask me what I would do, my reply is, I would arrest them; I would try them; I would convict them, and I would hang them. As humble as I am and have been, I have pursued but one undeviating course. All that I have—life, limb and property—have been put at the disposal of the country in this great struggle. I have been in camp, I have been in the field, I have been everywhere where this great rebellion was; I have pursued it until I believe I can now see its termination. Since the world began there never has been a rebellion of such gigantic proportions, so infamous in character, so diabolical in motive, so entirely disregardful of the laws of civilized war. It has introduced the most savage mode of warfare ever practiced upon the earth.

"I will repeat here a remark, for which I have been in no small degree censured. What is it, allow me to ask, that has sustained the nation in this great struggle? The cry has been, you know, that our Government was not strong enough for a time of rebellion; and in such a time she would have to contend against internal weakness as well as internal foes. We have now given the world evidence that such is not the fact; and when the rebellion shall have been crushed out, and the nation shall once again have settled down in peace, our Government will rest upon a more enduring basis than ever before. But, my friends, in what has the great strength of this Government consisted? Has it been in one man power? Has it been in some autocrat, or in some one man who held absolute government? No! I thank God I have it in my power to proclaim the great truth that this Government has derived its strength from the American people. They have issued the edict; they have exercised the power that has resulted in the overthrow of the rebellion, and there is not another Government upon the face of the earth that could have withstood the shock. We can now congratulate ourselves that we possess the strongest, the freest and the best Government the world ever saw.

"Thank God that we have lived through this trial, and that, looking in your intelligent faces here, to-day, I can announce to you the great fact that Petersburgh, the outpost of the strong citadel, has been occupied by our brave and gallant officers, and our untiring, invincible soldiers. And not content with that they have captured the citadel itself, the stronghold of the traitors. Richmond is ours, and is now occupied by the forces of the United States! Death to the conspirators—clemency to their victims. One word more, and I have done. It is this: I am in favor of leniency; but in my opinion, evildoers should be punished. Treason is the highest crime known in the catalogue of crimes; and for him that is guilty of it—for him that is willing to lift his impious hand against the authority of the nation—I would say death is too easy a punishment. My notion is that treason must be made odious, that traitors must be punished and impoverished, their social power broken, though they must be made to feel the penalty of their crimes. Hence I say this—the halter to intelligent, influential traitors. But to the honest boy, to the deluded man, who has been deceived into the rebel ranks, I would extend leniency. I

would say, return to your allegiance, renew your support to the Government and become a good citizen; but the leaders I would hang. I hold, too, that wealthy traitors should be made to remunerate those men who have suffered as a consequence of their crimes—Union men who have lost their property, who have been driven from their homes, beggars and wanderers among strangers. It is well to talk about things here to-day, in addressing the well-informed persons who compose this audience. You can, to a very great extent, aid in moulding public opinion and giving it proper direction. Let us commence the work. We have put down these traitors in arms; let us put them down in law, in public judgment and in the morals of the world."

In the spirit of these declarations President Johnson, shortly after his inauguration, addressed Governor Oglesby of Illinois, and a number of eminent citizens of the State as well as other delegations from the East and West To the expressions of sympathy and confidence by Gov. Oglesby he replied: "To an individual like myself, who has never claimed much, but who has, it is true, received from a generous people many marks of trust and honor, for a long time, an occasion like this, and a manifestation of public feeling so well-timed, are peculiarly acceptable. Sprung from the people myself, every pulsation of the popular heart finds an immediate answer to my own. By many men in public life such occasions are often considered merely formal. To me they are real. Your words of countenance and encouragement sink deep in my heart, and were I even a coward I could not but gather from them strength to carry out my convictions of the right. Thus feeling, I shall enter upon the discharge of my great duty firmly, steadfastly, if not with the signal ability exhibited by my predecessor, which is still fresh in our sorrowing minds. Need I repeat that no heart feels more sensibly than mine this great affliction? In what I say on this occasion, I shall indulge in no petty spirit of anger, no feeling of revenge. But we have beheld a notable event in the history of mankind. In the midst of the American people, where every citizen is taught to obey law and observe the rules of Christian conduct, our Chief Magistrate, the beloved of all hearts, has been assassinated; and when we trace this crime to its cause, when we remember the source whence the assassin drew his inspiration, and then look at the result, we stand yet more astounded at this most barbarous, most diabolical assassination. Such a crime as the murder of a great and good man, honored and revered, the beloved and the hope of the people, springs not alone from a solitary individual of ever so desperate wickedness. We can trace its cause through successive steps, without my enumerating them here, back to that source which is the spring of all our woes. No one can say that if the perpetrator of this fiendish deed be arrested, he should not undergo the extremest penalty the law knows for crime; none will say that mercy should interpose. But is he alone guilty? Here, gentlemen, you perhaps expect me to present some indication of my future policy. One thing I will say. Every era teaches its lesson. The times we live in are not without instruction.

The American people must be taught— if they do not already feel—that treason is a crime and must be punished; that the Government will not always bear with its enemies; that it is strong, not only to protect, but to punish. When we turn to the criminal code and examine the catalogue of crimes, we there find arson laid down as a crime with its appropriate penalty; we find there theft, and robbery, and murder, given as crimes; and there, too, we find the last and highest of crimes—treason. With other and inferior offences our people are familiar; but in our peaceful history treason has been almost unknown. The people must understand that it is the blackest of crimes, and will be surely punished. I make this allusion, not to excite the already exasperated feelings of the public, but to point out the principles of public justice which should guide our action at this particular juncture, and which accord with sound public morals. Let it be engraven on every heart that treason is a crime, and traitors shall suffer its penalty. While we strain our minds to comprehend the enormity of this assassination, shall we allow the nation to be assassinated?"

The presidential term of President Johnson will occupy a peculiar place in the political history of the country. The war being ended, his sympathies, which had been so strongly enlisted in upholding the National Union, and had led him to an alliance with the Republicans—now returning to their old channel—brought him again in concert with the Democratic party. It was his fortune thenceforth during his term of office to be in a state of perpetual disagreement with the measures which

Congress adopted in the government of the late disaffected States and otherwise in the work of reconstruction. Want of confidence and suspicion led to hostility; there was but little reticence on either side; the leaders of the House of Representatives were unsparing in their denunciations; the President, who never practised any concealment of his thoughts, indulged freely in recrimination, by pen and speech; laws were passed, to receive, time and again, the Presidential veto, and to be re-adopted and made the law of the land by constitutional majorities. The work was thus thrown on the Executive of putting into operation and enforcing enactments which he over and over demonstrated, from his own point of view—following his best convictions—to be illegal, and contrary to the true interests of the country. In the maintenance of his opinion he was stubborn and unyielding. Congress, holding him firmly to his executive duties, constantly imposed new conditions and contrived safeguards by which he should be bound to carry out their will without regard to any "policy" of his own. This in time led to an open rupture and a resort by Congress to the extreme resource of impeachment.

Among the more important acts of Congress which called forth the veto of the President was the Civil Rights Bill, in 1866—an act for the benefit of the emancipated colored race, declaring all persons, of every race and color, born in the United States and not subject to any foreign power—excluding Indians not taxed—to be citizens of the United States, entitled to the full and equal benefit of all laws and proceedings for the security of person and property enjoyed by white citizens, and guaranteeing to the late slaves protection in their newly-acquired rights under the exclusive jurisdiction of the United States Courts. To this act President Johnson, among other things, objected the impolicy of immediately conferring citizenship upon the recently emancipated race, urging the discrimination in their favor against foreign residents, who were required to "undergo a probation of five years," and especially the interference of the bill with the peculiar rights and legislation of the several States concerned. The bill was passed in April over the veto in the Senate by a Republican vote of 33 against 15—mainly Democratic, and in the House by 122 against 34.

The adjustment of the Freedmen's Bureau Bill gave rise to other vetoes, the President, among other points, objecting to the conflict of jurisdiction between the military tribunals of the bill and other constituted authorities. The bill abolishing the distinction of race or color in the elective franchise in the District of Columbia met with like opposition; so, too, the act providing military government for the insurrectionary States, which, like the others, was passed over the President's veto. Thus the conflict went on between the executive and legislative departments of the Government, culminating in the passage, of course in like manner, over the President's veto, of the Tenure-of-Civil-Office Act, by which the power of removal of incumbents was taken away from the President, save on the terms of their original appointment "by and with the advice of the Senate." The act was made specially applicable to the members of the Cabinet, the Secretaries of State, of the Treasury, of War, of the Navy, and of the Interior, the Postmaster-General and the Attorney-General, whose term of office was continued, subject to the control of the Senate, during the term of the President by whom they may have been appointed. Under certain circumstances of alleged misconduct, or legal disqualification, or incapacity, the President might, during a recess of the Senate, suspend such officer and appoint a temporary incumbent until the case should be acted upon by the Senate at its next meeting. This bill was passed by the requisite majorities in March, 1867. The alleged violation of this act formed the ground of several articles of the formidable "Impeachment" of the President, brought by the House of Representatives exactly a year afterwards. In August, 1867, President Johnson suspended Secretary Stanton from office as Secretary of War, and appointed Gen. Grant as his successor *ad interim*. Stanton strongly protested, but yielded the office to Grant, who discharged its duties till, at their next meeting in January, the Senate refused to concur in Mr. Stanton's suspension, upon which Grant retired, thus reinstating Stanton in office, whilst President Johnson endeavored to prevent this result, appointing and seeking to establish Adjutant-General Thomas in the position. Stanton, however, took and kept possession of the office till the failure of the impeachment, in May, induced his resignation. The Impeachment trial began in the Senate on the 30th March, 1867, and terminated in a final vote on the 26th May, the question having been taken on only three of the articles of the eleven. The verdict was a close one, just failing the requisite two-thirds vote—35 voting guilty, 19 not guilty, on the test articles. The Court then adjourned *sine die*.

On the eve of retiring from the office of the Presidency, Johnson sent forth a farewell address "To the People of the United States," bearing date March 4, 1869, the day of the inauguration of his successor. The document went forth to the country, and was published in many of the newspapers simultaneously with the Inaugural Address of Gen. Grant. In this paper President Johnson dwelt in his usual unhesitating manner upon his difficulties with Congress, and, in return for the "impeachment" which had been inflicted upon him, charged that body with a formidable array of grievances, the enumeration of which, as it fell from his pen, exhibited in the most striking light his utter alienation from that branch of the National Government. With these and other bitter parting words, President Johnson retired from office, and a few days afterwards left Washington for his old home in Tennessee. On his way at Baltimore and elsewhere, and on his arrival in his adopted State, he was received with distinguished attention by his friends and supporters, whom he addressed in various speeches on the political affairs of the day.

In 1875 he was elected United States Senator, and during the brief extra session of March he spoke against the resolution to recognize the Kellogg government in Louisiana. He died in Carter County, East Tennessee, July 31, 1875, aged 66 years.

U. S. Grant

ULYSSES SIMPSON GRANT.

The ancestry of General Grant is traced to an early Pilgrim emigrant, .Matthew Grant, who came to Massachusetts with his wife, Priscilla from Dorsetshire England, in 1630. After a few years' residence at Dorchester, having lost his wife, Matthew settled at Windsor, iu Connecticut, where he became a man of consequence, and was a second time married.

Ulysses Simpson Grant was the seventh in descent from this alliance. Members of the family served in the old Indian and French wars, and in the war for Independence, Noah, the grandfather of Ulysses, having entered the service at Lexington, and attained the rank of captain. After the war was over, he was settled for a while in Pennsylvania, and subsequently established himself in a house in Ohio. His son, Jesse Root Grant, then in his childhood, accompanied him, and after various youthful adventures, entered upon manhood with the occupation of a tanner. At the age of twenty-seven he married Hannah Simpson, and of this alliance was born at the family residence, Point Pleasant, Clermont County, Ohio, on the 27th of April, 1822, Ulysses Simpson Grant. This, however, was not the baptismal name of the child. He was christened Hiram Ulysses Grant, the first name apparently exhibiting a trace of the ancestral Puritan associations of the family; the second, Ulysses, having been inspired by a no less classical authority than the Telemachus of Fenelon, a stray copy of which had brought the fame of the Homeric hero to the homestead on the Ohio. We shall see presently by what accident the name was changed. The boy grew up in the Buckeye state, under the paternal training, accustomed to the industry of the tan-yard, and outside of the labors of this sturdy pursuit finding ready relief in the manly rural sports and adventures of Western life, with an especial zest for all that related to horsemanship. He became in fact so great an adept in riding, that he practised some of the daring feats of the ring. In such hardy pursuits Grant grew up a rather quiet, self-reliant youth, and on his approach to manhood exhibited a spirit of inde pendence in an uncompromising disrel ish of the somewhat rough toil of the tannery. On his rejecting this mode of life, his father, looking round for a pursuit for his son, the thought happily occurred to him of a cadetship at West-Point. Accidentally there was a vacancy in the district, and an appli cation to the representative in Congress secured it. The member confounding the family names, sent in the application for Ulysses Simpson Grant. Under this name the appointment was made out, and the authorities at the Military academy being indifferent or unwilling to correct the error, the candidate was compelled to accept the designation. He entered West-Point in 1839, at the age of seventeen, and graduated in due course in 1843, the twenty-first in a class of thirty nine. He had no great reputation in the academy as a student, though he displayed a taste for mathematics; while his general abilities and moral qualities were undoubted. The skill in horsemanship which he carried with him, distinguished him in the exercises of the riding school. His biographer, Albert D. Richardson, to whom we are indebted for many interesting personal notices of General Grant, has recorded an anecdote of his proficiency in this accomplishment. "There was nothing," says he, "he could not ride. He commanded, sat, and jumped a horse with singular ease and grace; was seen to the best advantage when mounted and at a full gallop; could perform more feats than any other member of his class, and was altogether one of the very best riders West-Point had ever known.

"The noted horse of that whole region, was a powerful, long-legged sorrel, known as York. Grant and his classmate, Conts, were the only cadets who rode him at all, and Couts could not approach Grant. It was his delight to jump York over the fifth bar, about five feet from the ground, and the best leap ever made at West-Point, something more than six feet, is still marked there as 'Grant's upon York.' York's way was to approach the bar at a gentle gallop, crouch like a cat, and fly over with rarest grace. One would see his fore feet high in the air, his heels rising as his fore feet fell, and then all four falling lightly together. It needed a firm seat, a steady hand, and a quick eye to keep upon the back of that flying steed. At the final examination, his chief achievement was with his famous horse York. In presence of the board of visitors he made the famous leap of six feet and two or three inches."

Grant left West-Point with the brevet appointment of second lieutenant in the 4th Infantry, and presently joined his regiment at Jefferson Barracks, St. Louis, Missouri, where he became acquainted, and formed an attachment to the sister of one of his academy classmates, Miss Julia Dent, the lady who subsequently became his wife. This was the period of meditated Texas annexation, which under the influences of Southern political necessities was being steadily forced upon the country. Portions of the small national army were gradually concentrated on the Southern frontier. The regiment to which Grant was attached, was pushed forward in the movement, tarrying a year at Fort Jessup, on Red river, when it was sent to Corpus Christi, Texas, forming a part of General Taylor's army of observation, Grant being now promoted full second lieutenant, and in the spring of of 1846, reached the Rio Grande. It was a challenge to the Mexican forces on the right bank of the river, which they were not long in accepting. The contest fairly began in May, with the battles of Palo Alto and Resaca de la Palma, in both of which actions Grant was actively engaged. He was also in the thick of the fight in the severe assault of Monterey, in September. Shortly after the arrival of General Scott at Vera Cruz, in the beginning of the following year, Grant joined that commander, his regiment with others having been withdrawn from the forces of General Taylor, to take part in the expedition against the capital. He was with the army of Scott in the successive battles from Cerro Gordo, onward, which marked the victorious progress to the City of Mexico, ever active in the field and as quartermaster, and was brevetted first lieutenant and captain for gallant and meritorious conduct at Molino del Rey and Chapultepec.

The war being ended, Grant on a visit to St. Louis married his betrothed in August, 1848, and was subsequently stationed for two years with his regiment at Detroit, with a brief interval of service at Sackett's Harbor, discharging the duties of quartermaster. In 1852, his regiment was sent to the Pacific, and stationed in the vicinity of Portland, Oregon, where in 1853, he was promoted to a full captaincy. He was then ordered with his company to Fort Humbolt, in northern California. Here having been subjected to certain animadversions from Washington, on the ground of intemperate drinking, on an intimation of the charge in the summer of 1854, he resigned his commission. He now passed several years in farming operations with his wife's family in Missouri, and in 1859, became engaged with a friend in business at St. Louis as real-estate agent, with the firm of Boggs & Grant. At this time he made an application to the authorities of the city for a local office. The characteristic letter addressed to the Hon. County Commissioners, in which he presented his claims, has been preserved by his biographers; it reads as follows: "Gentlemen; I beg leave to submit myself as an applicant for the office of County Engineer, should the office be rendered vacant, and at the same time to submit the names of a few citizens who have been kind enough to recommend me for the office. I have made no effort to get a large number of names, nor the names of persons with whom I am not personally acquainted. I enclose herewith also, a statement from Prof. J. J. Reynolds, who was a classmate of mine at West Point, as to qualifications.

"Should your honorable body see proper to give me the appointment, I pledge myself to give the office my entire attention, and shall hope to give general satisfaction.

Very respectfully,
Your obedient servant,
U. S. GRANT."

This application though backed by a goodly number of business friends was rejected, his competitor for the office succeeding, it is said, through greater political influence, though it must be admitted there was but a feeble recognition at this time of the talents and character by which Grant subsequently became so famous. "There was no other special objection to him," says his biographer Richardson, "than his supposed democratic proclivities from his political antecedents. His ability as an engineer was accorded. He was not much known, though the commissioners had occasionally seen him about town, a trifle shabby in dress, with pantaloons tucked in his boots. They supposed him a good office man, but hardly equal to the high responsibility of keeping the roads in order. He might answer for a clerk, but in this county engineership, talent and efficiency were needed."

A partial amend for this disappointment was made by a minor position in the Custom House at St. Louis, out of which he was thrown after a few weeks possession by the death of his superior, the collector. On the prospect of a vacancy in the County Engineership in 1860, he sent in a second application to the commissioners, but the office was not vacated, and of course nothing came of it. In this extremity of his fortunes having a family to support, he removed to Galena, Illinois, where his father had established a profitable leather business. In this store Grant was employed at the very humble salary of eight hundred dollars. In this position he was found when the attack on Sumter in the Spring of 1861 summoned the country to arms for the preservation of the integrity of the Union. The news that this first blow was struck, in Illinois, as elsewhere in the North and West, fired the heart of the people. Grant's town of Galena was not behind in this national emotion. A meeting on the instant was held, at which Washburn, member of Congress of the district, and Rawlins a young lawyer of the place, destined to become distinguished in the United States army, were speakers, and gave expres-

sion to the enthusiasm of the hour. Their voice was for the uncompromising maintenance of the National Union, and their expressions were unequivocal that this involved an armed struggle. Grant was present, quite willing to accept the conclusion, and expressed his intention again to enter the service. At a second meeting he was called upon to preside, and being apparently the only one in the region who knew anything of military organization, unfolded some of the details required in raising troops, which was now the order of the day. He was active in the preliminary local movements, in getting together volunteers, and Washburn, who began to appreciate his merits, presented his claims to command unsuccessfully in these first days to Governor Yates, at Springfield. Grant meanwhile, had offered his services to the War Department at Washington, and the application remained unanswered; nor had an application to the Governor of Ohio met a better fate. Governor Yates, now of necessity gave him employment as clerk in his military office, and under a like exigency, though still without a commission, became actively engaged in the work of military organization. Nearly two months had now passed, and Grant was on a visit to his father in Covington, opposite Cincinnati, when General McClellan was in command. It is related that Grant called upon him twice without "proposing to ask for an appointment, but thinking that McClellan might invite him to come on his staff." * The accident of not meeting McClellan, offers a curious subject of speculation as to the

---

* Richardson's Personal History of Grant.

probable results in diverting a man of mark from the future great destiny which awaited him. Before he reached Illinois, on his return, a dispatch from Governor Yates to Grant was on its way appointing him colonel of the twenty-first Illinois volunteers. In this capacity Grant began his actual service in the war, marching his men to northern Missouri, where he discharged the duties of acting Brigadier General. Congress was now in session in July, and the organization of the national army of volunteers was proceeding at Washington, and at the urgency of Washburn, Grant received the commission of Brigadier General. He was now placed in command of the district of southeastern Missouri, including the neighboring territory at the junction of the Ohio and Mississippi, with his head-quarters at Cairo. He began by rendering an important service to the country. In the nick of time, in advance of orders from General Fremont, commander of the Western Department, and in anticipation of the Confederate General Polk, who was bent on appropriating the district, and was about moving on from his headquarters below at Columbus, Grant detailed a portion of his command to take possession of Paducah, Kentucky, an important station for military purposes, at the mouth of the Tennessee. Thus promptly securing this station, he addressed a proclamation to the citizens of Paducah, dated Sept. 6th, well qualified by its courtesy and firmness to vindicate his course in allaying the jealousies, and at the same time repressing any hostility which might be expected from the border State, a portion of whose territory he was occupying. "I am come among you," says he, "not as an enemy, but as your fellow-citizen; not to maltreat you, nor annoy you, but to respect, and enforce the rights of all loyal citizens. An enemy, in rebellion against our common government, has taken possession of, and planted his guns on, the soil of Kentucky, and fired upon you. Columbus and Hickman are in his hands. He is moving upon your city. I am here to defend you against this enemy, to assist the authority and sovereignty of your government. I have nothing to do with opinions, and shall deal only with armed rebellion and its aiders and abettors. You can pursue your usual avocations without fear. The strong arm of the government is here to protect its friends, and to punish its enemies. Whenever it is manifest that you are able to defend yourselves, and maintain the authority of the government, and protect the rights of loyal citizens, I shall withdraw the forces under my command."

Grant's friend Rawlins joined him at Cairo, as assistant adjutant general. A participation in friendship and military duty continued during the struggle, and which led to his appointment in the Cabinet as Secretary of War. The sudden death of General Rawlins was an irreparable loss to the President.

In November, Fremont having taken the field on the Arkansas border, where he was opposed to the rebel general Price, ordered Grant to make a demonstration in the direction of Columbus to prevent the co-operation of Polk with the enemy in Arkansas. Grant, accordingly gathering his newly recruited forces, about three thousand men, embarked with them on transports on the 6th, and moved down the river. Resting for the night at a point on the shore, he learnt that Polk had thrown over a force from Columbus to Belmont, immediately opposite on the Missouri side. To carry out the object of the expedition, and to test the valor of his troops, he resolved upon an attack. He landed his men about three miles above Belmont, out of range of the guns at Columbus, and leaving a batallion of infantry to protect his boats, advanced on the enemy's camp, where General Pillow had concentrated about twenty-five hundred men. Meeting the confederates on the way, the land was swampy and covered with timber, there was considerable miscellaneous firing, in which Grant's horse was shot under him. This was carried on through the morning hours, ending in a determined push upon the enemy, and the capture of their camp, with its artillery and personal spoils. The raw recruits, elated by success, began the work of plunder, and presently the tents were set on fire. As all this was visible at headquarters at Columbus, Polk directed his guns at the spot and brought over reinforcements to intercept the Union troops on their return, which Grant and his officers, fully aware of the situation, with energy, though not without difficulty were conducting. The men were brought through a fire of skirmishers to the boats, carrying off a number of prisoners, with all possible care for the wounded, Grant being the last man on the bank to re-embark. It is said that while he was riding slowly along in the dress of a private, he was pointed out by General Polk, as a target to his men, who were too intent on firing upon the crowded transports to take advantage of this opportunity within their reach. This was the battle, as it was termed, of Belmont, with the result which fully justified the movement, a heavy loss having been inflicted on the enemy, in killed, wounded, and prisoners, the indicated diversion having been effected, and what was more, at the time, in the words of Grant in a private letter to his father immediately after the engagement: "confidence having been given in the officers and men of this command that will enable us to lead them in any future engagement, without fear of the result."

The next military movement of consequence in which Grant was engaged, grew out of his timely proceeding in gaining command of the Tennessee river at Paducah. Halleck was now Grant's superior in the Western department, and was planning a comprehensive scheme of attack upon the enemy on the Kentucky and Tennessee frontier, proportionate to the importance and magnitude which the conflict had now assumed.

January, 1862, saw these plans perfected; the design was to dislodge the enemy on the upper waters of the Tennessee and the Cumberland, and thus gain possession of the river communication with the interior. Grant moved with a land force on the 2nd of February, ascending the Tennessee in transports from Paducah, supported by a flotilla of gunboats under Com. Foote. Fort Henry was the immediate object of attack, and the position was gained in the preliminary assault by the gun-

boats in a close encounter, General Til-
man, the commander of the garrison,
making a timely escape with his men
to Fort Donelson, distant but twelve
miles on the Cumberland, which thus
far pursued a parallel course with the
Tennessee. Grant now saw his opportunity to strike a blow by advancing immediately upon Fort Donelson.
With characteristic energy he would
have moved at once, but was prevented
by a rising of the Tennessee, which put
the roads under water, and made them
impracticable for artillery. On the
12th, he moved upon the position, and
began the investment of the place.
Weather of intense severity set in, and
the men suffered fearfully from exposure; still the work went on, with sharp
skirmishing, reinforcements meanwhile
arriving, and Foote bringing up his
gunboats on the Cumberland. An attack of the latter upon the works, failed of success, on account of the high
position of the enemy's guns above the
river. On the 15th, the enemy despair-
ing of maintaining their position, though
numbering a large force, ably defended
by artillery, attacked the right of
the investing army, held by McCler-
nand. They had gained some advan-
vantage when Grant came upon the
ground, arriving from an interview
with Foote. Detecting by his military
sagacity, from the fact that the prisoners' haversacks were filled with rations,
the intention of the enemy to cut their
way out, he resolved upon an immediate assault upon the works, ordering
the veteran General C. F. Smith in command on the left, to begin the attack.
This was made late in the afternoon
with great gallantry, and ended in

Smith's gaining a position which commanded the fort. That night the enemy
evacuated the position, the rebel generals Floyd and Pillow escaping with
a large portion of the force by boats
up the river, leaving General Buckner
to arrange the conditions of surrender.
He accordingly, at daylight on the morning of the 16th, sent a dispatch to General Grant proposing an armistice with
a view of entering on negotiations.
To this Grant on the night after sent
the following reply: " Yours of this
date proposing armistice, an appointment of commissioners to settle terms
of capitulation, is just received. No
terms except an unconditional and immediately surrender can be accepted.
I propose to move immediately upon
your works" Stript of his troops by
the flight of the rebel-generals, Buckner had no choice left, but submission.
The United States flag was raised at
Fort Donelson, and fourteen thousand
prisoners were transported to Cairo.
For that good day's work Grant was
made a major-general of volunteers.

Notwithstanding Grant's brilliant
success at Donelson, his character appears to have been so little understood
by General Halleck that after several
annoying complaints Grant felt compelled to ask to be relieved from further duty in the department. This
however Halleck would not accept and
ordered a disposition of the forces
which soon brought Grant again into
action. Two months later occurred the
battle of Pittsburgh Landing, on the
Tennessee River. Under the orders of
his superior, Grant had brought together at this place all the troops in
his command, numbering 38,000 men,

and he was expecting Buell from Nashville to join him with about the same number. The enemy was assembling his forces at Corinth, an important railway junction twenty miles distant. Exaggerated reports of their strength were current in the Union Camp, and as the position was badly defended, and an immediate attack was feared Grant began to look with anxiety for the arrival of his reinforcements. At last, on the 5th, of April the van of Buell's army reached the Tennessee a few miles below the camp, and were ordered to hold themselves in readiness for immediate action, as skirmishing had already commenced. On Sunday the 6th of April, the rebel General A. S. Johnson made an attack in force. General Prentiss was in command of that side of the camp where the attack began, and he had only time to form his line before he was driven back by the advancing columns. The field was soon swept by the enemy and the Union forces pushed to the river where they were partially protected by the gunboats. The reinforcements which had arrived the day before, and the rest of Buell's army which had followed them, did not come upon the ground until too late to be of service on that day. At the beginning of the battle, General Grant was at his headquarters at Savannah, but hearing of the action, immediately reached the ground and was engaged on the field in the afternoon in rallying his broken divisions. When he perceived that the ardor of the enemy's attack had somewhat abated, and that they did not pursue their advantage as they might, he determined to renew the fight on the next morning,

believing, as he said, that in such circumstances when both sides were nearly worn out, the one that first showed a bold front would win. Such was his determination, when the arrival of Buell's 20,000 fresh troops placed the hoped for success almost beyond a doubt. The next day the fight was accordingly resumed, and after a series of severe contests, Beauregard, who had succeeded to the command of General Johnson, who was killed in the first day's engagement, retired with his army to Corinth. The fatigue of the troops, and the roads rendered impassible by the showers of rain, made pursuit impossible.

Soon after this, General Halleck, the head of the department, took the field, and Grant became second in command. After the evacuation of Corinth by the enemy, when Halleck was called to Washington, as General-in-Chief, the force which had been gathered on the Tennessee was divided up into different commands. Buell was sent with his army to the east, and General Grant was assigned to the army of West Tennessee. The battles of Iuka, and the second battle of Corinth, in September and October, proved the successful management of his department. His command having been greatly increased, he established his headquarters, in December, at Holly Springs in Mississippi, and henceforth was engaged in the arduous operations in that State, which for many months employed the forces on the Mississippi, till final victory crowned their efforts in the capture of Vicksburg, with its garrison, a triumph doubly memorable by its association with the day of independence—the full surrender being made and the flag raised over the vaunted stronghold on the 4th of July, 1863. The campaign of General Grant immediately preceding the close investment of the city gained him the highest reputation as a commander, at home and abroad. After the Union forces had been disappointed in repeated efforts to take the city with its formidable works by direct assault or near approach, General Grant, at the end of April, landed a force on the Mississippi shore, about sixty miles below, defeated the enemy at Port Gibson, thus turning Grand Gulf, which consequently was abandoned to the naval force on the river; advanced into the interior, again defeated the enemy at Raymond, on the 12th of May; moved on and took possession of Jackson, the capital of the State; then marched westward towards Vicksburg, defeating the forces General Pemberton, the commander of that post, sent out to meet him, at Baker's Creek, and again at Black River Bridge. All this was the work of a few days, the eighteenth of the month bringing the army in the immediate vicinity of Vicksburg, in command of all its communications with the interior. The siege followed; it was conducted with eminent steadfastness and ability, and surrendered as we have stated in an unconditional triumph. For this eminent service, General Grant was promoted Major-General in regular army.

This great success finally determined Grant's position before the country, and the estimation in which he was now held was all the more enthusiastic and secure in consequence of the distrust which in spite of his successes, had in a great degree attended his course. It had in fact been with difficulty that he had been retained in his command before Vicksburg; and it had been wholly owing to his self reliance that he had carried out his own plan of throwing himself in his final successful movement upon the passage of the river below the fortress. President Lincoln unreservedly acknowledged Grant's superior prescience and his own want of confidence. When all was over and the Mississippi was virtually opened to the sea he wrote to the General, " When you got below and took Port Gibson, Grand Gulf, and vicinity, I thought you would go down the river and join General Banks; and when you hurried northward east of the Big Black, I feared it was a mistake. I now wish to make the personal acknowledgement that you were right and I was wrong."

This period also practically saw an end on the part of his opponents of the scandal which had at different times been revived against Grant on the charge of intemperance in drinking. During the protracted siege of Vicksburg an impatient grumbler, we are told by Richardson, demanded his removal from the President. "For what reason?" asked Lincoln. "Because he drinks so much whiskey," " Ah! yes," was the reply, "by the way can you tell me where he gets his whiskey? He has given us about all the successes, and if his whiskey does it, I should like to send a barrel of the same brand to every General in the field." In fact Grant, as his biographer just cited states, "was never under the influence of drinking to the direct or indirect detriment of the service for a single moment, and after the restoration of peace planted his feet on the safe and solid ground of total abstinence."

In October, Grant was again called to the field. Rosecrans had been badly defeated by Bragg and Longstreet at Chickamauga in Tennessee, and Thomas who had superseded him was now closely hemmed in by the enemy at Chattanooga. Grant, while on a visit to New Orleans in the summer, had been thrown by a restive horse, sustaining severe bruises which confined him to his bed for several weeks, and at the time he received his orders to join the army of the Tennessee, he was only able to move about on crutches, but his bodily suffering in no way subdued his characteristic energy. He immediately brought up Sherman with a large reinforcement, and at the same time Hooker with his army was sent by General Halleck from Virginia. In the succeeding battle of Chattanooga Grant attacked the enemy in his own position, and after a series of conflicts, among the severest in the war, the Union troops led by Hooker and Sherman drove the rebels from their lines, forcing Bragg to retreat into Georgia, and thus exposing the centre of the Confederate States.

In consequence of these brilliant successes, the grade of Lieutenant-General was revived by Congress and conferred upon General Grant. He was now Commander-in-chief of all the armies of the United States. That he fully appreciated how much in attaining this rank he owed to his subordinates, is shown by the following letter addressed to Sherman on quiting the west. After announcing his promotion, he says

"Whilst I have been eminently successful in this war, in at least gaining the confidence of the public, no one feels more than I, how much of this success is due to the energy, skill, and harmonious putting forth of that energy and skill of those whom it is my good fortune to have occupying subordinate positions under me.

"There are many officers to whom these remarks are applicable to a greater or less degree, proportionate to their ability as soldiers; but what I want is, to express my thanks to you and to M'Pherson, as the men to whom, above all others, I feel indebted for whatever I have had of success.

"How far your advice and assistance have been of help to me you know. How far your execution of whatever has been given to you to do, entitles you to the reward I am receiving, you cannot know as well as I.

"I feel all the gratitude this letter would express, giving it the most flattering construction.

"The word *you* I use in the plural, intending it for M'Pherson also."

Grant had now the whole country before him to chose his own field of operations. His first thoughts were turned to Georgia, where the opportunities opened up by the success at Chattanooga invited him to a campaign in the interior, but looking round he saw that the head and front of the rebellion was still at Richmond, and he determined to face the enemy upon the ground where, hitherto undefeated, a victory gained over him would be most decisive in breaking the power of the Confederacy.

Grant's design was now to make a

simultaneous attack along the whole Union line, from the James River to New Orleans. He took the command of the army of the Potomac in person, and moved from his headquarters at Culpepper Court-House on the 4th of May, with the object of putting himself between Richmond and Lee's army which was then a few miles distant at Orange Court-House. The enemy, however, apprised of his movement, fell upon his flank and the two days fighting in the Wilderness that ensued were among the bloodiest conflicts of the war. Grant barely held his ground, but although the losses he sustained were as great as those which had driven Hooker and Meade back to Washington, he held on to the design of cutting the rebel line, and before the last gun was fired in the Wilderness, his front had again encountered Lee's troops at Spottsylvania. Here the contest was renewed, and lasted with various movements and great slaughter for twelve days. It was now evident that success, however determined the onset, and with whatever sacrifice of life, was not to be determined by a first or a second blow. Grant, however, was not to be deterred from his purpose, which he expressed in a memorable despatch. "I propose to fight it out on this line if it takes all summer." The line, however, as at another earlier crisis of the war, proved not so direct as was anticipated by the public, which learnt only by degrees the full measure of the enemy's strength and resolution. By a flank movement, Grant now directed his forces to strategic points of importance on the road to Richmond, successfully

accomplishing though not without opposition the passage of the North Anna to encamp again on the old battlegrounds of McClellan. The struggle was renewed in a desperate but impracticable assault on the enemy's line at Chickahominy.

From this point the contest was rapidly transferred to the James River; Petersburg was invested and the effort henceforth was to command the enemy's supplies and draw closer the lines of the siege by cutting off his communications by railroad with the granaries of the South. When that region was devastated by the march of Sherman to the sea, and the force of the Rebellion in men and provisions was fairly exhausted, then, and not till then, he yielded to the steady and repeated blows of Grant and his generals. The surrender took place at Appomattox Court-House, on the 9th of April, 1865, in a personal interview between the two commanders, Grant accepting liberal terms of capitulation.

These successes of Grant in the field, in terminating the war, with the good sense and ability, mingled firmness and moderation which he had uniformly displayed as a leader of events, marked him out as the inevitable candidate for the presidency of the party to whom had fallen the conduct of the war. The interval which elapsed saw him steadily engaged at Washington, occupied with his duties as Lieutenant-General, and for a short time during the suspension of Stanton acting Secretary of War.

When the Republican National Convention met at Chicago in May, 1868, Grant was unanimously nominated for the presidency on the first ballot. In his letter of acceptance, after endorsing the resolutions of the Convention, he added,—"If elected to the office of President of the United States, it will be my endeavor to administer all the laws in good faith, with economy, and with the view of giving peace, quiet, and protection everywhere. In times like the present, it is impossible, or at least eminently improper, to lay down a policy to be adhered to, right or wrong, through an administration of four years. New political issues not foreseen, are constantly arising; the views of the public on old ones are constantly changing, and a purely administrative office should always be left free to execute the will of the people. I always have respected that will, and always shall.

"Peace, and universal prosperity—its sequence, with economy of administration, will lighten the burden of taxation, while it constantly reduces the national debt. Let us have peace."

At the election in November, Grant was chosen President by the vote of twenty-six states; Mississippi, Florida, Texas, and Virginia not voting, and the Democrats carrying Delaware, Georgia, Kentucky, Louisiana, Maryland, New Jersey, New York, and Oregon; his popular majority over Horatio Seymour, in the direct vote, being something over three hundred thousand.

President Grant's inaugural address on assuming the Presidency was marked by a tone of moderation and deference to the will of the people as expressed in the Acts of Congress. His administration has been in accord with their measures. Among the leading features of its domestic policy, has been the gradual restoration to the South of its privileges, forfeited by the necessities of the war, and the reduction of the national debt; while its foreign policy has secured the negotiation of the treaty of arbitration with England for the settlement of claims, arising from the negligence or wrong-doing of that country in relation to certain questions of international law, during the Southern rebellion. When, in 1872, at the approaching conclusion of his term of office, a new nomination was to be made for the Presidency, he was again chosen by the convention of the Republican party as their candidate.

The result of the election was equally decided with that following his first nomination. He received the vote of thirty-one states, with a popular majority, over Horace Greeley, of 762,991. The second inauguration on the 4th of March, 1873, though the day was severely cold, was celebrated by an imposing civil and military procession, with a large attendance at the capitol. In his address, the President alluded to the restoration of the Southern States to their federal relations; the new policy adopted towards the Indians; the civil service rules, and other topics of foreign and domestic administration, with a general reference to the tendency of the world towards Republicanism.

After the expiration of his second term of office, General Grant proceeded to carry out a long projected tour around the world. He left Philadelphia on May the 17th, 1877, and was received in London with the honors befitting his military and civil reputation. Queen Victoria invited him to Windsor Castle, and princes and nobles vied with each other in their respects. From England he went to the Continent, and after a visit to Switzerland and North Italy, traversed Egypt and the Holy Land, arriving at Constantinople just after the treaty of San Stefano had been signed by the Sultan and the Czar. The remainder of the year was occupied by visits to the Courts of Europe. Rome and Berlin, Madrid and St. Petersburg welcomed with magnificence our great soldier. In 1879 General Grant sailed to India. In that splendid Viceroyalty he received the greatest attention from native princes as well as the English authorities. Perhaps the highest compliment he received was paid him by the Chinese Government, which invited him to mediate between China and Japan respecting the Loo-Choo difficulty. His visit to these great and wealthy empires undoubtedly strengthened American influence in the East.

General Grant's return was greeted by an ovation, and he was at once made a prominent candidate for the Presidential nomination on the Republican ticket. But although he had the support of the strongest leaders of his party, the prejudice against a third term was too strong to be overcome and General Garfield received the nomination. In the ensuing campaign General Grant took a prominent part, and contributed in no small measure to the victory. As soon as the election was over his energy took another direction. He placed himself at the head of several powerful financial organizations which seek to develop the immense resources of our Southern neighbor, Mexico, by opening up her extensive provinces to lines of railroads connecting with our own, by working her valuable mines in a more business way, and, in fact, by promoting in every manner commercial relations between the two countries. "Peace has its victories as well as war."

RUTHERFORD BIRCHARD HAYES.

Rutherford Birchard Hayes was born on the 4th of October, 1822, in Delaware, Ohio. Ezekiel Hayes, his great-grandfather, claimed to be descended from the great Norman and Scottish family De la Haye or Hay, and he was fond of telling the legend of the battle of Loncarty, where the Hay of the period smote down the stoutest champions of the Danes with the yoke which he had taken from his plow. Coming down to sober fact, we find that in 1682 George Hayes left England and settled in Windsor, Conn., whence he removed to Granby. In 1712 his son Daniel was carried off captive to Canada by the Indians and was ransomed from them for the sum of seven pounds paid by the public treasury of the State. His grandson, the first Rutherford in the family— the name came from a maternal ancestor of Scotch descent—migrated to New Hampshire and then to Vermont, where in the town of West Brattleborough he plied his trade as a blacksmith, acquiring money and land, and died in 1836, the father of eleven children. His fifth child, another Rutherford, was more enterprising than his ancestors, and the Great West tempted the adventurous son of New England to seek a new home in Ohio. He was already a man of means, when in 1817 he bought land in Delaware, Ohio, and was prospering with every prospect of a successful career, when he died in 1822, leaving two children and a wife, who was soon to give birth to another. This posthumous child received the name Rutherford, in memory of his father, and Birchard from his maternal uncle, who proved himself a tender and careful guardian of his sister's fatherless children.

It is to the wife of the first Rutherford that the later Hayes ascribe their best traits. This lady, Chloe Smith, was the daughter of Israel Smith, a steady Whig, who served under Washington. She was sternly religious, intolerant of idleness, and a notable housekeeper. "She knit more stockings, mittens, and gloves, wove more rag carpets, spun and wove more cloth, made more wonderful rugs, lamp-mats, and bags than any woman of her generation." are the words of one of her grandsons. To labor truly and to walk humbly before her God were the principles of their austere ancestress. The mother of the late President, Sophie Birchard, was born in Connecticut. After the death of her husband the widow lost her eldest son. The surviving brother and sister were henceforth all in all to each other.

The children were together at the school of Daniel Granger, "a little wiry Yankee," who flogged his pupils till they "danced like parched peas." Their first separation was when he went to the Academy at Norwalk, Ohio, and they were seldom together during his college life at Middletown, Connecticut, and at Kenyon, Ohio. At college he determined on his profession. He would be a lawyer and let politics alone. Yet in one of his letters he writes: "I was *never* more rejoiced than when it was ascertained that Harrison's election was certain. I hoped we should then have a stable currency of uniform value." Then he speaks of his aspirations, and exclaims: "Give me the popularity that runs after, not that which is sought for." His legal studies commenced in the office of Messrs. Sparrow and Matthews, of Columbus, in 1842. After ten months' practical study in the office of these prominent lawyers, he entered, in 1843, the Harvard Law School, in which Story and Greenleaf were then teachers. At Harvard his interest in public affairs was developed. He listened with all the impressibility of youth to Webster and Choate, to John Quincey Adams, to Winthrop, and to Bancroft. He was a passionate admirer of Henry Clay. "I would start in the world without a penny," he wrote, "if by my sacrifice Clay could be elected President." After graduating at Harvard he commenced to practice in conjunction with Mr. Ralph P. Buckland, at Lower Sandusky. His health, however, failed, and he thought of joining

29

the Mexican expedition in 1847, but his physician forbade it. Restored to health by prolonged travels through New England, Canada, and Texas, Rutherford B. Hayes settled in Cincinnati. In 1852 he supported Scott, of whom two years before he had said after meeting him: "He'll do for President." The first legal argument that brought him into notice was the defence of the insane murderess, Nancy Farrer, and henceforth his business, especially in fugitive slave cases, increased steadily. In 1854 he formed a partnership with R. M. Corwine and W. R. Rogers. Though now a successful lawyer, he found mere legal success unsatisfying. He was active in the Fremont campaign and two years after was chosen City Solicitor, his first public office. When his term expired, in 1861, the state of affairs was such that he resolved that the only place worthy of a citizen was the place of a soldier in the field. "This is a just and necessary war," he said. "I would prefer to go into it if I knew I was to be killed in the course of it, rather than to live through it without taking any part in it."

In June, 1861, Rutherford B. Hayes became Major of the Twenty-third Ohio Regiment, and two days after he went into camp at Columbus, with S. Rosecrans as his Colonel, and Stanley Matthews as his Lieutenant-Colonel. On the 25th of July the regiment went to Western Virginia, and after the retreat of General Floyd before the Union forces, the Major became General Rosecrans' Judge Advocate. But he soon returned to active service as Lieutenant-Colonel and took part in the battle of South Mountain, where he was severely wounded. His wound quickly healed, and on the 30th of November he rejoined the army as Colonel, and in the following summer routed the guerrilla Morgan, who had crossed the Kenawha into Ohio. In 1864, Colonel Hayes took part in all the fighting near Winchester, and won his rank as Brigadier-General by the way in which he handled his men in the disaster of Cedar Creek. During the very hottest period of the struggle in the Shenandoah Valley, General Hayes was nominated by the Republicans for Congress for the second Cincinnati district, but he did not take his seat till the war was over. In October, 1865, he returned to his old home in Cincinnati, and in December quietly took his seat in Congress, where he soon became conspicuous as an indefatigable worker.

We need not describe the compromise which led to the nomination of Rutherford B. Hayes by the Republican National Convention at Cincinnati, for the office of President of the United States. His letter of acceptance was dated July 8, 1876, from Columbus, Ohio. He declared himself for a thorough, radical, and complete reform of the Civil Service; he stated it to be his inflexible purpose not to be a candidate for a second term, and to use all his efforts to accomplish a return to specie payments. Finally he added, " Let me assure my countrymen of the Southern States that I shall use my best efforts in behalf of a civil policy which will wipe out forever the distinction between North and South in our common country."

The Democratic candidate for the Presidency was Mr. Samuel J. Tilden, the ex-Governor of the State of New York. The canvass was energetic on both sides, and both sides confidently anticipated success.

Both sides claimed the victory. It was, however, necessary in order to give the majority to the Republicans, that both Louisiana and Florida should have gone Republican, while the Democrats with 184 unquestioned votes, wanted only one to have a majority in the electoral college. Accusations of bribery, fraud, and violence were mutually made ; men's passions became fiercer at the prospect of a disputed election. In any other country but our own a bloody civil war would have blazed forth. Three days afterward, President Grant gave orders to General Sherman to see that General Auger at New Orleans, and General Ruger in Florida " preserve order, and take steps to keep the legal Board of Canvassers in those States unmolested." He added, "Should there be any grounds of suspicion of fraudulent count on either side, it should be refuted and denounced at once. *No man worthy of the office of President should be willing to hold it if counted in or placed there by fraud. Each party can afford to be disappointed in the result. The country can not afford to have the result tainted by the suspicion of illegal or false returns.*"

By the words of the Constitution the certificates of the voting at the Presidential election in the various States shall be opened by the President of the Senate in the presence of both Houses and the votes shall then be counted. The question then arose who was to make the count.

This was the first, and it is to be hoped will be the last, disputed Presidential election in our history. Measures were introduced into both houses to settle the disputed point in the Constitution. Finally a committee of seven members of the House and seven members of the Senate were instructed to discover a solution of the difficulty. On the 18th of January, 1877, this committee reported; it consisted of Senators Edmunds, Frelinghuysen, Morton, and Conkling, and Representatives M'Crary, Hoar, and Willard, belonging to the Republican party, and Senators Thurman, Bayard, and Ransom, with Representatives Payne, Hewitt, Hunter, and Springer belonging to the Democratic party. These men, the most eminent statesmen of their parties, reported "that in the cases of more than one return from a State all such returns should be, upon objection made, submitted to the judgment and decision of a committee of fifteen consisting of five Senators, five members of the House, and five Associate Judges of the Supreme Court. A bill in accordance with this report was passed by both houses, the chief opposition being made by prominent Republicans. The Electoral Commission thus created consisted of Senators Edmunds, Morton, Frelinghuysen, Thurman, and Bayard, Representatives Payne, Hunter, Abbott, Garfield, and Hoar, and Justices Clifford, Miller, Field, Strong, and Bradley. The committee, by a strict party vote of eight to seven, declared that the votes of Louisiana and Florida had been cast for Rutherford B. Hayes, who thus received the requisite number of 185 votes.

On the 2d of March, Rutherford Birchard Hayes was declared President, and William A. Wheeler Vice-President of the United States. His inaugural address repeated with emphasis the declarations of his letter of acceptance. He at once inaugurated a conciliatory policy toward the Southern States. The leaders of the South were summoned to Washington, and consulted with the President. The result was that the military forces under Federal officers in Louisiana and South Carolina were withdrawn. The withdrawal of the troops involved the loss to the Republican party of the Republican legislatures in those States, but the country felt that a great step had been made towards the pacification of the South. It is one of the first maxims of constitutional government that the military must be subordinate to the civil power, and that even when it is used in the last resort it ought to be employed only for the protection of Government, not as a means of influencing ordinary political action. The action of President Hayes was an avowal that the employment of the military in civil affairs should now, once, and forever cease, and that no extraordinary dangers existed or were threatened. At the same time the President expressed a steady purpose to repress disorders by whomsoever committed, and the practical recognition of the great principle that no class or race of men should be regarded as the peculiar friends of the Government, no class as its enemies; that, in other words, there should be equal laws for all.

The action of the President was, however, highly displeasing to many of the party which had elected him; and his difficulties were increased by the fact that the organizations of both houses were in the hands of the Democrats. Thus his term is more remarkable for the failure of good intentions than for any great successes. In one thing, however, the policy of President Hayes and his Secretary of the Treasury, John Sherman, was triumphant against all enemies. They had never wavered in their advocacy of the resumption of specie payments, and their denunciation of greenback and other financial heresies. The country began to recover from the panic of 1873 — that recoil from the inflation of the war times —and gold, which on the 11th of July, 1864, was at 285 per cent., sold at par on the 17th of December, 1878. The attainment of this result was, however, undoubtedly facilitated by the confidence felt by the whole banking and commercial community in the sound " honest money " principles of the President and the Secretary, a confidence which before the expiration of his Presidency enabled him to refund at 3½ and 4 per cent. large amounts of the public debt. During this period of recovery from financial depression the office of Secretary of the Treasury was

the most important branch of the Government, and by President Hayes' support of all measures tending to lighten the burden of taxation and to give confidence to our large trading interests, much of our present prosperity must be attributed; for without confidence in the consistency and integrity of a Government, commerce will not spread her sails.

President Hayes had repeatedly to exercise his power of veto. He vetoed the bill to restrict Chinese immigration, alleging " general considerations of interest and duty which sacredly guard the faith of the nation in whatever form of obligation it may have been given." When an attempt was made to carry, attached to the army bill, some legislative clauses respecting the use of the army, President Hayes rejected the bill as being " a dangerous violation of the spirit and meaning of the Constitution." The bill to prevent military interference at elections was also vetoed, as " it required an abandonment of its obligations by the National Government, a subordination of national authority and an intrusion of State supervision over national duties which amounts in spirit and tendency to State supremacy." The last official act of Mr. Hayes was to veto the funding bill, some of the clauses in which deeply affected the national banking system.

Mr. Hayes married, in 1852, Lucy W. Webb, daughter of Dr. James Webb. This lady is a devoted advocate of total abstinence, and carried out her principles during her reign at the White House, much to the discomfiture of her guests. Mr. Hayes is the father of eight children, of whom five are alive. Without being a great or a strong man, Mr. Hayes has been a conscientious and honest Chief Magistrate, who has served his country rather than his party, and preferred national to sectional aims. Party spirit and party corruption frustrated his best efforts, but Mr. Hayes deserves high credit for steadfastly insisting on the paramount necessity of reform. Mr. Hayes inherited from his uncle, Mr. Sardis Birchard, an ample fortune, and a well-selected collection of French, German, and American paintings. With his pictures and his books, and amid the groves of Fremont, may he enjoy the repose he has earned by his services!

JAMES ABRAM GARFIELD.

As we trace these lines, over all this wide land emblems of mourning darken the streets, and sadness hushes the din of traffic. The nation is in mourning for its head. Tragic has been the end of President Garfield, but tragic with no common form of tragedy. He was the typical American; the man who had worked his way upward till he sat with princes, without wealth and without a patron, and who till the last retained those domestic virtues which the poorest and most obscure of us can feel.

James A. Garfield is descended from a good New England family. He was born at Orange, Ohio, on the 19th of November, 1831, the youngest of four children. Before he was two years old, his father died from his efforts to save his poor homestead from a forest fire. The care of the bereaved family now fell to the widowed mother, and nobly did she discharge her duties. She made the fences, cultivated the crops, sewed for a living among the neighbors, and thus paid the father's debts and supported the infant family. If General Garfield derived from his father his powerful and robust frame, he derived from his mother his energy, courage, and perseverance. Her character formed his, her principles guided his steps.

230

Poor as she was, Mrs. Garfield resolved to give her son the best education within her reach. The school teacher of the vicinity perceived the talents of his child-pupil and said: "If you learn, my boy, you may grow up to be a general." But the circumstances of the family were too straitened to allow the boy to go regularly to school, and for some time he worked as a carpenter, till he became clerk in a store. His employer possessed Marryat's novels and "The Pirate's Own Book." The clerk devoured these fascinating works, and when he quitted his employment, set out for Lake Erie, with the intention of becoming a sailor on that inland sea. At Cleveland he met his cousin, Amos Letcher, who commanded a boat on the Ohio and Pennsylvania Canal. The cousin's boat, the "Evening Star," was then lying at the dock when the lad presented himself. He asked for employ ment, adding, "I came here to ship on the lake, but they bluff me off, and call me a country greenhorn, and ask me if I can climb a mast in a storm."

"And what did you tell them?" asked the captain.

"I told them I would try."

Pleased with the grit of the reply the captain gave him charge of two

J. A. Garfield

horses, and the future President was soon on his first trip on the tow-path. During one of the following days the captain said, as he tells the story, "'Jim, I should like to ask you a few questions.'

"'Proceed,' said Jim, 'but don't ask too hard ones.' I asked him several, and he answered them all, and then turned on *me*, and asked me several that I could not answer, and I was like the boy who got into a row and said, 'If you'll let me alone, I'll let you alone.'

"'Jim,' I said, 'you have too good a head on you to be a wood-chopper or a canal-driver. You go to school one term more, and you will be qualified to teach a common school, and then you can make anything you have a mind to out of yourself.'

"'Do you think so, captain?' And it set him a thinking, I know."

He remained four years on the tow-path, but the exposure and labors of this life were too severe for his growing frame. Long months he lay sick and helpless; his mother opposed his return to the canal, advised him to qualify himself to teach, and gave him seventeen dollars to start him as a pupil in the Academy at Chester. Here he studied hard, and managed when his mother's little hoard was expended to earn his living by working in the carpenters' shops in the village. During his stay at this academy he met Lucretia Rudolph, "a quiet girl, of a sweet disposition, and a warm heart," and the hope of gaining her hand urged the young student to even harder work. In 1851 he pre-

sented himself to the board of trustees of Hiram College; he was admitted and defrayed the expenses of his tuition by acting as janitor, lighting the fires, sweeping the floor, and ringing the bell. While he was a student here he connected himself with the "Church of the Disciples," a sect commonly called from its founder's name, the Campbellites.

A lady who was one of the pupils at the academy writes:

"In those days the faculty and pupils were in the habit of calling him 'the second Webster,' and the remark was common, 'He will fill the White House yet.' In the Lyceum he early took rank far above the others as a speaker and debater."

"He is," she says, "a man who, in the belief of any one who ever knew him, could not be corrupted, and who considers his honor above his life."

In 1854 he was admitted to Williams College, and during the vacation taught in the neighboring towns, among others in North Pownal, where two years before his successor, Chester A. Arthur, had taught English. Graduating in 1856, at the age of twenty-five, he returned to Hiram as Professor of Greek and Latin, and married his old sweetheart, Miss Lucretia Rudolph. At this time the Kansas-Nebraska question, involving the question of slavery, claimed general attention. Garfield, who very soon became President of the College, joined the newly-born Republican party. He became a most efficient speaker, and in 1859 was elected, at the early age of twenty-eight, to the State Senate. When secession took place and the President's call for 75,-000 men was read, he sprang to his feet and moved that 20,000 men and $3,000,000 should be the quota of Ohio. Governor Dennison offered him the command of a regiment, and he resigned his Presidency of Hiram College to place himself at the disposal of the National Government. "Go, my son," were his mother's words, "your life belongs to your country."

During the war he distinguished himself by his defeat of General Marshall at the Big Sandy. His superior officer, General Buell, committed to him all questions of detail, and in an admirably planned series of operations Colonel Garfield hurled back the invaders of Kentucky.

President Lincoln, when he heard of it, said to a distinguished army officer who happened to be with him:

"Why did Garfield, in two weeks, do what would have taken one of you Regular folks two months to accomplish?"

"Because he was not educated at West Point," answered the West-Pointer, laughing.

"No," replied Mr. Lincoln; "that wasn't the reason. It was because, when he was a boy, he had to work for a living."

A few weeks later, Garfield, with a commission as Brigadier - General, joined the army of the Cumberland. With the battle of Chickamauga, his service in the field ended. General Rosecrans, in his official report, writes: "To Brigadier-General Garfield, Chief of Staff, I am especially indebted for the clear and ready manner in which he seized the point of action and movement. He possesses the instincts and energy of a great commander." A fortnight later he received his commission as Major-General for "gallant conduct and important services." While he was still in the field he had been unsolicitedly elected to Congress from the nineteenth district of Ohio. He hesitated whether he should, in the hour of our country's peril, abandon his duties as a soldier, or endeavor to promote her interests by devoting to her his services in a civil capacity. He consulted General Rosecrans; the latter said: "The war is not yet over, nor will it be for some time to come. Many questions will arise in Congress which will require not only statesmanlike treatment, but the advice of men having an acquaintance with military affairs; for that reason you will, I think, do as good service to the country in Congress as in the field. I not only think that you can accept the position with honor, but that it is your duty to do it." This, for the time, decided Garfield, and before the interview closed Rosecrans said to him: "Garfield, I want to give you some advice. When you go to Congress, be careful what you say. Don't talk too much; but when you talk, speak to the point. Be true to yourself, and you will make your mark before the country." As we go on with his life, we shall see how Garfield profited by these instructions. He took his seat December 4, 1863, the youngest member of the House of Representatives, as he had been the youngest Brigadier in the army. His voice uttered no uncertain sound in the war-legislation of the period, and his manly eloquence carried the bill allowing Lincoln to draft five hundred thousand men, while his speech on the Constitutional Amendment to abolish slavery, gave him a prominent position among his colleagues. Of his power over a popular audience, one of his biographers gives a striking account. When the death of Lincoln by the assassin's dagger was announced in New York, a mass meeting was convoked. General Butler addressed the excited assemblage; cries of "Vengeance" rose on all sides, and when the telegram, "Seward is dying," arrived, shouts of "*The World*," "*The World*," were heard, and a mob began to move to the office of that journal. At that juncture, a man stepped forward with a small flag in his hand, and beckoned to the crowd. "Another telegram from Washington!" And then in the awful stillness of the crisis, taking advantage of the hesitation of the crowd, whose steps had been arrested a moment, a right arm was lifted skyward, and a voice, clear and steady, loud and distinct, spoke out: "Fellow-citizens: Clouds and darkness are round about Him! His pavilion is dark waters and thick clouds of the skies! Justice and judgment are the establishment of His throne! Mercy and truth shall go before His face! Fellow-citizens! God reigns, and the Government at Washington still lives." The effect, says an eye-witness, was tremendous. The crowd paused awestruck. Men asked, "Who is he?" The answer was, General Garfield, of Ohio. His words

30

saved New York from a scene of horrible disorder.

In the Thirty-ninth Congress, Garfield requested to be dropped from the Military Committee, and to be put upon that of Ways and Means. "I would like to serve," he said, "where I can study finance. That is to be the great question of the future." He at once devoted all his energies to master the science of finance, and his speech on the Public Debt and Specie Payments, March 16, 1865, displayed a thorough mastery of this intricate subject, and it was followed, in 1866, by a most able discussion of the whole question of Protection and Free Trade.

In 1867, General Garfield, broken in health by his labors, visited Europe, and in a journey of four months saw all those famous spots which had been rendered familiar places to him by his early reading. Returning with renewed vigor, he showed by his speeches on the Tariff, the Currency and the Banks, the Public Expenditure and the Civil Service, what a statesman-like mind he possessed. In 1872 the Credit Mobilier scandal disgusted the whole country. The revelations that were made implicated men of the highest position in the country. Guilt was clearly brought home to some of them. Others suffered from their connection with the guilty. Garfield was among those who were accused of receiving the bribes of Oakes Ames. He and his friends asseverated his innocence, and the popular verdict, as shown by his election as President, must be regarded as a verdict of acquittal. With regard to the Salary

Bill, by which members of Congress voted into their own pockets $4,500 apiece, he may have been injudicious in voting for the obnoxious measure, but there is no doubt that he was actuated by honest considerations of duty.

During the four years in which General Garfield was Chairman of the Committee on Appropriations he labored toward the restoration of business, trade, commerce, industry, sound political economy, hard money, and honest payments of all obligations. Both in and out of Congress he was a consistent advocate of honest money, and opposed to every form of inflation.

One of the great questions which are looming up in the dim future, is that of our railway system. Garfield in 1874 put his views on record, and claimed for the State the right of restraining and regulating these powerful associations.

No less boldly did he express himself respecting Civil Service Reform:

"No man whose vision is not utterly blinded by partisan feeling will deny that our civil service has fallen far below the high place which the founders intended it should occupy; and it is no doubt true that the doctrine of 'spoils,' introduced in the days of Jackson, has been the chief motive power in dishonoring and degrading that service. But a careful study of the subject has led me to conclude that at the present moment another element is at work even more dangerous than the doctrine of 'spoils'; it is the tendency of the different parts of the Government to interfere with the independence of each other. . . . . . I do not hesitate to declare that we are now in greater danger of disturbing the balance and distribution of power, by the interference of Congress with the executive office, than we were in the days of Johnson from executive usurpation."

One of Garfield's greatest oratorical efforts was his reply to Mr. Lamar, of Mississippi, in which he argued that the administration of the Government could not be safely entrusted to the Democratic party. "The Democracy as a political organization," he urged, "can not accomplish any reform. During sixteen years the Democratic party has not advanced a single doctrine which has not been exploded." He arraigned its action after it had attained a majority in the House, as being "factious and corrupt, an army of schemers, seeking for spoils and clamoring for appropriations, subsidies, and the payment of Southern claims."

The term of President Hayes was about to expire. A very influential portion of the Republican party had been working steadily with a view of obtaining the nomination of ex-President Grant as the Republican candidate for the next presidency. Another almost equally numerous party advocated the nomination of Senator Blaine, of Maine. A third and weaker section, which, however, had the support of the Government of Mr. Hayes, was pledged to vote for Mr. Secretary Sherman. Ballot after ballot, and day after day, the phalanx of Grant and the phalanx of Blaine remained unbroken. The forces of Sherman, had they been added to either side, would have carried victory; but as the deadliest hostility existed between the three rivals, such a result could not be expected. Finally, one vote was given to James A. Garfield, then the Sherman votes and other scattering votes were added, and ultimately when the Grant leaders, Conkling, Cameron, and Logan, showed no sign of letting their three hundred and six "stalwart" delegates escape from the bonds of discipline, the Blaine delegates went over to the Garfield party. Their accession decided the affair, and on the motion of Mr. Conkling the nomination of Garfield as the Republican candidate was made unanimous. The Democratic convention at Cincinnati nominated General Winfield Scott Hancock as the candidate of the party. General Hancock, a distinguished soldier, who gained his brightest laurels at the fight at Gettysburg, was a gentleman of unspotted character, but lacked entirely the training requisite for an occupant of the highest post under our Constitution. Above all, his ignorance of all financial science, and the Greenback proclivities of many of the Democratic party, alarmed the business community. The result was that in November James Abram Garfield, of Ohio, was elected President by an overwhelming majority. The Vice-President on the ticket was Chester A. Arthur, of New York.

The first appointment in the Cabinet made by President Garfield after his inauguration, which took place with unusual pomp and ceremony, was the nomination of Mr. Blaine as his Secretary of State. The other Cabinet officers were Mr. Windom, Secretary of the Treasury; Mr. Hunt, Secretary of the Navy; Mr. Robert Lincoln, a son of the martyr President, Secretary of War; Mr. Kirkwood, Secretary of the Interior; Mr. James, Postmaster-General; and Mr. McVeagh, Attorney-General.

Soon the day of his inauguration arrived. President Garfield showed that he was resolved to be President in fact as well as in name, and not to submit to the dictation of party leaders or a party machine. His independence roused the hostility of the stalwart faction of the Republicans, and Senator Conkling, of New York, used all his great influence to induce the Senate to reject the nominations sent in by the President to that body for confirmation. A custom had arisen, it was argued, which had acquired the force of an unwritten law, by which the federal appointments in each State were to be made by the President in accordance with the recommendations of the Senators of each State. This custom, known as the Courtesy of the Senate, was violated, in Mr. Conkling's opinion, by the nomination of Mr. Robertson for the office of Collector of Customs of New York, and the stalwart leader therefore opposed the confirmation of all the nominations. Garfield boldly accepted battle. He withdrew the nominations of Mr. Conkling's friends, and left that of Robertson the only question before the Senate. An unseemly deadlock had been existing in the Senate with no immediate prospect of its being broken. The President's action at once narrow ed the issue to a conflict between the Executive and a single Senator. Hopeless of success as he then stood, Conkling took the unprecedented course of resigning his Senatorial office, a step in which he was followed by his colleague. The expectation of Mr. Conkling and Mr. Platt was that they would be re-elected by the State Legislature, and would thus re-enter the Senate chamber triumphantly endorsed by the constituency of the Empire State. They were doomed to disappointment. The opposition to their return developed unexpected strength, and the contest between the two Republican wings was transferred to the Capital at Albany. It was an envenomed struggle, in which foul calumnies, violent threats, and every means of corruption were unsparingly employed. The language in which the stalwarts assailed their opponents, whom they styled the "half breeds," surpassed even the ordinary license of political debate. Week after week passed at Albany, as week after week had passed at Washington, in mutual recriminations and denunciations. Men's passions rose to fever heat. Finally Messrs. Lapham and Miller were elected Senators from New York to succeed Messrs. Conkling and Platt. By this time the appointment of Robertson had been confirmed, and Congress had adjourned. On the 2d of July the President prepared to join his family at Elberon on the New Jersey coast. His wife had suffered severely from malaria during her residence in the White House, and had sought the healthy breezes of the ocean. The President was intending to spend in his domestic circle the festival of the 4th of July. As he was taking his ticket at the railroad depot in Washington, a man named Guiteau fired at him with a pistol of the kind called an English bulldog. The ball struck the unfortunate President in the back, to the right of the spine. He sank to the ground, in the midst of the Cabinet officers who had come to the depot to bid him good-bye. The ball, it was thought, had penetrated the liver, and death was considered imminent in a few hours. The news of this assassination, when flashed along the wires, was received with incredulity at first, then with the utmost horror and deepest indignation. Business everywhere was temporarily suspended. Such an assault at such a time and on such a man, seemed an attack on the whole nation, and was felt by every citizen an outrage on himself personally; as being an attack on the Constitution for which so many had died, and which so many were prepared to defend with their lives. Lincoln had fallen beneath the pistol of an assassin, at the end of a long, bloody, and fratricidal strife; but now when the country was at perfect peace, when the old sectional antipathies were dying away, when an era of unexampled prosperity was blessing the nation, the action of the assassin was seen to be one of unexampled atrocity. The miscreant was at once seized. He gloried in what he had done, stated that he had meditated it for some time, and affirmed that he as a "stalwart" could see no other salvation for the Republican party than the death of the man who had betrayed it. It is needless to say that no one but the madman himself was involved in the affair. Guiteau had led for years an erratic, disreputable life, now lecturing, now professing law, now fleeing from justice, always swindling. He claimed to have been active in the electoral campaign—of course falsely—and had haunted the public offices of Washington, seeking an office as minister, as consul, as clerk. The assassination was the murder of a Civil Service Reformer by a disappointed place hunter.

Fortunately for the country, the wounded President did not die at once. His firm will, his robust frame, his temperate habits, enabled him to linger till the 19th of September. During the eleven weeks in which he lingered patiently and uncomplainingly the whole world displayed its sympathy with the martyr. The telegrams which told every vicissitude of his sickness were eagerly read by every people and every sovereign in Europe. The days passed slowly on, and hope alternated with despondency. It was thought that the air of the White House delayed his convalescence; he requested, with a pathetic love for his quiet home, to be removed to Mentor, but the distance was too far. It was decided to take him to Elberon. The road was lined with tearful crowds, who had come even from long distances, as the train conveying the wounded man sped onward, and a silent throng was gathered at every depot. At Elberon hope again revived; he sat up in a reclining-chair once or twice and watched the ocean as it rolled in to the shore. But all that nature or all that skill could do were of no avail. Fresh complications betrayed their fatal presence, and on Monday, September 19th, he quietly passed away. The body, after lying in state beneath the dome of the rotunda at Washington, was transferred to Cleveland, and interred September 25th, in the Lake View Cemetery. Such a spectacle has never been presented as the mourning with which the whole civilized world honored our late President. Emperors and kings, senates and ministries, were in spirit his pall-bearers, and their peoples from the highest to the lowest were equally visible and audible as sorrowing assistants. The Queen of England all through the dreary time of trial had evinced the deepest concern and sympathy not only for the President, but for the devoted wife who so hopefully and patiently nursed him, and as his remains lay in state the wreath she had sent lay on the head of the coffin. The British court was ordered to go into mourning, and this unprecedented act precisely expressed the universal feeling that an Englishman who was in the place of a king and worthy to rank with kings had passed away. Nor is it an exaggeration to say that of the eighty-three millions of people who now think in English there were not fifty men who would not have made some sacrifice to aid him in his struggle for life.

"Rhetoric relative to President Garfield's noble end," said Mr. Lowell, our ambassador to London, "is out of place. If we were allowed to follow the promptings of our own hearts we should sum all up in the sacred words, 'Well done, good and faithful servant!' The death scene was unexampled. The whole civilized world gathered about. Let us thank God that it was through the manliness, the patience, the religious fortitude of the noble victim that the tie of human brotherhood was thrilled. That 'touch of nature that makes the whole world kin' is the touch of heroism, our sympathy with which dignifies and ennobles. There were few," he continued, "who could die well daily for eleven weeks. He was good-natured even when dying, although there were few from whom death wrenched a nobler heritage. The fibre that could stand such a strain is only used in the making of heroic natures. General Garfield, twenty years ago, offered his life for his country. He has now died for her as truly as if he had fallen then. His blood has cemented the fabric of the Union. His example is a stimulus to his countrymen forever."

There must have been something far above the ordinary in a man at whose grave a united nation stands as it were "contracted in one brow of woe," whose burial-day was observed by fifty millions of people with funeral rites and for whom the kings and counselors of the earth were mourners together. It was not alone that he was the head of a powerful Government and stood for the authority of a great nation. It was not the ruler that excited all this sympathy and admiration and whose death arrayed the Republic in mourning; it was the man who in a lofty station had risen to the full height of greatness, and displayed those heroic qualities which forever command the fealty of human nature. Another might have attained the same high station and been stricken down without exciting more than formal regret and the demonstration of sorrow which decency requires. The circumstances attending the death of Garfield were calculated to arouse the sentiments which have found such profuse expression only so far as they wrought upon a nature whose greatness and nobility were thereby brought into relief. The position of the man, the act of the assassin, the lingering and painful illness, could have wrought no such effect as we have seen except that the victim was one whose life and character endeared him to the universal heart of mankind.

" After life's fitful fever he sleeps well ;
  Treason has done his worst ; nor steel nor
      poison,
  Malice domestic, foreign levy, nothing,
  Can touch him further."

President Garfield was a man of powerful frame, six feet high, broad-shouldered and deep-chested, with a massive head and a full, closely-trimmed beard. His strength and endurance were great, and his physical robustness enabled him to do an enormous amount of work. His general culture was broad, his patience in accumulating facts equalled his skill in arranging them and his art in expounding them. The generosity of his nature had not been spoiled by public life, and no more loving family circle could be found than that which used to gather at his home at Mentor.

His character had been largely formed by the devotion and teachings of his mother, and she was repaid by as true a love as ever son had for a mother. Amidst the brilliant ceremonies of the inauguration at Washington, she was a prominent figure, and when her son had taken the oath of office and publicly assumed his high functions, he turned and embraced the mother who had made him what he was.

We cannot more fitly close our notice of the brief Presidential career of James Abram Garfield than with the lines of the poet which he himself quoted so effectively in reference to the death of Lincoln:

"Divinely gifted man,
Whose life in low estate began,
And on a simple village green,
  Who breaks his birth's invidious bars,
And grasps the skirts of happy chance,
And breasts the blows of circumstance,
  And grapples with his evil stars ;
Who makes by force his merit known,
  And lives to clutch the golden keys,
  To mold a mighty State's decrees,
And shape the whisper of the throne ;
And moving up from high to higher,
  Becomes, on Fortune's crowning slope,
  The pillar of a people's hope,
The center of a world's desire."

CHESTER ALLAN ARTHUR.

CHESTER ALLAN ARTHUR, elected Vice-President of the United States in 1880, became, by the death of President Garfield, the twenty-first President of the United States. He was born in 1830, in Fairfield, Franklin County, Vermont. His father was a Baptist minister, who came to this country from Ballymena, in the County Antrim, Ireland, and preached in Vermont and Canada. So frequent were his changes of residence between our own country and the adjacent British province, that doubt has been expressed whether his son was an American by birth. There is, however, no doubt that he was born in the place above mentioned and fulfils that requisite in a President, birth on American soil. Chester Allan Arthur received his first instruction from his father, who for years had been a teacher of youth, and at an early period entered Union College, where the celebrated Dr. Eliphalet Nott was at the height of his fame. A schoolfellow describes him as being the most popular boy in his class, always genial and cheerful, a good scholar, and apt in debate. Even in those days he took an interest in politics. He was a Whig, and afterward a Republican. While he was studying at Union, the young man contributed to his own support by teaching during the winter. He graduated in 1848, and taught the village school at his old home till he had acquired a sum sufficient to take him to New York, and to enable him to study law. After a few years of partnership with Mr. Culver, in whose office he had studied, he formed a new business association with Henry D. Gardner. The idea of the young men was to go out West, but after prospecting for a couple of months they returned to New York, and soon acquired a large practice. The most important case in which young Arthur was engaged was in 1852. The case is an historical one, and is worthy of a full report. The facts were as follows:

Jonathan Lemmon and Juliet, his wife, who had been residents of the slaveholding State of Virginia, determined to move to Texas. They sailed from Norfolk to this city, bringing eight slaves with them. Their intention was to remain in this city until a vessel sailed for a Texas port. They went to an hotel upon their arrival here, and engaged board and lodging for their slaves at 3 Carlisle Street. A free colored man living in this city, and known as Louis Napoleon, presented, through counsel, an application to Judge Elijah Paine of the Superior Court for a writ of habeas corpus to

compel Mr. and Mrs. Lemmon to produce their slaves in court, and show
cause why they should not be set at
liberty. The writ was issued, and the
slaves were taken before Judge Paine.
In their answer to the order to show
cause, Mr. and Mrs. Lemmon averred
that the slaves were brought to the
city of New York from a slaveholding
State with the sole purpose of procuring transportation to another slaveholding State, Texas; and they claimed
that this transit was lawful, and that
any interruption of it was unlawful.
Judge Paine decided that the slaves
could not be held in this State, and
they were freed. General Arthur was
interested in this case, first as the associate of Judge Culver, senior counsel,
and later as the associate of William
M. Evarts, when an appeal was taken
from Judge Paine's decision. The Supreme Court of the United States
affirmed the decision, and the first
telling blow in the courts against the
slaveholding power was struck.

Mr. Arthur was henceforth regarded
as the champion of the colored people,
and his aid was consequently invoked
to establish the right of colored people
to ride in the street cars in the State
of New York.

One Sunday in 1855 a neatly-dressed
colored woman named Lizzie Jennings,
who had just come from fulfilling her
duties as superintendent of a colored
Sunday-school, hailed a Fourth Avenue car. The car stopped, she took a
seat and the conductor took her fare—
thus silently acknowledging her right
to ride in the car. The car went on a
block and then a drunken white man
objected to her riding in the car. She
was thereupon ejected. Influential
colored people soon heard of the woman's treatment, and going to the office
of Messrs. Culver, Parker & Arthur,
told them all about it. They at once
told them that her wrongs should be
righted. A suit was brought against
the railway company in her behalf in
the Supreme Court in Brooklyn. Public sentiment was still on the side of
the slaveholder, however, and even the
Judge seemed prejudiced. When Mr.
Arthur handed him the papers in the
case he said, "Pshaw! do you ask me
to try a case against a corporation for
the wrongful act of its agent?" Mr.
Arthur immediately pointed out a
section of the revised statutes under
which the action had been brought,
making the corporation liable for the
acts of its servants. The case was tried
before a Brooklyn jury, which gave
the plaintiff a verdict for $500.

In the following year he made his
first prominent appearance in politics
as inspector of election. He had
always been a staunch Henry Clay
Whig, and as such was a delegate at
the Saratoga Convention that founded
the Republican party. In 1861 he was
made Quartermaster-General by Governor Morgan, his warm friend, and in
1862 he went with a commission as
Inspector-General to inspect the New
York posts in the army of the Potomac. This was the darkest period of
the war, and in June a meeting of the
Governors of the loyal States was held
in New York, at which Arthur acted
as Secretary. The advice of the meeting
resulted in Lincoln's call for 300,000

volunteers, and 300,000 militia. In organizing the New York quota of 60,000 men, General Arthur displayed admirable activity. In 1862 a Democratic administration in the State relegated him to private life, and he renewed the active pursuit of his profession, for some years in his old partnership, for some years alone. In 1871 the firm of Arthur, Phelps, Knevals & Ransom was formed.

He gradually, however, re-entered public life, and was very much interested in promoting the first election of President Grant, being chairman of the Central Grant Club of New York. He also served as chairman of the Executive Committee of the Republican State Committee of New York. He re-entered official life on November 20, 1871, being appointed Collector of the Port of New York by President Grant. So satisfactory was his work that upon the close of his term of office in December, 1875, he was renominated by President Grant. The nomination was unanimously confirmed by the Senate without referring it to a committee—a compliment never given before except to ex-Senators. He was removed by President Hayes on July 12, 1878, despite the fact that two special committees made searching investigation into his administration, and both reported themselves unable to find anything upon which to base a charge against him. In the following winter, however, charges against him were presented to the Senate by Mr. Sherman.

In reply to the charges, General Arthur wrote a letter to Senator Conkling reviewing his administration. He produced statistics to show that during his term of over six years in office the percentage of removals was only $2\frac{3}{4}$, against an annual average of 28 per cent. under his three predecessors; and all appointments to clerkships commanding $2,000 a year except two were made on a system of advancement from lower to higher grades on the recommendation of heads of bureaux. General Arthur averred that the commission cited by Secretary Sherman had drawn conclusions not based on evidence, and had failed to notice the efficient reforms effected during his administration.

General Arthur's nomination for Vice-President was as much a surprise as that of General Garfield for the first place on the ticket. He had not been mentioned as a candidate, and his own delegation had not thought of presenting his name until the roll was called in the Convention. Nor was he himself anxious for the nomination, as his ambition was to become the Senator from his State. When New York was reached in the call, her delegation asked to be excused from voting for a time. During the recess Arthur's reluctance was overcome, and then General Stewart L. Woodford cast the vote for Arthur. The leading candidate had been Elihu B. Washburne, but the tide quickly turned. The Ohio men were disposed to be conciliatory, and swung over to Arthur, who was nominated on the first ballot. The vote stood: Arthur, 468; Washburne, 193; Marshall Jewell, 44; Horace Maynard, 30.

General Arthur married, soon after he began legal practice, Miss Herndon, daughter of Lieutenant Herndon, of the *Central America*, who went down with his ship at sea. His wife died two years ago, but both of his children, a son and daughter, are living.

General Arthur took a very active part in Mr. Conkling's recent canvass for re-election to the United States Senate. It was in his house in this city that the conference of influential Republicans was held at which it was determined that Messrs. Conkling and Platt should be candidates for re-election. He accompanied Mr. Conkling to Albany on the day after that conference, and remained there, working hard for the ex-Senator's return to the Senate until the evening preceding the day on which President Garfield was shot. On that night, accompanied by Mr. Conkling, he took the steamboat to New York. He received the news of the attempt upon the President's life just after the boat had reached her dock in this city. He was greatly shocked by the intelligence, and driving to his house in Lexington Avenue, remained there until night. At midnight he started for Washington, in response to the request of the President's Cabinet. He remained in the Capital until the President was pronounced by his physicians to be in a fair way to recover, and then returned to New York.

On receipt of the sad news that Garfield had died, it was resolved that it was advisable for the new President to take the oath of office. Judge Brady was sent for, and administered the oath according to the Constitution at 1 o'clock in the morning, at the President's private residence in Lexington Avenue, New York. The new Executive proceeded as soon as possible to Washington, and there renewed his oath in presence of the Chief-Justice of the United States, and the Cabinet officers.

As the elevation of Vice-President Arthur to the Presidency has vacated the Presidency of the Senate and left him without the successor designated by the Constitution, his first official act was to summon the Senate to elect a President *pro tempore*, and at its meeting, October 10th, Senator Bayard, of Delaware, was chosen; who on the 14th was succeeded by David Davis, the Senator from Illinois.

Chronological List of the Presidents and Vice-Presidents of the U. S.

The First Administration—1789 to 1797—Eight Years.

PRESIDENTS.	VICE-PRESIDENTS.
GEORGE WASHINGTON, Virginia.	JOHN ADAMS, Massachusetts.

The Second Administration—1797 to 1801—Four Years.

JOHN ADAMS, Massachusetts.　　THOMAS JEFFERSON, Virginia.

The Third Administration—1801 to 1809—Eight Years.

THOMAS JEFFERSON, Virginia.　　AARON BURR, New York.
　　GEORGE CLINTON, New York.

The Fourth Administration—1809 to 1817—Eight Years.

JAMES MADISON, Virginia.　　GEORGE CLINTON, New York.
　　ELBRIDGE GERRY, Massachusetts.

The Fifth Administration—1817 to 1825—Eight Years.

JAMES MONROE, Virginia.　　DANIEL D. TOMPKINS, New York.

The Sixth Administration—1825 to 1829—Four Years.

JOHN QUINCY ADAMS, Massachusetts.　　JOHN C. CALHOUN, South Carolina.

The Seventh Administration—1829 to 1837—Eight Years.

ANDREW JACKSON, Tennessee.　　JOHN C. CALHOUN, South Carolina.
　　MARTIN VAN BUREN, New York.

The Eighth Administration—1837 to 1841—Four Years.

MARTIN VAN BUREN, New York.　　RICHARD M. JOHNSON, Kentucky.

The Ninth Administration—1841 to 1845—Four Years.

WILLIAM HENRY HARRISON, Ohio. (Died　　JOHN TYLER, Virginia.
April 4, 1841.)
JOHN TYLER, Va., (from April 4, 1841).

The Tenth Administration—1845 to 1849—Four Years.

JAMES K. POLK, Tennessee.　　GEORGE M. DALLAS, Pennsylvania.

The Eleventh Administration—1849 to 1853—Four Years.

ZACHARY TAYLOR, Louisiana. (Died July　　MILLARD FILLMORE, New York.
9, 1850.)
MILLARD FILLMORE, New York. (From
July 9, 1850.)

The Twelfth Administration—1853 to 1857—Four Years.

FRANKLIN PIERCE, New Hampshire.　　WILLIAM R. KING, Alabama. (Died
April 18, 1853.)

The Thirteenth Administration—1857 to 1861—Four Years.

JAMES BUCHANAN, Pennsylvania.   JOHN C. BRECKENRIDGE, Kentucky.

The Fourteenth Administration—1861 to 1869—Eight Years.

ABRAHAM LINCOLN, Illinois.   HANNIBAL HAMLIN, Maine.

ABRAHAM LINCOLN, (Assassinated, 2d Term,
    April 15, 1865.) Succeeded by   ANDREW JOHNSON, Tennessee.
ANDREW JOHNSON, Tennessee. (From
    April 15, 1865.)

The Fifteenth Administration—1869 to 1873—Four Years.

ULYSSES S. GRANT, Illinois.   SCHUYLER COLFAX, Indiana.
    Entered on his Second term
      March 4, 1873.   HENRY WILSON, Massachusetts.

The Sixteenth Administration—1877 to 1881—Four Years.

RUTHERFORD B. HAYES, Ohio.   WILLIAM A. WHEELER, New York.

The Seventeenth Administration—1881 to 1885—Four Years.

JAMES A. GARFIELD, Ohio. (Assassinated   CHESTER A. ARTHUR, New York.
    July 2, 1881. Died September 19, 1881).
CHESTER A. ARTHUR, New York. (From
    September 19, 1881).

UNITED STATES CAPITOL, WASHINGTON, D.C.

The Constitution of the United States.

We, the people of the United States, in order to form a more perfect union, establish justice, ensure domestic tranquillity, provide for the common defence, promote the general welfare, and secure the blessings of liberty to ourselves and our posterity, do ordain and establish this Constitution for the United States of America:

ARTICLE I.

Sect. 1. All legislative powers herein granted shall be vested in a Congress of the United States, which shall consist of a senate and house of representatives.

Sect. 2. The house of representatives shall be composed of members chosen every second year by the people of the several states; and the electors in each state shall have the qualifications requisite for electors of the most numerous branch of the state legislature.

No person shall be a representative, who shall not have attained to the age of twenty-five years, and been seven years a citizen of the United States, and who shall not, when elected, be an inhabitant of that state in which he shall be chosen.

Representatives and direct taxes shall be apportioned among the several states which may be included within this union, according to their respective numbers, which shall be determined by adding to the whole number of free persons, including those bound to service for a term of years, and excluding Indians not taxed three-fifths of all other persons. The actual enumeration shall be made within three years after the first meeting of the Congress of the United States, and within every subsequent term of ten years, in such manner as they shall by law direct. The number of representatives shall not exceed one for every thirty thousand, but each state shall have, at least, one representative; and until such enumeration shall be made, the state of New Hampshire shall be entitled to choose three, Massachusetts eight, Rhode Island and Providence Plantations one, Connecticut five, New York six, New Jersey four, Pennsylvania eight, Delaware one, Maryland six, Virginia ten, North Carolina five, South Carolina five, and Georgia three.

When vacancies happen in the representation from any state, the executive authority thereof shall issue writs of election to fill such vacancies.

The house of representatives shall choose their speaker and other officers; and shall have the sole power of impeachment.

Sect. 3. The senate of the United States shall be composed of two senators from each state, chosen by the legislature thereof, for six years; and each senator shall have one vote.

Immediately after they shall be assembled in consequence of the first election, they shall be divided, as equally as may be, into three classes. The seats of the senators of the first class shall be vacated at the expiration of the second year, of the second class at the expiration of the fourth year, and of the third class at the expiration of the sixth year, so that one-third may be chosen every second year; and if vacancies happen by resignation or otherwise, during the recess of the legislature of any state, the executive thereof may make temporary appointments until the next meeting of the legislature, which shall then fill such vacancies.

No person shall be a senator who shall not have attained to the age of thirty years, and been nine years a citizen of the United States, and who shall not, when elected, be an inhabitant of that state for which he shall be chosen.

The vice president of the United States shall be president of the senate, but shall have no vote, unless they be equally divided.

The senate shall choose their other officers, also a president pro tempore, in the absence of the vice president, or when he shall exercise the office of president of the United States.

The senate shall have the sole power to try all impeachments. When sitting for that purpose, they shall be on oath or affirmation. When the president of the United States is tried, the chief justice shall preside; and no person shall be convicted without the concurrence of two-thirds of the members present.

Judgment in cases of impeachment shall not extend further than to removal from office, and disqualification to hold and enjoy any office of honor, trust, or profit, under the United States; but the party convicted shall nevertheless be liable and subject to indictment, trial, judgment, and punishment, according to law.

Sect. 4. The times, places and man-

ner of holding elections for senators and representatives, shall be prescribed in each state by the legislature thereof; but the Congress may at any time by law, make or alter such regulations, except as to the places of choosing senators.

The Congress shall assemble at least once in every year, and such meeting shall be on the first Monday in December, unless they shall by law appoint a different day.

Sect. 5. Each house shall be the judge of the elections, returns, and qualifications, of its own members; and a majority of each shall constitute a quorum to do business; but a smaller number may adjourn from day to day, and may be authorized to compel the attendance of absent members, in such manner, and under such penalties as each house may provide.

Each house may determine the rules of its proceedings, punish its members for disorderly behavior, and, with the concurrence of two-thirds, expel a member.

Each house shall keep a journal of its proceedings, and from time to time publish the same, excepting such parts as may, in their judgment, require secrecy; and the yeas and nays of the members of either house on any question, shall, at the request of one fifth of those present, be entered on the journal.

Neither house, during the session of Congress, shall, without the consent of the other, adjourn for more than three days, nor to any other place than that in which the two houses shall be sitting.

Sect 6. The senators and representatives shall receive a compensation for their services, to be ascertained by law, and paid out of the treasury of the United States. They shall in all cases, except treason, felony, and breach of the peace, be privileged from arrest during their attendance at the session of their respective houses, and in going to and returning from the same; and for any speech or debate in either house, they shall not be questioned in any other place.

No senator or representative shall, during the time for which he was elected, be appointed to any civil office under the authority of the United States, which shall have been created, or the emoluments whereof shall have been increased during such time; and no person holding any office under the United States, shall be a member of either house during his continuance in office.

Sect. 7. All bills for raising revenue shall originate in the house of representatives; but the senate may propose or concur with amendments as on other bills.

Every bill which shall have passed the house of representatives and the senate, shall, before it become a law, be presented to the president of the United States. If he approve, he shall sign it; but if not, he shall return it, with his objections, to that house in which it shall have originated, who shall enter the objections at large on their journal, and proceed to reconsider it. If, after such reconsideration, two-thirds of that house shall agree to pass the bill, it shall be sent, together with the objections, to the other house, by which it shall likewise be reconsidered, and if approved by two-thirds of that house it shall become a law. But in all such cases, the votes of both houses shall be determined by yeas and nays, and the names of the persons voting for and against the bill shall be entered on the journal of each house respectively. If any bill shall not be returned by the president within ten days, (Sundays excepted) after it shall have been presented to him, the same shall be a law, in like manner as if he had signed it, unless the Congress. by their adjournment prevent its return, in which case it shall not be a law.

Every order, resolution, or vote, to which the concurrence of the senate and house of representatives may be necessary, (except on a question of adjournment) shall be presented to the president of the United States; and before the same shall take effect, shall be approved by him, or, being disapproved by him, shall be repassed by two-thirds of the senate and house of representatives, according to the rules and limitations prescribed in the case of a bill.

Sect. 8. The Congress shall have power—

To lay and collect taxes, duties, imposts, and excises:

To pay the debts and provide for the common defence and general welfare of the United States; but all duties, imposts, and excises, shall be uniform throughout the United States:

To borrow money on the credit of of the United States:

To regulate commerce with foreign

nations, and among the several states, and with the Indian tribes:

To establish a uniform rule of naturalization, and uniform laws on the subject of bankruptcies throughout the United States:

To coin money, regulate the value thereof, and of foreign coin, and fix the standard of weights and measures:

To provide for the punishment of counterfeiting the securities and current coin of the United States:

To establish post offices and post roads:

To promote the progress of science and useful arts, by securing for limited times, to authors and inventors, the exclusive right to their respective writings and discoveries:

To constitute tribunals inferior to the supreme court:

To define and punish piracies and felonies committed on the high seas, and offences against the law of nations:

To declare war, to grant letters of marque and reprisal, and make rules concerning captures on land and water:

To raise and support armies; but no appropriation of money to that use shall be for a longer term than two years:

To provide and maintain a navy:

To make rules for the government and regulation of the land and naval forces:

To provide for calling forth the militia to execute the laws of the union, suppress insurrections, and repel invasions:

To provide for organizing, arming, and disciplining the militia, and for governing such part of them as may be employed in the service of the United States—reserving to the states respectively, the appointment of the officers, and the authority of training the militia according to the discipline prescribed by Congress:

To exercise exclusive legislation in all cases whatsoever, over such district (not exceeding ten miles square) as may, by cession of particular states, and the acceptance of Congress, become the seat of government of the United States, and to exercise like authority over all places purchased, by the consent of the legislature of the state in which the same shall be, for the erection of forts, magazines, arsenals, dock yards, and other needful buildings:—and,

To make all laws which shall be necessary and proper for carrying into execution the foregoing powers, and all other powers vested by this constitution in the government of the United States, or in any department or officer thereof.

SECT. 9. The migration or importation of such persons as any of the states, now existing, shall think proper to admit, shall not be prohibited by the Congress prior to the year 1808, but a tax or duty may be imposed on such importation, not exceeding ten dollars for each person.

The privilege of the writ of habeas corpus shall not be suspended, unless when, in cases of rebellion or invasion, the public safety may require it.

No bill of attainder, or ex post facto law, shall be passed.

No capitation, or other direct tax shall be laid, unless in proportion to the census or enumeration herein before directed to be taken.

No tax or duty shall be laid on articles exported from any state. No preference shall be given by any regulation of commerce or revenue to the ports of one state over those of another; nor shall vessels bound to, or from one state, be obliged to enter, clear, or pay duties in another.

No money shall be drawn from the treasury, but in consequence of appropriations made by law: and a regular statement and account of the receipts and expenditures of all public money shall be published from time to time.

No title of nobility shall be granted by the United States: and no person holding any office of profit or trust under them, shall, without the consent of the Congress, accept of any present, emolument, office, or title of any kind whatever, from any king, prince, or foreign state.

Sect. 10. No state shall enter into any treaty, alliance, or confederation; grant letters of marque and reprisal; coin money; emit bills of credit; make any thing but gold and silver coin a tender in payment of debts; pass any bill of attainder, ex post facto law, or law impairing the obligation of contracts, or grant any title of nobility.

No state shall, without the consent of the Congress, lay any imposts or duties on imports or exports, except what may be absolutely necessary for executing its inspection laws; and the nett produce of all duties and imposts, laid by any state on imports or exports, shall be for the use of the treasury of the United States; and all such laws shall be subject to the revision and control of the Congress. No state shall,

without the consent of Congress, lay any duty of tonnage, keep troops or ships of war in time of peace, enter into any agreement or compact with another state, or with a foreign power or engage in war, unless actually invaded, or in such imminent danger as will not admit of delay.

ARTICLE II.

Sect. 1. The executive power shall be vested in a President of the United States of America. He shall hold his office during the term of four years, and, together with the Vice President, chosen for the same term, be elected as follows:

Each state shall appoint, in such manner as the legislature thereof may direct, a number of electors equal to the whole number of senators and representatives to which the state may be entitled in the Congress; but no senator or representative, or person holding any office of trust or profit under the United States, shall be appointed an elector.

The electors shall meet in their respective states, and vote by ballot for two persons, of whom one at least shall not be an inhabitant of the same state with themselves. And they shall make a list of all the persons voted for, and of the number of votes for each; which list they shall sign and certify, and transmit sealed to the seat of the government of the United States, directed to the president of the senate. The president of the senate shall, in the presence of the senate and house of representatives, open all the certificates, and the votes shall then be counted

The person having the greatest number of votes shall be the president, if such number be a majority of the whole number of electors appointed; and if there be more than one who have such majority, and have an equal number of votes, then the house of representatives shall immediately choose, by ballot, one of them for president; and if no person have a majority, then from the five highest on the list, the said house shall, in like manner, choose the president. But in choosing the president, the votes shall be taken by states, the representation from each state having one vote. A quorum for this purpose shall consist of a member or members from two-thirds of the states, and a majority of all the states shall be necessary to a choice. In every case, after the choice of the president, the person having the greatest number of votes of the electors shall be the vice president. But if there should remain two or more who have equal votes, the senate shall choose from them, by ballot, the vice president.

The Congress may determine the time of choosing the electors, and the day on which they shall give their votes; which day shall be the same throughout the United States.

No person, except a natural born citizen, or a citizen of the United States at the time of the adoption of this constitution, shall be eligible to the office of president; neither shall any person be eligible to that office, who shall not have attained to the age of thirty-five years, and been fourteen years a resident within the United States.

In case of the removal of the president from office, or of his death, resignation, or inability to discharge the powers and duties of the said office, the same shall devolve on the vice president; and the Congress may by law provide for the case of removal, death, resignation, or inability, both of the president and vice president, declaring what officer shall then act as president, and such officer shall act accordingly until the disability be removed, or a president shall be elected.

The president shall, at stated times, receive for his services a compensation, which shall neither be increased nor diminished during the period for which he shall have been elected, and he shall not receive within that period any other emolument from the United States, or any of them.

Before he enters on the execution of his office, he shall take the following oath or affirmation:

"I do solemnly swear, (or affirm) "that I will faithfully execute the "office of president of the United "States, and will, to the best of my "ability, preserve, protect, and de-"fend the constitution of the United "States."

Sect. 2. The president shall be commander-in-chief of the army and navy of the United States, and of the militia of the several states, when called into the actual service of the United States; he may require the opinion, in writing, of the principal officer in each of the executive departments, upon any subject relating to the duties of their respective offices; and he shall have power to grant reprieves and pardons for offences against the United States, except in cases of impeachment.

He shall have power, by and with the advice and consent of the senate, to make treaties, provided two-thirds of the senators present concur: and he shall nominate, and by and with the advice and consent of the senate, shall appoint ambassadors, other public ministers, and consuls, judges of the supreme court, and all other officers of the United States, whose appointments are not herein otherwise provided for, and which shall be established by law. But the Congress may by law vest the appointment of such inferior officers as they think proper in the president alone, in the courts of law, or in the heads of departments.

The president shall have power to fill up all vacancies that may happen during the recess of the senate, by granting commissions, which shall expire at the end of their next session.

Sect. 3. He shall, from time to time, give to the Congress information of the state of the union, and recommend to their consideration such measures as he shall judge necessary and expedient; he may, on extraordinary occasions, convene both houses, or either of them, and in case of disagreement between them, with respect to the time of adjournment, he may adjourn them to such time as he shall think proper; he shall receive ambassadors and other public ministers; he shall take care that the laws be faithfully executed; and shall commission all the officers of the United States.

Sect. 4. The president, vice president, and all civil officers of the United States shall be removed from office on impeachment for, and conviction of treason, bribery, or other high crimes and misdemeanors.

ARTICLE III.

Sect. 1. The judicial power of the United States shall be vested in one supreme court, and in such inferior courts as the Congress may, from time to time, ordain and establish. The judges, both of the supreme and inferior courts, shall hold their offices during good behavior; and shall, at stated times, receive for their services a compensation, which shall not be diminished during their continuance in office.

Sect. 2. The judicial power shall extend to all cases in law and equity, arising under this constitution, the laws of the United States, and treaties made, or which shall be made under their authority; to all cases affecting ambassadors, other public ministers, and consuls; to all cases of admiralty and maritime jurisdiction; to controversies to which the United States shall be a party; to controversies between two or more states, between a state and citizens of another state, between citizens of different states, between citizens of the same state, claiming lands under grants of different states, and between a state, or the citizens thereof, and foreign states, citizens, or subjects.

In all cases affecting ambassadors, other public ministers and consuls, and those in which a state shall be party, the supreme court shall have original jurisdiction. In all the other cases before mentioned, the supreme court shall have appellate jurisdiction, both as to law and fact, with such exceptions, and under such regulations as the Congress shall make.

The trial of all crimes, except in cases of impeachment, shall be by jury; and such trial shall be held in the state where the said crimes shall have been committed; but when not committed within any state, the trial shall be at such place or places as the Congress may by law have directed.

Sect. 3. Treason against the United States shall consist only in levying war against them, or in adhering to their enemies, giving them aid and comfort. No person shall be convicted of treason unless on the testimony of two witnesses to the same overt act, or on confession in open court.

The Congress shall have power to declare the punishment of treason; but no attainder of treason shall work corruption of blood, or forfeiture, except during the life of the person attainted.

ARTICLE IV.

Sect. 1. Full faith and credit shall be given in each state, to the public acts, records, and judicial proceedings of every other state. And the Congress may, by general laws, prescribe the manner in which such acts, records and proceedings shall be proved, and the effect thereof.

Sect. 2. The citizens of each state shall be entitled to all privileges and immunities of citizens in the several states.

A person charged in any state with treason, felony, or other crime, who shall flee from justice, and be found in another state, shall, on demand of the executive authority of the state from which he fled, be delivered up, to be removed to the state having jurisdiction of the crime.

No person held to service or labor in one state, under the laws thereof, escaping into another, shall, in consequence of any law or regulation therein, be discharged from such service or labor; but shall be delivered up, on claim of the party to whom such service or labor may be due.

Sect. 3. New states may be admitted by the Congress into this union; but no new state shall be formed or erected within the jurisdiction of any other state, nor any state be formed by the junction of two or more states, or parts of states, without the consent of the legislatures of the states concerned, as well as of the Congress.

The Congress shall have power to dispose of and make all needful rules and regulations respecting the territory or other property belonging to the United States; and nothing in this constitution shall be so construed as to prejudice any claims of the United States, or of any particular state.

Sect. 4. The United States shall guarantee to every state in this union a republican form of government, and shall protect each of them against invasion; and on application of the legislature, or of the executive (when the legislature cannot be convened) against domestic violence.

ARTICLE V.

The Congress, whenever two-thirds of both houses shall deem it necessary, shall propose amendments to this constitution; or, on the application of the legislatures of two-thirds of the several states, shall call a convention for proposing amendments, which, in either case, shall be valid to all intents and purposes, as part of this constitution, when ratified by the legislatures of three-fourths of the several states, or by conventions in three-fourths thereof, as the one or the other mode of ratification may be proposed by the Congress: Provided, that no amendment which may be made prior to the year 1808, shall in any manner affect the first and fourth clauses in the ninth section of the first article; and that no state, without its consent, shall be deprived of its equal suffrage in the senate.

ARTICLE VI.

All debts contracted and engagements entered into, before the adoption of this constitution, shall be as valid against the United States under this constitution as under the confederation.

This constitution, and the laws of the United States which shall be made in pursuance thereof; and all treaties made, or which shall be made, under the authority of the United States, shall be the supreme law of the land; and the judges in every state shall be bound thereby, any thing in the constitution or laws of any state to the contrary notwithstanding.

The senators and representatives before mentioned, and the members of the several state legislatures, and all executive and judicial officers, both of the United States and of the several states, shall be bound by oath or affirmation, to support this constitution; but no religious test shall ever be required as a qualification to any office or public trust under the United States.

ARTICLE VII.

The ratification of the conventions of nine states shall be sufficient for the establishment of this constitution between the states so ratifying the same.

Done in convention, by the unanimous consent of the states present, the 17th day of September, in the year of our Lord 1787, and of the independence of the United States of America, the twelfth. In witness whereof, we have hereunto subscribed our names.

GEORGE WASHINGTON,
President,
And deputy from Virginia.

New Hampshire.
JOHN LANGDON,
NICHOLAS GILMAN,

Massachusetts.
NATHANIEL GORHAM,
RUFUS KING.

Connecticut.
WILLIAM SAMUEL JOHNSON,
ROGER SHERMAN.

New York.
ALEXANDER HAMILTON.

New Jersey.
WILLIAM LIVINGSTON,
DAVID BREARLY,
WILLIAM PATTERSON,
JONATHAN DAYTON.

Pennsylvania.
BENJAMIN FRANKLIN,
THOMAS MIFFLIN,
ROBERT MORRIS,
GEORGE CLYMER,
THOMAS FITZSIMONS,
JARED INGERSOLL,
JAMES WILSON,
GOUVERNEUR MORRIS.

Delaware.
GEORGE READ,
GUNNING BEDFORD, Jun.
JOHN DICKINSON,
RICHARD BASSETT,
JACOB BROOM.

Maryland.
JAMES M'HENRY,
DANIEL OF ST. THOMAS JENIFER,
DANIEL CARROLL.

Virginia.
JOHN BLAIR,
JAMES MADISON, Jun.

North Carolina.
WILLIAM BLOUNT,
RICHARD DOBBS SPAIGHT,
HUGH WILLIAMSON.

South Carolina.
JOHN RUTLEDGE,
CHARLES COTESWORTH PINCKNEY,
CHARLES PINCKNEY,
PIERCE BUTLER.

Georgia.
WILLIAM FEW,
ABRAHAM BALDWIN.

Attest.
WILLIAM JACKSON, *Secretary.*

AMENDMENTS TO THE CONSTITUTION.

The first ten of these Amendments were proposed to the legislatures of the several States by the first Congress, which assembled at New York, in March, seventeen hundred and eighty-nine; the eleventh article was proposed at the second session of the third Congress; the twelfth article at the first session of the eighth Congress; and the thirteenth in eighteen hundred and sixty-five. Having been ratified according to the provisions of the fifth article of the Constitution, these Amendments form an integral portion of that great charter of American liberty and law.

ARTICLE I.

Congress shall make no law respecting an establishment of religion, or prohibiting the free exercise thereof; or abridging the freedom of speech, or of the press; or the right of the people peaceably to assemble, and to petition the government for a redress of grievances.

ARTICLE II.

A well-regulated militia being necessary to the security of a free State, the right of the people to keep and bear arms shall not be infringed.

ARTICLE III.

No soldier shall, in time of peace, be quartered in any house without the consent of the owner; nor in time of war, but in a manner to be prescribed by law.

ARTICLE IV.

The right of the people to be secure in their persons, houses, papers, and effects, against unreasonable searches and seizures, shall not be violated; and no warrants shall issue, but upon probable cause, supported by oath or affirmation, and particularly describing the places to be searched, and the persons or things to be seized.

ARTICLE V.

No person shall be held to answer for a capital or otherwise infamous crime, unless on a presentment or indictment of a grand jury, except in cases arising in the land or naval forces, or in the militia, when in actual service, in time of war or public danger; nor shall any person be subject for the same offence to be twice put in jeopardy of life or limb; nor shall be compelled, in any criminal case, to be a witness against himself; nor be deprived of life, liberty, or property, without due process of law; nor shall private property be taken for public use without just compensation.

ARTICLE VI.

In all criminal prosecutions, the accused shall enjoy the right to a speedy and public trial, by an impartial jury of the state and district wherein the crime shall have been committed, which district shall have been previously ascertained by law, and to be informed of the nature and cause of the accusation; to be confronted with the witnesses against him; to have compulsory process for obtaining witnesses in his favor; and to have the assistance of counsel for his defence.

ARTICLE VII.

In suits at common law, where the value in controversy shall exceed twenty dollars, the right of trial by jury shall be preserved; and no fact tried by a jury shall be otherwise re-examined in any court of the United States, than according to the rules of the common law.

ARTICLE VIII.

Excessive bail shall not be required, nor excessive fines imposed, nor cruel and unusual punishments inflicted.

ARTICLE IX.

The enumeration in the Constitution of certain rights shall not be construed to deny or disparage others retained by the people.

ARTICLE X.

The powers not delegated to the United

States by the Constitution, nor prohibited by it to the States, are reserved to the States respectively, or to the people.

ARTICLE XI.

The judicial power of the United States shall not be construed to extend to any suit in law or equity, commenced or prosecuted against one of the United States by citizens of another State, or by citizens or subjects of any foreign State.

ARTICLE XII.

The electors shall meet in their respective States, and vote by ballot for president and vice-president, one of whom, at least, shall not be an inhabitant of the same State with themselves; they shall name in their ballots the person voted for as president, and in distinct ballots the person voted for as vice-president; and they shall make distinct lists of all persons voted for as president, and of all persons voted for as vice-president, and of the number of votes for each, which lists they shall sign and certify, and transmit, sealed, to the seat of the government of the United States, directed to the president of the senate; the president of the senate shall, in the presence of the senate and house of representatives, open all the certificates, and the votes shall then be counted; the person having the greatest number of votes for president, shall be the president, if such number shall be a majority of the whole number of electors appointed; and if no person have such majority, then, from the persons having the highest numbers, not exceeding three, on the list of those voted for as president, the house of representatives shall choose immediately, by ballot, the president. But in choosing the president, the votes shall be taken by States, the representation from each State having one vote; a quorum for this purpose shall consist of a member or members from two-thirds of the States, and a majority of all the States shall be necessary to a choice. And if the house of representatives shall not choose a president, whenever the right of choice shall devolve upon them, before the fourth day of March next following, then the vice-president shall act as president, as in the case of the death or other constitutional disability of the president.

The person having the greatest number of votes as vice-president shall be the vice-president, if such number be a majority of the whole number of electors appointed; and if no person have a majority, then, from the two highest numbers on the list, the senate shall choose the vice-president; a quorum for the purpose shall consist of two-thirds of the whole number of senators, and a majority of the whole number shall be necessary to a choice.

But no person constitutionally ineligible to the office of president, shall be eligible to that of vice-president of the United States.

ARTICLE XIII.

Adopted January 31st, 1865.

SECTION 1.—Neither slavery nor involuntary servitude, except as a punishment for crime, whereof the party shall have been duly convicted, shall exist within the United States, or any place subject to their jurisdiction.

SEC. 2.—Congress shall have power to enforce this article by appropriate legislation.

ARTICLE XIV.

Fully adopted July 28th, 1868.

SECTION 1.—All persons born or naturalized in the United States, and subject to the jurisdiction thereof, are citizens of the United States, and of the State wherein they reside. No State shall make or enforce any law which shall abridge the privileges or immunities of citizens of the United States; nor shall any State deprive any person of life, liberty, or property, without due process of law, nor deny to any person within its jurisdiction the equal protection of the laws.

SECTION 2.—Representatives shall be apportioned among the several States according to their respective numbers, counting the whole number of persons in each State, excluding Indians not taxed. But, when the right to vote at any election for the choice of electors for President and Vice-President of the United States, Representatives in Congress, the Executive and Judicial Officers of a State, or the members of the Legislature thereof, is denied to any of the male inhabitants of such State, being twenty-one years of age, and citizens of the United States, or in any way abridged, except for participation in rebellion, or other crime, the basis of representation therein shall be reduced in the proportion which the number of such male citizens shall bear to the whole number of male citizens twenty-one years of age in such State.

SECTION 3.—No person shall be a Senator or Representative in Congress, or elector of President and Vice-President, or hold any office, civil or military, under the United States, or under any State, who, having previously taken an oath, as a member of Congress, or as an officer of the United States, or as a member of any State Legislature, or as an Executive or Judicial Officer of any State, to support the Constitution of the United States, shall have engaged in insur-

rection or rebellion against the same, or given aid or comfort to the enemies thereof. But Congress may, by a vote of two-thirds of each House, remove such disability.

SECTION 4.—The validity of the public debt of the United States, authorized by law, including debts incurred for the payment of pensions and bounties, for services in suppressing insurrection or rebellion, shall not be questioned. But neither the United States, nor any State, shall assume or pay any debt or obligation incurred in aid of insurrection or rebellion against the United States, or any claim for the loss or emancipation of any slave; but all such debts, obligations and claims shall be held illegal and void.

SECTION 5.—The Congress shall have power to enforce, by appropriate legislation, the provisions of this article.

ARTICLE XV.
Fully adopted March 30th, 1870.

SECTION 1.—The right of citizens of th United States to vote shall not be denied or abridged by the United States, or by any State, on account of race, color, or previous condition of servitude.

SECTION 2.—The Congress shall have power to enforce this article by appropriate legislation.

Washington's Farewell Address.

WASHINGTON in 1796 expressed his fixed determination not to continue at the head of affairs any longer; yet, in the unsettled position of matters with France, he was urgently entreated to withhold the announcement of his determination for a time at least. But his purpose was not to be changed. He had already sacrificed enough for his country to be entitled to his discharge from public life, and never did a weary and careworn pilgrim more earnestly covet rest and retirement, than he, to whom his country was so large a debtor. In accordance with every propriety therefore, Washington determined to avail himself of the opportunity to address to his countrymen his parting words of wise and fatherly counsel. Accordingly, early in September, nearly six months before his term of office expired, he completed his Farewell Address, and gave expression to the views which he entertained on public affairs, and the principles by which he had ever been governed in the service of the state. This noble and manly document, the invaluable legacy of the father of his country to the people whom he loved, and for whom he labored all his life long, is too important not to be held up continually before the eyes of the countrymen of Washington, and the inheritors of the manifold blessings of liberty and law, which Washington expended his best energies to secure to all generations.

"TO THE PEOPLE OF THE UNITED STATES.

"FRIENDS AND FELLOW CITIZENS:—The period for a new election of a citizen to administer the executive government of the United States being not far distant, and the time actually arrived when your thoughts must be **1796.** employed in designating the person who is to be clothed with that important trust, it appears to me proper, especially as it may conduce to a more distinct expression of the public voice, that I should now apprise you of the resolution I have formed, to decline being considered among the number of those out of whom the choice is to be made.

"I beg you at the same time to do me the justice to be assured, that this resolution has not been taken without a strict regard to all the considerations appertaining to the relation which binds a dutiful citizen to his country; and that in withdrawing the tender of service, which silence in my situation might imply, I am influenced by no diminution of zeal for your future interest; no deficiency of grateful respect for your past kindness; but am supported by a full conviction, that the step is compatible with both.

"The acceptance of, and continuance hitherto in, the office to which **1796.** your suffrages have twice called me have been an uniform sacrifice of inclination to the opinion of duty, and to a deference for what appeared to be your desire. I constantly hoped that it would have been much earlier in my power, consistently with motives which I was not at liberty to disregard, to return to that retirement from which I had been reluctantly drawn. The strength of my inclination to do this, previous to the last election, had even led to the preparation of an address to declare it to you; but mature reflection on the then perplexed and critical posture of our affairs with foreign nations, and the unanimous advice of persons entitled to my confidence, impelled me to abandon the idea.

"I rejoice that the state of your concerns, external as well as internal, no longer renders the pursuit of inclination incompatible with the sentiment of duty or propriety; and am persuaded, whatever partiality may be retained for my services, that in the present circumstances of our country, you will not disapprove of my determination to retire.

"The impressions with which I first undertook the arduous trust, were explained on the proper occasion. In the discharge of this trust I will only say, that I have, with good intentions, contributed toward the organization and administration of the government the best exertions of which a very fallible judgment was capable. Not unconscious, in the outset, of the inferiority of my qualifications, experience in my own eyes, perhaps still more in the eyes of others, has strengthened the motives to diffidence of myself; and every day the increasing weight of years admonishes me more and more, that the shade of retirement is as necessary to me as it will be welcome. Satisfied that if any circumstances have given peculiar value to my services, they were temporary, I have the consolation to believe, that while choice

and prudence invite me to quit the political scene, patriotism does not forbid it.

"In looking forward to the moment which is to terminate the career of my political life, my feelings do not permit me to suspend the deep acknowledgment of that debt of gratitude which I owe to my beloved country, for the many honours it has conferred upon me; still more for the steadfast confidence with which it has supported me; and for the opportunities I have thence enjoyed of manifesting my inviolable attachment, by services faithful and persevering, though in usefulness unequal to my zeal. If benefits have resulted to our country from these services, let it always be remembered to your praise, and as an instructive example in our annals, that, under circumstances in which the passions, agitated in every direction, were liable to mislead—amidst appearances sometimes dubious—vicissitudes of fortune often discouraging—in situations in which not unfrequently want **1796.** of success has countenanced the spirit of criticism—the constancy of your support was the essential prop of the efforts, and a guarantee of the plans, by which they were effected. Profoundly penetrated with this idea, I shall carry it with me to my grave, as a strong incitement to unceasing wishes, that heaven may continue to you the choicest tokens of its beneficence—that your union and brotherly affection may be perpetual—that the free Constitution, which is the work of your hands, may be sacredly maintained—that its administration in every department may be stamped with wisdom and virtue—that, in fine, the happiness of the people of these states, under the auspices of liberty, may be made complete, by so careful a preservation and so prudent a use of this blessing, as will acquire to them the glory of recommending it to the applause, the affection, and the adoption, of every nation which is yet a stranger to it.

"Here, perhaps, I ought to stop. But a solicitude for your welfare, which cannot end but with my life, and the apprehension of danger natural to that solicitude, urge me, on an occasion like the present, to offer to **1796.** your solemn contemplation, and to recommend to your frequent review, some sentiments, which are the result of much reflection, of no inconsiderable observation, and which appear to me all-important to the permanency of your felicity as a people. These will be offered to you with the more freedom, as you can only see in them the disinterested warnings of a parting friend, who can possibly have no personal motive to bias his counsel. Nor can I forget, as an encouragement to it, your indulgent reception of my sentiments on a former and not dissimilar occasion.

"Interwoven as is the love of liberty with every ligament of your hearts, no recommendation of mine is necessary to fortify or confirm the attachment.

"The unity of government, which constitutes you one people, is also now dear to you. It is justly so; for it is a main pillar in the edifice of your real independence; the support of your tranquillity at home, your peace abroad; of your safety, of your prosperity, of that very liberty which you so highly prize. But as it is easy to foresee, that from different causes and from different quarters, much pains will be taken, many artifices employed, to weaken in your minds the conviction of this truth; as this is the point in your political fortress against which the batteries of internal and external enemies will be most constantly and actively, (though often covertly and insidiously,) directed, it is of infinite moment, that you should properly estimate the immense value of your national union, to your collective and individual happiness; that you should cherish a cordial, habitual, and immovable attachment to it; accustoming yourselves to think and speak of it as of the palladium of your political safety and prosperity; watching for its preservation with jealous anxiety; discountenancing whatever may suggest even a suspicion that it can in any event be abandoned; and indignantly frowning upon the first dawning of every attempt to alienate any portion of our country from the rest, or to enfeeble the sacred ties which now link together the various parts.

"For this you have every inducement of sympathy and interest. Citizens, by birth or choice, of a common country, that country has a right to concentrate your affections. The name of AMERICAN, which belongs to you in your national capacity, must always exalt the just pride of patriotism, more than any appellation derived from local discriminations. With slight shades of difference, you have the same religion, manners, habits, and political principles. You have in a common cause fought and triumphed together; the independence and liberty you possess, are the work of joint councils, and joint efforts, of common dangers, sufferings, and successes.

"But these considerations, however powerfully they address themselves to your sensibility, are greatly outweighed by those which apply more immediately **1796.** to your interest. Here every portion of our country finds the most commanding motives for carefully guarding and preserving the union of the whole.

"The *north*, in an unrestrained intercourse with the *south*, protected by the equal laws of a common government, finds in the productions of the latter, great additional resources of maritime and commercial enterprise, and precious materials· of manufacturing industry. The *south*, in the same intercourse, benefiting by the agency of the *north*, sees its agriculture grow and its commerce expand. Turning partly into its own channels the seamen of the *north*, it finds its particular navigation invigorated—and while it contributes, in different ways, to nourish and increase the general mass of the national navigation, it looks forward to the protection of a maritime strength, to which itself is unequally adapted. The *east*, in like intercourse with the *west*, already finds, and in the progressive improvement of interior communications by land and water, will more and more find a valuable vent for the commodities which it brings from abroad, or manufactures at home. The *west* derives from the *east*

supplies requisite to its growth and comfort; and, what is perhaps of still greater consequence, it must of necessity owe the secure enjoyment of indispensable outlets for its own productions, to the weight, influence, and the future maritime strength of the Atlantic side of the Union, directed by an indissoluble community of interest as one nation. Any other tenure by which the *west* can hold this essential advantage, whether derived from its own separate strength, or from an apostate and unnatural connection with any foreign power, must be intrinsecally precarious.

"While, then, every part of our country thus feels an immediate and particular interest in union, all the parts combined cannot fail to find in the united mass of means and efforts, greater strength, greater resource, proportionably greater security from external danger, a less frequent interruption of their peace by foreign nations; and, what is of inestimable value, they must derive from union an exemption from those broils and wars between themselves which so frequently afflict neighboring countries, not tied together by the same government; which their own rivalships alone would be sufficient to produce, but which opposite foreign alliances, attachments, and intrigues, would stimulate and embitter. Hence likewise they will avoid the necessity of those overgrown military establishments, which, under any form of government, are inauspicious to liberty, and which are to be regarded as particularly hostile to republican liberty. In this sense it is, that your union ought to be considered as a main prop of your liberty, and that the love of the one ought to endear to you the preservation of the other.

"These considerations speak a persuasive language to every reflecting and virtuous mind, and exhibit the continuance of the Union as a primary object of patriotic desire. Is there a doubt whether a common government can embrace so large a sphere? Let experience solve it. To listen to mere speculation in such a case were criminal.

1796. We are authorized to hope that a proper organization of the whole, with the auxiliary agency of governments for the respective subdivisions, will afford a happy issue to the experiment. It is well worth a fair and full experiment. With such powerful and obvious motives to union, affecting all parts of our country, while experience shall not have demonstrated its impracticability, there will always be reason to distrust the patriotism of those who, in any quarter, may endeavor to weaken its bands.

"In contemplating the causes which may disturb our union, it occurs as matter of serious concern, that any ground should have been furnished for characterizing parties by geographical discriminations—*northern* and *southern* —*Atlantic* and *western*: whence designing men may endeavor to excite a belief that there is a real difference of local interests and views. One of the expedients of party to acquire influence, within particular districts, is to misrepresent the opinions and aims of other districts. You cannot shield yourselves too much against the jealousies and heart-burnings which spring

from these misrepresentations; they tend to render alien to each other, those who ought to be bound together by fraternal affection. The inhabitants of our western country have lately had a useful lesson on this head. They have seen, in the negotiation by the executive, and in the unanimous ratification by the Senate, of the treaty with Spain, and in the universal satisfaction at that event throughout the United States, a decisive proof how unfounded were the suspicions propagated among them of a policy in the general government, and in the Atlantic states, unfriendly to their interests in regard to the Mississippi. They have been witnesses to the formation of two treaties, that with Great Britain, and that with Spain, which secure to them every thing they could desire, in respect to our foreign relations, towards confirming their prosperity. Will it not be their wisdom to rely for the preservation of these advantages on the Union by which they were procured? Will they not henceforth be deaf to those advisers, if such there are, who would sever them from their brethren, and connect them with aliens?

"To the efficacy and permanency of your union, a government for the whole is indispensable. No alliances, however strict, between the parts can be an adequate substitute; they must inevitably experience the infractions and interruptions which all alliances in all times have experienced. Sensible of this momentous truth, you have improved upon your first essay, by the adoption of a constitution of government, better calculated than your former, for an intimate union, and for the efficacious management of your common concerns. This government, the offspring of our own choice, uninfluenced and unawed; adopted upon full investigation and mature deliberation; completely free in its principles; in the distribution of its powers uniting security with energy, and containing within itself a provision for its own amendments, has a just claim to your confidence and your support. Respect for its authority, compliance with its laws, acquiescence in its measures, are duties enjoined by the fundamental maxims of true liberty. The basis of our political systems is the right of the people to make and to alter their constitutions of government. But the constitution which at any time exists, until changed by an explicit and authentic act of the whole people, is sacredly obligatory upon all. The very idea of the power and the right of the people to establish a government, presupposes the duty of every individual to obey the established government.

1796.

"All obstructions to the execution of the laws, all combinations and associations, under whatever plausible character, with the real design to direct, control, counteract, or awe the regular deliberations and action of the constituted authorities, are destructive of this fundamental principle, and of fatal tendency. They serve to organize faction; to give it an artificial and extraordinary force; to put in the place of the delegated will of the nation, the will of a party, often a small, but artful and enterprising minority of the community; and according to the alternate triumphs of different parties, to make the public administration the mirror of the ill-concerted and incongruous projects of faction, rather than the organ of consistent and wholesome plans, digested by common councils, and modified by mutual interests.

"However combinations or associations of the above description may now and then answer popular ends, they are likely, in the course of time and things, to become potent engines, by which cunning, ambitious, and unprincipled men, will be enabled to subvert the power of the people, and to usurp for themselves the reins of government; destroying afterwards the very engines which have lifted them to unjust dominion.

"Towards the preservation of your government, and the permanency of your present happy state, it is requisite not only that you steadily discountenance irregular oppositions to its acknowledged authority, but also that you resist with care the spirit of innovation upon its principles, however specious the pretexts. One method of assault may be to effect in the forms of the Constitution alterations which will impair the energy of the system, and thus to undermine what cannot be directly overthrown. In all the changes to which you may be invited, remember that time and habit are at least as necessary to fix the true characters of governments, as of other human institutions—that experience is the surest standard, by which to test the real tendency of the existing constitution of a country—that facility in changes upon the credit of mere hypothesis and opinion, exposes to perpetual change from the endless variety of hypothesis and opinion; and remember, especially, that for the efficient management of your common interests, in a country so extensive as ours, a government of as much vigor as is consistent with the perfect security of liberty, is indispensable. Liberty itself will find in such a government, with powers properly distributed and adjusted, its surest guardian. It is, indeed, little else than a name, where the government is too feeble to withstand the enterprises of faction, to confine each member of the society within the limits prescribed by the laws, and to maintain all in the secure and tranquil enjoyment of the rights of person and property.

1796.

"I have already intimated to you ne danger of parties in the state, with articular reference to the founding f them on geographical discriminations. Let me now take a more comprehensive view, and warn you in the most solemn manner against the baneful effects of the spirit of party generally.

"This spirit, unfortunately, is inseparable from our nature, having its root in the strongest passions of the human mind. It exists under different shapes in all governments, more or less stifled, controlled, or repressed; but in those of the popular form, it is seen in its greatest rankness, and is truly their worst enemy.

"The alternate domination of one faction over another, sharpened by the spirit of revenge natural to party dissension, which in different ages and countries has perpetrated the most horrid enormities, is itself a frightful despotism. But this leads at length to a more formal and permanent despotism. The disorders and miseries which result, gradually incline the minds of men to seek security and repose in the absolute power of an individual; and sooner or later the chief of some prevailing faction, more able or more fortunate than his competitors, turns this disposition to the purposes of his own elevation on the ruins of public liberty.

"Without looking forward to an extremity of this kind, (which nevertheless ought not to be entirely out of sight,) the common and continual mischiefs of the spirit of party are sufficient to make it the interest and duty of a wise people to discourage and restrain it.

"It serves always to distract the public councils, and enfeeble the public administration. It agitates the community with ill-founded jealousies and false alarms; kindles the animosity of one part against another; foments occasional riot and insurrection. It opens the door to foreign influence and corruption, which find a facilitated access to the government itself, through the channel of party passions. Thus the policy and the will of one country are subjected to the policy and will of another.

"There is an opinion that parties in free countries are useful checks upon the administration of the government, and serve to keep alive the spirit of liberty. This, within certain limits, is probably true; and in governments of a monarchical cast, patriotism may look with indulgence, if not with favor, upon the spirit of party. But in those of the popular character, in governments purely elective, it is a spirit not to be encouraged. From their natural tendency, it is certain there will always be enough of that spirit for every salutary purpose; and there being constant danger of excess, the effort ought to be, by force of public opinion, to mitigate and assuage it. A fire not to be quenched, it demands a uniform vigilance to prevent its bursting into a flame, lest, instead of warming, it should consume.

"It is important, likewise, that the habits of thinking in a free country should inspire caution, in those intrusted **1796.** with its administration, to confine themselves within their respective constitutional spheres, avoiding in the exercise of the powers of one department to encroach upon another. The spirit of encroachment tends to consolidate the powers of all the departments in one, and thus to create, whatever the form of government, a real despotism. A just estimate of that love of power, and proneness to abuse it, which predominate in the human heart, is sufficient to satisfy us of the truth of this position. The necessity of reciprocal checks in the exercise of political power, by dividing and distributing it into different depositories, and constituting each the guardian of the public weal against invasions of the others, has been evinced by experiments ancient and modern; some of them in our country, and under our own eyes. To preserve them must be as necessary as to institute them.

If, in the opinion of the people, the distribution or modification of the constitutional powers be in any particular wrong, let it be corrected by an amendment in the way which the Constitution designates. But let there be no change by usurpation; for though this, in one instance, may be the instrument of good, it is the customary weapon by which free governments are destroyed. The precedent must always greatly overbalance, in permanent evil, any partial or transient benefit which the use can at any time yield.

"Of all the dispositions and habits which lead to political prosperity, religion and morality are indispensable supports. In vain would that man claim the tribute of patriotism, who should labor to subvert these great pillars of human happiness—these firmest props of the duties of men and citizens. The mere politician, equally with the pious man, ought to respect and to cherish them. A volume could not trace all their connections with private and public felicity. Let it simply be asked, where is the security for property, for reputation, for life, if the sense of religious obligation desert the oaths which are the instruments of investigation in courts of justice? And let us with caution indulge the supposition that morality can be maintained without religion. Whatever may be conceded to the influence of refined education on minds of peculiar structure, reason and experience both forbid us to expect that national morality can prevail in exclusion of religious principles.

"It is substantially true, that virtue or morality is a necessary spring of popular government. This rule indeed extends with more or less force to every species of free government. Who that is a sincere friend to it can look with indifference upon attempts to shake the foundation of the fabric?

"Promote, then, as an object of primary importance, institutions for the general diffusion of knowledge. In proportion as the structure of a government gives force to public opinion, it is essential that public opinion should be enlightened.

"As a very important source of strength and security, cherish public credit. One method of preserving it is to use it as sparingly as possible, avoiding occasions of expense by cultivating peace; but remembering also, that timely disbursements to prepare for danger, frequently prevent much greater disbursements to repel it; avoiding likewise the accumulation of debt, not only by shunning occasions of expense, but by vigorous exertions in time of peace to discharge the debts which unavoidable wars may have occasioned, not ungenerously throwing upon posterity the burden which we ourselves ought to bear. The execution of these maxims belongs to your representatives; but it is necessary that public opinion should co-operate. To facilitate to them the performance of their duty, it is essential that you should practically bear in mind, that towards the payment of debts there must be revenue; that to have revenue there must be taxes; that no taxes can be devised which are not more or less inconvenient and unpleasant; that the intrinsic embarrassment inseparable

from the selection of the proper objects, (which is always a choice of difficulties,) ought to be a decisive motive for a candid construction of the conduct of the government in making it, and for a spirit of acquiescence in the measures for obtaining **1796.** revenue, which the public exigencies may at any time dictate.

"Observe good faith and justice towards all nations; cultivate peace and harmony with all. Religion and morality enjoin this conduct; and can it be that good policy does not equally enjoin it? It will be worthy of a free, enlightened, and, at no distant period, a great nation, to give to mankind the magnanimous and too novel example of a people always guided by an exalted justice and benevolence. Who can doubt, that, in the course of time and things, the fruits of such a plan would richly repay any temporary advantages which might be lost by a steady adherence to it? Can it be, that Providence has not connected the permanent felicity of a nation with its virtue? The experiment, at least, is recommended by every sentiment which ennobles human nature. Alas! it is rendered impossible by its vices.

"In the execution of such a plan, nothing is more essential than that permanent inveterate antipathies against particular nations, and passionate attachments for others, should be excluded; and that in place of them, just and amicable feelings towards all should be cultivated. The nation which indulges towards another an habitual hatred, or an habitual fondness, is in some degree a slave. It is a slave to its animosity or to its affection, either of which is sufficient to lead it astray from its duty and its interest. **1796.** Antipathy in one nation against another disposes each more readily to offer insult and injury, to lay hold of slight causes of umbrage, and to be haughty and intractable when accidental or trifling occasions of dispute occur.

"Hence frequent collisions, obstinate. envenomed, and bloody contests. The nation, prompted by ill-will and resentment, sometimes impels to war the government, contrary to the best calculations of policy. The government sometimes participates in the national propensity, and adopts through passion, what reason would reject; at other times it makes the animosity of the nation subservient to projects of hostility instigated by pride, ambition, and other sinister and pernicious motives. The peace often, sometimes perhaps the liberty, of nations has been the victim.

"So, likewise, a passionate attachment of one nation for another, produces a variety of evils. Sympathy for the favorite nation, facilitating the illusion of an imaginary common interest in cases where no real common interest exists, and infusing into one the enmities of the other, betrays the former into a participation in the quarrels and wars of the latter, without adequate inducements or justification. It leads also to concessions to the favorite nation of privileges denied to others, which are apt doubly to injure the nation making the concessions, by unnecessarily parting with what ought to have been retained; and by exciting jealousy, ill-will, and a disposition to retaliate, in the parties from whom equal privileges are withheld; and it gives to ambitious, corrupted, or deluded citizens, (who devote themselves to the favorite nation,) facility to betray or sacrifice the interests of their own country, without odium, sometimes even with popularity; gilding with the appearances of a virtuous sense of obligation to a commendable deference for public opinion, or a laudable zeal for public good, the base or foolish compliances of ambition, corruption, or infatuation.

"As avenues to foreign influence in innumerable ways, such attachments are particularly alarming to the truly enlightened and independent patriot. How many opportunities do they afford to tamper with domestic factions, to practise the arts of seduction, to mislead public opinion, to influence or awe the public councils! Such an attachment of a small or weak, towards a great and powerful nation, dooms the former to be the satellite of the latter. Against the insidious wiles of foreign influence, (I conjure you to believe me, fellow-citizens,) the jealousy of a free people ought to be constantly awake; since history and experience prove, that foreign influence is one of the most baneful foes of republican government. But that jealousy, to be useful, must be impartial; else it becomes the instrument of the very influence to be avoided, instead of a defence against it. Excessive partiality for one foreign nation, and excessive dislike of another, cause those whom they actuate to see danger only on one side, and serve to veil and even second the arts of influence on the other. Real patriots, who may resist the intrigues of the favorite, are liable to become suspected and odious; while its tools and dupes usurp the applause and confidence of the people, to surrender their interests.

"The great rule of conduct for us, in regard to foreign nations, is, in extending our commercial relations, to have with them as little political connection as possible. So far as we have already formed engagements, let them be fulfilled with perfect good faith. Here let us stop.

1796.

"Europe has a set of primary interests, which to us have none, or a very remote, relation. Hence she must be engaged in frequent controversies, the causes of which are essentially foreign to our concerns. Hence, therefore, it must be unwise in us to implicate ourselves by artificial ties, in the ordinary vicissitudes of her politics, or the ordinary combinations and collisions of her friendships or enmities.

"Our detached and distant situation invites and enables us to pursue a different course. If we remain one people, under an efficient government, the period is not far off, when we may defy material injury from external annoyance; when we may take such an attitude as will cause the neutrality we may at any time resolve upon, to be scrupulously respected; when belligerent nations, under the impossibility of making acquisitions upon us, will not lightly hazard the giving us provocation; when we may choose peace or war, as our interest, guided by justice, shall counsel.

"Why forego the advantages of so peculiar a situation? Why quit our own to stand upon foreign ground? Why, by interweaving our destiny with that of any part of Europe, entangle our peace and prosperity in the toils of European ambition, rivalship, interest, humor, or caprice?

"It is our true policy to steer clear of permanent alliances with any portion of the foreign world; so far, I mean, as we are now at liberty to do it; for let me not be understood as capable of patronizing infidelity to existing engagements. I hold the maxim no less applicable to public than to private affairs, that honesty is always the best policy. I repeat it, therefore, let those engagements be observed in their genuine sense. But in my opinion, it is unnecessary, and would be unwise, to extend them.

"Taking care always to keep ourselves, by suitable establishments, on a respectable defensive posture, we may safely trust to temporary alliances for extraordinary emergencies.

"Harmony, and a liberal intercourse with all nations, are recommended by policy, humanity, and interest. But even our commercial policy should hold an equal and impartial hand; neither seeking nor granting exclusive favors or preferences; consulting the natural course of things; diffusing and diversifying by gentle means, the streams of commerce, but forcing nothing; establishing, with powers so disposed,—in order to give trade a stable course, to define the rights of our merchants, and to enable the government to support them,—conventional rules of intercourse, the best that present circumstances and mutual opinion will permit, but temporary, and liable to be from time to time abandoned or varied, as experience and circumstances shall dictate; constantly keeping in view, that it is folly in one nation to look for disinterested favors from another; that it must pay with a portion of its independence for whatever it may accept under that character; that by such acceptance, it may place itself in the condition of having given equivalents for nominal favors, and yet of being reproached with ingratitude for not giving more. There can be no greater error than to expect or calculate upon real favors from nation to nation. It is an illusion which experience must cure, which a just pride ought to discard.

"In offering to you, my countrymen, these counsels of an old and affectionate friend, I dare not **1796.** hope they will make the strong and lasting impression I could wish; that they will control the usual current of the passions, or prevent our nation from running the course which has hitherto marked the destiny of nations. But if I may even flatter myself, that they may be productive of some partial benefit, some occasional good; that they may now and then recur to moderate the fury of party spirit; to warn against the mischiefs of foreign intrigue; to guard against the impostures of pretended patriotism; this hope will be a full recompense for the solicitude for your welfare, by which they have been dictated.

"How far, in the discharge of my official duties, I have been guided by the principles which have been delineated, the public records and other evidences of my conduct must witness to you and to the world. To myself, the assurance of my own conscience is, that I have at least believed myself to be guided by them.

"In relation to the still subsisting war in Europe, my proclamation of the 22d of April, 1793, is the index to my plan. Sanctioned by your approving voice, and by that of your representatives in both houses of Congress, the spirit of that measure has continually governed me; uninfluenced by any attempts to deter or divert me from it.

"After deliberate examination, with the aid of the best lights I could obtain, I was well satisfied that our country, under all the circumstances of the case, had a right to take, and was bound in duty and interest to take, a neutral position. Having taken it, I determined, as far as should depend upon me, to maintain it with moderation, perseverance, and firmness.

"The considerations which respect the right to hold this conduct, it is not necessary on this occasion to detail. I will only observe, that according to my understanding of the matter, that right, so far from being denied by any of the belligerent powers, has been virtually admitted by all.

"The duty of holding a neutral conduct may be inferred, without any thing more, from the obligation which justice and humanity impose on every nation.

in cases in which it is free to act, to maintain inviolate the relations of peace and amity towards other nations.

"The inducements of interest for observing that conduct will best be referred to your own reflections and experience. With me, a predominant motive has been to endeavor to gain time to our country to settle and mature its yet recent institutions, and to progress, without interruption, to that degree of strength and consistency, which is necessary to give it, humanly speaking, the command of its own fortunes.

"Though in reviewing the incidents of my administration, I am unconscious of intentional error, I am nevertheless too sensible of my defects not to think it probable that I may have committed many errors. Whatever they may be, I fervently beseech the Almighty to avert or mitigate the evils to which they may tend. I shall also carry with me the hope that my country wil never cease to view them with indulgence; and after forty-five years of my life dedicated to its service, with an upright zeal, the faults of incompetent abilities will be consigned to oblivion, as myself must soon be to the mansions of rest.

"Relying on its kindness in this as in other things, and actuated by that fervent love towards it, which is so natural to a man who views in it the native soil of himself and his progenitors for several generations; I anticipate with pleasing expectation that retreat, in which I promise myself to realize, without alloy, the sweet enjoyment of partaking, in the midst of my fellow-citizens, the benign influence of good laws under a free government—the ever favorite object of my heart, and the happy reward, as I trust, of our mutual **cares** labors, and dangers.

"UNITED STATES, *Sept.* 17, 1796.

www.ingramcontent.com/pod-product-compliance
Lightning Source LLC
Chambersburg PA
CBHW031031120726
47905CB00007B/2137